Praise for Pauline Gedge

"Gedge excels at setting the scene and subtly evoking a sense of the period as she tells a timeless story of greed, love, and revenge."　　　　　　　　—*Kirkus Reviews*

"Gedge makes the past so accessible. You can imagine walking between the pillars into a magnificent hall and watching it come alive with the smell of the fresh paint on the frescoes."　　　　　　　　—*The Globe and Mail*

"Gedge vividly renders the exotic, sensuous world of ancient Memphis, the domestic rituals of bathing and dressing, the social ambience of superstition and spells."
　　　　　　　　—*Publishers Weekly*

"Gedge has such a terrific feel for ancient Egypt that the reader merrily suspends disbelief and hangs on for the ride."
　　　　　　　　—*Calgary Herald*

"Her richly colourful descriptions ... hit the reader with photographic clarity."　　　　　　　　—*The Ottawa Sun*

"Gedge has brought Egypt alive, not just the dry and sandy Egypt we know from archaeology, but the day-to-day workings of what was one of the greatest and most beautiful kingdoms in the history of the world."
　　　　　　　　—*Quill & Quire*

PENGUIN CANADA

THE HORUS ROAD

PAULINE GEDGE is the award-winning and bestselling author of eleven previous novels, eight of which are inspired by Egyptian history. Her first, *Child of the Morning*, won the Alberta Search-for-a-New Novelist Competition. In France, her second novel, *The Eagle and the Raven*, received the Jean Boujassy award from the Société des Gens des Lettres, and *The Twelfth Transforming*, the second of her Egyptian novels, won the Writers Guild of Alberta Best Novel of the Year Award. Her books have sold more than 250,000 copies in Canada alone; worldwide, they have sold more than six million copies and have been translated into eighteen languages. Pauline Gedge lives in Alberta.

ALSO BY PAULINE GEDGE

THE
HORUS
ROAD

Lords of the Two Lands
VOLUME THREE

PAULINE
GEDGE

PENGUIN
CANADA

PENGUIN CANADA

Published by the Penguin Group

Penguin Group (Canada), 90 Eglinton Avenue East, Suite 700, Toronto, Ontario, Canada M4P 2Y3
(a division of Pearson Canada Inc.)

Penguin Group (USA) Inc., 375 Hudson Street, New York, New York 10014, U.S.A.
Penguin Books Ltd, 80 Strand, London WC2R 0RL, England
Penguin Ireland, 25 St Stephen's Green, Dublin 2, Ireland (a division of Penguin Books Ltd)
Penguin Group (Australia), 250 Camberwell Road, Camberwell, Victoria 3124, Australia
(a division of Pearson Australia Group Pty Ltd)
Penguin Books India Pvt Ltd, 11 Community Centre, Panchsheel Park, New Delhi – 110 017, India
Penguin Group (NZ), 67 Apollo Drive, Rosedale, North Shore 0632, Auckland, New Zealand
(a division of Pearson New Zealand Ltd)
Penguin Books (South Africa) (Pty) Ltd, 24 Sturdee Avenue, Rosebank, Johannesburg 2196, South Africa

Penguin Books Ltd, Registered Offices: 80 Strand, London WC2R 0RL, England

First published in a Viking Canada paperback by Penguin Group (Canada),
a division of Pearson Canada Inc., 2000
Published in Penguin Canada paperback by Penguin Group (Canada),
a division of Pearson Canada Inc., 2001
Published in this edition, 2007

1 2 3 4 5 6 7 8 9 10 (OPM)

LIBRARY AND ARCHIVES CANADA CATALOGUING IN PUBLICATION

Gedge, Pauline, 1945–
The Horus road / Pauline Gedge.

(Lords of the two lands ; v. 3)
Originally publ.: Toronto : Viking, 2000.
Includes bibliographical references.
ISBN 978-0-14-316747-1

1. Ahmose I, King of Egypt—Fiction. 2. Egypt—History—To 332 B.C.—Fiction.
I. Title. II. Series: Gedge, Pauline, 1945– Lords of the two lands ; v. 3.

PS8563.E33H67 2007   C813'.54   C2007-903368-7

ISBN-10: 0-14-316747-2
ISBN-13: 978-0-14-316747-1

Visit the Penguin Group (Canada) website at **www.penguin.ca**

Special and corporate bulk purchase rates available; please see
www.penguin.ca/corporatesales or call 1-800-810-3104, ext. 477 or 474

This trilogy is dedicated to Prince Kamose, one of the most obscure and misunderstood characters in Egyptian history. I hope that in some small way I have contributed to his rehabilitation.

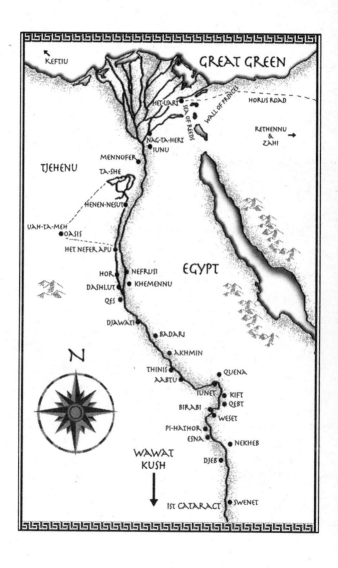

CHARACTER LIST

Yuf—Aahotep's personal priest
Pa-she—Tutor to Ahmose-onkh
Hekayib—Ahmose's body servant

Isis—Tetisheri's body servant
Hetepet—Aahotep's body servant
Heket—Tani's body servant
Raa—Ahmose-onkh's Nurse
Senehat—a servant

Hor-Aha—a native of Wawat and leader of the Medjay
Makhu of Akhmin
Mesehti of Djawati
Ankhmahor of Aabtu
Harkhuf—his son
Sebek-nakht of Mennofer
Antefoker of Iunu

Tetaky—Mayor of Weset
Dagi—Mayor of Mennofer
Pahesi—Mayor of Nekheb
Amunmose—High Priest of Amun
Turi—Ahmose's childhood friend and General of the
    Division of Amun

Ramose—son of Aahotep's relatives, a close friend to Ahmose, and once Tani's betrothed

Baba Abana—a naval officer

Kay (later Ahmose) Abana—his son, also a naval officer

Zaa pen Nekheb—Kay Abana's young cousin

Qar—Captain of the ship *North*

EGYPTIAN MILITARY PERSONNEL

DIVISION OF AMUN

Prince Ahmose—Commander-in-Chief

Turi—General

Ankhmahor—Commander of the Shock Troops

Idu—Standard Bearer

division of ra

Kagemni—General

Khnumhotep—Commander of the Shock Troops

Khaemhet—Standard Bearer

DIVISION OF PTAH

Akhethotep—General

DIVISION OF THOTH

Baqet—General

Tchanny—Commander of the Shock Troops

Pepynakht—Standard Bearer

INTRODUCTION

AT THE END of the Twelfth Dynasty the Egyptians found themselves in the hands of a foreign power they knew as the Setiu, the Rulers of Uplands. We know them as the Hyksos. They had initially wandered into Egypt from the less fertile eastern country of Rethennu in order to pasture their flocks and herds in the lush Delta region. Once settled, their traders followed them, eager to profit from Egypt's wealth. Skilled in matters of administration, they gradually removed all authority from a weak Egyptian government until control was entirely in their hands. It was a mostly bloodless invasion achieved through the subtle means of political and economic coercion. Their kings cared little for the country as a whole, plundering it for their own ends and aping the customs of their Egyptian predecessors in a largely successful effort to lull the people into submission. By the middle of the Seventeenth Dynasty they had been securely entrenched in Egypt for just over two hundred years, ruling from their northern capital, the House of the Leg, Het-Uart.

But one man in southern Egypt, claiming descent from the last true King, finally rebelled. In the first volume of this trilogy, *The Hippopotamus Marsh*, Seqenenra Tao, goaded and humiliated by the Setiu ruler Apepa, chose revolt rather than obedience. With the knowledge and collusion of his wife, Aahotep, his mother, Tetisheri, and his daughters, Aahmes-nefertari and Tani, he and his sons, Si-Amun, Kamose and Ahmose, planned and executed an uprising. It was an act of desperation doomed to failure. Seqenenra was attacked and partially paralyzed by Mersu, Tetisheri's trusted steward who was also a spy in his household. Regardless of his injuries he marched north with his small army, only to be killed during a battle against the superior forces of the Setiu King Apepa and his brilliant young General Pezedkhu.

His eldest son, Si-Amun, should have assumed the title of Prince of Weset. But Si-Amun, his loyalty divided between his father's claim to the throne of Egypt and the Setiu King, had been duped into passing information regarding his father's insurrection to Teti of Khemmenu, his mother's relative and a favourite of Apepa, through the spy Mersu. In a fit of remorse he killed Mersu and then himself.

Believing that the hostilities were over, Apepa travelled south to Weset and passed a crushing sentence on the remaining members of the family. He took Seqenenra's younger daughter, Tani, back to Het-Uart with him as a hostage against any further trouble, but Kamose, now Prince of Weset, knew that his choice lay between a continued struggle for Egypt's freedom or the complete impoverishment and separation of the members of his family. He chose freedom.

The second volume of this trilogy, *The Oasis*, tells how Kamose renewed his father's fight with the assistance of other Princes of Egypt. Necessity made him a vengeful and merciless warrior who was unable to tell friend from foe. He tore the country apart in his desire to restore Egypt to its former glory, but he was ultimately betrayed and murdered by several of his princely allies who became disillusioned with his methods and made a bargain with Apepa for their own profit. Seqenenra's youngest son, Ahmose, was wounded at the same time that Kamose was killed. While he was recovering, the women of the family came into their own, putting down the mutiny and re-establishing control over the army. It was then left to Ahmose to develop a strategy that might bring the domination of the Setiu to an end.

THE
HORUS
ROAD

I

DURING THE REMAINING DAYS of mourning for Kamose, Aahmes-nefertari saw little of her husband. She had expected the solemnity of grief to finally descend on the household now that the rebellion had been put down, and it was true that peace of a kind embraced the family, but it was more a silent sigh of relief than a quiet tribute to her brother. The weight of bitterness, the constant urge for revenge that had driven Kamose to so much killing and destruction, had pervaded them all for so long that they had become accustomed to living in a state of underlying tension. Now the source of that strain was gone, and they felt its withdrawal as a strange cleansing.

Nevertheless they had loved him, and as Mekhir flowed into Phamenoth and every small field around Weset came alive with the songs of the sowers as they flung their seed onto the glistening dark soil, they each grieved for him in their own way. Tetisheri kept to her rooms, the incense that accompanied her private prayers blurring the passage outside her door in a thin haze. Aahotep moved about the house with her usual calm regality, but she could often be seen sitting motionless under the trees of the garden, her chin sunk into her palm and her gaze fixed unseeingly before her.

Aahmes-nefertari found that her own sorrow made her restless. With a servant holding a sunshade over her head and a patient Follower plodding behind her, she took to walking. Sometimes she paced the river road between the estate and the temple. Sometimes she ventured into Weset itself. But more often she found herself skirting the fields where the germs of new life were being trodden into the wet earth by sturdy, naked feet. It was as though purposeless movement might enable her to escape from the misery that dogged her, but everywhere she carried with her the curve of his smile and the sound of his voice.

Ahmose would rise early, eat quickly, and disappear just after dawn. In answer to his wife's remonstrations he smiled absently, kissed her gently, assured her that he was feeling stronger every day, and left her. At one time he would have been fishing, she knew, but he had kept to his vow and had even given away his favourite rod and his net. Occasionally she happened to be passing the mangled gates leading to the old palace and glancing inside she caught a glimpse of him, once standing with hands on hips staring up at the frowning edifice and once emerging from the gloom of the huge reception hall. Several times she saw him coming along the edge of the canal that joined the temple forecourt to the Nile, surrounded by his retainers. Then he would wave and smile. She did not wonder what was in his mind. There was no room in her for anything but memories.

The strange serenity of those weeks was broken by the return of Ramose, Mesehti and Makhu. They came sailing up the river one warm afternoon, a small flotilla of servants' crafts behind them, and Aahmes-nefertari knew that the time of introspection was over. A herald had arrived the

day before to warn Ahmose of the Princes' arrival and he
was waiting for them above the watersteps with Hor-Aha
and Ankhmahor. Aahmes-nefertari was there also, acutely
conscious of her husband's stiff stance and the expression-
less set of his features as he watched the boat nudge the
steps and the ramp slide out.

Ramose was the first to disembark. Climbing the steps,
he strode to Ahmose and extending his arms in a gesture of
submission and reverence he bowed. Ahmose beckoned
him forward and then pulled him close. "My friend," he said
quietly. "Welcome home. I do not know yet how I may
repay the debt to you that has accumulated since my
father's day. Nor can I describe the pain your mother's
execution caused me when I recovered enough to hear
about it. I am well aware of how much agony a man can
suffer when he must choose where to place his loyalty and
you have been forced to make that choice too often. I pray
that never again will such a bitter cup be offered." Ramose
smiled sadly.

"It is good to see you restored to full health, Majesty," he
replied. "With your permission I must go at once to the
House of the Dead and make sure that my mother is being
correctly beautified." Turning to Aahmes-nefertari, he took
the hand she offered. "You are not yet wearing a commander's armbands," he said lightly, and she laughed and
hugged him impulsively.

"Dear Ramose!" she exclaimed. "In spite of our common
grief it is wonderful to see you smile."

The two Princes had been standing silently behind
Ramose and as Ahmose's attention became fixed on them
they knelt on the paving. Pressing their foreheads against

the stone and sweeping the ever-present grit into a tiny pile before them, they sifted it over their heads in a gesture of repentance and submission. Ahmose watched them for a moment, one eyebrow raised. "They have redeemed themselves, Ahmose," Ramose said in a low voice. "You spoke of the distress of divided loyalties. They have made their choice. They are here, not in Het-Uart. I beg you …" Ahmose held up a peremptory hand.

"Do you realize," he said to their dusty skulls, "that the woman standing beside me has shown more courage and performed more deeds of desperate loyalty than either of you? That if you had managed to find one drop of such bravery in your pale and watery blood my brother would still be alive? If you had warned him, Kamose would still be alive!" he shouted, bending over them. "But no! You closed your mouths! You made no choice! You recoiled from the responsibility and slunk away like a couple of hyenas! Amun's curse on you for the cowards that you are!" He straightened and for a moment his eyes wandered to the second boat, now moored, where the servants crowded watching the scene avidly. "Well, get up," he ordered more calmly. "That is, if your feeble spines will hold you. Tell me what I am supposed to do with you." Slowly they came to their feet and bowed.

"Majesty, you are correct in all you say." It was Mesehti who answered him. "We listened to Meketra and the others and did not take our knowledge to the Osiris one. Yet we did make a choice. We chose to withdraw. We could not support our fellow nobles although we owed them the fidelity of our common station, but neither could we betray them. If we erred, it was not through cowardice but from uncertainty."

"Uncertainty," Ahmose repeated. He sighed. "Uncertainty dogged Kamose from the start and his greatest uncertainty was always the true temper of his Princes." Suddenly he swung to his wife. "Aahmes-nefertari, you have the right to speak on this matter, you know. You were compelled to risk your life on the training ground. You stood and watched the executions. You have been harmed and changed. What do you advise?"

She looked at him, startled both by his generous public acknowledgement of her importance and his sensitivity to the turmoil that had raged and then subsided in her ka. All at once she knew that the substance of her answer would determine whether or not that importance was maintained. I must speak honestly and wisely, she thought in a panic. He has heard what I did but he was not there. He wants a validation he can see and hear for himself. Three pairs of eyes were fixed on her. Two were anxiously enquiring. The third was amused and Aahmes-nefertari, meeting her husband's quizzical gaze, realized that his vehement speech to the prostrate men had been an act. But how much of an act? she wondered. What does he want? Further retribution? Two more executions? A reason to pardon them?

No, she told herself resolutely. I will not try to fathom what he expects of me. I will speak from my own judgement and mine alone. "The bestowal of mercy can be interpreted as a weakness," she began carefully. "Yet mercy is greatly prized by Ma'at and together with justice is a quality every King must possess." She turned fully to Ahmose. "Justice has been done to the fullest extent, Majesty," she went on. "Our brother is dead. His murderers were executed. Mesehti and Makhu have pursued and slain the last remnants of a rebellion that belonged to an old order, Kamose's order, and in doing so they have rediscovered the portion of Ma'at that they once threw away. A new order begins. Let your first act as a King be one of forbearance." He was squinting at her now, his eyes alight.

"Forbearance, perhaps, but not pardon," he retorted. "Not yet. Trust must be earned, Aahmes-nefertari, don't you agree?" He swung to the Princes. "Where are your soldiers?"

"They march on the edge of the desert, Majesty," Makhu said hastily. "They should arrive tomorrow."

"Well, get yourselves out of the sun and into the guest quarters," Ahmose ordered. "Thanks to your Queen you have one last chance to prove yourselves. Do not fail again. And do not go near the barracks or I shall suspect yet another plot!" He turned away from their bows, and taking Aahmes-nefertari's arm he began to stroll towards the house. Ramose had already left in the direction of the House of the Dead.

"I do not understand, Ahmose," his wife said hesitantly. "You shouted your anger at them but I sensed that it was forced. Did you intend to spare them all along and I simply told you what you had already decided?"

"No," he replied. "My anger was real, is real, deep inside me, my dearest, but I wanted it to appear forced. If you had recommended their execution I would have taken your advice, but I am glad that you appreciate both the power and the trap of mercy. Let us hope it has not been a trap in this case."

"I still do not understand."

"Then I will tell you." He took a moment to lift his face to the brilliant blue of the sky and his hair fell back, revealing the jagged scar behind his ear, still rough and red. "I loved Kamose," he went on slowly. "He was brave and intelligent and he inspired an awed respect, but that respect was tinged with fear. In this he was foolish. His manner was harsh. His method of revenge was implacable. The ordeal we have suffered was the direct result of that inexorable drive towards the extermination of the Setiu. It frightened the people and insulted the Princes. I loved him," he repeated, a tremor in his voice, "but the result of his terrible need was entirely predictable."

"Ahmose," Aahmes-nefertari broke in urgently. "Are you saying that you will abandon the fight? Give Egypt back to Apepa?"

"Gods no! Do not be deceived. My own hatred and desire for revenge against Apepa burns just as strongly as Kamose's did. But I have a new policy. I will strew smiles like lotus petals. I will toss titles and preferments and rewards like so many brightly painted baubles. I will not make my brother's mistakes, and thus I will flog every Setiu back to Rethennu where they belong." They had reached the shade of the pillared portico before the main entrance to the house and Aahmes-nefertari shivered in the sudden chill.

"I think I see," she said cautiously. "Kamose ruled the Princes by coercion. You will control them more subtly. But, Ahmose, if our brother had not flayed Egypt with the whip of his pain and rage, if he had not prodded and shamed the Princes into action and drenched Egypt in blood, your strategy would not work. He drew the poison for you. He cleared the way for a gentler approach."

"And I owe him that? You were afraid to finish your thought, Aahmes-nefertari. You are right. I owe him a great deal. He was like a farmer who takes possession of a field which has been left untended for hentis. His task was to slash and burn the weeds. I know this. I honour it. But I owe him nothing more. He was mildly insane." One ringed finger crept up to his scar and rubbed it absently. It was a gesture that was becoming a habit and Aahmes-nefertari was beginning to recognize it as a signal of speculative thought.

"But Amun loved him!" she blurted, alarmed. "He sent him dreams! Take care that in hardening your heart against his memory you do not blaspheme against the god, Ahmose!" For a moment the face he turned to her was blank. Then it lit with his guileless smile.

"He died in trying to save my life," he said. "I slept beside him, fought beside him, and in our youth he was always there to protect me. My heart will never harden against him. I speak facts, Aahmes-nefertari, not feelings. The emotion is for you and me alone. But a new order begins, as you said, and there is great danger to me if I present even a hint to the nobles that I am prepared to continue the brutal policies of my brother." He leaned close to her. "I intend to render them impotent, every one of them, and make them thank me for doing it. I will never trust them again. I also intend to put a torch to Het-Uart, that stinking nest of rats, and thus Kamose will be twice justified. But I must never allow one drop of the acid of blind revenge to stir in my veins or we will not be allowed a second chance at salvation." He straightened. "I trust you, Aahmes-nefertari. I have opened my mind on this matter to no one else. When I ask you for advice, I expect you to give it to me without fear, as you did a short while ago. I have requested a meeting with Hor-Aha this evening in the office. I want you and Mother there." Aahmes-nefertari blinked in surprise.

"You want me to be present at a discussion about strategy?" He put a thumb against her chin, and lifting her face he kissed her firmly on the mouth.

"Of course," he replied. "I need a Queen who can do more than sip pomegranate wine and listen to servants' gossip." He stifled a yawn. "Now I need an hour on my couch. My head has begun to ache."

Aahmes-nefertari stifled an impulse to put a hand on his forehead. A shyness had overtaken her as she looked at this man, so sweetly familiar and yet so suddenly alien, and he must have divined her aborted inclination, for he put an arm across her shoulders and propelled her firmly towards the doorway. "Akhtoy can nurse me now," he said. "That is his job. You will have other responsibilities." Releasing her, he strode away down the corridor and she watched him go. He did not say Tetisheri, she thought. Was it an oversight or a deliberate exclusion? If he antagonizes Grandmother, the house will be full of wrangling. Then she laughed aloud, shrugged, and set off towards the nursery. I doubt if a quarrelsome house has a place in the new order, she mused. Our King will insist on domestic peace.

She approached the office just after dusk, greeting the servants who were lighting the torches bracketed in the passage as she went and returning the salutes of the guards taking up the first watches of the night. Outside the imposing cedar door she paused, momentarily intimidated. She had never before been invited into the place where her father and later Kamose had dealt with the myriad affairs that made up the world of men: dictating directives to the headmen of the villages under their care, going over the tallies of grain, wine and oil, discussing judgements regarding the often petty grievances the peasants brought to them, and later wrestling with the agonizing decisions that had resulted in the Weset uprising. She knew what the room contained, of course, having often inspected it for tidiness and cleanliness after the servants had swept it, but to enter it for the purpose of business—that was different. She could hear voices within, her husband's rich treble followed by Hor-Aha's rough, rare chuckle, and with a frown of irritation at her own hesitation she knocked and, without waiting to be bidden, let herself in.

Aahotep was already there, sitting quietly at one end of the heavy table. Hor-Aha had his back to the door and, as Aahmes-nefertari walked across the floor, he rose and turned to reverence her. Ahmose, seated opposite with Ipi already cross-legged by his knee, smiled at her and waved her to the empty chair at the other end. Light filled the sparsely furnished space from two standing lamps in the corners and one on the table at Ahmose's side. Three walls were full of nooks from which the ends of rolled papyri protruded and below which were the chests containing records not in current use. The fourth wall was simply a line of pillars giving out onto the darkening sky.

For one second, as she settled herself facing her mother, Aahmes-nefertari could have sworn that she inhaled a faint whiff of her father's perfume, a mixture of sweet persea and oil of frankincense. Wondering if it somehow lingered deep in the very grain of the table where he had so often placed his hands, and resisting the desire to put her nose to its surface, she linked her own fingers in her lap and waited. Ahmose cleared his throat. "Ipi, are you ready?" he enquired. The man glanced up at him and nodded and Aahmes-nefertari heard him whispering the scribes' preparatory prayer to Thoth beneath Ahmose's next words. "Good. As you can see, Akhtoy has provided us with wine and sweetmeats but you will have to serve yourselves. This discussion is not for servants' ears." He already had a cup before him and he drank briefly before continuing. "While I lay on my couch regaining my strength, I had many hours to ponder the course my rule should take," he said. "And it seemed to me that the most urgent project confronting us is a reorganizing of the army. Without a coherent, efficient fighting force we are nothing. We cannot even defend ourselves, let alone mount effective campaigns. Kamose performed a very difficult task in taking raw peasants and turning them into soldiers. He began with one unit, the Medjay, and a motley collection of peasants. He had officers who had never drawn a sword and commanders who were reluctant to command. In short, what he did must have earned him the wonder and applause of the gods themselves." He shot a glance at his wife. "But he was hampered by a peasant's need to till his soil in the spring and a prince's need to assert the superiority of his blood. The rebellion has taught us the danger of both. Peasants whose minds are full of worry about their arouras and Princes who chafe to return to the luxury of their estates are not to be trusted."

He already uses that word a great deal, Aahmes-nefertari thought, hearing the mildly disdainful emphasis he had placed on it. It has become a preoccupation for him. I pray that it may not become an obsession. She turned her attention back to what he was saying. "Therefore I intend to implement a standing army. Give me your response." Aahotep pulled the wine jug towards her and carefully filled her cup.

"Egypt has never maintained a standing army," she said slowly. "The peasants have always been conscripted temporarily, either for war or for building purposes, by the King or the temples. They have always known that no matter how long their services may be required they will eventually be allowed to go home. If they are told that they may not go home, you will have one mutiny after another."

"Surely that depends on how it is done," Aahmes-nefertari objected. "It might be possible to form a military core of permanent troops with their own village and then augment them with others during the Inundation. Or perhaps take a census of all males and cull those not necessary for working the land. They would have to be supported and armed out of the royal treasury. You would have to create new orders of scribes and stewards who would do nothing else. You would need the authority to tax all Egypt. But it would mean that each man was fully trained, professional, and it would remove the threat of another revolt."

"Hor-Aha?" Ahmose looked at his General, who had been listening with his head down, one finger tracing an intricate and invisible pattern on the table before him. Now he pursed his lips and, folding his arms, he nodded.

"It could be done. I consider my Medjay first. I know them, Majesty. They would be willing to leave their villages to be cared for by their women and slaves, if they were allowed several weeks of freedom a year and sufficient beer and bread. As for the rest, you already have the embryo of such a core in your Weset contingent." He stirred and Aahmes-nefertari saw him take a slow, quiet breath. "But what will you do for commanders?" he asked smoothly— too smoothly, Aahmes-nefertari thought. This is the question closest to his strange heart. This is where his true interest lies. "Will you promote the sons of those who have died?"

"Been executed for treason you mean!" Ahmose retorted. "No, I do not wish to train their offspring in the art of command. A professional army needs professional officers at its pinnacle. I want to promote from the ranks." But that is not your real reason, Aahmes-nefertari told him silently. You have already expressed that to me. You will never trust a nobleman again.

"The ranks?" Aahotep expostulated. "But, Ahmose, what common soldier will have any respect for a commander who has no noble blood in him? There must be distance between them!"

"I am inclined to disagree, Mother," Ahmose told her mildly. "Perhaps a lowly fighting man will have more confidence in the directives of someone he has already seen in action. He may also dream of his own promotion if such an avenue becomes open." He spread his hands. "In any event it is worth the gamble. Kamose attempted the traditional way. He did great harm to Apepa but came close to destroying us in the process. We lose nothing by changing the rules."

"I would like to come back to the matter of support," Aahmes-nefertari said. "The war has cost us and the rest of

Egypt. We have had two harvests since Kamose removed the peasants from the land and the granaries are filling again, but our situation will not bear any extra burden. Not yet. Do we not invite a future disaster by scrambling to fill the mouths of thousands of troops who will fall idle once the war is over?" He favoured her with one of his wide, benign smiles of approval.

"A good point," he responded. "Firstly I do not envisage the soldiers idle. With their training and skills they will be invaluable in policing the towns and villages, escorting caravans; we can even sell their time to the temples, all in rotation of course. And if an emergency arises, they can be recalled to Weset already armed and proficient."

"Majesty, will you also allow them to be used as private soldiers?" Hor-Aha interrupted. There was a pause during which Ahmose appeared to be considering the question, but Aahmes-nefertari suspected that he was merely hiding his annoyance at it.

"When Egypt has been scoured and peace returns, there will be no necessity for private armies," he answered with the exaggerated docility he used to hide disapproval, anger or boredom. Mother and daughter caught each other's eye, but Hor-Aha seemed unaware that he had put Ahmose on his guard. "However, escorts will surely be permissible, although they will not be privately recruited nor staffed with officers who are not answerable to me. This is a detail, Hor-Aha." He turned to his wife. "Secondly," he went on, "I have no intention of raping Egypt in order to preserve her! Don't forget the gold routes, Aahmes-nefertari. We have blocked the passage of gold to the Delta. Now we can take it for ourselves. Also I intend to send emissaries to

Keftiu. They are an eminently practical people. They care nothing for our internal squabbles. Trade is what they like, and trade with Het-Uart has become sporadic since Kamose captured the treasure ships. I believe that they will be eager to draw up new agreements with Egypt, particularly after the next campaign, when I hope to clear the Delta of the Rethennu troops dribbling in."

"Our ancestor Senwasret erected the Wall of Princes between the Delta and Rethennu hentis ago to keep the Setiu out and to protect the Horus Road into the east," Aahotep reflected. "He could not have imagined that they would still come seeping past his defences, first as sheep herders pasturing their flocks and then as traders, that they would become masters of Egypt through commerce. Perhaps through commerce you may slowly strangle them, my son. How ironic that would be!"

"It is certainly one weapon I have considered," Ahmose agreed. "But Apepa's fellow Princes in Rethennu, those he calls his 'brothers,' do not want him to relinquish Egypt without a fight. We provide them with too many riches. Spies in the Delta from the navy at Het nefer Apu tell me that their soldiers continue to trickle in."

"They can keep coming steadily while we are hampered by the Inundation and are immobilized," Hor-Aha put in gruffly. "It may eventually be necessary to fight them even while Egypt lies under the flood."

"That is why Kamose was anxious to form a navy," Ahmose pointed out. "He foresaw such an eventuality from the moment we learned of the influx of Setiu from Rethennu. And that is why, General, I need an army that will not disband and scatter every year." Hor-Aha frowned.

"I do not think you will defeat them this year, Majesty," he offered.

"Neither do I," Ahmose admitted. "But my grip can tighten around their fat necks. I have the upper hand and I intend to keep it." He poked about intently in a dish of shat cakes and honeyed figs encased in pastry. "Ipi, are you following us?" he asked.

"Yes, indeed, Majesty." The scribe's voice floated up from his position on the floor. "But I hope I have a sufficient supply of papyrus sheets."

"Ah, papyrus," Ahmose commented, abandoning the food for the wine jug. "Now that is something the Keftiu crave." He glanced around at them all. "I wish to pass now to the reconstruction of our forces. We can still call upon fifty-five thousand men, eleven divisions, can we not, General? Apart from the few hundred Ramose, Mesehti and Makhu pursued and killed during the rebellion."

"Yes, Majesty. But only one division is quartered here."

"I know. I want you to arm yourself with scribes and go to every nome. Begin to interview every officer I have. Talk to them about the men under them. Note any that have impressed their superiors either by their expertise in weaponry or by an ability to lead. Judge the officers' own fitness to continue as such and weed out those with direct allegiance to any prince, living or dead. Bring all names and descriptions to me. Until the Delta is completely mine I need all eleven divisions active, but I want to retain five divisions of infantry and one of marines permanently, all officers to be answerable only to me as Commander-in-Chief. We will discuss the breakdown of troops later, but it will be far more precise than ever before."

"May I include the Medjay in this survey?" Hor-Aha enquired with a hesitation Aahmes-nefertari had never seen in him before, and Ahmose shook his head.

"No. The Medjay will return to being an irregular force, adaptable to any situation, with their own officers. Any Medjay officers at present commanding Egyptians will be replaced. And before you open your mouth to protest, Hor-Aha, think about it. A large part of the unrest that boiled up into revolt stemmed from resentment against both you and the Medjay. Egyptian soldiers are not ready to place their confidence in black skin, and Egyptian nobles consider you inferior to them in every way." He leaned across the table and grasped Hor-Aha's forearm. "I speak of harsh realities, my friend. I must. To me you are Egyptian, and not only Egyptian but one of the finest. I love you. I will not deprive you of the title of Prince my brother gave you, but it will not be used until the Double Crown sits on my head and the Horus Throne rests on the dais of the old palace. Forgive me and try to understand."

"Oh, I understand," Hor-Aha said huskily. He did not withdraw his arm, but Aahmes-nefertari saw its muscles tighten. "I have risked my life for your family. First Seqenenra, then your brother, received all the worship and loyalty I had to give. Indeed, your father was more to me than my own life and I loved him deeply. I have endured the arrogance and condescension of men who could not walk without falling over their own swords and who, when it came to military strategy, could see no farther than the end of their own aristocratic noses. And for this I am rewarded with contempt. It stings, Ahmose." He swallowed. "Yet I am the greatest tactician you have and as such

I know that if you are to build and control an army out of Kamose's half-disciplined, half-trained rabble you must indulge its ignorance." He fixed Ahmose with a cold stare. "Do not forget that I am Egyptian. Ny mother, Nithotep, was Egyptian. Regardless of the colour of my skin I belong here, and because I do and for no other reason, I will trust you to fulfil the promise Kamose made to me at the appropriate time and I will continue to be yours to command. You need me." Now he took his arm away, pushing his silver bracelet up over the place where Ahmose's fingers had grasped him, and Ahmose sat back.

"Of course I need you!" he repeated vehemently. "What else can I say? This meeting is at an end. Come to me tomorrow, Hor-Aha, before you leave. You have a month to gather the information I want. I will give you a more detailed list of the officer positions I intend to create. I would like to leave for the Delta as soon as Kamose is buried." He came to his feet and the others followed. Bowing, Hor-Aha strode from the room and the door slammed behind him. Aahotep blew out her breath.

"Gods, Ahmose, I pray that you have not made an enemy of our most precious ally. Do you no longer trust him?"

"I love him, Mother," Ahmose replied wearily. Dark smudges had appeared under his kohled eyes and his pallor betrayed more healing to be done in spite of his insistence that he had fully recovered from his wound. "I love him but I do not trust him. I have often sensed the kind of pride in him that must be bridled. He muzzles it, but without a firm hand on him it will bolt and destroy him." Aahotep came around the table and, kissing him on the cheek, she drew her linen cloak around her and crossed to the door.

"I am astounded at the foresight and cunning you have shown this evening," she said. "I should not be, for I birthed and raised you, but I am. Egypt will be safe with you. Sleep well, Majesty." This time the door closed with a demure click. Ahmose's shoulders slumped.

"I am suddenly very tired," he murmured. "My head is pounding. I think I will drink poppy tonight, but I want you to sleep with me, Aahmes-nefertari. I need the feel of your body against mine. I would make love to you but I do not have the energy." Going to him, Aahmes-nefertari put an arm around his waist.

"We can always lie side by side and pretend," she teased him. Then more soberly she asked, "Ahmose, why did you exclude Ramose from this discussion?"

"Oddly enough Ramose is one man I do trust completely," he replied. "But he is not a soldier. Besides, he is mourning for his mother and I do not wish to interfere with his grief." But you interfere with ours for Kamose, she wanted to retort. Instead she said, "Will you send him to spy in Het-Uart instead? And what of Mesehti and Makhu? And Ankhmahor for that matter!" Holding each other, they moved towards the passage.

"I do not need a spy in Het-Uart after all," he told her as they left the office. A cool draught blew through the passage beyond, making the torches gutter, and the guard on the door straightened into a respectful salute. "Hor-Aha is correct in his surmise that the city will not fall to me this season. It is well defended. I will concentrate on killing the fresh Setiu entering the Delta. As for my two Princes, I will offer them new titles and keep them beside me, but I have already taken their divisions away from them, although they do not know it yet. And Ankhmahor ..." They were passing the open doorway to the rear garden and he slowed to inhale the gusts of scent-laden air before walking on. "Ankhmahor is a jewel. He will continue to order my Followers and act as Commander of the Shock Troops of the Division of Amun. He is one Prince for whom I make an exception. Would you like to captain the household guards, Aahmes-nefertari?" He was smiling down at her, his eyes sparkling in spite of their shadows.

"Yes, I would," she responded immediately. "I have come to know our local soldiers well. If I can select them myself, I will feel quite safe. Some of them will be Medjay, Ahmose." Akhtoy was rising from his stool as they approached Ahmose's quarters.

"That is fine," Ahmose said. "You, my dearest sister, I do trust implicitly! Akhtoy, bring in hot water and send to the physician for poppy. Aahmes-nefertari, return as soon as you can."

She left him then and walked the short distance to her own quarters. Tetisheri will be furious when she learns how she was excluded tonight, she thought as Raa came forward to undress her. He ought to do his best to placate her. A new title perhaps? She laughed aloud as she raised her arms and the sheath was lifted up over her head.

That night she dreamed of the death of Ramose's mother, Nefer-Sakharu, and woke sweating and trembling in the thick darkness. Sitting up, she wiped her neck and breasts with the crumpled sheet, thankful that she was not alone. Turning to drink from the water jug by the couch, she was startled to hear Ahmose's voice. "What is the matter?" he mumbled. "Are you all right?"

"A bad dream, nothing more," she whispered back, feeling for the reassurance of his warm flesh and finding the curve of his hip. "Why are you not sleeping, Ahmose?"

"I did sleep," he replied more clearly. "Until your muttering and tossing woke me up."

"I am sorry." She lay back down on her pillow. "Can you sleep again, do you think?" He stirred and rolled towards her.

"I could," he said. "But my headache has gone. Let us make love now, Aahmes-nefertari. Do you want to? It will be a unique experience. I have never made love to a soldier before." Go away, she said silently to the image of the Medjay with Nefer-Sakharu's blood spurting over him, and she opened her mouth to her husband's kiss.

The expected outburst from Tetisheri did not come, much to Aahmes-nefertari's surprise. She wondered whether perhaps her grandmother was not aware that the meeting had taken place, but doubted it. Tetisheri had always kept a sharp ear for the casual conversation of the servants. It was more likely that she sensed a shift in the hierarchy of the family and, not wishing to find herself on the bottom rung of the ladder, she had decided to keep her wounded pride to herself. She showed her displeasure, however, by questioning Ahmose sharply regarding the state of Kamose's tomb at dinner one evening. "You have been absent from the house on many occasions," she said to him abruptly as he was feeding morsels of roast duck to Behek. The dog had spent the days since Kamose's murder wandering disconsolately from his master's empty rooms to the watersteps and back as though he hoped Kamose might return at any moment from some river voyage, until

Ahmose had the animal leashed and led behind himself as he went about his business. Ahmose affected to ignore Tetisheri, continuing to tear pieces of meat from the bones on his plate and slip them between Behek's strong teeth, but she persisted. "Have you been overseeing the completion of Kamose's tomb?"

"No, Grandmother," he finally said patiently. "Actually I have had matters to attend to in the temple."

"Matters that are more important than your brother's resting place?" she pressed. "Do you want him to lie amid stone chips and unfinished inscriptions?" Ahmose straightened and dipped his fingers in the fingerbowl.

"You presume a great deal, Tetisheri," he said with mild rebuke. "You would like to think that I am capable of such a petty revenge. You have always chosen to believe that I was jealous of Kamose, but it was never so. We disagreed on many things, but I loved him just as much as you did."

"I doubt that," she responded tartly. Aahmes-nefertari saw her husband's jaw tighten at her tone, but he did not rise to her bait. Drying his hands, he indicated that his plate could be removed and sat back.

"I have been to the tomb twice," he said evenly. "It will not be entirely ready but that is no one's fault. Kamose did not expect to die so young. The inner chamber with all the correct inscriptions is complete because I commanded the artisans to work at night as well as during the day, but the carving along the passage to it cannot be done before the funeral. The pyramid stands finished but unfaced. That can be completed later. The enclosing wall of the courtyard is also finished. The men are exhausting themselves, but there is a limit to what I can ask of them, Tetisheri."

"So the prayers and incantations that will surround his body are correct but his mighty deeds will not be recorded," she grumbled. "It is disastrous."

"The prayers and divine protections were far more important," Ahmose retorted. His forefinger was straying to his scar, betraying his tension, and Aahotep spoke up before Aahmes-nefertari could pour a little oil on the exchange.

"You are being deliberately disagreeable, Tetisheri," she said. "Would you rather have Kamose protected from evil in the next life or lost because Ahmose insisted on having his deeds chronicled? There is no time to do both!"

"I know what you are thinking." Ahmose had turned to his grandmother and was looking at her coolly. "In your secret heart you fear that I will begin to claim Kamose's victories, all his great attempts to free us, all the pain of his heart, as my own. But even if I wanted to, I could not. The archives are full of his letters and dispatches to you, and unless I burned them all I could not assume my brother's sad history. Nor would the gods approve of such dishonesty." He sighed. "I pity you, Tetisheri. You think so ill of me that you are unable to lift up your head and see either Kamose or me as we really are. But I also warn you. I am now the King as well as your grandson. Try to curb your tongue if you cannot curb your thoughts, or you may find yourself accused of blasphemy." She glared at him for a moment before slumping forward.

"You are right," she managed through stiff lips. "I apologize to you, Majesty. I am an obstreperous old woman." But Aahmes-nefertari, seeing the glint of mutiny in her hooded eyes, knew that the words she spoke were not the ones churning in her mind. Presently Tetisheri left the dais, stalking through the lamplight in the direction of her quarters.

"Forgive her, Ahmose," Aahotep pleaded. "She grieves terribly for Kamose."

"Grief can excuse much, but not everything," was all Ahmose replied.

He continued to be absent a great deal, sometimes vanishing in the direction of the temple, sometimes walking with his ever-present guard of Followers to the barracks and the training ground. Several times in the month that followed, heralds arrived at the watersteps with messages for him, and Aahmes-nefertari, passing the closed door of the office, heard his voice interspersed with the rumble of other men's tones. But she did not fret because she was excluded from their news. She had his confidence, and if anything of importance was reported to him she knew he would tell her at once.

Rising late one morning, she requested that her first meal be brought to her in the garden, and after being bathed, dressed and painted she made her way to the pool, only to find Ahmose already there, lying on his back under a billowing canopy. Hent-ta-Hent was sprawled naked on his stomach, deeply asleep, one tiny thumb still resting between her half-open lips, her wisps of soft black hair stirring in the breeze. Ahmose had one hand across her chubby back to prevent her from slipping and with the other he was gesticulating at Hor-Aha who sat cross-legged beside him. They were surrounded by Ipi and three of his under-scribes, all bent industriously over their palettes. Ahmose-onkh, also naked, stood by the water under the watchful eye of a servant, his shaved head, but for the wet and bedraggled youth lock straggling to his shoulder, gleaming in the strong light. When he saw his mother coming over the grass, he toddled towards her beaming, palms cupped. "Look, look!" he exclaimed in his excited high treble. "This frog jumped onto my foot!" Squatting, Aahmes-nefertari kissed his round cheek and admired his catch.

"But you must throw it back into the pond," she cautioned him. "If you hold it too long its skin will become dry and hot and you will make it sick. It is special, Ahmose-onkh, and you must not harm it. Frogs are tokens of rebirth and we honour them." He shrugged, already bored, and pouted, but he did as he was told, pausing on the edge of the pool to stroke the creature before tossing it carelessly away. It struck the water with scarcely a splash and Aahmes-nefertari, rising, saw it kick its way beneath the green spread of a lotus pad. She beckoned to the servant.

"Braid his youth lock," she said. "He looks very untidy. And put him in a loincloth. He is three years old now. He must become used to being dressed." Ahmose had turned his head at her approach, smiling broadly, and Hor-Aha had come to his feet to reverence her.

"Hor-Aha returned with his lists last night," Ahmose said as she moved in under the shade of the canopy. "It was too beautiful a morning to waste in the gloom of the office, so I am listening to them out here. Later I must question the more senior men recommended myself, but I cannot move until Hent-ta-Hent wakes up." He glanced fondly down at his daughter. "I think she is teething, Aahmes-nefertari. She was dribbling and crying a great deal and the nursery servant could not calm her. What will you do today?"

"I thought I might take a litter and go out beside the fields," she replied. "I want to see how this season's crops are growing." Then she burst out laughing. "Ahmose, you look ridiculously domestic with a baby draped over your belly!" Hent-ta-Hent stirred at the sound, made little smacking noises, and half-opened her eyes before relaxing into slumber once more. The thumb that had been in her mouth slid out to rest on her father's chest.

"Yes, but the beat of my heart soothes her and the warmth of her body pacifies me," he replied. "Your food is coming, Aahmes-nefertari. Sit and eat here while I finish my business. Then I think I will come with you. The officers are settling into the barracks. I can talk to them this evening."

Surprised and pleased, she accepted his offer, savouring her meal with her eyes on the play of sun and shadow across the verdant spring glory of the garden and her ears open to Hor-Aha's voice as he submitted a seemingly endless array of names together with descriptions of their strengths and weaknesses. Ahmose had eleven divisions to staff. That meant everything from Commanders to Standard Bearers, Charioteers to Captains of a Hundred, Greatest of Fifty to Instructors of Retainers.

Many of the rankings were entirely new to her, and she realized as she listened that Ahmose was creating them as he went. The army would indeed be different, rigidly codified and completely under his control. The knowledge brought her a certain peace, but sadness also. Kamose had done everything he could, but he had not had either the time or the foresight for something like this. He had prepared the way for his brother, hewing a crude beginning, but Ahmose would refine and perfect it, building on the foundation Kamose had left, and perhaps in time Kamose's contribution would be forgotten. After all, he had been a mystery to his family, a dictator to his nobles, and a terror to the peasants whose villages he had destroyed. If Ahmose were able to bring about freedom and prosperity for Egypt, his brother might even become an embarrassment whose memory would be allowed to dwindle until he faded from the annals of the nation. Aahmes-nefertari shuddered. You would not have made a good King, dearest Kamose, she thought for the first time. The gods knew it, and that is why they used you to plough the ground and then took you away. It was not your destiny to rule.

Ahmose-onkh was emerging from the house, his youth lock decorously braided, a white loincloth around his small hips, and Raa followed him, several scrolls in her grasp. She is going to read him stories, Aahmes-nefertari mused, but he is almost old enough to begin to learn to read and write for himself. Soon we must find him a good tutor. He must know the history of this country if he is to succeed Ahmose on the throne. The connection of her ideas depressed her for a moment and she shook off her reverie. Hent-ta-Hent was waking, moving restlessly in her father's grip, and Aahmes-nefertari rose. "Let the nursery servant have her before she makes you wet," she said to Ahmose. "I will order the litters and wait for you by the river path." He nodded, passed the grumbling baby up to the patient attendant without pausing in his speech, and Aahmes-nefertari left the men to their deliberations.

For several precious hours she and Ahmose had themselves carried around the environs of the estate, talking lightly across the space between their litters of how thickly green and healthy the crops were and leaning out to peer at their blurred reflections in the canals that criss-crossed the fields. One of the Tao's farmers had invented a method to raise water from the Nile, lift it over the dams that prevented the annual flood from spilling out of the canals as the river shrank, and pour it back into the channels. Aahotep had made him Overseer of Granaries and his invention was now in common use. Ahmose often had the litters halted so that he could watch the shadufs in motion, fascinated at their efficiency, but Aahmes-nefertari simply enjoyed the glitter of sunlight as the water cascaded from the buckets.

Later they left the litters and walked along the palm-shaded river road hand in hand, commenting idly on the skiffs tacking by, the fragile long legs of the white ibis standing lazily in the shallows, the heat shimmer of the barren cliffs they could glimpse on the west bank. Often they met citizens of Weset bound on various errands, who bowed respectfully and stood aside as they passed. "I do not think that we will do this much more," Ahmose said as they neared their watersteps. "It is not good for the King to be so visible and available to the people. He must, of course, be ready to hear their problems through his judges, but in these times it is better that they do not envision him with muddy feet and sweat-stained kilt. While I am gone, have the wall enclosing the estate built higher, Aahmes-nefertari, and a solid gate put in above the watersteps so that those passing cannot look into the edge of the garden."

"You are planning many changes, aren't you, Ahmose?" she said, and he nodded solemnly.

"Yes, but first I must address the enemy in the Delta. That is my priority." He pulled her arm through his and together they turned away from the river towards the house that lay familiar and welcoming in the afternoon heat.

2

 ON THE TWENTY-NINTH DAY of Pharmuthi the family and all the servants gathered at the watersteps on the west bank to escort Kamose to his tomb. He had given no thought to the crafting of his sarcophagus and there were none suitable in the storerooms of the House of the Dead, so the sem-priests laid his cocooned body in a plain wooden coffin carved in the shape of a man with features crudely resembling Kamose's own and the facsimile of a kingly beard attached to the chin. His name, where it appeared, hastily painted, was not enclosed in the cartouche of royalty. Aahmes-nefertari, standing watching the coffin being lifted from the raft that had borne it across the river and loaded onto the sled that would carry it, was shocked at its anonymous poverty. He deserves better than that, she thought angrily. "Did you choose it?" she whispered to her husband over the wails of the blue-clad women around her.

"No!" he hissed back. "I was told that he had not made provision for his coffin and there was no time to have one properly constructed and adorned. Poor Tetisheri. She will see this as just another insult to Kamose on my part."

"Well, it is insulting, even though it is not your fault," she breathed. "Oh, Kamose! Forgive us all!" Ahmose did not reply. Up ahead the High Priest had begun to walk, chanting the haunting and beautiful litany for the dead, a host of acolytes with censers raised surrounding him. When his voice quavered once, Aahmes-nefertari was reminded of how he had loved Kamose, but he quickly recovered and under the power of his song the rest of the procession followed. The sled went first, drawn by the two red oxen of sacred tradition, and Aahotep, Tetisheri, Ahmose and Aahmes-nefertari followed.

The children had been left with Raa in the house and Aahmes-nefertari missed them with a sudden pang. They would have been a promise of new life in the midst of this terrible death. She also felt the lack of Ramose's presence. He had gone north to Khemmenu to see to the preparations for his mother's burial there and had sent word that he could not return until tomorrow. Behind the family the servants clustered and at the rear were the professional mourners, keening and scooping up sand to place on their dishevelled heads. They were hired by custom, for the importance of the person to be buried was measured by the number of women weeping for him or her. Aahotep had engaged two hundred, every one that Weset could provide, and their sobbing and strange, wild wailing rolled across the river to be echoed by the thousands of citizens who crowded the east bank to bid their King and protector farewell.

At least Weset loved and honoured him, Aahmes-nefertari's thoughts ran on. All at once she began to cry and, bending as she went, she took a handful of Egypt's desert, pressing the hot grains against her palm before trickling them above her forehead and grinding them into her face.

The barren land sloped up between the river and the high, sharp tumble of the western cliffs in a long rise.

Kamose's small pyramid lay to the south on the edge of the place of the dead, its forecourt open to the east to greet the sun. Behind it loomed the much larger mortuary temple and tomb of his ancestor Osiris Mentuhotep-neb-hapet-Ra at the very foot of the serried Cliff of Gurn, and the remainder of the arid plain to the north was dotted with similar structures, their little pyramids capping the quiet mysteries within. Aahmes-nefertari, in the pause that came while the coffin was removed from the sled and canted upright against the wall of the tomb, let her gaze wander over them. You are in mighty company, dear Kamose, she said to him. Here lie the gods of happier times. You deserve to rest among them, for like them you loved Egypt and revered Ma'at, and for both you sacrificed your life.

The members of the cortege fell silent as the lid of the coffin was removed and for several moments the wind could be heard fluttering the blue mourning linens of the assembly and stirring the dust into spirals that formed from nothing and as quickly vanished. Taking a deep, uneven breath, Aahmes-nefertari raised her eyes to the thing standing within the shadow of the wooden box, her imagination questing beyond the layer upon layer of tightly complex bandaging and the amulets of protection to the beloved man beneath. He was there in her mind's eye as she had seen him in sleep, lying on his back, his hands crossed on the light rise and fall of his chest, his face immobile but suffused with a steady, quiet animation. She knew that she was fostering an illusion, that the reality of what Kamose had become was something brown and desiccated and stiff, but she could not confront it yet and she clung to Kamose asleep while Amunmose stepped up with the adze in his hand to begin the incantation for the Opening of the Mouth so that her brother's senses might be freed once more. "He was only twenty-five years old," she said more loudly than she had intended. She felt Ahmose take her hand, his own fingers moist, and she realized that he was weeping too.

When the High Priest had finished, the women began to wail afresh and one by one the members of the family knelt to kiss the linen-wound feet that smelled of myrrh and the unguents of preservation. The coffin was lifted and at last Kamose was carried down the long, bare passage to the tiny room whose walls glowed with colours that no one living would ever see again. There was a stone plinth in its centre to receive him and around it was placed his furniture and the personal belongings he would need. They were pitifully few.

Aahmes-nefertari had an armful of spring flowers to lay on his breast, blue cornflowers and red poppies, and his mother also showered him with blooms she had culled from the garden, but Tetisheri stood rigidly with tears pouring down her wrinkled cheeks and her hands behind her back. "I gave him everything in life," she had said earlier when they had gathered at the watersteps to cross the river. "I will offer no token of his death. I do not accept this day." Ahmose went to her, pity in the tenderness with which he encircled her frail shoulders, and to Aahmes-nefertari's dull surprise she did not pull away but allowed him to support her as the lid was replaced and nailed down and they finally turned away. Aahmes-nefertari, inhaling the dank, stale air of the passage, looked back. Kamose was already shrouded in darkness, the coffin with its lifeless burden no more than a bulky shape that would remain immobile in a stygian blackness forever.

Tents had been pitched a short distance away from the tomb's forecourt and here for three days his family and household feasted, eating and drinking to his memory, praying for his ka's safe journey, and shedding many tears. On the second night Aahmes-nefertari could not sleep. After tossing restlessly on her cot opposite a slumbering Ahmose, feverish and increasingly uncomfortable, she rose, wrapped herself in a cloak, and left their shelter. The night was cool and still. Across the river a few faint orange lights marked the environs of Weset and the Nile itself flowed peacefully, a narrow, fluid darkness from where she stood.

It was no more than a few steps to the low wall of the court and she crossed the uneven, shadow-hollowed ground quickly with a word of reassurance to the Follower who had materialized by her side. He moved back and she went on alone to the black, gaping hole in the side of the pyramid that would be filled and sealed the next day.

Here she sank down, and drawing up her knees she began to speak in a whisper, telling her brother how much she loved him, reminding him of their childhood together, putting into words how it felt to hear his voice issuing from another room as she walked along a passage, to go out into the garden and look up to see him perched motionless on the roof of the old palace, to be warmed by one of his rare smiles. "You were our rock, our touchstone, obdurate and unyielding, and I did not realize how closely we clung to you," she said softly. "Somehow we took it for granted that your very obstinacy would always protect us. Ahmose is King now and his way is not your way. It never was. You know this, dear Kamose. Yet I think that if Ahmose had gone first he would have failed. That will not happen now because his time has come, but you did the right thing, the only thing, and you will be justified before the gods.

"Do you remember sailing down to Khemmenu one year when we were still very young, to celebrate the Feast of Thoth on the nineteenth of his month with Mother's relatives? And on our first night out Si-Amun accidentally pushed me off the boat and I had not learned to swim? The Inundation had barely begun. The servants were rushing about screaming and Si-Amun started to cry and Father came out of the cabin not knowing what the uproar was about. You just calmly ran down the ramp, waded into the shallows, and dragged me to the bank. I was coughing and spitting. 'Silly Aahmes-nefertari,' you said. 'Swimming is easy. I will teach you how and by the time we come home you will be faster than the fish.' Even then you took charge of our safety. I will not let you be forgotten. I will not let your memory be distorted. The history of Egypt will not be allowed ..."

The words died in her throat from pure terror, for something moved in the darkness of the tomb entrance. A shape detached itself from the void and came panting towards her and with a low cry of relief she recognized Behek. Whining, he settled onto his haunches beside her and laid his grey head in her lap. She flung her arms around him. "How did you get across the river?" she scolded him. "Did you push your way onto one of the servants' skiffs? You should not have been down there. You might have found yourself immured behind a wall of rubble tomorrow, unable to escape, and no one would ever have known what had

become of you. But I understand. Oh, I do understand."
And, burying her face in his warm neck, she began to sob.

In the morning the last rites were chanted, the tents
struck, and the remains of the feast buried. Masons stood
waiting to fill in the doorway that seemed to exhale a cold
loneliness into the sparkling air. "Amunmose will see that
the seals are attached when the men have finished,"
Ahmose said to a quiet Aahmes-nefertari. "It is over and we
must go on. The boats are waiting to take us back to the
house and there is much to do. How did Behek get here?"
He gave a sharp order to a guard standing nearby and, with
a last glance at the stubby pyramid rearing solidly against
the clear blue of the sky, Aahmes-nefertari got onto her
litter and pulled the curtains closed.

Ahmose disappeared in the direction of the temple once
they had gained the eastern bank, and the women also
separated to their several quarters. To Aahmes-nefertari the
house seemed cleansed, empty of all the currents of
emotion that had swirled invisibly along its corridors, and
she was immediately exhausted. Going to her couch, she
closed her eyes and fell into a deep, dreamless sleep.

In the evening she was summoned to her mother's
rooms, where Ahmose already sat drinking water while he
talked with Aahotep. He rose to greet her with a kiss. "You
look better," he said, eyeing her critically. "Kamose has
gone now. His heart has been weighed and he has left the
Judgement Hall to take his place in the Holy Barque with
our ancestors. Can't you feel it?"

"Yes," she answered, coming forward with a short bow to
her mother. "That is why the house feels so ... so scoured."
She wrinkled her nose at the force, the appropriateness of

the word. "I am sorry for Ramose. He still must accompany Nefer-Sakharu to Khemmenu and endure her funeral. Did he return, Ahmose?" He waved her to the stool before Aahotep's cosmetics table.

"Yes. Nefer-Sakharu's beautification is complete, but I cannot release Ramose for a couple of days. Tomorrow is the last day of Pharmuthi. On the first day of Pakhons, which is also of course the first of Shemu, I have planned a great ceremony in the temple and Ramose must be here for it. I cannot be crowned King," he went on heavily. "The atef-crown and the Double Crown are in Het-Uart. But I intend to declare myself King of Upper and Lower Egypt with every solemn rite of purification and acclamation and to date the Anniversary of my Appearing from the first day of summer. It is entirely appropriate." He grinned suddenly. "Every Weset notable, every new military officer, every official, will be called upon to swear allegiance to me, including Ramose. Then he can go. As I travel north with the army, I will require the same act of loyalty from the governors of the nomes and the sons of those who betrayed Kamose, and from the navy. You, my dearest, will sit beside me in the temple as my Queen and will also receive the homage of those who owe it." He reached over to stroke her cheek. "Make sure that Raa dresses Ahmose-onkh as sumptuously as possible. He can stand between us, a visible Hawk-in-the-Nest. This must be a ritual with all the pomp and magnificence we can muster. We need a show of power."

He sobered and turned to his mother. "Aahotep, I want you to wear as much jewellery and glitter as you like but your garment must be the sheath you were wearing when you slew Meketra. I know that you have kept it."

"Ahmose!" she cried out in shock. "No! Never! Quite apart from the fact that it is stiff and encrusted with old blood and probably smells, I could not bear its touch against my body!" He leaned towards her, elbows on his knees.

"I want them all to see the triumph of the Taos. I want them to ponder our victory in the midst of all the incense and dancing and ritual, a victory won not with fine words and harmless gestures but with knives and blood. I want our strength to be before their eyes during all the hours in the temple. Disloyalty brings death. That is what I want them to finally understand."

"There are a thousand ways in which you can press your message home," Aahotep objected hotly. Her own cheeks had become flushed and her eyes glinted angrily. Aahmes-nefertari had never seen her poise so shaken. "It is not only an utterly distasteful request, Ahmose, it smacks of insanity. No. I will not wear it." He got up slowly and folded his arms.

"I realize that the prospect is abhorrent," he responded firmly, "but I have more than one reason for asking you to do it. This is not a request from your son, Aahotep. It is a command from your King." She went very pale, the hectic colour draining from her face.

"And if I still refuse?"

"Then not only will you incur my extreme displeasure but you will spoil a surprise I have for you. Please trust me, Mother. I love you more than any son could ever worship the one who gave him life, because not only did you give it, you also preserved it from the assassin's club. Trust me and do not refuse." She gazed long and searchingly into his face, her hands linked loosely in front of her, and gradually her features softened.

"No one but your father could ask such a thing of me, nay even demand it, and be obeyed," she said at last. "Very well, Ahmose. I will wear the sheath." At once he beamed, and striding to the door he was gone.

The two women looked at each other. "The blow to his head ..." Aahotep began haltingly, but Aahmes-nefertari broke into her sentence.

"No, I do not think so. There has been a steady rationality to everything he has said and done since his recovery. He knows what he is asking of you, and why."

"Nevertheless the prospect is disgusting." She shuddered. "Stay with me for a while, Aahmes-nefertari. We can play sennet and talk. I have seen little of you lately and nothing of Tetisheri at all. Is Hent-ta-Hent well and gaining weight as she should?" At her summons Hetepet came in, set up the sennet board, and trimmed the lamps. Mother and daughter soon became engrossed in the game and their easy conversation but occasionally Aahotep cast a surreptitious glance in the direction of the chest where, Aahmes-nefertari knew, the besmirched sheath lay. She did not blame her mother for her apprehension.

The morning of the first day of Pakhons dawned and with it a flurry of frenetic activity in the house. Ahmose had spent the night in one of the anterooms of the temple, taking with him Akhtoy and his body servant, so that he might pray and meditate during the dark hours, be purified, and watch Amunmose perform the god's first ablutions for the last time. Once officially King, he also acquired the privilege of entering the sanctuary alone and tending to

Amun's ritual needs instead of the High Priest if he wished, but on this important day, as he told his wife before he left her quarters, he wished to savour the last of his youth.

It was a curious turn of phrase and Aahmes-nefertari pondered it while Raa laid out the red, gold-shot sheath she would wear and the cosmetician expertly dropped a bead of water onto the powdered black kohl in his tiny dish. To her it had been Meketra's blow that had ended Ahmose's youth, for there was no doubting the subtle but definite changes that had taken place in him since then. But perhaps he saw a weight of responsibility descending on him with the kingly titles he would take and, together with the detachment from his old self divinity would bring, it would serve to separate him not only from every other Egyptian but also from his young self. He is only twenty-one, she mused, closing her eyes at the cosmetician's murmured request. So much has happened in the last five years to change us all. Sometimes I forget that I am not as ancient as Tetisheri, sixty-five at least, and I expect that Ahmose feels the same.

She had chosen a belt of thin gold links for the sheath, and white leather sandals studded with jaspers. Her wig was heavy, fifty braids falling almost to her waist, brushing gently against arms laden with golden bracelets on whose gleaming surfaces likenesses of Hathor, goddess of love and beauty, and linked hoops of ankhs were delicately etched. Clasping one of her upper arms in the golden embrace of her wings was Mut, the vulture goddess, totem of Queens, her predatory beak facing the rear to protect Aahmes-nefertari from any attack. Green scarabs set in gold graced her fingers and blue lapis lazuli scarabs hung from her earlobes.

Before the wig was placed on her head, Raa carefully settled a heavy pectoral around her neck, a sturdy golden chain holding Mut's spread wings that fanned out over her breasts. Each feather had been meticulously enamelled in a different colour—red, green, blue, yellow—so that the piece would blaze with life when sunlight struck it. Ahmose had given it to her the previous day and she had taken it wonderingly. "I am sorry that there is no silver in it," he had apologized. "I have taken all the silver I could lay my hands on for other purposes. But it is beautiful nonetheless. The temple jewellers have been sweating over it for a long time. Wear it as the Queen you are."

She was too dazzled to enquire what he was doing with silver, a metal prized for its rarity and in short supply at Weset, but now as she felt the pectoral bump against her skin through the gossamer linen of her sheath, the unasked question formed. Raa set the wig over her own pinned hair and handed her a mirror. Taking it, Aahmes-nefertari inspected her copper-coloured reflection critically. Her mouth, usually oddly pale, was bright with orange henna, but paint could not disguise its haughty downward curve, a physical characteristic that had often misled guests into believing that even as a child she was cold and arrogant. When in fact I was intensely shy, she thought fleetingly. The rich dark brown eyes blinked back at her, exotically outlined in kohl and lidded in gold-speckled blue, and the crinkled fringe of the wig brushed winged eyebrows also blackly shiny with kohl.

Ahmose had told her not to wear any gems on her head. But I feel undressed on such a solemn occasion, she thought again, tilting her face from side to side. The wig needs

something. He means to crown me, doesn't he? At that
realization a pang of anxiety went through her and she
passed the mirror back to her servant. It is one thing to run
out to the training ground and browbeat soldiers before
hurrying back to my household duties, she said to herself
rather grimly. It is quite another to assume the lofty iden-
tity of a goddess. "Raa, go and see if my mother is ready and
make sure Ahmose-onkh has not pulled off his sandals," she
ordered. "Tell Uni to somehow make Grandmother hurry.
Ankhmahor can have the litters brought to the entrance
now."

In the small silence that followed the servant's departure
Aahmes-nefertari drew in a deep, slow breath and gingerly
fingered the pectoral. She was already thirsty but did not
want to smudge her freshly hennaed lips by drinking. This
day is the last of your youth too, she told herself. You have
been a Princess, you have married twice, you have borne
children, but you were still very much a girl. The rebellion
gave your youth a mortal wound, but it will finally die
today.

Outside the servants had gathered to see their mistresses
in all their unaccustomed finery and the litters, ribboned
and garlanded with fresh flowers, waited on the grass.
Ankhmahor, in his capacity as Captain of the Followers,
bowed to Aahmes-nefertari as she left the shadow of the
pillars and walked towards him. He too was carefully
painted, his large eyes ringed in kohl, his mouth hennaed.
On his head he wore a linen helmet striped in blue and
white, the ancient colours of royal Egypt, and a ceremonial
dagger, its hilt filigreed gold, the black leather of its scabbard stitched in gold, hung from his belt. He wore white

leather gloves. Behind him the escort waited, the men he and she had selected together to guard the household, each in similar helmets and brown leather sandals and gloves, but the weapons nudging their thighs were for use not display. Gravely they saluted her and she smiled at them all, moving quickly to her litter.

As she was lowering herself onto the cushions, Uni and Kares appeared. In spite of their many tasks that morning, they were both attired in the formal garb of a steward, plain white voluminous tunics falling from one shoulder to their ankles and edged in gold thread. On their upper arms they wore the plain, thick gold bands that denoted their exalted station in the household hierarchy and ribbons of blue and white went around their short wigs. Aahmes-nefertari spared them one admiring look before her eyes found the two women pacing at their heels.

Tetisheri was clad in gold from her head to her tiny brown feet. Gold leaves glinted on her yellow sheath, golden lotus flowers swung from her earlobes, gold glistened in her wig, and gold dust sparked from her painted cheeks. But it was not her grandmother who caused Aahmes-nefertari a stab of sympathy and alarm. Aahotep wore no jewellery at all. Her wig was straight and shoulder-length. Her arms and neck were bare and on her feet were a pair of well-worn and rather scruffy sandals. She came forward slowly, chin high, not trying to hide the hideous brown stains slashed across the plain white sheath. Even as Aahmes-nefertari watched, a flake that had been encrusting its skirt became detached and spiralled onto the path. A murmur of shock went through the assembly but Aahotep ignored it. Ankhmahor sprang to hold back the curtains of her litter and as soon as she was safely inside he closed them firmly. Tetisheri bent to peer in at Aahmes-nefertari. She was grinning impishly, the gold particles in the henna of her lips making tiny points of fire as she spoke. "I know why Ahmose made her wear it," she said happily. "He came to me last night and explained. We had a most interesting discussion." That was clever of you and wise too, my husband, Aahmes-nefertari thought. Make Grandmother your accomplice, smooth her ruffled feathers, and you remove her claws. "I could not tell Aahotep what he said, of course, but I did assure her that this would be the proudest day of her life," Tetisheri went on. "She decided not to adorn herself although Ahmose said she could. Jewellery simply looked ghoulish with all that dried blood." She chuckled and straightened.

"Does it have something to do with the silver Ahmose told me he was amassing?" Aahmes-nefertari asked, momentarily inquisitive in spite of herself. "Is he dedicating a shrine or a statue in her name in the temple?" Tetisheri looked blank.

"Silver?" she said sharply. "No, I didn't know that. But I hope he is not going to make an expensive gesture to Amun's priests, not with silver. It is too scarce. When he defeats Apepa and can open normal trade routes, we will have all the silver we can afford, but not yet." She would have gone on, but Ahmose-onkh interposed himself between them, one hand still imprisoned in a nurse's fist.

"You look pretty, Mother," he said. Aahmes-nefertari smiled at him. His clear brown eyes had been ringed in kohl. A long golden tear ending in a tiny hawk with folded wings hung from one of his little earlobes, and both wrists were encircled in gold bracelets.

"And you look very handsome in your pleated kilt and new sandals," she answered. "No, Ahmose-onkh, leave your youth lock alone or you will lose the clasp and the plaiting will come undone."

"But the netting scratches my neck," he grumbled. "When can I take the sandals off? My feet are hot."

"Come in here beside me." She patted the cushions. "I have things to tell you. I will give him back to you when we reach the temple," she called up to the patient girl as she relinquished Ahmose-onkh's hand. "Ankhmahor, let us go!"

At once he shouted an order. The litters were lifted, the guard fell in behind and before, and the cavalcade started towards the river road. As they went, Aahmes-nefertari took her son's small hand in her own and began to explain to him why he had been painted and carefully dressed, why he must keep his sandals on, the significance of what was about to happen in the temple. He listened soberly, his bright, intelligent eyes fixed on her face, and when she had finished he wriggled thoughtfully on his cushion, looking down at his red-hennaed palms. "Father is King over all of Egypt now that my uncle Kamose is dead?" he queried.

"Yes," she replied. "He is going to tell everyone today, and they will promise to do everything he says, and not rebel against him like some of the nobles and soldiers did to your uncle."

"They killed him, didn't they?" he said with more relish than regret. "They shot him dead."

"Yes, they did."

"And you and Grandmother punished them." He slapped his brown knees cheerfully. "And when Father dies I will be King?"

"Yes."

"Good. When I am King and everyone must do as I say, I shall put all the soldiers and nobles in prison once a year, just to be sure."

"It is not that easy to be King, Ahmose-onkh," she said with a sigh. "Even Kings must be obedient to the laws of the gods, and Ma'at decrees that no one may be imprisoned without a cause. Egyptian kings are not like the savages of other countries who rule without Ra." But he was no longer paying attention. He was peering through a crack in the curtains.

"Mother, look at all the people!" he exclaimed excitedly. "Let me open the curtains!" He was tugging at them and she reached past him and slid them wide.

Beyond the sheltering phalanx of guards pacing to right and left, both edges of the river road were thick with shouting, jostling citizens. As the litter curtains were drawn back and Aahmes-nefertari and her son appeared, the clamour grew. Weset knew what she and Aahotep had done and they were grateful. The link, always strong between the Taos and their people, was now well-nigh unbreakable. Ahmose-onkh was laughing and waving back at them but Aahmes-nefertari, though she smiled and inclined her head, was seized with a fleeting melancholy. The Setiu still hold the Delta, she thought. Ahmose can declare himself King of Upper and Lower Egypt, but the truth is that the country is still divided.

The litter bearers were forced to slow as they turned left along the short canal leading to Amun's pylons, for here the throng was thick, and when the family alighted just within the outer court they found it also packed, though with a more dignified gathering of prominent Weset dwellers who bowed to them gravely. Aahmes-nefertari was reminded of a field of grain bending to the wind as she relinquished Ahmose-onkh to the nurse and proceeded towards the inner court, her mother and grandmother beside her. The atmosphere around them changed as Aahotep's sheath became visible and a ripple of whispers followed them until they vanished into the inner court.

The air here was hazed with fragrant incense. Aahmes-nefertari, who loved the smell, inhaled appreciatively as she peered through it to the open doors of the sanctuary beyond. Amun smiled enigmatically back at her, his hands on his knees, his feet hidden in flowers, a wreath of blossoms resting against his smooth chest. It was a rare privilege to see him. Hidden from impious eyes in the dim security of his sanctuary for most of the year, ruling through his priests and oracles, he was a benignly invisible presence to most of his subjects.

Aahmes-nefertari knelt, and together with Tetisheri and Aahotep, prostrated herself before him. As they rose, Aahotep stumbled and fell, a small, quiet movement that went virtually unnoticed under the tinkle of the finger cymbals and the rattle of the systra held by the temple singers. By the time Aahmes-nefertari had noticed her mother's distress, a young man had darted out from the ranks of priests ranged just outside the sanctuary and had dropped to his own knees beside her. "Pretend that you are making a second reverence, Majesty," Aahmes-nefertari heard him say. "That way you will transform a blunder into

a mark of deep respect and the god will bless you for it."
Aahotep was obviously too shaken to disobey. He joined
her in her obeisance and unobtrusively helped her to rise
with a hand under her elbow. Aahmes-nefertari expected
her to shake him off with a quiet reprimand but she did no
more than nod once without looking at him and he
resumed his place with his fellows.

Two chairs with a stool between them had been set
before the sanctuary, facing the men and women filling the
inner court. Behind the chairs were the priests and to either
side the holy singers and dancers were ranged. Aahmes-
nefertari would have liked to turn around and scan the
crowd, but she did not dare and indeed she would scarcely
have had time, for Amunmose was approaching from one of
the anterooms lining the court, accompanied by his
incense-laden acolytes. He was wearing the leopard skin
denoting his exalted position draped over one shoulder and
his staff of holy office was in one hand. Following him was
Ahmose in a plain white kilt, his feet bare, his head
covered by a square of knotted white linen. Then came
three priests, each solemnly bearing a box. The singers
burst into harmony. Regally the High Priest led Ahmose to
one of the chairs and bowed.

Ahmose did not sit. For a moment his gaze travelled
across the assembly, met his wife's eyes, and acknowledged
her with a grin that flashed out and was gone so quickly
that Aahmes-nefertari wondered if she had imagined it. He
held up a hand and immediately the singing stopped. There
was a breathless hush. "Favoured ones of Egypt," Ahmose
called, his voice echoing to the stone ceiling. "Today I
succeed my brother as Lord of the Two Lands and Beloved

of Amun. From henceforth, the first day of summer will mark the Anniversary of my Appearing as the god's Divine Incarnation here on earth. I pledge to uphold the laws of Ma'at, reward those who serve me well, and punish justly those who do not. I take to myself the kingship of Egypt as the legitimate inheritor of my ancestors' right to rule. Aahotep, come here." His mother stepped forward, and gently taking her arm he swung her to face the gathering. "This is the price of treachery," he said, pointing at her sheath, "and it was exacted ruthlessly by this woman, herself the wife of a King without a crown. Can any deny the claims of the house of Tao in the presence of such courage and nobility? Mark this well, and ponder what you see." Aahmes-nefertari felt a tug on her own sheath and glanced down to see Ahmose-onkh.

"Why is Grandmother wearing a dirty sheath?" he whispered fiercely. "Is Father giving her a reprimand?" Aahmes-nefertari pressed a finger to his hot little mouth.

"Not now," she whispered back. "I will explain later."

"I too am a King without a crown," Ahmose was saying. "The sacred Regalia—the hedjet, the deshret, the atef, the heka and the nekhakha—lie in blasphemous foreign hands. Even the Lady of Flame and the Lady of Dread are in the north. But I will rescue the White Nefer and the Red, the atef and the sceptre and the flail, and when I do there will be a fitting coronation here, before Amun, in the midst of his city." He had released Aahotep but she had not moved. She continued to stand, straight and pale, the brown splashes on her foul linen sending out both a warning and a testimony. "Today I will only take the nemes, a symbol of concord with my people," Ahmose went on. "And I will accept new sandals in order to walk the new path the god has decreed for me. But let there be no mistake. Power does not reside in the Double Crown but in the person of the god who wears it. Let us continue. Bring stools for my mother and grandmother."

He signalled. Aahmes-nefertari noticed anxiously that Aahotep was trying to hide a limp as they went to him and she heaved a secret sigh of relief when they were all seated. But blood was seeping slowly from beneath Aahotep's broken toenail and Aahmes-nefertari experienced a surge of the superstitious horror that used to often overtake her. It is a bad omen for the start of Ahmose's reign, she thought. No one must see it. What shall I do? She had been waved to one of the two chairs and knew she could neither rise nor bend down without drawing attention to herself.

But the same young priest who had come to Aahotep's rescue before had been watching. Boldly he approached, fell gracefully before her, and while seeming to kiss her feet in an impulse of respectful submission managed to use the hem of his garment to wipe away the drops. Aahotep stared before her grimly, giving no sign, and while he was walking away Aahmes-nefertari saw her pull her feet in under the protection of her own voluminous garb.

Ahmose now sat. The first box was opened and Amunmose withdrew a pair of magnificent sandals that, like Ankhmahor's dagger, were not meant for any but ceremonial purposes. Covered in gold leaf and encrusted with lapis and jasper, they were slipped reverently onto Ahmose's feet while a prostrate Amunmose intoned the correct litany and the priests formed the responses. Aahmes-nefertari had time to notice that a startling likeness to Apepa had been painted on their soles before the High Priest stood, waved a censer over Ahmose, and lifted the lid of the second box.

He drew out a pectoral, and with a shock Aahmes-nefertari recognized the ornament Kamose had commissioned for himself. There, hanging regally from Amunmose's fingers, was Heh, god of eternity, kneeling on the heb sign with the notched palm ribs in his hands signifying myriad years, but the cartouche above him had been altered. It no longer encircled Kamose's name. Nekhbet and Wadjet embraced Ahmose's name instead. A lump came into Aahmes-nefertari's throat as the beautiful reminder of all Kamose's hopes was lowered over her husband's head. He does not mean it as a triumph over Kamose, she said to herself sadly. For him it is a link with his brother, a promise that all Kamose began will be brought to fruition. But for me it is only heartache.

The last box contained a nemes headdress exquisitely fashioned in stripes of dark blue and gold, its rim a band of plain gold above which the simple facsimile of the uraeus, the vulture Lady of Dread, protectress of the south, and the cobra Lady of Flame, protectress of the north, reared gleaming. With solemn words Amunmose removed the square of linen from Ahmose's head and replaced it with the nemes, settling the lappets to either side of his neck. It was the last time that the King's sacred head would be seen naked in public.

Then Ahmose stood and raised his arms. A tide of applause began and swelled to a roar of approval and homage and with one accord the company went to the ground, foreheads against the stone floor. On rising they continued the tumult until at Ahmose's nod the herald Khabekhnet stepped forward. "Hear the desires of the King!" he called, and rapidly the furore died away. "Firstly His Majesty wishes it to be known that of the five titles which are his prerogative he will take up only the three pertaining to his godhead until Egypt is cleansed. At that time, when he sits upon the Holy Throne with Steps under the weight of the Double Crown, he will be pleased to receive the title of nesw-bit, He of the Sedge and the Bee, and the appellation He of the Two Ladies. Thus, for the time being, he is Uatch-Kheperu Ahmose, Son of the Sun, Horus, the Horus of Gold. The King has spoken." He paused. "Secondly His Majesty wishes now to place a Queen's crown upon the head of his beloved Aahmes-nefertari, the Beautiful Daughter of the Moon, so that Egypt may do homage to her as God's Wife and worship her as first among the glories of our land. The King has spoken."

He retired and Ahmose rose. From beside his chair he took up a fourth box Aahmes-nefertari had not noticed before and opening it he brought out a diadem of gold, a solid cap in the likeness of the goddess Mut whose wings were draped to either side of the head of the wearer and whose claws each gripped a shen-sign, signifying infinity, eternity and protection. Mut's vulture head reared back, her curved beak sharp, her eyes with their black onyx pupils glittering dangerously. With great care, with the tenderness of love and pride, Ahmose lowered it onto Aahmes-nefertari's wig. "The booty from the treasure ships must be lamentably depleted by now, Majesty," she murmured as his face came close to hers and he grinned slowly.

"Wickedly so," he muttered in return. "But there will be much more before I am done. I adore you, my irresistible warrior." Once again the inner court resounded to loud cheers.

Ahmose did not resume his seat as Aahmes-nefertari thought he would. Instead he let the noise continue for a while. Then his ringed hand came up. "I now have a solemn and vital duty to perform," he said, his voice ringing out over the expectant crowd. "Aahotep, my mother, come and stand before me." Aahotep left her stool and did as she was bidden. Aahmes-nefertari saw puzzlement in her eyes as she and her son faced one another. She was at least half a head shorter than Ahmose so that when he next spoke, all could see his hennaed mouth over the top of her plain, flat wig. "There are three awards bestowed by a King upon deserving subjects," he said. "One, the Gold of Favours, is given to any citizen for outstanding loyalty to his King, for devotion to his work for his King, or for excellence in his administrative capacity. The other two, the Gold of Valour and the Gold of Flies, are only conferred on soldiers, whether common or commanding, who have shown exemplary courage in battle. No woman has ever received the Gold of Valour or the Gold of Flies. Of those two, the Gold of Flies is the most rare. In the whole history of Egypt it has only been awarded four times. Today will mark its fifth." He thrust out a hand and Amunmose laid across it a thin loop of gold from which hung three golden flies. Aahmes-nefertari, watching them swing in her husband's grasp, marvelled at the skill of the jewellers who had given them such a semblance of animation. Their wings were solid, their eyes bulbous. But it was in the crafting of the bodies that the anonymous man had shown his genius. He had grooved them to simulate the stripes of a living fly so that when the wearer moved and breathed they would appear iridescent in the sunlight. "I have caused a stela to be erected here within the sacred precincts," Ahmose went on. "I will tell you all what it says. 'Aahotep is one who has accomplished the rites and cared for Egypt. She has looked after Egypt's troops and she has guarded them. She has brought back the fugitives and collected together the deserters. She has pacified Upper Egypt and expelled the rebels.' This I dictated to the one who carved the words. Nothing more needs to be said in stone, but you all know that not only did she save my life but she also took part in quelling the uprising among the soldiery. No man is more worthy than this woman to have such an exalted award hung about her neck to rest against the bloody emblem of her bravery. Aahotep, hold up your head. I award you the Gold of Flies and I give you a new title, nebet-ta, Mistress of the Land."

The necklet fastened with a simple golden hook. Ahmose undid it, reached around his mother and coupled it, giving it a pat before stepping back. Aahotep turned. She seemed dazed. The host erupted into a wild cacophony of yells, calling her name, whistling and shouting, and tears began to slip down her cheeks. Amunmose went to her, and taking her arm he led her back to her stool. Sinking onto it, she looked across at Ahmose, her fingers caressing the exquisite insects. She smiled at him through her tears.

"I am glad that my surprise meets with your approval," he said. "Now we will continue. Ahmose-onkh, come up here." Letting go his nurse's hand, the boy trotted eagerly forward and scrambled up onto his father's knees.

What a curious mixture of formality and spontaneity this ritual is, Aahmes-nefertari thought, as she watched her son wriggle to find a comfortable spot on Ahmose's muscled thighs. But it perfectly expresses Ahmose's character. Kamose would never have done this. For him every chant, every step, every sonorous pronouncement would have been executed according to rigid custom so that the past could flow seamlessly into the present without any taint of potentially perilous innovation. Kamose wanted to restore us to the past, but I am beginning to realize that my husband intends to not only restore but reanimate the structure of Egypt. He has been able to combine tradition with an instinctive talent for the impulse and has lost no dignity in doing so. It is like being married again to an intriguing stranger.

The din was lessening. Ahmose signalled. "Hor-Aha, bring the armbands," he ordered, and his General shouldered his way through the flock of priests carrying a chest which he opened but kept, going down on one knee beside Ahmose. Aahmes-nefertari shifted so that she could peer into it and saw that it was full of wide silver bracelets. "You will now, all of you, swear allegiance to me, to the God's Wife, and to the Hawk-in-the-Nest Ahmose-onkh." Ahmose raised his voice. "Every prince and noble, every governor and administrator. I have not singled you out. I will require the same submissions from each town and city I pass on my way north. I do not intend this rite to be merely a matter of form. Your oath will be regarded as completely binding. First I invite those whose names my herald calls. I have decided to employ five permanent army divisions to be stationed here in

Weset. All eleven divisions have new officers, but I will receive the permanent commanders first." He nodded at Khabekhnet.

"The Division of Amun. General Turi, the Commander of Shock Troops Prince Ankhmahor, the Standard Bearer Idu." The three men came forward, Ahmose's childhood friend in the lead. Kamose had sent him and his family south, out of harm's way, during the first desperate years of the insurrection and Ahmose had recently recalled them. Prostrating themselves, the men kissed Ahmose's feet and both his hands, straightening a little to perform the same act on Ahmose-onkh who laughed delightedly. Moving to Aahmes-nefertari, they reverenced her with the same humble respect. Ahmose bade them rise and handed each of them an armband.

"The badge of your responsibility," he said. "Do not use it like a club with which to beat your underlings nor as a tree to hide behind. The blessings of your Lord."

"The Division of Ra," Khabekhnet intoned. "General Kagemni, the Commander of Shock Troops Khnumhotep, the Standard Bearer Khaemhet." Once again the homage was offered and received and the armbands distributed. "The Division of Thoth," Khabekhnet shouted. "General Baqet, the Commander of Shock Troops Tchanny, the Standard Bearer Pepynakht."

Aahmes-nefertari watched and listened attentively. She recognized very few of the men whose bodies were crouched over her and whose mouths touched her flesh. He has done exactly as he said he would, she thought. Most of these soldiers are from the ranks. Their posture, their stride, the rough combination of awkward pride and hesitant self-consciousness, it all brands them as commoners. She stole a glance to where Mesehti and Makhu were standing, but she could read nothing on their faces. Ramose, close beside them, looked strained but calm. The other two divisions to be quartered at Weset were Horus and Montu, but six more had been newly formed and, by the time the non-military men had begun to file forward and bind themselves to their new King, the box Hor-Aha had steadily proffered was empty. Aahmes-nefertari was suddenly tired. The glorious Queen's crown had begun to chafe her behind her ears and her spine was aching. So that is where all the silver went, she thought, and my husband with it. No wonder he was spending so much time here in the temple. He and Amunmose, the masons and jewellers and overseers of sacred protocol must have worked like the slaves of the Setiu to prepare for this day.

Ahmose-onkh had begun to squirm and whine quietly. Ahmose hushed him peremptorily and after a wail of protest his thumb crept into his mouth and he fell asleep against his father's chest. When he woke in response to a gentle shake, his cheek had been imprinted with the design of Kamose's pectoral.

They proceeded out of the temple on a tide of music and renewed clouds of incense to be met by a shower of flower petals and a delirious congregation of citizenry. Ahmose-onkh was yawning. Aahotep was disguising a limp. All at once she halted and turned to her steward. "Kares, go back and fetch me that young priest. You know the one," she ordered. They waited, the guards struggling to hold back the clamorous people, the late afternoon sun dancing on the ripples of Amun's canal and making them blink after the relative dimness of the inner court. Presently Kares returned with the young man. When he saw Aahotep he bowed low several times, his palms uplifted in a gesture of supplication. "Don't worry," Aahotep said kindly. "I want to thank you, not punish you. What is your name and position?"

"I am called Yuf, Exalted One," he stammered. "I am a we'eb priest, servant to the servants of the god."

"Well, Yuf, you have shown great presence of mind today," Aahotep said. "Not to mention an impudent resourcefulness. I need a priest of my own. If you would like to serve me, come to the house tomorrow and ask for Kares." She did not wait for a reply but hobbled straight to her litter, leaving Yuf's startled face to be swallowed up in the crush. Aahmes-nefertari heard her rare, abrupt laugh from behind the closed curtains as she herself climbed into her own conveyance.

Late that night, after the feasting and the music, the congratulatory speeches, the garlands and wine and revelry, an exhausted Aahmes-nefertari lay on her husband's couch in the blissful silence of his quarters. They had finished making love and Ahmose had just snuffed out the lamp. Darkness rushed in, soothing and welcome. "Here," he said. "Put your head in the hollow of my shoulder and sleep beside me. Do you approve of what I did today, Aahmes-nefertari? Was it wise?"

"Yes, I think so," she replied drowsily. "Providing you remember to treat the Princes with more than your usual courtesy and give them the titles you promised. They are not stupid, Ahmose. They are surely aware that you have greatly curtailed their power. You must throw them a few bones." He grunted and there was silence for a moment. She thought that he had drifted to sleep but suddenly she felt him stir.

"Oh, by the way," he said casually. "I forgot to tell you earlier. I have appointed you the Second Prophet of Amun. Amunmose has agreed to my decision." Mild shock jerked her completely awake.

"But why?" she exclaimed. "You have given me enough duties with the household guards and overseeing the construction of a town for the new divisions! How am I supposed to add service in the temple to those chores?" He said nothing, and she realized that he was waiting for her to come to an answer herself. "You need a spy in the temple, don't you?" she said slowly. "You are fond of Amunmose but you do not trust him, or rather, you need to know that you can go on trusting him. The temple is a world unto itself. I am to link that world with this."

"Yes," he half-whispered. "It is honourable to serve the god, Aahmes-nefertari, and like Kamose I revere him and am ready to do his will. It is his servants who are full of the frailties of human nature. I do not want surprises. I do not want to come home to sedition, not ever." She bit her lip, an indication of mild distress that he could not see.

"You don't really trust anyone, do you, my husband?" she said.

"Only you, my lovely Queen," he responded, a quiver of mirth in his voice. "Only you."

3

AHMOSE, THE MEDJAY, and the Weset contingent of the army left for the north the following afternoon. Ahmose, standing above the watersteps with Ahmose-onkh's small hand enclosed within his own, felt weary but satisfied. I did not know if I could do it, he thought. It was a risk, all of it, but I have established the foundation for a new fighting force, proclaimed my hold over most of the country, and broken the power of the Princes, although they do not know it yet. Only Apepa remains between me and total control. Only. He smiled ruefully to himself. At least I can concentrate on this campaigning season without worrying about what is happening behind my back. Aahmes-nefertari and Mother are well capable of ruling here in my absence and I am taking my potential enemies with me.

He cast a sidelong glance at Hor-Aha. The man was talking quietly to Ankhmahor, one black hand resting loosely on the hilt of his sword, the other gesticulating lazily. Ankhmahor was looking at the ground, occasionally nodding gravely as he listened. He has not complained, Ahmose thought. Not since that first meeting when he said he understood. But it must be a bitter thing for him to find himself relegated to commanding nothing but the Medjay. I wish I did not need them so badly. Then it would not matter if he took them back to Wawat. As it is, I must take care to consult him as Kamose used to do, for it is true that his worth as a tactician is great. I wonder if he suspects that I have no intention of ratifying his noble title or of giving him an estate until I am completely assured of Egypt's submission.

Around them swirled the activity of embarkation. Last-minutes stores were being carried up the ramps of the reed ships, Scribes of Assemblage were bent over their lists as soldiers filed past them, and those men already on deck were leaning on the guard rails watching the groups of officers still on the bank. I shall be sorry to miss the harvest, Ahmose's thoughts ran on. How many years is it since I have seen the air full of flying chaff and heard the songs of the reapers as the stalks of grain fall under their blades? By the time I come home the Inundation will have begun, the granaries will be full, and the new wine will be fermenting in the vats.

He became aware that Ahmose-onkh was tugging at his arm. "I want to go with you, Father," he was piping. "I want to go to war." Ahmose smiled into the eager little face.

"I would gladly take you," he said, "but you must be able to draw the bow and wield the spear and sword, and most importantly, you must be able to read."

"Read?" Ahmose-onkh made a face. "Why?"

"Because before a battle all the generals and commanders gather round the maps the scribes have made, with the names of towns and villages and tributaries on them, and they decide what to do. Ipi writes it all down, but how would you know if he had made the right words and how would you tell those words to the men if you could not read them?" He went down on his haunches, straightening the warm black youth lock against the boy's thin collarbone, gently caressing the sun-heated skin. "One day if Amun wills it, you will be King," he went on kindly. "But a King must fight better than any other man in his kingdom and read and write better than any scribe. When you can do these things you can come with me. I shall miss you, my tiny Hawk-in-the-Nest."

"Well, at least tell Mother that I want a room of my own in the house," Ahmose-onkh grumbled. "I am too big to share with Hent-ta-Hent any more." Ahmose rose.

"When you are five and start your lessons, you will have your own quarters," he said. "I will have them built for you. Until then you must obey your mother and grandmother. A King must also learn self-discipline, Ahmose-onkh." The boy heaved a gusty sigh.

"Father, I am so glad you didn't tell me to obey Great-grandmother!" he exclaimed. "She is always grumpy and her nails dig into me when she makes me hug her." Ahmose bit back the admonishment rising to his tongue. I do not like her either, he wanted to say. All my life she has scorned me or simply tolerated me, depending on her mood. To her I will always be guileless Ahmose, innocent and rather stupid. The conversation we had all those months ago did not do much to change her mind, although we managed to arrive at a precarious truce, and when Kamose showed that he was strong enough to hold onto his sanity that truce dissolved. I should have acknowledged her in public yesterday, given her some trifling award, but the days of her active support belong to the Seqenenra and Kamose years, not to mine. I cannot count on her for sensible advice or even mute endorsement, but will she openly oppose me and my policies? It is too soon to say.

"Nevertheless," he said aloud to the upturned face whose features were beginning to mature into the likeness of his true father, Si-Amun, and therefore Kamose's also, "she is a great and noble lady who deserves your respect. A King must learn to hide his feelings, Ahmose-onkh, and yet not become deceitful while doing so …" But Ahmose-onkh had lost interest and was batting at a golden scarab that was whirring by in a flash of glinting carapace.

"Leave it alone, Ahmose-onkh!" his mother called. She came up to them and Ahmose kissed her painted cheek. She smelled of nutmeg and lotus oil.

"Aahmes-nefertari, you are so beautiful!" he said impulsively. She smiled at him delightedly, her kohled eyes narrowed against the blaze of the sun.

"Of course I am," she teased him. "For am I not almost a goddess? Ahmose, this village I am to build for the soldiers, it will need a canal linking it to the river for rapid abandonment when necessary. It cannot rise by the existing barracks. They are almost directly behind the house. Nor should it go on the other side of the town. That is too far for efficient supervision. Where do you want it?" He considered for a while, his arm around her taut waist, his gaze on the gradually diminishing chaos on the river.

"Put it to the south," he said at last. "The cultivable land between the Nile and the desert is narrow so the canal will be short. The soldiers can use it to irrigate the fields already there. They can grow some of their own food when they are not fighting or training. Give the existing barracks to your household guards and their families."

"The fields are ours anyway," she replied. "They were not included in the arouras Kamose promised as future payment to the men who built the reed boats so I will not need to move any peasants from their huts. Do you care what architect I hire to do this work?" He slipped his arm from her waist and began to stroke her hair, the burnished curve of her shoulder, the corded tendons of her neck, feeling an urgent need to store up memories of how she looked to him, how she felt to his touch.

"No," he answered. "Your judgement is sound. Bring one in from elsewhere if there are none qualified in Weset. Amunmose will recommend a man of experience." A sudden thought struck him and he dropped his arm. "When you find someone suitable, take him into the old palace," he told her in a low voice. "Ask him to draw up some plans for its restoration." She glanced at him keenly.

"You have been planning all these things for years, haven't you, my husband?" she murmured. "Apepa's defeat, bringing the old palace to life, making Weset the centre of the world and Amun its mightiest god. What if Kamose had lived?" A spasm of pain disfigured his face for a moment.

"Kamose held the same vision for the future," he said quietly. "We were as one in this. But long before the oracle's cryptic pronouncement I knew that Kamose would not survive to sit on the Horus Throne. He knew it too. Remember the omen of the hawk, Aahmes-nefertari? From then on I began to turn over in my mind what I would do if power came into my hands." He pursed his lips. "Do not mistake me," he went on, and his voice broke. "I loved my brother. Not even the whisper of treason ever entered my thoughts. It was a painful thing, a dreadful thing, Aahmes-nefertari, to prepare for his death, but I did. I know what must be done and how I will do it. This year will see another siege that will not succeed, but it will keep Apepa penned up in Het-Uart, and while he is rendered impotent I will clean out the soldiers of Rethennu from the rest of the Delta. Next year I will defeat him. Do not speak of these things to Mother and especially not to Grandmother," he urged. The other women were approaching along the path with Uni and Kares, and Aahmes-nefertari nodded her agreement and drew away from him. He turned to find Hor-Aha at his elbow.

"The men are all on board and the marchers are finally ranked, Majesty," he said. "It is time."

"Amun himself is coming to bless us," Ahmose reminded him. "We will wait a little."

Even as he spoke he heard the singing. Around him and out on the ships a sudden silence fell. The procession came into view, first the musicians with their finger cymbals and drums, then the singers. Behind them Amunmose was surrounded by his incense-wreathed acolytes, but for once Ahmose's glance slid over his friend and fled to the litter beyond. Borne on the wide shoulders of eight priests, heavily curtained, its sumptuous trappings swaying and glittering in the sun, it advanced until it reached the paving. The bearers set it down with reverent care and its entourage surrounded it protectively.

Amunmose stepped up and drew aside the curtain and at once the assembly went to the ground in worship. To Ahmose's surprise it was Aahmes-nefertari who immediately rose again, and walking to the litter and bowing to the smoothly golden profile of the god within, she turned to the prostrate company. "Hear the words of the Greatest of Greatest from the mouth of his Second Prophet, O King," she called, her voice ringing out clearly and proudly. "Thus says Amun, Lord of Weset. 'O my son Nebpehtira Ahmose, Lord of the Two Lands, I am thy Father. I set terror in the northlands even unto Het-Uart, and the Setiu are a stain beneath thy feet.'" She paused, bowed again, and retreated.

"When did you receive this oracle?" Ahmose whispered into her ear and she smiled.

"Amunmose sent it to me this morning early. Hush now, Ahmose. He is going to bless the troops." The High Priest had taken a censer and was holding it out in the direction of the ships, intoning the chants of benediction and protection, and two other priests waited with the flagons of milk and bull's blood to pour upon the flagstones. All at once a sense of enormous well-being flooded Ahmose. Everything was going to be all right.

It was a wrench to be separated yet again from his family and to see the panorama of the house in its shelter of trees, then the temple and the town itself, then the wide bend of the river pass out of sight, but there was none of the aching anxiety both he and Kamose had felt on previous partings. The fall of Het-Uart was assured. Next year or the year after would see Egypt united once more. It was simply a matter of time. Standing on the deck of his ship with Hor-Aha, Ankhmahor and Turi beside him and the long, uneven line of the other boats strung out behind, he had the strong impression that Kamose also hovered at his shoulder and in a moment he would hear his voice. "Well, Ahmose, we venture forth once more," he would say with that familiar blend of resignation and fortitude.

So powerful was the sense of his brother's presence that Ahmose gave a start when a bevy of ducks hidden in the reeds rose squawking at their approach and the spell was broken. All the same, he thought, you see us, don't you, Kamose? Your passion for our freedom will keep you here watching, your ba-self hovering invisibly as we go north. Oh how I miss you! I did not realize how comfortable it was to occupy a place in your shadow while the ultimate responsibilities of rule and command were yours. Now they are mine and I am naked under their weight. "We will not have long in the Delta this season, Majesty," Turi's words broke in on Ahmose's reverie. "It is a tedious, hot march for the infantry divisions. They will not reach Het-Uart until the middle of Epophi. That leaves us a little more than Mesore to siege and turn for home again before the river road floods." Ahmose gave his attention to his old friend. Turi's angular, rather uneven features were drawn together in a frown under the rim of his blue-and-white linen helmet and his dark eyes were fixed thoughtfully on the verdant bank sliding by.

"True," Ahmose replied. "But it is time to change tactics, Turi." He glanced at the sky, white with heat. "Come into the cabin, all of you. I will tell you what I want to do and you will give me your advice." They retired into the relative coolness of the cabin with alacrity and for the rest of the afternoon drank beer and argued Ahmose's strategy. By the time they emerged the sun was setting, a spreading pool of molten fire on the western horizon, and the sailors were manoeuvring the ships to a night mooring.

Before he prepared for sleep, Ahmose received a message from Het nefer Apu. Paheri and Abana were eagerly awaiting him and the navy was ready for engagement. He sat on the edge of his cot with the scroll in his hands, looking across at the empty space where Kamose used to lie. Akhtoy had set up his travelling Amun shrine there but its shape seemed ephemeral, as though it were temporarily displacing the more solid contours of a rumpled sheet and a black head resting on a pillow.

I am still lost without you, Ahmose spoke silently into the dimness. Despair lurks in these moments when I am idle or defenceless in that strange world between waking and sleep and I must fight it or it will render me impotent. Father, Si-Amun, and now you, all gone down into death, and I am alone. What satisfaction will there be in victory amid such ruination? Even if Aahmes-nefertari gives me a dozen male Taos to fill the house with their virile presence, it will never be the same. The past is a scroll rolled up and sealed and stored in some secret place. Inside it, where time has stopped, the hieroglyphs gleam slickly black, the colours hold their brilliance forever, but outside I am condemned to memories that gradually distort and fade until the recollections themselves are a lie.

Suddenly annoyed at his own self-pity, he called for Ipi, gave him the papyrus for noting and filing, and sent him to his own cot. Lying down, he closed his eyes and brought his wife determinedly to mind, the way she had looked only that morning, the things she had said, but behind her image there was only a melancholy greyness and he could not rest.

Their progress to the north was steady but slow, broken by the need to review the troops gathered from the towns and farms along the way and leave their new officers with them. Watching the chaos of jostling men and listening to the irate shouts of General Iymery's subordinates as they struggled to establish some order along the riverbank at Badari, the centre of Prince Iasen's holdings, Ahmose reflected grimly that it was a good thing the months of campaigning under Kamose had taught the peasants to fight. Those skills would not have to be learned, only honed after a winter and spring spent in their homes and fields.

He had gone to Iasen's house and confirmed Iasen's oldest son in his hereditary position as the new Prince, but he had made it clear that the adviser he had yet to appoint would make every action of the young noble answerable directly to himself. He had required the same oath of fealty from the Prince and the rest of the family as he had received from those gathered at Amun's temple. He had explained to the Prince that the newly created Division of Khonsu under General Iymery would be headquartered in Badari and the General was to be accorded every co-operation and respect. "But, Majesty," the young man had protested. "Iymery was nothing but an assistant to my father's Overseer of Cattle before your brother conscripted him into the army! I am now the Prince of the Uatchet-nome! The Division should be mine to command! My father died for his treason against Osiris Kamose, but I have just now promised my loyalty to you and I am insulted that you do not trust me!" Ahmose looked into the angry and bewildered face with an inward sigh.

"You are indeed the Prince of this nome," he said cautiously. "You are an erpa-ha. But my will for you is that you govern your nome with intelligence and justice together with the counsellor I shall send you from Weset, and my will for the army is that it be commanded by men who know how to fight, not govern. It is not a matter of trust. Can you fight, Prince?" The man looked at him coolly.

"No, Majesty, I have not had the opportunity. But my father trained me in the art of bow and sword. Egyptian nobles have always led the army in times of war!"

"I do not question your competence with weapons," Ahmose persisted patiently, trying to keep the irritation out of his voice. "But for this war I must have men in command who have already tasted battle under my brother and who consequently know the Delta. I trust you to do what Princes have always done, that is, govern with the efficiency for which they were born. Generals do not need noble blood to deploy and lead troops. They need the authority that commands obedience and the humility that bows the head before their King." Iasen's eyes, scornful and defeated, gazed back at Ahmose out of his son's proud face.

"I understand, Majesty," he said at last, and Ahmose received his bow and dismissed him. I can see that you do, he thought, watching him stalk away, his kilt swirling about his strong young thighs. But there is nothing you can do about it. I cannot afford the luxury of allowing you to prove yourself to me.

"Khonsu will be disbanded when Het-Uart falls. It will not be a part of the permanent army," Turi remarked as he and Ahmose were walking back to the river. "Perhaps that is not such a good idea, Majesty."

"You mean because of Iasen? Do you think that Badari will continue to be a weak link in my chain of control?"

"It might. But Hor-Aha and Ankhmahor and I have been talking about the disposition of your permanent troops over our evening wine. It seems sensible to keep two divisions, perhaps Amun and Ra, on alert at Weset, but build permanent quarters for the other three in carefully chosen towns along the Nile."

Ahmose smiled across at him. "And I suppose the three of you have suggestions?"

"Yes, Majesty." Turi hesitated. "You will not be offended?" Ahmose came to a halt.

"Of course not!" he exclaimed. "Gods, Turi, you and I have wrestled and raced our way from childhood together. We shared every thought until your father was sent away. Are you no longer my friend?"

"I am not sure that divine beings have friends," Turi replied. "You used to be the youngest son of the Prince of Weset, Ahmose, but now you are the King of Egypt."

"I need men who will give me their opinions without fear," Ahmose retorted. "If you like, I will make you Chief Wrestler to His Majesty as well as General of the Division of Amun. Let us walk on." They turned together as Turi laughed.

"I do not need another title," he said. "Look, Majesty, establish homes for divisions at Khemmenu, Mennofer and Nekheb as well as Badari. Khemmenu is only ten miles from Nefrusi. Teti and Meketra ruled there and they were executed. A division at Khemmenu would give you peace of mind. Mennofer is close to where the Delta begins. Nekheb will guard your southern flank." Ahmose nodded.

"Thank you, Turi," he said rather formally. "I will consider what you have said."

"You had the same response from Intef's two sons when we put in at Qebt as you did here at Badari," Turi pointed out. "Mesehti and Makhu know that they are on sufferance, but who can say what Djawati and Akhmin will spawn in the future if your campaigns are not clean and swift? Curb them also."

I intend to, Ahmose thought, as he regained the deck and lowered himself onto the cushions against the outside wall of the cabin. At once his body servant appeared, removing his sandals and setting hot water beside him so that he could wash his hands, but Ahmose scarcely acknowledged his presence. The Prince of Mennofer is still an unknown quantity, he told himself. I remember him well both from Apepa's visit to Weset and from Kamose's negotiations with him. I liked him, but that means nothing. As for Khemmenu, the princedom there rightly belongs to Ramose and I must give it to him at once, without the constraint of an adviser to spy on him for me.

He smiled wryly into the thin shade of the canopy that flapped desultorily above him. New generals, new officers and an army that must be reorganized on the march, he mused. It could be worse. At least I do not need a sophisticated strategy in order to siege a city and chase foreigners along the dry tributaries of the river. I wonder what Paheri and Abana will say when I tell them there will be no rest for them during the Inundation?

It was with an overwhelming sense of relief that Ahmose saw Het nefer Apu come drifting into sight on the twelfth day of Epophi. He felt that the weeks behind him had been spent in repairing some tattered piece of carpet, picking up the loose threads and weaving them back into the warp and woof of the design, cutting out the pieces too ragged to be saved, brushing away the accretions of grime so that the original pattern might be discerned.

He had made sure that each town received him with formality, each mayor, governor and noble was summoned to swear their loyalty, and every one of them was scrutinized and assessed for reliability. Some were dismissed. Ipi's lists of administrative positions to be filled and the men who might possibly be trusted to fill them grew longer by the day and Ahmose found himself longing for his wife's advice. Aahmes-nefertari would enquire into each candidate's lineage and background, what they had been doing during the Kamose years, what god they served, what reputation for family stability and piety they might have. She would do so efficiently and objectively, without any need to repay a favour or promote a relative. I do not have time for the task, Ahmose thought. Yet it is a vital one. Perhaps I should send her the lists and she and Mother can gather the necessary information and make their recommendations to me when I return home. Dealing with Het-Uart will take all my energy and ingenuity, yet the management of Egypt's affairs must go on. Crop assessments, taxes, court proceedings, local building projects, all of it. The government cannot lie fallow while I pursue the Setiu.

Kamose destroyed Egypt's structure. It was necessary and it has enabled me to reorganize far more than just the army, but the construction of a new order cannot wait. Aahmes-nefertari can also assemble a delegation to travel to Keftiu. The Keftians do not care about Egypt's politics. They are concerned with commerce, no matter what god sits on the Horus Throne. They must know what has been happening since trade with the Delta was disrupted, and I will wager that they feel no particular loyalty to Apepa and will be content to transfer their trading negotiations to Weset instead of Het-Uart.

When Ahmose put in at Khemmenu, he discovered that Ramose had been living in a tent he had pitched on the city's outskirts. "I had no right to occupy Meketra's estate, Majesty," he told Ahmose frankly, "and there was no other house available. In spite of Meketra's ultimate betrayal he worked hard to restore Khemmenu. Many refugees from Dashlut and the other villages that were burned have settled here and the city is enjoying a burst of vitality." They had met on the ship after Ahmose had been ceremoniously received by Khemmenu's mayor and councillors and had spent an hour in prayer at Thoth's temple under the wary eye of the High Priest who had so sharply refused Kamose and himself entrance to the inner court. Now he and Ramose leaned together against the rail, watching the bustle of Khemmenu's wharves in the dusty red haze of sunset. No smell of burning flesh, Ahmose thought. No splashes of blood in the sand, on the white walls, no debris in the streets; it is as if we dreamed it all, Kamose and I. Time and the thrusting force of life itself has closed over the wounds.

"What of Nefrusi?" he asked with an effort, wrenching his mind away from a contemplation of the past that was in danger of becoming a habit. Ramose laughed and shook his head.

"Nefrusi has become a tidy little village full of competent farmers," he said. "I believe that this year the Setiu soldiers are competing with one another to see who can thresh the most grain in the shortest time. Will you go there, Majesty?" Will I? Ahmose repeated the question to himself. Do I want to stand on the spot where your father fell, where thousands of bodies were dragged across the sand to be fired? I was sick to my soul almost every day and Kamose moved and spoke like someone who had been buried alive.

"No, I do not think so," he said slowly. "I will greet the officers in charge there, but on the bank." He turned to his friend. "Ramose, I want you to assume the governorship of the Un nome. I have already drawn up the document making you an erpa-ha prince. Fold up your tent and take possession of the estate where you were raised." Ramose paused for a long while before he answered. Then he looked Ahmose full in the face.

"Such an offer is right and honourable, Majesty," he said. "I deserve both the title and the property. I will indeed move into the house my parents loved and tended, and I will govern the Un nome under the edicts of Ma'at. But I know what you have done to every other noble in positions of administrative authority. You have emasculated them," and here he used a common expression used by the peasants to describe the removal of a man's testicles, "and the control over their jurisdictions has gone to the so-called advisers you are placing by their sides. I know what has caused your wariness and I think you are wise. But if I am to order Khemmenu and its nome I will do so with stewards and overseers of my own choosing, not yours. Either I am to be trusted or not." He had not spoken angrily or resentfully. His features were as calm as his words. Ahmose nodded.

"Good!" he said brightly. "I had no intention of having you spied upon, Ramose. Neither you nor Ankhmahor nor Turi. You will not hear me call my servants spies in public but I do so to you, for spies they will be until such time as my godhead is secure. Take the nome freely." Ramose let out a gust of relieved breath.

"Thank you for your confidence, Ahmose," he said. "Let me reciprocate. Unless you give me a specific command, I will not take up my responsibilities here until the war is over. I desire to remain beside you." Ahmose's gaze narrowed.

"You still hope to see Apepa dead and Tani back in your arms, don't you?" he remarked quietly. Ramose's mouth became a thin line. Stepping away from the rail he bowed shortly, turned on his heel, and walked away without replying. Ahmose watched him stride down the ramp and mingle briefly with the crowds on the dock before disappearing through the open city gates. You are either mad or holy, dear Ramose, he mused. Either way you are the most stubborn man I have ever known. It would never occur to you that perhaps Tani is no longer worthy of such frightening, uncompromising devotion.

That had been two days ago, and now Ramose, together with Turi, Hor-Aha, Kagemni, Baqet and the other generals, sat around a large table under the shade of a canopy a stone's throw from the Nile. Behind and around them the divisions continued to straggle into Het nefer Apu, where the Scribes of Assemblage were directing the men to their billets. Before them, on the river itself, the navy's ships cast pale intertwining shadows onto the listless bushes lining the bank. The noon heat was oppressive. Soldiers standing their watch at the feet of the many ramps linking vessels to land were visibly sweating. Aboard the boats themselves the sailors were clustered under huge awnings, invisible to the gathering on the shore, but their lazy conversation and occasional laughter could be heard. The town itself, a short way to the north, lay quiet in the drugged lull of the afternoon sleep. "We will be at full strength by this time tomorrow," Turi was saying. "The last contingents are drifting in. The Scribes of Distribution are already complaining about the amount of beer the late arrivals are drinking."

"It cannot be helped," Ahmose said shortly. "Marching is hot work. Let them drink beer while they may. When we leave for the Delta, it will be water only. I have heard your report on the navy's readiness, Paheri, and I am satisfied that you have not wasted the months I have been away. Now, Abana, tell me of the state of the Delta." For answer the older man indicated his son.

"Paheri and I have been fully engaged in the care and training of the eleven thousand marines here, Majesty," he said apologetically. "I did not want to delegate the responsibility for the task your brother assigned us to anyone for whom I would be reluctant to answer. Therefore I sent Kay north." The young man was flicking his whisk over his cup where a cloud of flies was trying unsuccessfully to settle. He put his hand over its rim and looked up with a smile.

"My men and I made the journey three times, Majesty," he said promptly. "Twice when the Inundation was at its height. Of course my ship is sturdy and my sailors entirely reliable, so I found the Delta tributaries to be reasonably navigable. We penetrated the Delta along its eastern branch, past the remains of the fort at Nag-ta-Hert, and then tied up some way below the Setiu strongholds. I sent out small sorties. Most of the swamps and lakes that become fully flooded are in the eastern portion of the Delta and the ditches and canals from which the water drains back into the Nile in the spring were full, but by making a detour around Het-Uart and poling our skiffs across the canals, we were able to reach the Horus Road."

Ahmose watched him with a secret humour and a great deal of astonishment. Kay was speaking nonchalantly, almost carelessly, of a foray that must have taxed him and his crew to the utmost. Sitting back with one sandalled foot planted on a hummock of grassy earth, shards of sunlight playing fitfully on the one small gold hoop he wore in his ear as the linen above him billowed and collapsed, he was the picture of confident self-possession. "There was no point in exploring the western Delta," he went on dismissively. "Het-Uart sits right on the eastern edge of the Nile's great eastern tributary and between that and the western tributary the Inundation is more polite. There are orchards and vineyards and grazing for cattle and of course beyond the western waterway itself there are the marshes and then the desert. The Osiris One Kamose devastated it all two years ago to try and prevent the Setiu from storing much food. I believed that your Majesty would be more interested in any activity along the Horus Road."

You have changed, Kay Abana, Ahmose thought. Your brashness is no longer a shower of arbitrary sparks. You were an eager, boastful child, and although you are still full of overweening confidence, it is being tempered by the intelligence of an approaching maturity. Kamose did right to give you your own command. "It was a courageous thing to do," he said aloud and Kay smiled delightedly.

"It was," he answered promptly. "But my men are fearless and I lead them well. Between us we only wish to please you, Majesty."

"The Horus Road," Turi put in bitterly. "What a two-edged knife it is! A lifeline from the eastern trading centres straight into the heart of the Delta in times of peace but in times of war it becomes a channel along which every danger can flow. Your ancestor Osiris Senwasret built the forts of the Wall of Princes across it to control the influx of foreigners, Majesty, but now the Wall is in Apepa's power and the Setiu pour into Egypt in a steady stream."

"I know," Ahmose said. "Go on, Captain. What did you see?" Kay crossed his legs, leaned forward, and again applied the whisk, this time to the insects seeking salt from the sweat that beaded in the crook of his arm.

"Setiu troops, heavily armed," he answered promptly. "They do not march in formation, they advance in loose groups with much noise and little discipline, but they keep coming. They cannot all be contained in Het-Uart. There is no room in that pest hole for even another rat. They are camping in groups as close to the city as they can. The Delta is liberally sprinkled with them."

"If Het-Uart is to fall, we must somehow clear the Delta and then hold the Horus Road," Hor-Aha said. "Kamose did his best to scour the Delta, but during the Inundation the Princes of the East sent more reinforcements along the Horus Road."

"Then the solution is obvious," Ahmose summed up. "Kamose did not speak of this, but I think that in creating the navy and insisting on its competence, he was preparing to begin a full year of campaigning, not just during the dry months. We cannot afford to keep gaining ground only to lose it. We will move north at once, as soon as the last soldiers have arrived. Five divisions will deploy around the mounds on which the city rests and besiege them together with the Medjay archers. The flood plains are dry and hard. Chariots can be used to advantage. The other six divisions will patrol the Delta and engage the contingents of fresh Setiu troops wherever they find them. Again, the ditches and canals will hold only the merest trickles of water and movement throughout the Delta should be relatively easy. Kay, can you estimate the number of Setiu soldiers coming in from Rethennu?"

"Not really, Majesty. I am sorry. A few days spent watching the road were not enough to give me an accurate count. But they came with regularity." He emptied his cup, setting it back on the table with a bang. "And what of the navy?" he asked with relish. "What is your desire for your most faithful fighting men, Majesty? The *North* is manned, equipped and ready for engagement!"

"The marines will become farmers until Thoth," Ahmose replied firmly. "There are ten thousand men here, Kay, and a whole town to be fed. The harvest must be conducted as efficiently as possible. The infantry divisions will plunder the Delta villages as they go."

"And at Thoth?" It was Paheri who interrupted this time, and Ahmose swung to him.

"Then if the gods will it, Isis will cry," he said. "The Inundation will spread. But we will not go home. The navy will proceed into the Delta by water and we will give the Setiu no time to rest and regroup." Paheri grunted and an expression of relief crossed Kay Abana's face. "I wish to discuss the details now," Ahmose went on. "Ipi, bring up the maps. Akhtoy, have the table cleared."

By the time each General had received his orders, questioned them, and had them elucidated, the sun had begun to set behind the town in a flood of molten bronze. Ahmose finally dismissed them, and walking wearily to his tent he passed his guards and entered, lowering himself into the collapsible travelling chair beside the cot with a sigh and lifting his feet so that his waiting body servant could remove his sandals. "Your feet are swollen, Majesty," the man commented as he wrestled with the ties. "I will bring warm water and a salve."

He went away and for a time Ahmose sat alone in the gathering dimness. Outside footsteps sounded. Men came and went. His guard barked a challenge that was answered. Somewhere close by a donkey began to bray hoarsely. The pleasant odour of roasting gazelle wafted through the tent flap. I suppose the soldiers have been out on the desert hunting, Ahmose thought. He looked about him at the lamp, soon to be lit, the neatness of his cot waiting for him to raise the sheets, his clothes chest against one wall, his closed shrine against another. Flax matting had been laid on the earth under him. He was in a protected oasis of orderliness and silence, and all at once a wave of loneliness overtook him. Its source was not the uniqueness of his position as King, he knew. Nor was it solely the absence of his brother in a situation they had always experienced together, or a homesickness for Aahmes-nefertari. I miss the way it was, he thought despondently. I miss all the Princes, Intef and Iasen and yes, even Meketra, all of us around the council table, Kamose with his moodiness and harshness, the grumbles of the nobles, the uncertainties and horrors of that time but a kind of comradeship all the same. I fashion a new order but I long for the familiarity of the old.

Akhtoy came into the tent with the body servant, and while Ahmose's feet were soaked and massaged he moved quietly about, lighting the lamp, putting fresh drinking water beside the cot, and gathering up the day's soiled linen. Ahmose watched him for a moment. Then he said, "Akhtoy, I do not want to be alone tonight. Please have another cot brought in and ask Turi to sleep here." Imperturbably the steward bowed and went out. The body servant eased papyrus slippers onto Ahmose's oiled feet and rose with the bowl of water in his arms. Ahmose thanked and dismissed him. A short time later Akhtoy returned.

"The General Turi's aides tell me that he has taken a bodyguard and gone night fishing with Idu, his Standard Bearer, Majesty," Akhtoy told him. "Is there anyone else Your Majesty wishes to see?" Night fishing, Ahmose repeated to himself with an inward pang. And why not? It is a pastime we both enjoyed before he went away, before we grew up. We would sit in a skiff under the stars, dangle our lines in the dark river, and talk and laugh the peaceful hours away. He has not forgotten, but the nature of the affinity between us has changed. We can no longer be equals in friendship no matter how much we desire it, and he is forming bonds within the Division I have entrusted to him. Akhtoy was regarding him with an understanding sympathy that Ahmose could not find insulting.

"No," he said slowly. "No, Akhtoy, I rather think that a King must draw a circle of detachment around himself. He cannot incite jealousy." Akhtoy's expression did not change.

"That is true," he replied. "However, a mere servant will incite no man's apprehension. With your permission I will bring my pallet in here." Ahmose said nothing, and taking his silence for consent Akhtoy leaned out into the new darkness and shouted an abrupt command. Presently his under-steward bowed his way to the far side of the tent and proceeded to unroll Akhtoy's mattress, laying sheets and a pillow on it before bowing himself out again. "Majesty, I have chores for the morning to perform," Akhtoy said, "but I will return quickly. There are pomegranates and black grapes, newly picked, and your cook has baked freshly ground reed bulbs today, mixed with plenty of honey, the way you like them. Let me bring you a light meal." Ahmose looked up at him reflectively.

"You are a compassionate and tactful man as well as a superior steward, Akhtoy," he said. "Tell me, are you happy?" Akhtoy's eyebrows rose into his rigidly even black fringe of hair.

"That is a large word, encompassing many lesser states of being, Majesty," he answered. "I am deeply honoured to be first among your servants, even as I loved and served your brother. I am content with my wife and daughters at home in Weset. My life is full and satisfying and the work on my tomb in West-of-Weset is progressing well. All these things make me happy."

"Then I am pleased." Ahmose got out of the chair. "No, do not bring me food, but if any scrolls have arrived from my family I want to see them before I retire."

Once Akhtoy had gone, Ahmose got onto his cot, and sliding between the cool sheets he lay back with a sigh. His depression had lifted. One day I will promote that man, he thought. We take the fidelity of our servants for granted but we ought not to. Their unobtrusive reliability deserves to be rewarded.

He was drowsing when Akhtoy returned. The lamp was extinguished. Ahmose heard the small sounds as the steward lowered himself onto his pallet and composed himself for sleep, and bidding him a good night he closed his eyes and surrendered to the feeling of security the other man's presence had brought. What is his wife's name? Ahmose's thoughts ran on. And his daughters? He keeps his other life very private, but I must ask him if there is anything I can do for them. I have a vague memory of two rather pretty girls holding his hands when I saw him once in the temple during a holiday. I wonder how my own little Hent-ta-Hent is faring?

Three days later the army left Het nefer Apu. Ahmose had decided to continue the journey north by ship rather than with his division, but it was with an odd sense of proprietary loss that he stood on the edge of the desert and watched the long phalanxes of men march away, the standards bobbing half-obscured by their dust, the whirling spokes of the chariots glinting dully in the sullen heat.

Just beyond him to the west, the track to the oasis ran away to vanish on the hazed horizon and, gazing along it with eyes half closed against the fierce morning light, he thought of the time when he and Kamose had waited for the remnants of Kethuna's parched and dying troops to come staggering out of that rock-pitted waste. But it was not of Kethuna that I was thinking then, Ahmose reflected. No, it was Pezedkhu, sitting just north of Het nefer Apu with his thousands of soldiers, waiting even as we did, to see what would happen. He had melted away as Kamose's men fell upon those hapless, half-crazed Setiu and cut them down, dissolving back towards the Delta like some silent phantom rather than risk an engagement that might have brought him failure. Pezedkhu. I wonder what he is doing right now, shut up in Apepa's palace, what his spies and scouts have been telling him. Does he think of me with a shiver of fear, as I do of him? Pezedkhu, the most formidable military mind brought against me. Apepa himself is nothing, a crude painting on papyrus beside the force and subtlety of this foreign General who looms like a towering statue behind my every decision.

Mentally shrugging, Ahmose turned his back on the blinding stretch of tumbled ground that now held no hint of the carnage that had once taken place there. On an impulse that was half instinct, half good sense, he had ordered a delighted Kay Abana to accompany his and the Medjay's vessels with the *North*. Kay and his marines had scouted the Delta. They might be useful in some way Ahmose could not foresee, although Apepa had few ships himself that were not trading vessels and Ahmose did not anticipate any hostile engagement on water. Not yet.

As he walked towards the river through the litter left by the army's camp, Kay himself approached, bowing profusely, one outstretched arm clutching a young boy who was trotting beside him. At Ahmose's signal his entourage came to a halt. Kay came up, fell to his knees, and touched his forehead to the earth. After a moment's hesitation the boy did the same. "Rise," Ahmose said. "What can I do for you, Captain? Nothing too complicated I hope. I am ready to embark and you should be also."

"Oh I am, Majesty!" Kay assured him, getting up and brushing the grit from his calves. "The *North* is victualled and prepared. I and my men are humbled by this opportunity to distinguish ourselves still further in your service. We fly the blue and white with unsurpassed pride." Ahmose smiled at him coolly.

"Abana, your sincerity is overwhelming," he said. "Only your incredible bombast exceeds it. What do you want?" For answer the young man thrust his companion forward.

"This is my cousin Zaa pen Nekheb," he said. "He looks older than he is. I will not lie to you, Majesty, he is only twelve, but he is clever and strong and will make a fine soldier. I beseech you to allow him on board the *North* with me."

A ripple of laughter ran through the watching group. Ahmose scrutinized the boy. He indeed looked older than his years. He was thin but there was a wiriness about him that suggested strength and, although his nervousness was betrayed in the clenching and unclenching of his fingers, he met Ahmose's gaze without flinching. His family resemblance to Kay was more a matter of hints than gestures, the sweep of the jawline, the stubbornly cleft chin, a similarly long peak to the hairline. Ahmose turned back to Kay.

"Why?" he enquired. Kay blinked, then recovered.

"Because it is his dream to be a soldier," he said promptly. "Ever since his youth he has talked of nothing else."

"His childhood, you mean," Ahmose contradicted him dryly. "But you have not answered my question. Every little boy wants to be either a soldier or a scribe. This one seems no different. You have a grave responsibility as the captain of one of my ships, Kay. I do not want that responsibility

weakened by being divided. What are you doing here, Zaa?"
he addressed the other. "Why are you not in school?"

"I ran away," Zaa answered rather breathlessly.

"Then you will be sent home to Nekheb at once. And I
am surprised at your fecklessness, Kay. I have no time for
this nonsense. Perhaps I should leave you here after all so
that you may learn a little maturity under your father's
supervision."

"Oh, Majesty, do not disgrace me!" Kay blurted, all trace
of cheerful bluster gone. "Hear me, I beg! My request is not
as frivolous as it seems."

"You have ten heartbeats." Kay faced him with a grim-
ness he had never seen before.

"Zaa is a rascal but a useful one. He has run away from
my uncle's house and from his school in Nekhbet's temple
countless times. Last time he was caught by my uncle's
steward he was almost at Weset, on his way to try to join
your army there. No one can do anything with him. My
aunt has cried over him ceaselessly since his birth. Finally
my uncle sent him here to my father. There is a scroll with
the permission. For several weeks he has been my servant
on board the *North*. He cleans weapons, scrubs the decks
and washes the sailors' kilts, helps the Scribe of
Distribution with our food supplies. My father approves. He
is inclined to hard work as a remedy for delinquency." Here
Zaa's glance fell shamefacedly to his feet. "But the *North*
may become engaged in a battle and I needed your permission to have a non-combatant on board." Ahmose stood
silent, considering.

"Has he done anything for which you have been forced
to punish him?" he asked at last. Kay shook his head.

"No, Majesty. He is simply so happy to be with fighting men that he is no longer eating his heart."

Ahmose crooked a finger. "Zaa, come here." The boy sidled closer and sketched a clumsy bow. "Are the words of my Captain true?"

"Yes, Majesty. I am sorry."

"All my soldiers must swear an oath to me. Do you know what that means?" Zaa's head came up and he looked at Ahmose with a dawning hope.

"Yes, Majesty. It means that a soldier will be loyal and respectful and brave and obey the King and his officers and do his duty," he almost stammered in his eagerness.

"It also means that if he breaks his oath he can have his nose removed and be exiled or even executed," Ahmose warned. "Will you risk swearing loyalty to me?"

"As your soldier?" Zaa's eyes were shining. "Oh yes, Majesty!"

"Not as my soldier," Ahmose retorted. "Not yet, not until you are sixteen. Until then you will continue in the care of your cousin and his father and do as they tell you. You may remain on board the *North* but I must tell you that you should be ashamed to put your parents to such pain and grief. Your actions are not worthy of a true Egyptian boy."

"No, Majesty. Thank you! Thank you!" Zaa's bare feet were performing a tiny dance of excitement in the dust while his body remained rigid with joy.

"Kiss my feet, then, and the palms of my hands in token of your bondage to me," Ahmose said. "You are no longer free to run wherever you choose, Zaa. Are you sure you understand this?" For answer the boy almost collapsed to the earth and pressed his lips fervently against Ahmose's toes. "As for you, Kay, I remind you that if you are forced to choose between an order in the heat of battle and saving your cousin's life, you must let him die." Kay nodded gravely.

"I have already considered this, Majesty," he said quietly. "So has he. You trusted me, young though I am, with an awesome responsibility. I promise you that in this thing too you will not be disappointed."

"Go then, both of you. You are dismissed." They bowed and backed away but when they turned Zaa whooped and broke into a run, vanishing along the path under the drooping trees towards *North*'s ramp. Kay followed more slowly.

"A child like that is either destined for a glorious military career or an early death," Hor-Aha remarked. Ahmose grinned wryly at him as they began to move on again.

"When I was twelve, I was getting drunk on date wine with Turi under the shrubbery beside the river," he said. "I think this child's ambition is more noble. Well, Hor-Aha, let us board our own ships and cast off for the Delta. We still have a long way to go."

4

AHMOSE WANTED HIS TROOPS to be deployed around Het-Uart by the beginning of Mesore, a scant two weeks away, but the infantry marching on the edge of the western cultivation would of necessity take longer to arrive than he and the Medjay in their boats, in spite of the prevailing north wind that was attempting to blow them back to Weset. Besides, he had already decided to put in briefly at Mennofer.

Prince Sebek-nakht had not been summoned to the ceremony at the temple. Ahmose had debated whether or not to send him a message but something, some voice of caution or tact, prevented it. Sebek-nakht was still an unknown quantity. He had kept the promise of non-involvement he had made to Kamose and there had been no suspicion that he had become entangled in the other Princes' treasonous machinations, but he was after all a breed apart, an Egyptian of ancient and noble blood, Priest of Sekhmet and an erpa-ha, but also the son of Apepa's vizier and an architect to the Setiu ruler.

Ahmose had liked him instinctively, but remembering Kamose's jibe that he would of course like anyone who could wield a throwing stick with enough skill to bring down a duck almost every time, he had hesitated to bring any pressure to bear on the governor of the Maten nome.

Mennofer was a rich and beautiful city, home of Ptah the Creator. If Sebek-nakht could be persuaded to commit himself actively to Ahmose, his support could be vital, and Ahmose suspected that he would not be won over by coercion. So no herald had travelled to Mennofer during the days of mourning for Kamose and no word of either sympathy or endorsement from Mennofer had come to Weset.

He is not an enemy, Ahmose thought, as his craft angled towards the west bank, where the city's wide watersteps were tiered with thick crowds waiting to catch a glimpse of him. He is either so completely wrapped up in his own security that he will take no definite position for or against me, or he has no love for military solutions. I rather think it is the latter. He did not strike me as a selfish or arrogant man.

It seemed that Ramose had been pondering the same questions, for as the boat bumped the tethering pole and the sailors leaped to run out the ramp he said, "I do not think that Kamose ever considered the fact that this Prince is one of Apepa's architects, Majesty. He must know the design of Het-Uart intimately. He could be invaluable in helping us to probe any weakness in its walls if he can be persuaded."

"I had not considered it either," Ahmose admitted. "But of course you are right. Don't forget, though, that as one of Apepa's high officials he will be reluctant to betray his master. Actually, Ramose, I would be rather disappointed if he did. He gave me the impression of a loyalty going far beyond the matter of service and its accompanying reward, a fidelity that exists for its own sake."

"Unlike Meketra," Ramose said dryly. "All the same, will you try to at least obtain maps or blueprints from him? We have battered at Het-Uart for far too long without success. If it was one walled bastion, we might have conquered it by now, but we fling ourselves against several of them, each separated by water that lies in deep canals. Admittedly only two of the mounds are significant, the one holding the city itself and the other full of soldiers. I have only been inside one of them, and I saw very little of its extent or pattern."

Khabekhnet had strode down the ramp and was now standing at the top of the watersteps facing the excited people, his herald's staff of office raised. Behind him the Followers poured, shields thrusting against the throng to provide an open pathway to the gleaming White Wall of Menes with its two high gates.

"On your faces before Uatch-Kheperu Ahmose, Son of the Sun, Horus, the Horus of Gold!" Khabekhnet shouted, as he had done at every stop along the Nile, and at once the furore died away. Everyone went to the earth. Ahmose glanced along the line of Medjay boats now also secured to the foot of the watersteps and smiled to see an occasional glint of gold among the naked black chests ranked proudly on the decks. The tribesmen who had been awarded the Gold of Valour were wearing their trophies. For once they were quiet, the bows slung on their shoulders ranged like a forest of sticks tipping the blue sky. With a terse word, he moved towards the ramp, Ramose, Hor-Aha, Ankhmahor and Turi at his heels.

One figure had risen and was waiting for his approach before the open gate that led, Ahmose remembered, directly to the Prince's residence and from there to the

District of Ptah. This city is beautiful, he thought, in the few moments it took to reach the man who was now bowing several times from his white-clad waist. The districts are clean and spacious and full of trees, the streets are wide, the buildings gracious. I am so glad that Kamose did not order its destruction. I would like to visit the temple of Hathor of the Sycamore before I sail on, but I don't suppose there will be time. There is good fishing, too, in the Pool of Pedjet-She on the edge of the desert. Perhaps Turi will go there. He halted and smiled.

"Welcome to the home of Ptah, Creator of the World, Majesty," the official said. "I am Dagi, mayor of Mennofer. There are litters waiting for you if you wish to be carried to the Prince's estate."

"No. I want to walk," Ahmose replied frankly. "I need the exercise. I do not remember you, Dagi." He gestured and they proceeded in under the shadow of the gate, the Followers running to form a protective cordon around them.

"I was a junior administrator when you and your brother came last to Mennofer," the man answered. "His Highness appointed me to my present position in the spring, when our previous mayor decided to retire. It is a great honour. Many kings made Mennofer their capital long ago." Ahmose found himself warming to Dagi's obvious love for his home and they talked easily, pacing under the dappling of the many trees along the city's broad thoroughfare. Beyond the warning bulk of the Followers, the citizens going about their own business stopped to bow and then to stare at the bejewelled company. Ahmose acknowledged them gravely with a half-raised hand as he went.

Prince Sebek-nakht stood at the entrance to his walled garden, flanked by his retainers. As Ahmose came up to them, they knelt in the dust, but Sebek-nakht put out his braceleted arms and bent low. "Majesty," he said, "I am honoured. Be pleased to enter my house."

"It is good to see you again, Sebek-nakht," Ahmose responded, "and to take my time in walking through the loveliness of Mennofer. You already know General Hor-Aha and Prince Ramose of Khemmenu. This is General Turi, my oldest friend. Let us go in." Two of the Followers fell in behind them, but Ankhmahor and the remainder of the guard took up their station in front of the estate's wall, under the interested eye of Sebek-nakht's gatekeeper, who peered out at them from his little room just within the gate itself.

The Prince's house with its brightly painted pillars lay directly ahead. He had laid out his garden to one side of the path leading to his entrance and on the other the shelter-ing wall was covered in flowering vines and fruit trees trained against its rough mud brick. House and garden filled the space so that nothing of the kitchen, granaries or servant's quarters that must surely lie in the rear could be seen, but a thin plume of smoke rose from that direction. As Ahmose came up to the pillars, a guard rose and rever-enced him, and beyond the man the cool shade of the doorway was suddenly filled with floating linens and the wink of light on gold. The Prince's wife and daughters had appeared to pay their respects.

After the sharing of wine and pleasantries by the lily-choked pool in the garden the women settled back on their cushions and drew together, and Ahmose, with Ramose,

Hor-Aha and Turi, followed Sebek-nakht into the house. It filled Ahmose's memory with its airy spaces, the cool green and white tiling of the reception hall, the gilded tables and curving ebony chairs with their flowers of inlaid ivory, the delicate painted lamps and the two elaborately chased house shrines to Sekhmet and Ptah. He remembered, too, the room to which the Prince led them, with its cedar desk, its walls painted to resemble spreading date palms whose fruit were cunningly camouflaged alcoves holding the scrolls that dealt with the administration of his holdings, its reed matting woven to resemble a fish-filled lake. Without waiting to be invited, he drew up a chair and the others did also. A servant appeared, gliding into the room and standing noiselessly. "Can I offer you anything more?" Sebek-nakht asked. "It is some hours until the evening meal." They declined, and with a wave Sebek-nakht dismissed the man. The door closed softly. Sebek-nakht turned to Ahmose.

"I am sorry about your brother," he said, "and ashamed of my fellow Princes. They were not honest enough to desert Kamose and come north to Het-Uart. Instead they resorted to murder. It was not in the way of Ma'at."

"No, it was not," Ahmose agreed, watching him carefully. "And I am not sure that they had any thought of placing themselves once more under Apepa's thumb when they killed Kamose and wounded me. I think they had some barely formed idea of treatying with Apepa while somehow holding onto the gains Kamose made, perhaps even of killing my stepson and electing a King from among themselves. In any case such a move would have been futile. Apepa would then have seized his chance to leave his city and flood the south with Setiu troops. Or would he?" The invitation was obvious. Sebek-nakht smiled.

"Majesty, I do not have Apepa's confidence, I only have his ear regarding his building projects and those are very few," he said smoothly. "The Setiu are not interested in erecting anything other than temples to their gods. I have drawn up plans for the extension of Apepa's palace in the past and seen them properly executed and I have done some work in the Delta for various other nobles, but that is all." Ahmose pulled his chair closer to the table and laid his arms across its surface. He leaned towards Sebek-nakht.

"No, I will not ask you to betray Apepa," he said with a sigh. "No matter where your heart lies in this matter, you will have nothing to tell me, will you?" Sebek-nakht touched his kohled temple in a curiously graceful movement.

"I do not keep my counsel because I am in sympathy with the Setiu," he remarked. "I am an architect and a priest, Majesty. I know nothing of military matters and care even less. I would rather serve you in those capacities than Apepa, but it has been Apepa who has used and rewarded my skill. I am of a very ancient Egyptian family and unlike many of my princely fellows who glory in ancestors who wielded weapons or power, I take pride in a history of architects and priests stretching back more hentis than I can count. Of course I have power," he emphasized. "I am a Prince. But I am not interested in using it to lead an army."

"What a pity," Ahmose murmured. "I was going to ask you to command one of my divisions." He was grinning and Sebek-nakht broke into laughter.

"If you require troops well versed in the merits of lime-stone over sandstone or how deep a foundation must go in order to support a column of a certain weight, then I am indeed a good choice," he said. "Otherwise, I would be a disaster."

"We have military minds in abundance," Hor-Aha put in sourly. "What we need are men who know how to tear down a glacis wall quickly and efficiently." His tone sobered the company and there was a moment of awkward silence. Hor-Aha flung up his hands. "Your pardon, Prince," he said to Sebek-nakht. "My words were not intended to offend. But I spoke the truth. The main mounds on which Het-Uart rests are girdled with such sloping designs. They are very high and as hard as rock. Egyptians do not build this way. Egyptian masons do not know what their flaws may be. The city's gates are also high and solid." He cast a dark glance at Ahmose. "Kamose took Nag-ta-Hert only after a month of sieging, and then only because the commander of the fort was running short of water and lost his nerve. Nag-ta-Hert's walls were torn down from the inside after our soldiers overran it, and not before."

"I do not take offence easily, General," Sebek-nakht assured him. "I understand your need. But you know from Kamose's success at Nag-ta-Hert that Setiu fortifications are not of stone. They are of sand and earth piled high and made stable with a canted facing of glacis. In my capacity as architect I am familiar with the advantages and weaknesses of various kinds of stone and I can plan structures composed of mud bricks, but that is all. I have no advice for you."

"Apepa's father doubled the height of the walls," Ahmose said. "I have often wondered why, seeing that in his day there was no threat to the city. Perhaps he received an oracle regarding his son's future."

"Perhaps." Sebek-nakht folded his arms. "But I think that the plague forty years ago frightened him. Het-Uart has always been a crowded, stifling warren of narrow alleys full of refuse and offal between row upon row of jumbled mud houses. No gardens except within the confines of the palace itself and a few tiny squares before the homes of the very privileged. No trees to speak of. Only noise and stench. Forty years ago the population had grown so vast that the city was choking on its own citizens. It was, it still is, overrun with rats and other vermin. The plague killed thousands of Setiu, so many that the dead were simply flung into open pits. At that time and for some time afterwards Het-Uart was vulnerable. Thus the improved defences."

"They are a dirty people," Turi said reflectively. "With the whole of the glorious Delta to settle, with room for houses with gardens, they chose to huddle together, pressed cheek by jowl in those girdled spaces. I do not understand it."

"Yes, you do," Ramose interposed. "They are foreigners. They do not know Egypt. They do not care for her beauty and her cleanliness. They are insects, ants teeming over an anthill." Sebek-nakht was gazing above their heads at the far wall. He seemed to find something interesting in the brown trunks and green fans of the date palms painted there.

"I have lately been ordered to oversee the safe disman-tling of Het-Uart's cemeteries," he said conversationally. "The small mortuary temples are of stone. They take up too much room. The citizens have been forced to bury their dead and even their donkeys under the floors of their houses." His gaze dropped to Ahmose. "My Lord is distressed but there is no solution to the problem of Het-Uart's limited size. It is only a matter of time before another plague breaks out or my Lord is forced to begin building extensions to the city on other mounds. Unfortunately for the common people, the northern fortified turtleback has become overrun with Setiu troops coming in from Rethennu to defend the Delta. Apepa had always stationed the overflow of his military contingents there, but now it is full to its limit and beyond. The few Egyptians who live on it, those who hold positions as administrators and overseers for Apepa and who have erected decent houses with irrigated gardens on the north-western edge of the mound where their small estates run down to one of the Nile's tributaries, are not happy with the steady influx."

Ahmose stiffened. The Prince had put a slight emphasis on some of his words. Irrigated gardens. North-western edge. He felt Hor-Aha's eyes flicker briefly in his direction and knew that the General had heard Sebek-nakht's almost imperceptible inflexion.

"Neither are we!" Turi exclaimed. "Before Het-Uart itself can be isolated and rendered naked, we must do battle with the infestation of these reinforcements. Our soldiers from the south do not relish having to negotiate the Delta's swamps and orchards in order to fight, let alone fling themselves at walls behind which thousands more are hiding." He sighed. "It is a disheartening task, Majesty."

"Yes it is," Ahmose admitted. "But time and the freedom to manœuvre are on our side, Turi. Eventually Apepa must concede defeat, unless the number of troops in Rethennu cannot be exhausted." He turned to Sebek-nakht who was now watching him steadily. "Thank you, Prince," he said simply. "Now I have a proposition for you. It seems to me that an architect in Het-Uart has few challenging assignments. If he has talent, he must become bored. I have need of such a one in Weset. The Queen is even now searching for someone to design a village, among other things involving far more than counting up mud bricks. Will you go and talk to her?" Sebek-nakht's eyes narrowed.

"I am still supervising the razing of the cemeteries, Majesty," he said with caution. "I am expected to return to Het-Uart very soon. I came home to confer with my Overseer of Crops regarding my harvest."

"You came home to greet me," Ahmose contradicted him. "I will not dissemble with you, Prince. I need you in Weset. Aahmes-nefertari needs you as soon as you have discharged your current obligation to Apepa. I am not asking for your sword, I am asking for your especial talent." He spread out his hands. "I humble myself before you, Sebek-nakht. Cast your lot with me. I swear that you will not be disappointed." A tiny, wry smile lit the Prince's face for a second.

"I have always liked you, Ahmose," he said, "and I respected your brother enough to give him my promise of non-intervention in his war. The Setiu do not belong here. This I do not dispute. It is also true that I long to work as my forebears worked, conceiving mighty monuments to the glory of the gods and the pleasure of the King. I tell you this. I will finish my commitment to my Lord in Het-Uart and then I will consider my commitment to my Lord in Weset. More than that I cannot promise."

"Well, will you at least travel to Weset and give the Queen some advice when you have finished in the Delta?"

Ahmose pressed. "She is facing several complex problems that might stimulate your architectural curiosity." He turned a bland face on Sebek-nakht, who shook his head and broke into a full grin.   .

"Very well, Majesty," he agreed. "And of course while I am there, I may very well be seduced by such problems." Ahmose slapped the table briskly and rose.

"I am an accommodating King, sensitive to the desires of his subjects," he said with humour. "See how readily I accept your terms, O Prince! Now let us go into your peaceful garden and relish the beginning of the sunset while the aroma of our feast gradually fills our nostrils. Do you have any Good Wine of the Western River? But of course you do, doubtless presented to you by Apepa himself. Have it opened at once."

Later that night, after the feasting and an amicable farewell to Sebek-nakht and his regal family, Ahmose sat on the deck of his ship with the men who had accompanied him to the Prince's house. Around them the hot darkness fought with the pools of yellow light cast by the lanterns strung from prow and stern and the motionless Followers were little more than uncertain silhouettes standing at intervals along the railing. Ramose was half-sitting, half-lying with his shoulders against the cabin wall, his eyes on the soft sky with its intricate patterns of stars. Beside him Turi lounged on a cushion. Ahmose himself was leaning forward from his camp stool, elbows on his knees, but Hor-Aha sat cross-legged on the bare planking, his spine straight, the hue of his skin blending into the surrounding darkness. Only the whites of his eyes and his gold bracelet caught the lamplight. He was fingering one of his thick braids and staring thoughtfully ahead. From one of the boats behind them music came floating over the rippling opacity of the water. The Medjay were singing quietly in their own tongue. Ahmose listened contentedly. It had been a very profitable day. "Majesty, do you think Sebeknakht will keep his word?" Turi's voice broke into Ahmose's drowsy reverie. "Will he go to Weset?"

"Yes, indeed he will," Ahmose answered. "He has spent the last year deciding where his loyalty lies, and long before he came home to Mennofer to meet me, he knew what he would do. Already he has given us valuable information."

"He has?" Turi looked puzzled, his brows drawn together, and Hor-Aha laughed harshly.

"You would make a very bad spy, Turi," he said, tossing the braid behind him. "The Prince gave us a clear picture of conditions on the northern turtleback where the Setiu troops are amassed, and a possible solution to the dilemma of how to get at them."

"Apepa's senior Egyptian servants, the aristocrats of the north, live on estates to the north-west of the mound," Ahmose ventured. "That was the first piece of useful knowledge, Turi. The second was that they have irrigated gardens."

"Well of course they do, Majesty," Turi said irritably. "They are, after all, still Egyptian nobles." Ahmose cuffed him on his bent head.

"Think, you idiot!" he said affectionately. "The mound is completely walled and yet those gardens are irrigated." Turi smoothed back his hair where Ahmose had ruffled it. He did not speak for a while. Ahmose waited. Then Turi clapped his hands.

"Of course! Wine has addled my brain. There must be breaches cut in the wall so that during the Inundation the ditches from which the nobles water their gardens may fill. Then when the Nile begins to recede the breaches are filled in again, both to re-establish the defences and to keep the precious water for irrigation during the summer." He looked up at Ahmose. "Those breaches are weak points in the wall. If they are opened and closed every year they cannot be very difficult to dig out."

"Award Turi the Gold of Intelligence," Hor-Aha said sarcastically. "The problem will not be a wall that will crumble easily. It lies in the fact that the Nile tributary does not dry out completely although its level falls. There cannot be much space between the water and the wall, and none at all in the winter. No room for more than a trickle of troops to gain the mound, and in winter a very wet task."

"But perhaps possible for Kay Abana and his men," Ahmose mused. "We will know more when we reach the Delta and the scouts have gone out." He rose from the stool and stretched. "Meanwhile we sleep. Tomorrow you rejoin your division, Turi, and march with them, and you, Hor-Aha, must sail with the Medjay. You are all dismissed. Sleep well."

Once on his cot he began to consider the information Sebek-nakht had given them and how it might be put to use, and his thoughts drifted to the man himself, how he would be going south soon, sailing on the summer wind out of the north into an Egypt where the parching heat of Shemu was suffused with the timelessness of eternity. Tomorrow I will dictate a message to Aahmes-nefertari, he told himself sleepily. She will be expecting him. He will be escorted into her presence. She will greet him graciously with that smile, the one that melts my heart. Perhaps they will meet in the garden, and all around them in the dazzling sunlight the drops of water on the grass from the gardeners' buckets will glint and shimmer. Perhaps Ahmose-onkh will be there also, lying on his stomach on the verge of the pond while the frogs shelter under the lily pads just out of his reach and the tiny fish flicker like fragments of coloured silver far down in the murky depths… . He slipped into unconsciousness with a gentle longing for the familiar sights of his home.

Two days of rowing brought the flotilla to the city of Iunu, Ra's home. Here the Nile divided into its two main tributaries, the eastern and the western arms. Ahmose waited there only long enough for the army to catch up to him before moving on. In another day he was passing the site where the fort of Nag-ta-Hert used to stand. He and Kamose had been delayed there for a month, trying to find a way past its deceptively simple walls. Nothing of them remained but an untidy mound of sand and earth in which young tree saplings and a few weeds were trying to take hold. Ahmose watched it slide by. The memories of that time were as fresh and vivid as ever, but examining them he found that the sharp bite of loss and grief for Kamose was beginning to be blunted. I am healing, he thought in surprise. Soon I will be able to say the prayers for the dead without weeping. Time can be a cruel enemy, but some-times I am grateful for its passing.

Het-Uart was still three or four days away, but already the Nile was sending out little branches that meandered from the main stem of the eastern flow to wander through tiny fields lined with shade trees and orchards laden with fruit. Their level was very low, leaving hard, dry land on either side where soldiers might march. Ahmose ordered the Medjay to stand to full alert, and carefully the fleet sailed on until the city was no more than a day ahead. Then he had the ships moored and sent for Kay Abana, waiting for him in the relative coolness of his cabin. Kay arrived with the alacrity Ahmose had come to expect of him, bowing respectfully and taking the stool Ahmose indicated. Akhtoy poured beer for them and then went out. "It is time to put you to work," Ahmose said to him. Kay nodded over the rim of his cup, drank deeply, and set it down on the floor beside him.

"Good beer, Majesty," he commented. "Somehow the humidity of the Delta makes me far more thirsty than the furnace that tries to burn us up at home." He wiped his mouth with one brisk swipe of a brown finger. "I smell this air and am immediately anxious, eager, and a little fearful, all at once. I hope that when Het-Uart finally falls, your Majesty will not choose to station the *North* up here. It may be beautiful but I hate it." Ahmose smiled.

"Is your cousin behaving himself?" he asked. Kay nodded.

"He has been tireless in carrying out my orders. All that may change when he sees the reality of war but I do not think so. Where is the army now, Majesty, and what would you have me do?"

"I expect the divisions to pass us in the night," Ahmose said. "Choose six of your scouts and have them ready to join the generals, one to each division that will be spreading out through the eastern Delta and along the Horus Road. The remaining five divisions will be sieging the city.

I want you and the *North* with me, Kay. I intend to destroy the docks at Het-Uart and you must give me your advice regarding access to the northern mound." Quickly he told the young man what Sebek-nakht had said. Kay listened with a frown of concentration.

"There must be thousands of Setiu troops crammed onto that accursed mound, Majesty," he remarked when Ahmose had finished. "It will be very difficult to hold them off while our soldiers crawl through a few muddy holes in the wall. Better to try and demolish the north-west portion of the wall completely before sending anyone in."

"I intend to keep them occupied by shooting at them on the eastern side," Ahmose said. "It is a slim chance. But my six divisions will be engaging the enemy contingents that are ranging freely in the eastern Delta. They will not be able to come at the rear of my besieging force."

"What of Het-Uart's main mound?"

Ahmose lifted his linen away from his sticky thighs. In spite of the slight breeze that was finding its way through the wooden slats of the cabin, the air was thick and hot. "The flood plains around it to the south and east are dry and I will fill them with archers," he explained. "Infantry will surround the gates. On its western side there is of course the tributary. The *North* will assist in defending the infantry who will demolish the docks." He sighed. "You and I both know that unless the gates open we cannot take the city. Not ever. We can almost certainly clear out the Delta of foreign troops, set a large guard on the Horus Road to prevent more coming in, and perhaps we may penetrate and wipe out the concentration on the northern mound, but that will still leave the city itself unscathed."

"If you stay up here through the winter, you can stop any food getting in," Kay offered. "They cannot hold out for long without food." Ahmose grimaced.

"It is all a puzzle of if and perhaps," he said. "For me there is only the next move. Are your orders clear, Kay?" It was a dismissal. Kay stood.

"The scouts will link up with the divisions as they go through," he assured Ahmose. "I presume that your Majesty requires regular reports from them?"

"Yes. Directly to me. If all goes well, we should sight Het-Uart the day after tomorrow. Have Hor-Aha sent to me on your way back to your ship, Kay. The Medjay must understand their deployment."

Ahmose had already mapped out a strategy in detail with the generals who would command the action against the new Setiu soldiers. Nevertheless he stayed up for a few final words with them as their troops marched doggedly past. Consequently he was still asleep when the curve of Het-Uart's southern wall came into sight, and Akhtoy woke him gently. Tying on a kilt and hurriedly thrusting his feet into his sandals, he left the cabin and walked across the deck through the group of protecting Followers to gaze out at Egypt's bane.

Already the top of the high, sloping fortification was thick with soldiers who were being jostled by crowds of shouting, pointing citizens. The naked flood plain before the wall was deserted. Obviously the city had been warned of their coming. "Turi, Kagemni, Baqet, Khety and Sebek-khu wait for your permission to board, Majesty," Ankhmahor said as he joined Ahmose at the rail. "They want your final orders. The Medjay have divided and the archers who are to surround the city are on the bank with the divisions. Hor-Aha is with the remainder."

"Have them come."

He watched his five generals run up the ramp, ignoring the furore from atop the wall and the hail of arrows being loosed hysterically in his direction even though he was well out of range. There was no sign of any threat from the ground. The six other divisions had entered the eastern Delta and any troops wandering outside the safety of their defences would have hurried inside the mounds hours ago.

The little throng strode up and bowed and Ahmose wasted no time. "Kagemni and Baqet, you are to take the Medjay waiting for you and deploy your men around the city to the south and east," he told them. "Set up camp well away from the walls. Put troops on the gates at once but let the rest pitch their tents and settle down. Have the chariots begin to patrol the perimeter. The ground is solid. They should have no trouble. Have the carts with the provisions arrived?" Kagemni nodded. "Good. Khety, march the Division of Horus straight to the eastern side of the northern mound and begin to shoot at anything that moves on the walls. Make a fuss. Raise the dust. I want the men inside to be distracted from Kay and his ship on the western side. At nightfall you can settle in. Turi, you and Sebek-khu will take the western edge of the mound, between the wall and the tributary. Ten thousand men should be enough to seal the Setiu inside. Your men will be constantly in range of their archers so you will be covered by the Medjay in the boats. You will begin work on the docks at once. If there are boats tied up there, seize the cargo and burn them. That is all." One by one they bowed and ran back the way they had come, and when they had gone, the ramp was drawn up. "Captain, take me closer in!" Ahmose called. Ankhmahor stepped up to him abruptly.

"Majesty, that is not wise," he protested. "A stray arrow could end all our dreams."

"Mine as well," Ahmose retorted with humour. "Don't worry. By the time we have rowed forward a little, the Medjay will have begun to pick the soldiers off the walls. Then see how quickly the cowards vanish. As soon as that happens, the *North* can slip past the city. I expect word on the irrigation channels by this evening."

Cautiously the oarsmen responded to the captain's command and the craft inched forward. Ahmose's gaze travelled from the swarm of soldiers pouring along the left-hand plain to the Medjay's boats moving swiftly ahead of them on their flank. In spite of the motion of the decks the archers were already at work, sending an erratic shower of arrows high into the cloud-flecked sky. Shrieks came from the walls as their arc disintegrated and they fell, finding their mark. Bodies slumped, some to tumble into the ranks of the Egyptians below. The press of people standing on the wide apex of the wall thinned suddenly and the Medjay sent up a triumphant yell.

Ahmose found his eyes straining to pick out individual faces from those still silhouetted high against the glare before with a mental shrug he lowered his attention to the progress of his two divisions. She would not be up there, exposing herself to danger, elbowed and pushed this way and that by excited commoners. Not Queen Tautha. Nevertheless he imagined her as a young girl leaning over the edge of that daunting slope and calling his name, waving at him frantically to attract his notice. Tani! He dismissed the spurt of anger and sadness.

Signalling curtly to his captain, he waited while his craft slowed and gently bumped the bank, then he ran down the ramp with Ankhmahor behind him. "Bring me a chariot if you can find one to spare," he ordered. "I want a clearer view of the docks. And I had better carry my shield. I have no faith in the accuracy of the Setiu archers, but to be struck dead by a stray arrow would be an ignominious end indeed." Ankhmahor pointed.

"There goes the *North*, Majesty!" he exclaimed. "She is beating past the Medjay, to their rear!" They stood watching for a moment until Kay's proud flag fluttered around the curve of the tributary and was lost to sight, then Ankhmahor sighed with relief. "She has negotiated the first peril," he said. "Khety will doubtless have engaged the interest of the troops on the northern mound by now."

Ahmose was about to comment when a roar went up from the soldiers lining the top of the wall. The civilians had disappeared, leaving rows of black-bearded men lying or crouching gingerly under the hail of lethal fire from the Medjay and attempting to bring their own arrows to bear on the soldiers milling beneath them.

"We have begun to attack the docks," Ahmose said. "How stupid the Setiu are! Boulders would effect more damage on our divisions than those arrows. Or perhaps hunks of stone from the cemeteries Sebek-nakht is dismantling." He laughed but the sound caught in his throat. A familiar figure had materialized and was striding behind the frustrated Setiu soldiers, ignoring the missiles clattering around him. Swarthy, coarse-featured, moving with a compact, athletic grace, he seemed to be berating them, although Ahmose could hear nothing of his words over the widespread clamour.

"Pezedkhu," Ankhmahor murmured. "What is he doing?"

"He is ordering them off the wall," Ahmose answered thickly. "He knows that they are no match for the Medjay and he does not want to lose any more of them. He also knows that such losses are stupid, seeing that no matter what we do we cannot enter the city. Once more he is showing caution at the expense of saving face." He swung to his commander. "Send to the Medjay to cease shooting but hold their positions," he said. "And get me that chariot." Do you think he saw me? he wanted to ask. Did his gaze light on me in recognition? Is that why I suddenly feel so naked? He watched Ankhmahor flick a hand at his Second as he walked briskly away and then the remainder of the Followers closed in around him.

The docks at Het-Uart were massive and numerous, great piers of wood thrusting into the tributary's current, but it was summer and the level of the water was low, revealing the carelessness of their construction. Like everything else the Setiu build, Ahmose thought with grim satisfaction as he stood in the chariot behind Ankhmahor, the shield held between himself and the city on his right. They appear sturdy but they are as flimsy as a child's twig house. What a waste of precious Rethennu timber!

Several large ships, some of reed, some of cedar, and one or two of clearly Keftian design with prows that curved into the likenesses of fish, lay berthed beside them. Fighting had broken out on their decks as the Egyptians boarded them. Many of their sailors, seemingly unarmed, were scrambling

over their sides and jumping into the shallow water, and
Ahmose was glad to see them struggle unmolested to the
farther bank between the Medjay craft. However, those
remaining who had weapons were trying to defend their
charges. Small skirmishes could be seen on the decks, while
around them the soldiers detailed to remove the cargo were
ignoring them, flowing into the holds empty-handed and
emerging again laden with sacks and boxes. It was impossible for Ahmose to determine what they held. Below and
beside the ships men waist-deep in water were already clus-
tering around the dock supports, axes glittering in the sun,
waiting for a word from their officers to begin hacking them
down, and on the bank a fire crackled. Critically Ahmose
surveyed an apparent chaos in the midst of which his strategy was smoothly being fulfilled.

All at once the steady thunder of noise increased. The
thousands of men crowding the plain between the city and
the docks began to sway and the standards of the two divisions, Amun and Montu, dipped and slewed before being
righted. Axe bearers, torch bearers and cargo bearers
faltered and turned towards the source of the disturbance.
"Gods!" Ahmose shouted as Ankhmahor bent quickly and
lifted the reins. "The gates are opening! They are going to
try to defend the docks!" He stamped in a paroxysm of
shock and glee. "Whip us forward, Commander!
Khabekhnet! Khabekhnet!" His Chief Herald came
running as the chariot picked up speed, and swung himself
up beside Ahmose. "Beat your way through that mess to the
generals," Ahmose went on, unaware that he was still
roaring. "Order them not to engage the Setiu. Order them
to keep those gates open at any cost and push their way

through, right into the city." Khabekhnet nodded and leaped away, pounding across the dusty earth, already calling. Tense in every muscle, Ahmose watched him disappear into the milling, screaming throng. Ten thousand troops, he though feverishly, excitedly. Ten thousand to flood Het-Uart, and another fifteen to throw after them if the gates can be held. Oh please, Amun, give Turi and Sebek-khu the presence of mind to see what must be done!

"Send for the other divisions, Majesty!" Ankhmahor called back over his shoulder. He was pulling on the reins, slowing the horses, and Ahmose did not object. It would do no good to be closer to that seething, struggling mass of men. He could see everything quite clearly. Panting and shaking, he gripped the sides of the chariot.

"Not yet," he said hoarsely. "We must not leave the North unprotected. The standards are moving, Ankhmahor. The Standard Bearers are closing on the gates. But will the troops be able to follow?"

Tensely they watched, oblivious of the noon sun pouring its heat on their heads, the sweat of apprehension trickling down their bodies, the stirring of the hot breeze in the blue and white ostrich feathers fastened between the twitching ears of the patient horses. At length Ankhmahor spoke. "The Medjay are trying to find targets but they are afraid of striking Egyptians," he said expressionlessly. "Such impotence must be driving Hor-Aha insane." Ahmose did not reply. He too could see the archers lining the boats drawn off from the conflict, arrows fitted to bows that jerked this way and that and could not be drawn. He glimpsed Hor-Aha standing with his fists pressed against his white-clad hips, his head down.

But in a moment the bows were raised as though the Medjay had suddenly been possessed by one thought. Ahmose looked up. Fresh Setiu soldiers had sprung onto the top of the wall, and kneeling, had begun to shoot down into the dense fighting. Pezedkhu was with them, and even from a distance Ahmose could sense his rage. The foray outside the gates was not his idea, Ahmose thought to himself immediately. Of course not. He would never command such rashness. Apepa must be behind this idiocy. Pezedkhu is trying to limit the damage, prevent us from storming the gates, slow us down. A surge of hope turned Ahmose's attention from the arrow-filled sky and back to the melee below.

The conflict had intensified. The gates still stood open but the mass of men packed before them had thickened. To Ahmose's dismay it was obvious that the Setiu, emerging to face a solid front of Egyptians, had been able to do no more than provide the gates with a human shield which the Egyptians were being forced to hack down before they could approach those mighty doors. The standards and the men following them could not circumvent the Setiu. The fighting had become fierce and merciless, the bodies of the slain crumpling to become yet another obstacle for the Egyptians who had now fallen silent and were wielding their weapons in a grim desperation to win through to that beckoning aperture that could mean the end of years of futility. "They will be forced to slay every Setiu soldier and clamber over their corpses before they can even touch the gates," Ankhmahor said in exasperation, voicing Ahmose's own surmise. "By then they will be too exhausted to do much more."

"Then they will be relieved," Ahmose said firmly. "Already the Setiu ranks are thinner. It is time to recall the other divisions." But even as he turned to give the command to one of his heralds waiting with the Followers, he saw Pezedkhu running along the top of the wall towards the gates, his shield raised high against the Medjay's arrows, his other arm ending in a fist. Coming to a halt he leaned over, and even above the noise of battle Ahmose could hear him screaming, "Close the gates you fools! What are you waiting for? Close them now! Imbeciles! Mindless dogs! Sons of perdition!" With a great gush of despair Ahmose saw the huge doors begin to inch shut. He cried out, and his exclamation of loss was echoed by the weary Egyptians. A howl went up. There was one last surge towards the wall, and then the boom of the gates coming together followed by the lesser sound of the mighty wooden beams falling into their cradles on the other side.

Within the next hour the last Setiu soldier stranded outside the city was cut down. Pezedkhu and his archers vanished. The axes resumed their work, biting into the precarious foundations of the docks. The cargo had been removed to be examined and stored by the Scribe of Distribution and the torch bearers waited their turn to fire the empty ships and thus whatever was left of the docks also.

The Medjay would remain in position until docks and ships were consumed and Kay Abana had brought the *North* back safely. Ahmose ordered the divisions back to their bivouacs for food and rest. He requested a tally of the Egyptian dead, reports on the wounded, a meeting with Turi and Sebek-khu, an inventory of the captured cargo, in a mood of bitter disappointment shared by the whole vast Egyptian camp.

Towards sunset the cooking fires were lit and the aroma of good food filled the air. Soldiers waded into the water to wash mired bodies and filthy linen or sat before their tents cleaning and sharpening dull weapons but there was none of the usual cheerful babble and banter. Ahmose, being driven along the lines before he himself ate, was enveloped in their dejection. He received their obeisances, speaking to them of their bravery and fortitude, and their answers were respectful but quiet. All of them understood the enormity of the chance that had been offered and then snatched away.

5

NO WORD HAD COME from Kay Abana. Ahmose, sitting later before his own tent, while behind him Akhtoy lit the lamp and before him the sun at last sank behind the profuse growth on the western side of the tributary, added that worry to his already dark mood. General Khety had sent word that his men had spent the day firing arrows and insults at the thick crowd of Setiu soldiers gathered on the walls of the northern mound and generally making a great noise and fuss, but in the late afternoon they had retired out of bowshot to make camp.

What were the orders for tomorrow? Ahmose did not know. He could formulate no plan for the Division of Horus until the *North* came sliding past Het-Uart. He did not expect any word from the divisions spreading out through the eastern Delta for some days. He was himself very tired but he sat on, a full wine cup on the small table beside him, a silent Ankhmahor and the Followers ranked watchfully in the shadows. Ramose had asked to be allowed to board the *North* and investigate the irrigation canals with Kay. Ahmose longed for his presence and added the fear for his friend's life to the already crushing weight of the day's discouragement.

But just as he had finished his evening prayers to Amun and was closing the doors of his travelling shrine, one of his heralds requested admittance. "The *North* has returned, Majesty," the man told him when Ahmose had come to the front of the tent. "Even now she is running out her ramp."

"Good!" Ahmose felt his bowels loosen with the intensity of his relief. "Then tell General Hor-Aha that the Medjay can stand down. Send Kay Abana and Prince Ramose to me as soon as the *North*'s crew has been given their rations and settled down." The man saluted and vanished into the fire-pricked dusk and Ahmose turned back. "Bring two stools, a flagon of wine and whatever meat and bread you can find," he told his steward. Akhtoy went out, and as Ahmose sank into his chair he was assailed by the first genuine hunger pangs he had felt in days.

It happened once, he thought with a resurgence of his customary optimism. It can happen again. Do not succumb to the gloom of the moment, you silly man! Amun will grant me the ultimate victory, I feel it in my very bones. The price has been paid. Father and Kamose paid it and the gods have willed that I may collect the reward.

By the time Kay and Ramose were admitted, Akhtoy had already placed wine and hot food on the table and had smoothly excused himself. Ahmose invited them to sit. They were both obviously freshly washed, their wet hair tied back, their clean linen rustling as they obeyed. Kay Abana had several cuts on the backs of his brown hands. His knees were grazed, like those of a child's who has tripped and fallen onto stones. A bruise was swelling, purple and ugly, on his cheek, and blood had dried in a thin line along one shin bone and across his calf. Ahmose indicated the roasted gazelle meat, barley bread and crumbled cheese. "Eat first," he advised. "Ramose, pour us some wine.

I see that you have been behaving rashly as usual, Captain Abana, but before you tell me why, we will fill our bellies." He smiled. "I am greatly heartened to have you both safe."

Not until the platters were scoured and the wine jug empty did Ahmose speak. "Now," he began. "Give me your report." Kay tutted.

"It is not good, Majesty," he said promptly. "There are indeed breaches in the wall, some twenty or thirty at most, where the irrigation canals inside the mound can be filled during the Inundation. They are of course closed up to keep water in at the moment but their locations are obvious. It appears that they are not large. Nor do they seem particularly firm, just mud and straw mixed perhaps with limestone powder and slammed into the gaps to harden without being smoothed. I would think that the Inundation itself would weaken them from the outside while the men within pick at them to make them crack." He folded his legs gingerly, the bloodied one over the other, and turned to face Ahmose directly. "My men endeavoured to scratch at them but it was hard work. When they have been softened by the flood it will be easier, but then the soldiers will be forced to hold their breath and wriggle through them underwater for a short way, one at a time. Then sopping and panting, they must draw wet weapons and face strong opposition on the other side." He shook his head. "The risk is too great."

"This coming from you, my rashest of officers?" Ahmose interrupted him lightly, although he was disappointed at Abana's assessment of the situation. "Perhaps the openings can be widened with the help of the flood and several hundred troops armed with picks."

"They would have to deal with a strong defence," Abana replied promptly. "The Setiu have cut slits in the wall above, from which they can fire down upon anyone trying to hack at the breaches, and in spite of the diversion you ordered to draw off the majority of men, the archers stationed above the bricked-up canals did not leave their posts. The Setiu officers are perhaps not as dull-witted as we believed. Or like baboons they can be trained to a task without having to use what little intelligence they might possess." He looked about. "Is there any more wine?" Ahmose ignored the question. He sat forward.

"Do you mean to tell me that you and your men attempted to open the breaches under fire from above and from the slits in the wall itself?"

Abana grinned happily. "Yes, we did," he said. "My faithful sailors kept up a steady rain of arrows from the deck of the *North* while we worked on our hands and knees. But it was useless," he finished regretfully. "We could hear troops massing in the gardens beyond, ready for us if by some chance we managed to chip our way to the water which," he pointed out with relish, "would have come pouring out on us if we had succeeded, and forced the inhabitants of those doubtless beautiful houses beyond to abandon all hope of sampling the last of their fruits and vegetables." He held out his hands. "I myself dug alongside my men," he continued, "and was grazed on the leg by a poorly aimed arrow. The Setiu archers shoot in a panic and their aim is wild."

"Nevertheless, their weapons are admirable," Ahmose reminded him. "The design of the bow they brought with them when they began to insinuate themselves into

Egyptian life was superior to anything we had seen before, and what of their axes with the broader blades than ours, and the scimitars?"

"A weapon is only as good as the man who wields it," Kay said loftily. "Now that we have learned to make those bows and axes and knives ourselves, we have been turning their own knowledge against them. They are not competent warriors." Ahmose regarded him with a mixture of mild irritation and affection.

"Give me your final assessment," he said. Kay sighed gustily.

"To attempt entrance to the northern mound through the irrigation canals would be a waste of effort and valuable men's lives, Majesty," he said regretfully. "I am loath to tell you this, but in my opinion another way needs to be found."

"Thank you." Ahmose nodded. "Go and sleep now, Kay. You have done well." Kay scrambled to his feet at once and bowed.

"I have left a gift for Your Majesty outside with the Follower on your door," he said as he backed towards the tent flap. "Or rather, several gifts. One of them is from my cousin Zaa. I wish you a restful night. You also, Prince." His wide smile flashed out again and then the flap closed behind him. Ahmose met Ramose's eye.

"You have been unusually silent," he ventured. "What is on your mind?" Ramose stirred.

"You have a brave and astute officer there, Ahmose," he said quietly. "The barrage of arrows from both the top of the wall and those lethal slits was constant and deadly, but Kay and his men went on hewing at the blocked-up breaches regardless of the danger. I watched it all from the relative safety of the *North*. The gift he has brought you is a sack of Setiu hands, twenty-seven in all, taken from the bodies of the defendants who were shot by the sailors on the boat and who tumbled down on this side of the wall. Many more fell backwards, out of sight. One of the hands belonged to a soldier young Zaa pen Nekheb managed to slay. It was a lucky shot, I think, considering that the boy is still struggling to learn how to draw the bow, but it was boldly done all the same." He rubbed at his forehead and looked across at Ahmose under weary lids. "Much of the enemy fire was understandably concentrated on the sailors. Thirty are wounded and another fifty were killed."

"Fifty!" Ahmose straightened in shock. "That is too many, Ramose. Far too many! Abana should have told me."

"He would have, if you had asked, but he is very proud of his ship and its men. He is ashamed that he could not protect them sufficiently. He had already summoned one of the army physicians to those injured before he came here."

"The irrigation breaches must be abandoned then," Ahmose said firmly. "I will not sacrifice Egyptians for such a slim chance of success. What do you think?"

He watched Ramose withdraw into himself for a time, his face entirely in shadow but the long, supple fingers of his right hand lying motionless on the table in the full play of the lamplight. Ahmose found himself remembering his sister at that moment, seeing that same hand, thinner and more youthful, bright with rings, curved protectively around Tani's bare shoulder on a morning full of warm sunlight. He waited. Presently the fingers tapped the table once and were withdrawn.

"I think you are right," Ramose said slowly. "However, Your Majesty might consider this. Reverse your strategy. Rather than trying to open the irrigation courses, station part of the navy on the tributary opposite them and prevent them from being opened when the Inundation begins. In fact, make sure that no water of any kind flows into either the northern mound or the other one." He leaned into the lamplight. "All the walled enclosures are crammed with people. You heard Sebek-nakht. Even the mortuary temples in Het-Uart are being razed for lack of living space. What do the people drink? There are no springs in the Setiu strongholds. Water must come from wells and be supplemented by the tributaries every winter when Isis cries. Cut them off. Stop the influx of fresh water. You have already decided to continue the siege and the Delta campaigns throughout the Inundation. Always before, we have retreated during the flood season and that is when Het-Uart augments its water supply. This year it will be different. Make them thirst!" Ahmose stared at him.

"Truly this has been a day of mingled frustration and hope," he murmured. He stood up and immediately Ramose rose also. "I will inspect Abana's rather grisly gift, and then we will fall gratefully onto our cots," he said. "Thank you for your advice." Ramose bowed in response and together they stepped out into the mild night air.

The sack lay at the feet of one of the Followers guarding the entrance to the tent. At Ahmose's command he bent down and pulled the neck wide revealing a mass of blood-ied, severed hands. Ahmose looked down on them thoughtfully. "Kamose did not take hands or penises for the tally in most of his battles," he said. "It never occurred to me to wonder why. But seeing these brings home to me the legitimacy of our struggle. We are not bandits slaying and thieving before moving on. This is an honourable war." His gaze rose to the Follower. "Have these taken to the Scribe of the Army so that he may note the number of the enemy killed by the ship *North*," he ordered. He was about to voice the realization that Kamose did not always keep the tally of enemy dead in the traditional way because he knew that his struggle resembled too closely the actions of a brigand, at least in the beginning, but he kept that reflection to himself. Bidding Ramose good night and asking the Follower to send Khabekhnet to him when he returned, he went back into the tent.

He waited quietly, listening to the sounds of his thousands of men gradually die away as they rolled themselves in their blankets until only the occasional protest of a donkey and the regular challenges of the sentries, some far, some near, broke the stillness.

The city also seemed subdued, its usual confusion of noise reduced to a low mutter. To Ahmose, sitting with arms and legs folded while Akhtoy and his assistant cleared the table, the tone held a quality of melancholy. He knew that his imagination was imbuing Het-Uart with an intimation of its fate, but he allowed himself to indulge his fancy anyway. I would dearly love to know the tenor of the commoners within, he mused. Are they still complacent when they hear my soldiers marching below their walls? Does any quiver of apprehension give them pause in the middle of their daily comings and goings? Akhtoy had finished wiping the table and folding it away. "Do you require anything else, Majesty?" he asked. Ahmose shook his head.

"No," he answered. "Wake me at dawn, Akhtoy, with food."

As Akhtoy left, he held the tent flap open for Khabekhnet. The Chief Herald came forward and bowed. "I want you to arrange shifts for all your heralds," Ahmose told him. "Not including you, of course, Khabekhnet. You will remain at my summons. They are to make chariot circuits of the city from sunset until dawn, calling for Apepa's surrender. Het-Uart believes itself inviolate, but we will do our best to disturb its dreams." Khabekhnet's black eyebrows rose.

"What would Your Majesty have them shout?"

"Let us make it a threat." Ahmose stood and stretched. "They must say this. 'Uatch-Kheperu Ahmose, Son of the Sun, Horus, the Horus of Gold, demands the surrender of the foreign usurper Apepa, unless he wishes to see the city of Het-Uart burned to the ground.' Every night, Khabekhnet. You are dismissed."

"Very good, Majesty."

When he had gone, Ahmose climbed onto his cot, and snuffing the lamp he closed his eyes. There should be reports soon from the divisions warring free in the Delta, he thought as his body began to relax, and perhaps some word from Weset. I must have Ipi make a note regarding the Gold of Valour for the crew of the *North*. I can do little more with the city until the Inundation and then I must send for the navy. Ramose is right. Keep fresh water out of Het-Uart. With that he fell asleep, half-waking several times before morning to hear, far off but very clearly, the voices of his heralds as they circled the flood plain, crying his warning.

But it was the Scribe of the Army who came to him with the first light of Ra, brandishing the lists of hands taken from the enemy dead who had been shot by the Medjay and fallen outside the walls and who had perished in the battle before the open gates.

Ahmose was more concerned with the numbers of his own men who had died and with any soldiers qualifying for an award due to bravery. There were several. The fighting in front of that tantalizingly open gate had been fierce and sustained. Greasy black smoke was already hazing the bright morning from the piles of burning Setiu bodies, but the Scribe of the Army assured Ahmose that the Egyptian dead were being washed and wrapped in clean linen before being buried. There were not many of them, for the Setiu had been grossly outnumbered. Their names had been meticulously recorded so that later they might be carved into stone; otherwise the gods would not be able to find them and give them life in the next world. It was the greatest hazard in war, Ahmose reflected as the scribe gathered up his papyrus and bowed himself away from the table under the willows where Ahmose had eaten his first meal of the day. A soldier risked dying twice, the second death being the more appalling.

The rumble of the city seemed louder this morning, the sound of its activity somehow more frantic. Ahmose, sipping his beer and watching his officers moving among the thousands of men squatting in the dirt with their rations in their hands, wondered if the heralds' stern message had done more than he had hoped. He did not underestimate the way in which the mood of the population could influence the ultimate decisions of those in authority, and it could be that the vermin of Het-Uart, waking to lie half-conscious and vulnerable in the darkness, had heard words that troubled the remainder of their sleep. No archers had appeared atop the wall. The city was ignoring the teeming host outside, as it had done when Kamose had surrounded it. Yet Ahmose sensed, very faintly, a change.

Hor-Aha and General Khety had both sent to him for orders and he had told them to simply hold their positions, firing upon anyone foolish enough to raise his head above the level of the wall but otherwise maintaining a watchful inactivity. No word had yet come from the six divisions ranging to the east, and Ahmose expected none for some time. Mesore was almost over. Thoth would mark the beginning of winter and the flood, and until the Inundation filled the tributaries of the Delta he could do little but drill his men and wait.

Mounting his chariot with Ankhmahor, he spent several hours inspecting the troops, talking with General Turi and General Sebekh-khu, and boarding the Medjay's vessels. He would have liked to invite Hor-Aha to keep him company through the day but purposely he refrained from showing the man any particular favour.

He sought out those officers of the Medjay who had been given command over Egyptian soldiers by Kamose and who had since been returned to the company of their own kind, and in talking to them he found no evidence of rancour. They responded to his carefully worded questions simply and respectfully but absently, and when he sent them away, they went back happily to the tasks he had interrupted. It is not that they lack intelligence, he mused, as he swung down one ramp and walked towards another.

They are quick to grasp a practical idea or solve a functional problem. But most of them seem to live entirely in the present, discarding both the disappointments and the triumphs of the past. Such an innate ability must give them a primitive contentment. Hor-Aha isa glaring exception, perhaps because his mother is Egyptian.

The sun was high overhead when he retraced the steps to his tent and the drooping willow beneath which he lowered himself again. Akhtoy at once emerged from his own shelter, sending for hot water and the noon meal, and Ahmose found himself approached by a herald who saluted and presented him with a scroll bearing Aahmes-nefertari's seal. Delighted, he broke the seal and began to read. "To my dear husband and King, greetings," she had dictated. "It seems as though you have been gone for many hentis and I and the children miss you very much, but there is plenty to keep me occupied on the estate and in Weset. I received your letter regarding the architect Prince Sebek-nakht of Mennofer. You have obviously decided to trust him and I suppose that while he is here in Weset he cannot be fomenting sedition farther north. Several days after your scroll arrived, he himself wrote to me explaining your invitation and expressing his regret that he has work to do for Apepa in Het-Uart before he can comply with your request for his services, but since you are now sieging that city and no one can enter or leave it, he must wait for the Inundation to complete the assignment his master had given him. I wrote back to him explaining that you were not withdrawing your armies this year, therefore he should travel to Weset as soon as possible. I thought it could do no harm, as the flood is little more than a month away."

Here Ahmose paused and smiled to himself. Clever Aahmes-nefertari, he thought, pleased. Once she has Sebek-nakht in her grasp, she will treat him like a brother and give him such satisfying work that he will never want to leave the pleasures of the estate or the challenge of the tasks. And if Amun wills it, there will be no mortuary temples left to be razed in Het-Uart. There will be no Het-Uart left at all. He lowered his gaze once more.

"Work has begun on raising the height of the wall surrounding the entire estate," the letter went on, "and I have taken it upon myself to order the one dividing our house from the old palace torn down. I have commissioned gates to be hung above the watersteps as you desired. Ahmose-onkh is much occupied in watching all this activity. I have been forced to detail a guard to accompany him so that he does not wander into danger. I have dictated an official letter in my capacity as your Queen to the ruler of the Keftiu, requesting the opening of trade negotiations that will entirely omit any dealings through the Setiu. I have also received a shipment of gold from Wawat which has been stored in the temple. I do not think that we can expect regular consignments from the mines there until you are able to turn your attention to the southern forts that used to guard the gold routes, and I have insufficient men and officers under me to send out such an expedition."

"Gods, I should hope so!" Ahmose exclaimed aloud with mingled shock and amusement. "Does the Commander of the Household Guard yearn to be created a General? General Aahmes-nefertari!" He shook his head, still chuckling. "What next, my beautiful warrior?"

"The children are well," he read on. "Your mother is overseeing the tallying of the harvest and the winemaking and she and I have been assessing the taxes to be levied this year. My duties in the temple are not onerous. Amunmose begs me to convey to you his greatest respect. He tells me that the omens for a successful conclusion to our long struggle are excellent.

"The scrolls I call for at night and read on my couch before I sleep are no longer love poems or the tales of our ancestors. They contain the lists of men you have drawn up for my investigation and judgement. My scribe, Khunes, sits on the floor beside me and records my thoughts regarding each one. He is, incidentally, a very talented and efficient young man. I found him among Amun's scribes in the temple where I go to perform the duties of a Second Prophet with which you charged me."

Once more Ahmose's eyes left the papyrus and strayed blankly to the delicately stirring tracery of thin branches. A moment of jealousy moved within him, echoing the fitful motion of the willow's fingers. Khunes, his mind whispered. A very talented and efficient young man, sitting on the floor of her bedchamber in the night with his undoubtedly handsome head bent obediently over his palette. I asked you to be my eyes and ears in the temple, Aahmes-nefertari. Is this man another link you have forged with those you must watch, or a little diversion for you? A pleasant titillation? He grunted and slapped the scroll against his knee, pushing the unworthy emotion away. Take care that you do not become unbalanced in your suspicions, Ahmose Tao, he reprimanded himself. The pit of madness waits for you as it did for Kamose, and the first step down into that darkness has "lack of trust" rendered large upon it. Swallowing, he bent over his wife's words.

"I thought it best not to use one of the household scribes to do this work," she silently explained. "I trust them all, of course, for they are trained to keep their master's counsel, but as their masters include our indomitable grandmother, it seemed wiser to recruit someone answerable to me alone. Khunes also brings the life of the temple to me when I am buried under my tasks and cannot attend there myself. When you come home, dearest husband, I shall remove him from Amun's care entirely. He instructs those who must delve into the suitability of the names I select to act as your representatives with the Princes and governors. You have given me many difficult tasks, Ahmose, but this is the hardest. It is being slowly accomplished."

The remainder of the letter was taken up with small gossip regarding the doings of the children, the health of their mother, and finally an outpouring of her love for him before she placed her name and titles at the end. Ahmose let the scroll roll up, called for Ipi, and then sat biting his lip and frowning. The one reference Aahmes-nefertari had made to Tetisheri had been innocuous enough, but it made him uneasy. Was there a struggle for control taking place in the house? Was Tetisheri attempting to assert her own authority over the many enterprises he had left in his wife's hands? I will not be returning to Weset for a very long time, he thought, as a shadow fell over him and he looked up to see Ipi come to a halt and bow. Aahmes-nefertari knows it, and that is why her letter was so full. I must remind her to seal her communications to me as soon as they are written and place them directly into the hands of the herald who will bring them. I must tell her to dictate everything done and said under her jurisdiction in the greatest detail. Better still, she must write the letters herself.

Then he laughed abruptly. That would require more time and effort than she had, and the mute suggestion had come straight from the muddy pool of jealousy still rippling inside him. I should be pleased that she has found someone on whom she may rely, he thought. This Khunes is a scribe, a useful and necessary tool. Nothing more. If he enters her bedchamber, if he bows before her as she sits propped up on her couch, her filmy white sleeping robe spread out around her and her hair loose upon the pillows, it is because it is the only time in her crowded day when she is able to address this particular matter.

I used to love her calmly, unreflectively, his thoughts ran on. I took her and that comfortable emotion for granted. She was my shy, pretty wife for whom I felt an indulgent, rather patronizing protectiveness. I made love to her with tenderness and enjoyment but passion for her was unknown to me. All that has changed. War and suffering has made me a man and brought out in her the qualities I ought to have seen in the beginning if I had not been so complacent with regard to her affection for me.

Now I am in love with her and I did not realize it fully until this moment. I am jealous of her scribe, the officers of her household guard, the priests with whom she worships in the temple. The women who clothe her, the men who feed her, the cosmetician who is privileged to touch her face, I envy them all. I want to bury my face in her hair, her neck, between her breasts, inhale the scent of her, lap up the warmth of her, not sanely curbed within myself but to burn, to be lost. Not wife, not mother, but woman, you are woman to me, Aahmes-nefertari, and I want you with a ferocity I did not know I possessed.

Ipi cleared his throat and Ahmose glanced up, dazed. "You wish to dictate, Majesty?" the scribe asked politely. Ahmose wrenched his attention back to the present.

"No. No, Ipi," he said huskily. He held out the scroll. "A letter from the Queen. Put a date on it and file it away. Tell me," he went on as Ipi took the papyrus, "do you know anything of a temple scribe called Khunes? Her Majesty has recently hired him as her personal assistant." Ipi frowned, considering.

"I know every under-scribe in your employ, Majesty," he replied, "but it is some time since I took notice of Amun's servants. The name seems familiar. Would Your Majesty like me to make a few discreet enquiries into the character and ability of this person?" At once Ahmose felt besmirched.

"No," he answered slowly. "The Queen's judgement is sound. I simply wondered what you could remember of him if you had ever met him. Thank you, Ipi. That is all." Yet his eyes stayed fixed on the scroll in Ipi's hand as the man hurried away, and he rose from his chair with reluctance. His head had begun to ache and the scar behind his ear to itch. He fingered it irritably. "Akhtoy!" he called. "Bring a sunshade! I will swim and then lie on the bank for a while before I eat."

Both the letter and the revelation that had followed it made him restless. He did not want the food Akhtoy placed before him, nor could he fall asleep in the hour when the sun seemed to stand still and the heat was greatest. He was almost glad when Ankhmahor requested admittance to tell him that Mesehti and Makhu were waiting outside to speak with him. Leaving his cot, he pulled on the linen cap of custom and wound a kilt about his waist before allowing the Princes entrance.

They came up to him and prostrated themselves, pressing their foreheads to the carpeted floor, before rising at his curt word. He studied them carefully and they gazed back at him solemnly, Mesehti's eyes steady in his weathered face, Makhu betraying anxiety in the clenching of his strong jaw. "Well," Ahmose said at last. "What do you wish to say to me?" Mesehti, as Ahmose might have expected, came straight to the point.

"Majesty, you have brought us with you to the Delta and you have kept us idle," he began. "We have no designated office here. We understand that we are under your divine discipline, that we accompanied you because you do not trust us, but we chafe at our inactivity. We humbly beg you to tell us how long we must dwell in the coldness of your disapproval." He glanced at Makhu. "We are aware that Your Majesty reads our letters to our families in Djawati and Akhmin and their letters to us. They dictate nothing more than the affairs of our estates, the abundance of the harvest, the progress of our tombs and suchlike. As for us, we wander about the camp with our shame displayed for every active officer to see. We would rather be imprisoned than that!"

"Would you indeed?" Ahmose broke in, his tone deceptively mild. "You were greatly averse to any such fate when you returned to Weset with Ramose and fell on your knees before me and the Queen. You were a hair's breadth away from losing your heads. Indeed, if it had not been for the Queen's clemency, you would even now be lying beautified in your tombs. And you dare to complain of such a small matter as your shame?" Makhu took one step forward.

"It is not a small matter, our shame," he said earnestly. "It is a disfigurement that we will carry on our kas for the rest of the lives the Queen so mercifully gave back to us. But, Majesty, we are not peasants. We are not stupid men. We erred from a confusion of loyalties, not from cowardice or indecision. We are Princes, with knowledge and skills that are at your disposal as our King. Do not waste us, Divine One! Give us work. Let us earn your trust once again!"

Ahmose turned away from them and began to pace. Letters and trust, he thought grimly. Perhaps it is I who need to learn a lesson today. Are you speaking to me, Amun, King of Gods? Are you admonishing me or giving me a warning? "It is certain that I cannot send you to your homes," he said, hands behind his back as he measured out the confined space of the tent. "It is also certain that I would be pleased to restore two nobles to my favour by allowing them to make amends for their mistakes. Such an indulgence would be most agreeable to Ma'at. But what atonement should I command?" He was half-playing with them, having already decided to bend his back to the caution of the god. "Oh sit down, both of you!" he snapped. "Take those stools. I understood your dilemma weeks ago and I fully expect you to understand mine. I can risk no more rebellions." They loosened, pulling up the stools and lowering themselves even as Ahmose flung himself into his chair. "Akhtoy left some wine on the table," he said. "Makhu, pour for us. I know that the divisions are short of charioteers and few Egyptians apart from the Princes know anything about horses. I desperately need someone to train drivers and organize the stables. It is an honourable position, well suited to ancient blood. You can both begin by becoming Overseers of the Stables, inspecting the state of the horses belonging to each division and putting the fledgling charioteers through their paces. With the Inundation imminent the chariots will soon be of little use but next summer they will come into their own and one day, I hope, they will be matched with the Setiu chariots right here on the flood plains outside Het-Uart. Is this acceptable to you?" They nodded gravely, relief on their faces but not the servility that would have hidden an insincerity Ahmose feared. "Good. Then let us drink to the restoration of Ma'at and the health of our loved ones." But I will still order your letters unsealed and read to me, Ahmose said to them silently as all three of them drank. And my eye will be on you constantly.

It was another week before reports from the six divisions fighting in the Delta began to dribble in and Ahmose read them with increasing disquiet. The situation was less reassuring than he had hoped. It was not dire, as Hor-Aha pointed out during the strategy meeting Ahmose had called to discuss the news, but it was troubling nonetheless. "Kamose ignored the Horus Road for too long," Turi remarked as the five men sat about the table in the shade of Ahmose's tent. "It is like an untended hole in an irrigation dyke. As long as troops from Rethennu keep flowing into Egypt, we will be unable to lure Apepa from the safety of his stronghold. His fellow Princes in the east will keep us in a state of impotence."

"He had little choice," Khety objected. "His immediate concern was the need to secure the rest of Egypt and that is where his energy went. He accomplished that goal."

"It seems as though Rethennu has an unlimited supply of men and arms," Sebek-khu said irritably. "Where are they coming from?"

"Do not forget that Rethennu is an alliance of several tribal chieftains who call themselves Princes," Ahmose reminded them. "Apepa's grandfather Sekerher was only one of them. I have no doubt that they are pledged to help one another in times of war."

"And in trade," Hor-Aha put in. "Much of the wealth of the Delta has surely been channelled into their coffers. We must plug up that hole."

"These foreign soldiers are not phantoms," Ahmose said. "Nor can the women of Rethennu produce them fully grown on demand." He went on speaking through a ripple of laughter. "There must be a time when the supply is exhausted. But we cannot wait. Het-Uart must fall, and soon."

He had a quick vision of discouraged generals, discontented and homesick troops, desertions, and through it all his enemy feasting at a table laden with all manner of delicacies in an impregnable palace, the Double Crown on his head and Tani at his right hand, weighed down with the gold of Wawat. Mentally shaking himself, he placed both hands flat on the table."I must venture farther into the Delta and see for myself what is happening," he told them. "You all know what must be done here. Hor-Aha, keep the soldiers and citizens from the walls. Have the Medjay shoot at anyone who shows his head. The docks are destroyed. No

Keftian or Asi trading vessels will be appearing until the Inundation fills the tributary, but if you spot any coming in from the Great Green to the north have them boarded, denuded and sent home politely. We do not wish to antagonize our future partners in prosperity." Hor-Aha nodded. Ahmose turned to the others. "Khety, defend the perimeter of the northern mound. Keep the soldiers bottled up inside it and prevent anyone from entering. Turi, Sebek-khu, see that the gates of Het-Uart do not open. Nothing must pass in or out."

For a while longer they discussed details, then Ahmose left them, signalling to Khabekhnet as he went. "Delegate your position to your second and prepare to travel with me," he ordered. "Make sure that your heralds continue their nightly challenge. Send to Kay Abana. If I do not return before the Nile begins to rise, he is to do his utmost to prevent the irrigation canals from being opened. He has my authority to summon other ships from Het nefer Apu if necessary. Bring me the Scribes of Victualling, the Army and Distribution." Khabekhnet saluted. Ankhmahor, conferring with a group of the Followers, turned to Ahmose inquiringly as he strode up. "We are moving into the Delta," Ahmose told him. "Your men can strike their tents. Have them ready to leave tomorrow morning."

He found Akhtoy and Ipi sitting together on the bank where several of the army's servants were washing linen, standing knee-deep while they beat the surface of the placid water with skeins of sopping white cloth. "Pack up my belongings," he said to Akhtoy, "and you, Ipi, bring plenty of papyrus and ink. It is time to see what my other thirty thousand men are doing."

He did not sleep much that night. His tent was empty, his effects shut away in the chests Akhtoy had piled up outside. Drowsing occasionally, he would wake to a series of random but worrying thoughts that flitted in succession across his mind and would not let him rest. Mesore was almost over. Thoth would mark the beginning of a new year and, if the gods willed it, a copious flood. The Horus Road wound tortuously between pools that would become lakes and reed-filled moist ground that turned into treacherous swamps, a thoroughfare that never became impassable, but that would have to be held by infantry alone without the aid of chariots. And what of the Wall of Princes? he asked himself, as he turned and turned again, his body tense. Can it be reinforced against the Setiu infiltrators without bleeding my army dry of men? Those are the keys to the eventual destruction of Het-Uart, the Wall of Princes and the Horus Road, and I am condemned to remain in the north until they are utterly mine.

Towards dawn he was finally able to drift into an unconsciousness broken only by the regular calling of the heralds as they drove around the towering walls of the city, and a dream in which he stood on one side of a Nile that was dangerously and uncharacteristically raging. Aahmes-nefertari stood on the other, pale and motionless, staring at him, while darkness grew between them and eventually she was lost to sight. Akhtoy's voice mingling with the new sunlight and the aroma of warm bread woke him, and he swung his legs over the edge of his cot and greeted his steward with massive relief. "I must make sure that Mesehti and Makhu travel with us," he said aloud as the cloud of preoccupations returned. Akhtoy did not reply, and Ahmose began his morning meal.

6

IT WAS A FULL SIX WEEKS before Ahmose turned his chariot back towards Het-Uart, and in that time the river had begun its swift rise towards the fullness of its flood two months away. The celebration of the new year took place on the first day of Thoth, when the rising of the Sopdet Star was marked by the solemn panoply of ritual in the temples and the full festivity of a holiday throughout the country.

Ahmose hardly noticed its passing, for the soldiers from Rethennu had no knowledge of true religion and no respect for its necessary observances. The fighting in the Delta did not stop for gods or men. Ahmose found himself plunged into the kind of frustrating, unresolved warfare he had thought left behind in the years with Kamose and before that, his father. Sallying forth from the outskirts of Het-Uart with Ramose, Ankhmahor and the Followers—Akhtoy, Ipi and his personal staff behind and Khabekhnet and his scouts ahead—he had rapidly been made aware of his defencelessness. A contingent of troops from the Division of Ptah intercepted him three days east of the city as he was about to enter a deceptively peaceful village of whitewashed huts and shady groves of tamarisk and acacia. Their senior officer pushed past the Followers' challenges and came up to Ahmose's chariot, while his men quickly formed a protective cordon around Ahmose's entourage. "General Akhethotep sent me to escort you to his headquarters, Majesty," he explained. "Your scouts found the Division yesterday, but we are continually on the move and the General was afraid that you might come too late to find him." He pointed at the cluster of little houses half-hidden amongst the random trees. "We fought the Setiu in that place," he said. "In and out of the dwellings. But we had to leave it before the whole area was secure. The Division of Khonsu needed our support."

"Why?" Ahmose asked sharply. "Where were they?" As he looked down into the officer's strained face, he felt the first intimations of genuine anxiety.

"Twenty-five miles farther along the Horus Road, Majesty," the man replied. "General Iymery was attempting to hold off a large force of the enemy that had converged by one of the lakes. Most of the fighting is a matter of small skirmishes," he went on, almost apologetically, "but this was a standing battle for which Iymery was not prepared. None of the generals expected such concerted opposition."

Ahmose's gaze wandered over the sun-drenched walls of the village without seeing them. All my time and energy has been bent on the siege around Het-Uart while the real battle for Egypt is taking place elsewhere, he thought with a spurt of panic. How could I have been so blind? Even while my mouth was speaking of the necessity for scouring the Delta of foreign troops, my mind was fully on a vision of the city's daunting gates. I was not listening. What was I imagining? That Kamose had cleaned out the Delta once and for all? That somehow the foreigners would dissolve and melt away once their feet touched Egyptian soil? Or is it simply that my brush with death has left me afraid to face yet again the sheer sweat and terror and brutality of first-hand combat? A siege is relatively bloodless. It is a slow and predictable enterprise. Amun help me, I cannot yet afford to slip comfortably into any slow and predictable enterprise. I have been deluding myself. Realizing that his men had fallen silent and were watching him inquiringly, he gestured.

"Come up and stand behind me," he ordered the officer. "Let your charioteer drive on alone and we will follow. Tell me what has been happening." The soldier sketched a bow and swung himself onto the floor of Ahmose's chariot. Ahmose signalled and the cavalcade began to move. The slumbering village gradually receded, lost behind a dappled confusion of dense foliage.

As they rolled over the flood plain, as yet still dry and hard-packed, although bordered by a swamp full of dark green reeds and noisy with water birds on one side and a young orchard criss-crossed with irrigation ditches on the other, the officer from the Division of Ptah spoke of the battle for control of the eastern Delta. His words were terse, his descriptions unadorned, yet he gave Ahmose a vivid and chilling picture of hand-to-hand combat in knee-deep quagmires, of sudden ambushes among fields of grazing cattle, of massacres in the white dust of the Horus Road itself. "We no longer pitch tents, Majesty," he said with an offhandedness that told Ahmose far more than his statements. "We have all become Shock Troops, free-wheeling, forced to adapt to any situation that may arise. That is why my General sent me out to greet you."

"Who is attempting to cut off the flow from Rethennu along the Road?" Ahmose wanted to know. The man smiled grimly.

"General Neferseshemptah with the Anubis Division had intended to do so," he answered. "But there are nests of Setiu everywhere. He has not yet managed to reach so far." The chieftains of Rethennu are throwing every army they have at us, Ahmose concluded to himself as the officer fell silent. They are emptying their lands to keep Apepa safe in his stronghold, hoping that in the end we will become exhausted and demoralized and go home, leaving the north to him. Egypt will be won or lost right here. And I have been too stupid to see it.

He had anticipated a dignified progression from one of his six divisions to another, an inspection of his eastern forces combined with leisurely consultations by lamplight in orderly camps. What he found were preoccupied, hard-pressed men sleeping on the ground in full battle attire with one ear open for the erratic reports of their scouts and one eye on the possibility of dawn attacks. The Setiu did not march in formation. They surged past the Wall of Princes and then broke up into small, compact units, moving quickly and easily among the Delta's many pools and marshes, often lost but still able to hide and inflict damage on Egypt's more disciplined forces by their sheer manœuvrability. And there are so many of them, Ahmose thought dismally, as he himself became part of the ebb and flow of the vicious, elusive shadowy war. The villages remember Kamose, the looting and burning and killing. They shelter the Setiu as their kinsmen, and the gods know that I do not want to rape the Delta again unless as a last resort.

Other gods' days came and went, the Uaga Feast on the eighteenth day of Thoth, the Feast of the Great Manifestation of Osiris on the twenty-second. But they belonged to a reality of peace and uniformity where families gathered in the outer court of their local temples before going home to mark the holiday with festive food and games. For Ahmose they were simply periods between dawn and dusk filled with the urgent words of dishevelled scouts, hurried and sketchy deliberations with officers who knew that in the end they could only adapt to the vicissitudes of the moment, and long, nerve-racking treks through a maze of pools whose thickly choked verges could hide any number of desperate Setiu.

Sometimes scouts from Het-Uart found him with their news. Sometimes not. They were risking their lives to bring him word that nothing had changed around the city, and Ahmose considered ordering the link between himself and his western commanders temporarily broken, but decided against it. Circumstances could change very rapidly, or so he told himself. But he also admitted that the scouts returning to Turi, Sebekh-khu and Hor-Aha were taking his presence back with them. His unspoken fear of another rebellion was irrational, he knew. He was too tired to suppress it.

Then it was Paophi, the second month of the year, and the flood plains began to narrow imperceptibly. Far away to the south, Isis was crying. Reluctantly Ahmose decided to turn back. The fighting around him had lessened in frequency if not in intensity. His soldiers were gaining the upper hand in the Delta and could now give their attention to sealing off the Horus Road. He dictated his orders to that effect, commanding four divisions to make a winter camp where the road veered to the north-east between two large bodies of water and the other two divisions to continue the hunt for any stray Setiu cut off by the rising waters.

Few of the thousands of foreign troops headed for Het-Uart had been able to evade the Egyptians. Many were dead and the rest were hiding in scattered villages or wandering in the marshes. But the price had been high in both casualties and fatigue. I must begin a rotation of the men, Ahmose thought, as he at last faced west with his weary Followers and saw the Horus Road winding towards Het-Uart. I must allow them to go home and plant their crops if all goes well. It is time to summon the navy. He glanced across at Ramose. "We will pray for a good flood," he said. Ramose smiled.

"Today is the Eve of the Amun-feast of Hapi," he remarked, "and the rest of this month is also devoted to the god of the Nile. We ought to pause and make sacrifice, Ahmose." Why, so it is, Ahmose remembered with a shock. Today is the seventeenth day of Paophi and I have been away from Het-Uart for only six weeks. It feels like six years. Nodding briefly at Ramose, he turned to Ankhmahor.

"Drive on," he said.

It seemed to him that nothing had changed when he finally dismounted stiffly from his chariot beside the familiar campsite outside Het-Uart and his retainers scattered to their old duties. Akhtoy began to issue a flood of orders that would result in the erection of the royal tent, hot food, a cot with clean sheets, a replenished container of incense grains beside the Amun shrine. The mighty tributary was perhaps flowing a little faster but the city still squatted

fortress-like upon its wide mound, its sloping walls towering
to the sky, the air above it hazed from the smoke of its innu-
merable cooking fires, its mysterious life coming to him in
a low susurration of constant noise. His soldiers were still
coming and going, the Medjay's ships still rocked gently on
the water's breast; it was as though he had never left.
Except that I feel dazed and battered, he thought ruefully.
Removing his sword belt and handing it to his body
servant, he lowered himself into the chair Akhtoy had set
in the shade of the trees and beckoned to Khabekhnet,
waiting patiently for instructions. "Send to Paheri at Het
nefer Apu," he said. "I want the navy here as soon as
possible. Enquire of your heralds whether or not there has
been any response from the city to their challenges. Ask
the three generals and Hor-Aha to present themselves to
me after the evening meal. That is all, Khabekhnet." The
Chief Herald bowed and walked briskly away. Ramose had
gone to see to his own living quarters. Ipi had also disappeared, but just as Ahmose's tent was raised in a graceful
unfolding of heavy linen, he returned, his arms full of
scrolls.

"There are letters from the Queens Tetisheri, Aahotep
and your wife, Majesty," he said as he came up. "Also one
from Prince Sebek-nakht. One from Paheri. One from the
mayor of Aabtu." Ahmose sighed. Out of the corner of his
eye he saw Makhu go past, leading one of his chariot
horses towards the water, a stable servant trailing behind
with a brush in each hand. The flies of winter, always
thickening as the river rose, were gathered in a black cloud
around the beast's head and Makhu was irritably waving
them away as he went. His own servant was unrolling the

carpet that covered the floor of his tent and another was unpacking his lamps.

"What does the mayor of Aabtu want?" he asked. Ipi set his burden on the grass, selected the appropriate scroll, and broke its seal with practised efficiency. He scanned it quickly.

"He wants to know if Your Majesty is able to be present at the sacred Osiris plays this year. Most of the month of Khoiak is devoted to the god. He has four feast days."

"Aabtu is in the Abetch nome and is under Prince Ankh-mahor's jurisdiction," Ahmose mused. "But the flood will have reached its apex during Khoiak and I cannot predict what that will mean for us here. We have never continued the siege through a winter before. Tell the mayor that due to circumstances here in the Delta, of which I am sure he is aware, I cannot commit myself to be present at the plays but that if possible I will send Prince Ankhmahor as my representative. Now Sebek-nakht." Ipi bent and lifted another scroll.

"The Prince wishes you to know that he has arrived in Weset and has assessed the work the Queen requires of him. He has been accorded the greatest courtesy, is occupying quarters within your house itself, and confers daily with the Queen whom he calls 'Egypt's most beautiful and illustrious lady.'" Ipi looked up. "He has no request, Majesty." Jealousy shot through Ahmose but he forced it back. Sebek-nakht is both handsome and accomplished, he thought darkly. He is far from his home, as I am. He sees her every day. They hold intimate discussions. Amun have mercy, what is wrong with me? The scar behind his ear prickled and he scratched at it with annoyance.

"The rest can wait until I can read them myself at my leisure," he said. "Thank you, Ipi. Be ready to record my meeting with the generals this evening." I cannot go home, let alone journey all the way to Aabtu for the sacred plays, he thought grimly as his Chief Scribe gathered up the scrolls and hurried away. If I begin to entertain these evil imaginings, I shall go mad. Aahmes-nefertari loves me and I trust her utterly. I must hold to those two beliefs alone and firmly reject all else. Yet the phantom pain continued to lurk at the back of his mind, its source grounded in nothing but his own sick fantasy, and he could not purge it away.

The navy did not arrive until the end of the following month, and Ahmose spent the time until then in making sure that the irrigation canals into the city could not be opened. The mighty ditches around the mounds slowly filled with the life-giving water the citizens of Het-Uart so desperately needed and which Ahmose was determined to deny them. He stationed contingents of men protected by Medjay archers at every point along the walls where corrugations showed old breaches.

At first men could be heard digging on the city side, loosening the stone-like mud, but where they broke through they were faced with a hail of well-placed arrows through the new apertures and soldiers who stood ready to struggle against the tug of the higher water in the ditches as it tried to flow into the lower canals and who quickly stopped its passage with boulders and earth. Ahmose knew that Apepa would order the digging of more wells and that water would be struck without much trouble, but he also knew that no matter how many wells were sunk the supply would never be enough.

Space inside Het-Uart was distressingly limited. The city was a tightly packed warren of narrow streets and rows of tiny houses. Where was there room for delving, if the inhabitants were being forced to bury their dead, and even their pack animals, under their floors? And suppose enough water was found for drinking if the populace lined up to collect it? The docks were gone and the city surrounded by Egyptian troops. The rich fertility of the Delta was now denied to the people. No goods would be unloaded. No fruits of any harvest would find their way inside to fill hungry bellies. In the past hostilities were broken off during the Inundation and resumed in the summer when the Nile had returned to its normal level and the crops had been sown. That was tradition. But Ahmose, alert to any changes in the quality of sounds emanating from Het-Uart and hearing them become gradually more subdued, reflected that such a tradition was gravely flawed. He had rejected it and in doing so he knew in his bones that Het-Uart would fall.

The navy's arrival completed the city's blockade. High water and ships surrounded it. Thousands of soldiers patrolled the narrow perimeter between its walls and the flood and kept watch over its stubbornly closed gates. The northern mound where the bulk of the Setiu army was quartered was faring no better. In the eastern Delta the fighting went on, but news from his divisions there was encouraging. The Horus Road was at last being held, although his troops were spread too thinly to attempt a recovery of the forts that constituted the Wall of Princes. That will come later, Ahmose thought on a tide of elation. For the first time since my father refused to bow to Apepa's insulting demand to slay the hippopotamuses in the Weset marshes, I can smell victory, and the odour is very sweet.

The memory of the hippopotamuses made him think of Tani. He had wondered, as winter dragged on, whether there would be a communication from her or from Apepa at last, if not a declaration of surrender then perhaps a plea for clemency on behalf of the citizens, a request for a meeting. But the palace within Het-Uart was dumb, either from misery or from stubbornness, and as day followed uneventful day its very silence prompted Ahmose's recollections to multiply.

He began to share them with Ramose in the long nights when nothing but the calling of the heralds and the sighing of the city disturbed the dark hours. The two men would sit in the glow of Ahmose's lamps, wine in their hands, and speak of Tani and Kamose and the agony of the years behind them. It was a cleansing of a kind, a release for Ramose, and for Ahmose a time when he could forget that a God-King may not draw too near to another human being. He was a Prince again, with friends to fish and wrestle with, a sister to love and protect, a brother who both baffled him and inspired his admiration.

"It is as though Tani has been turned to stone behind those walls," Ramose remarked one night. "For weeks I have half-expected some message from her to be tossed down to us, even if it was just an appeal for water or food. She must know that we are here. She could mount the walls and shout down to us if she wanted." He swirled the wine dregs slowly in his cup. "I suppose that she may be dead or ill but I do not think so. I fancy I would feel such things in my soul if they were so." He glanced at Ahmose warily but Ahmose did not laugh at him. "There is a wailing from the city tonight," he went on. "Did you hear it earlier, Ahmose?"

"Yes, I did," Ahmose replied gravely. "It is possible that disease has broken out. If that is so, then we may indeed receive a message from Apepa. But I do not believe he will make it that easy for us." He sat forward. "I judge that he has been commanded by his fellow Princes in Rethennu to hold out against us at any cost. They know that if Het-Uart falls, they will never be able to gain a foothold in Egypt again. All its wealth will be lost to them. Gold, grain, papyrus, everything. They are spending their own armies in this conflict with alarming abandon. They expect nothing less from their brother here." There was a silence during which he sipped his wine, pursed his lips, and set his cup back carefully on the table. I am a little drunk, he thought with surprise. But it is good, this slight removal from myself.

"And you expect nothing less from your divisions," Ramose countered. "But you will have to send some of your men home to the sowing when Mekhir comes, Ahmose. There is grumbling already in the ranks."

"I know." Ahmose said tersely. "I intend to. And I long to go home myself, Ramose. I dream that I am already there, but the garden is dim and the outline of the house is hazy and although I can hear Aahmes-nefertari's voice calling to me I cannot see her in the mist. I want this war of reclamation to be over." He spoke with a sudden and uncharacteristic bitterness and Ramose glanced at him, startled by the intensity of his words.

"You have done more towards seeing that goal accomplished than your brother ever could," he said simply.

Ahmose did not reply. The lamp was guttering, and as he reached out to snuff it, the flame died of its own accord.

Khoiak began with a light sprinkling of rain, not unknown in the Delta, and a sky cluttered with streamers of long, grey-tinged clouds driven by a brisk wind. The Medjay took shelter where they could, shaking the drops of moisture from their hair and crouching disgruntled together like flocks of bedraggled birds, but the Egyptians stood with faces raised and eyes closed, enjoying the unexpected drizzle. Afterwards the ground steamed. Hungry mosquitoes joined the phalanx of flies already tormenting naked skin in the rising humidity. The flood was at its highest, turning Egypt into a vast, placid lake beneath which new silt was settling onto the used-up soil. Het-Uart itself was an island girt about by water and the equally obdurate Egyptian army.

Yet to Ahmose, who had taken to standing on the verge of the swollen tributary and staring at the city when the routine of his daily duties was over, the atmosphere was charged with suspense. It was as though a storm was brewing far out in the desert, the slowly multiplying power of its birth generating the heavy expectancy he felt. Flicking his fly whisk absently he brooded, scarcely aware of the ordered activity constantly going on around him, his eyes travelling Het-Uart's awesome defences. He was becoming increasingly frustrated, at times even disheartened, by the inertia of his situation but overlying this was a breathless certainty that the impasse was about to be broken. It was in the stultifying air, in the lapping of the flood at his feet, filtering through men's actions and infusing their voices.

Soon he must begin to rotate his troops, he knew. By the end of the following month the Nile would have regained its banks and the earth would be waiting for the seed. Ankhmahor had already gone home to Aabtu to be present at Osiris's feasts, leaving his son to command the King's personal bodyguard. Ahmose wondered if Apepa was possessed by this same strong sense of anticipation. He pondered his enemy's state of mind, seeing him pacing out the boundary of his citadel, captured by a premonition he did not know they shared.

He was woken one morning just before dawn by a tide of anguish he had not felt since Kamose had ravaged Dashlut. Sitting up in the darkness, his heart fluttering, he was about to call for Akhtoy when a light wavered outside the tent and he heard Ramose's voice addressing the soldier standing watch. He swung his feet to the carpet and groped for a kilt, but then he stood still sniffing the air around him. It was filled with a sweetish stench that seemed to feed the grief by which he had been roused and he recognized it at once. I have paid it no attention when it has invaded my nostrils during the day, he thought as he wrapped the linen around his waist. But this time it must have begun while I dreamed. Dashlut. I will never forget my first whiff of burning human flesh. Pushing on a pair of sandals, he strode to the tent flap and lifted it cautiously.

His guard saluted and Ramose bowed, his face pale and shadowy. "I can smell it," Ahmose said. "It is very strong out here. Where is it coming from?"

"From the city," Ramose answered curtly. "You can see a dull glow even above the walls and when the sun rises I expect a pall of black smoke to be visible. They are burning bodies." Ahmose took his arm and together they walked to where the tributary lay motionless, its surface glassy black, and turned towards Het-Uart. The walls bulked dark against a slightly lightened sky, but the stars usually visible above them were eclipsed by a sullen orange rim. Ahmose shivered. The ground struck cold through his thin reed sandals and the pre-dawn air was chill.

For some time the two men watched. Then Ahmose said, "What do you think is happening, Ramose?"

"I think that people are dying," Ramose replied. "It is inevitable that a scarcity of water has resulted in the birth of disease, particularly in a place like this. Also there is no fresh food other than the handfuls of grain the citizens can grow on the rooftops. The poor, the farmers and traders visiting Het-Uart who became trapped inside when the siege began, the children, these will die first. Apepa's stockpiles are limited by space. They are becoming depleted. He and his nobles will not be suffering, but I pity the inhabitants with no resources at all."

"They would have done better to fling the bodies over the wall for us to deal with," a deep voice cut in, and Ahmose turned to find Hor-Aha at his elbow with Paheri and Kay Abana behind. "Thus they would have saved precious fuel and reduced the swift spreading of disease. The mayor is not a clever man."

"Perhaps Apepa does not want us to know the rate of human attrition," Paheri suggested. "That fire may represent a hundred bodies or a thousand. How they stink!" Oh, Tani, Ahmose thought in despair. How much of the city's agony are you able to see and hear? Did you lie awake last night with that first rank odour curling into your bedchamber so that you could not sleep? Are you deafened by the cries and wailings that do not drift down to us here? Or are you tightly held in Apepa's lavish cocoon, in his remorseless arms? Do you speak out to him against this horror or has your heart become too hard?

"Put the navy on full alert today, Paheri," he said huskily. "And you, Hor-Aha, do not let the Medjay leave their ships. Khabekhnet, are you here?" His Chief Herald detached himself from the shadows and came forward. "Warn General Khety to beware of any archers appearing on the walls of the northern mound. He is to prepare for battle. General Turi and General Sebek-khu must likewise deploy their divisions as though the gates were about to open."

"Your Majesty expects this?" Kay asked hopefully. "Then I beg Your Majesty's permission to anchor the *North* across from the gates leading to Apepa's citadel." Ahmose was too disturbed to smile.

"Your superiors will decide where the *North* is to be placed," he said. "As for what I expect, I can only believe that we are seeing the beginning of Apepa's ruin and therefore we must be ready for anything he might do." He shrugged. "Surrender is unlikely. Ramose, have my chariot brought round when you are ready." They reverenced him and scattered, and he walked back to his tent with one hand pressed to his nose. It seemed to him that the smoke from the city had a more pungent reek than that of the burning Setiu soldiers two months before. His imagination was magnifying his sense of smell, that he knew, but he could not control his revulsion.

He, his generals, and all his host waited in a state of battle readiness and tense anticipation while night after night the shifting blush of that macabre fire replaced the dwindling rose of sunset and blotted out the stars. Sometimes it sank to a few intermittent flares but it did not die completely, and its smell permeated hair, clothing and food so that the Egyptians wore, breathed and ate the testimony of death.

Two weeks went by and Khoiak ended. The level of water in the tributary and the canals around the city began to recede. On the first day of Tybi the rest of Egypt, the sane, clean, Ma'at-filled land blessed by the gods, celebrated the Feast of the Coronation of Horus. Ahmose had ceased to think of the Delta as belonging to that privileged country. It was an aberration, a place without a name where he was condemned to live in a continual haze of greyness and try to confront an enemy who would not show his face.

The troops shared his mounting apprehension. Increasingly he saw it in the eyes that turned to him as he was driven among them and heard it in the tones of his officers as they met him each morning to receive their orders. What shall I do if Apepa does nothing? he asked himself in the endless dark hours when sleep was a memory. How long can he withstand the suffering of his people? How stubborn is his will? What shall I do when the tributary shrinks to its summer level and the ditches to the east of the mounds dry up and I am forced to withdraw the navy?

No answers came to him, no dream in which his father or brother appeared with words of wisdom, no image of Amun holding symbols of victory to be interpreted by a grateful son. He remembered with envy the woman who had dominated Kamose's thoughts and ultimately stolen his heart with the timely visions that had enabled him to accomplish so much. Was Kamose less intelligent, less astute than I, that you should have favoured him so? he asked the god as he knelt before the shrine in his tent. Or did you value him more highly for his sheer obsessiveness? And yet I am the one you have appointed to be King. Hear me, great Amun. I do not want rewards. I do not even want a vision. Give me this city, this prize for which my brother died. Give it to me and name your price, for I am tired and I have come to a place from which there is no escape save by retreating.

He waited, but the silence around him remained unbroken and the thin column of incense rose from his outstretched hand undisturbed by any puff of ghostly wind. In the end he rose, prostrated himself before closing the doors of the shrine, and went to empty the spent incense holder outside the tent. Het-Uart still glowed. The air still stank. Bidding the Follower a good night, Ahmose retired to the tent. He listened to the small, innocuous noises beyond while his mind churned with alternatives, each more ludicrous than the last, and try as he might, he could not quiet his thoughts.

But he was jerked to full awareness by a sound he had not heard in a long time and his body responded to it, tumbling to rush outside before he recognized it as the tuneless blaring of horns. The sun had just lipped the eastern horizon and the cool air was full of glittering dust motes. Birds crowded above the water, noisily engaged in their morning feeding, and the surface of the water itself was broken into tiny rippling circles as fish rose to snap at the hovering clouds of newly hatched mosquitoes. The trees glistened wetly with dew. Ahmose noticed none of these things for the harsh, tuneless music was coming from the city and all around it the Egyptians were running to and fro as though a stone had been hurled into an anthill. Ahmose's heart skipped a beat and then thudded painfully in his chest. "Khabekhnet!" he shouted. "Where are you?"

"Here, Majesty," the man panted. He was loping towards Ahmose, fastening his kilt, one sandal still in his hand. Stumbling up, he sketched a bow, balancing precariously on one foot while he thrust the sandal onto the other.

"Run to Makhu. I want my chariot at once. You will need one also. Send your heralds to the generals. I want reports. I want Ramose. Tell him so, but do it last." The herald spun away. Ahmose turned to Harkhuf, Ankhmahor's son, temporarily in command of the Followers. He too was half-dressed but clutching his sword belt. His bow and quiver were slung over one naked shoulder. "Assemble the Followers, Harkhuf," Ahmose told him. "Have them fully armed. I am going to walk a little way towards the city but do not be distressed. Bring them when they are ready." The young man hesitated, doubt in his eyes.

"Majesty, my father … I do not think …"

"You will do very well," Ahmose said firmly. "Your father trained you and I approved you as his replacement while he is at Aabtu. You will protect me. Now go." Harkhuf bit his lip and nodded. Ahmose left, wanting to take to his heels and pelt along the tributary bank in the direction of the uproar but forcing himself to stand straight and stride calmly. No one must suspect that the King might be in a state of agitation.

Someone came rushing up behind him, and he paused to see Akhtoy burdened with a variety of objects. He waved the steward away impatiently but Akhtoy stood his ground. "Your pardon, Majesty, but you have time for this," he said obstinately. "The Followers are not yet ready and your chariot has not appeared." He handed Ahmose a small bowl of white cheese and fresh dates and a cup of beer. At once Ahmose became aware of his hunger. Grunting his thanks, he drank quickly and began to toss the food into his mouth. When he had finished, Akhtoy took back the bowl, saying, "Your Majesty cannot fight on an empty stomach. Nor with your sleeping cap on your head and no insignia for the troops to recognize." Ahmose's hand went to his head and he laughed, pulling off the covering. Akhtoy held out the great pectoral, its gold glinting in the new light, its lapis and turquoise gleaming dully, and Ahmose settled it around his neck.

As he felt its weight against his naked chest, all consternation left him. Akhtoy now passed him a starched blue-and-white striped linen helmet. Its rim was of gold surmounted by the vulture of Nekhbet. Ahmose set it on his shaved scalp and held out his arms so that the steward could slip the golden Supreme Commander's armbands onto his wrists. Akhtoy had not forgotten the sword belt from which both sword and dagger hung. Ahmose buckled it on and smiled into Akhtoy's eyes.

"Thank you," he said simply. On the periphery of his vision he saw the spokes of a moving chariot flashing in the sun. Akhtoy gestured.

"Your chariot comes and the Followers are right behind you, Majesty," he said. "May Amun give us victory." He melted unobtrusively away. The chariot came to a halt, Makhu holding the reins, and Harkhuf and his men came running up. Ahmose stepped onto the vehicle's floor.

"There is no need for haste, I think," he said. "Harkhuf, deploy your men to either side of me and be ready to move as I move. Makhu, let us go."

The brazen voice of the horns had fallen silent so that now even the roar of the thousands of Egyptian soldiers as they milled about on the flood plain seemed muted. The sun was fully risen. A brisk breeze was shredding the omnipresent plume of grey smoke rising above Het-Uart and in its murk Ahmose could see hundreds of figures spreading out along the rim of the wall. He glanced left and was reassured. Already the Medjay were lining the decks of their boats, bows bristling, and even as he looked a forest of arrows soared aloft, their tips catching the light before they began their deadly descent. Ahmose had full confidence in the Medjay's skill. He knew that no missile would fall among his own men crowding the foot of the walls.

But the Setiu had learned a painful lesson. This time they were crouching or squatting to fire, drawing upward before swinging their bows down and loosing their arrows at the soldiers below so as to provide the Medjay with a less visible target. Some were even lying on their stomachs, holding their bows sideways over the outer edge of the wall. Makhu snorted. "The idiots!" he said scornfully. "They bring into Egypt the most powerful and accurate bows ever invented but they use them so clumsily that one might imagine the weapons were of our own devising. We have certainly surpassed them in proficiency."

"They will rake their inner arms and the leather armguards will deflect their aim," Ahmose murmured. "Those crouching will almost certainly nick their knees. It is impossible to fire lying down. At the least they are in danger of dropping their arrows. They are afraid to stand."

"I would be afraid also if I had to expose myself to the Medjay," Makhu admitted. "Here comes Ramose, Majesty." At Ahmose's invitation Ramose clambered up beside him. He was sweating and out of breath.

"I could not sleep, so I got up and rode the perimeter of the city with the heralds," he explained in answer to Ahmose's enquiring glance. "I had left one of them on the far side of the mound and was talking to one of the sentries just as the sun began to rise. Then the horns sounded. I ran here."

"What did you see?" Ahmose wanted to know. Ramose considered.

"Not much," he answered. "The smoke. The archers beginning to flood the walls. Our tents emptying. Men running to their assembly points. There is order in that chaos."

"I would expect nothing less." Ahmose deliberated for a moment, his eyes on the turbulent scene ahead. "What is Apepa hoping to achieve?" he wondered aloud. "Is this simply a pointless exercise, a prideful gesture, what?"

Suddenly a great swelling howl went up mixed with a frenzied yelping that made Ahmose's skin prickle. Ramose's arms shot out, gripping both sides of the chariot in a paroxysm of excitement. "The eastern gate is opening!" he screamed. "Look, Ahmose! I cannot believe it!" Neither could Ahmose. With a kind of dazed incredulity he watched as the massive doors began to swing inward. He leaned forward to shout to Makhu to move closer but Makhu had already tightened the reins and the horses were picking up speed, the Followers running beside them. "The Setiu are coming out! Look at them, look at them!" Ramose was shouting against the wind whistling past Ahmose's ears and Ahmose, eyes narrowed, feet apart, bent over, felt a rush of pure joy mingled with pure terror.

Makhu brought them to a halt as another chariot came careening towards them. It was Khabekhnet. He leaped down and came running. "I have placed a herald with every general, Majesty," he cried. "Give your orders."

"I need to know if the gates of the northern mound are also open," Ahmose said. "If more troops are coming out. Tell General Khety that if they are I want them beaten and the northern mound occupied at any cost. At any cost. If he needs reinforcements, he has my permission to take them from Sebekh-khu or Turi. Tell Paheri to support him with the navy. The Medjay have control of the western edge of Het-Uart and therefore can aid in the push to the western gate." Khabekhnet saluted, and his chariot rolled away in a cloud of dust.

"Why the northern turtleback?" Ramose wanted to know.

"Because it is full almost exclusively with Setiu soldiers," Ahmose replied. "There are very few civilians living on it. If we can overrun it and slay them, we will have completely defeated Apepa. The eastern Delta is rapidly falling back into our hands. Think of it, Ramose. All he will have left is the city itself. Routing the troops is more important than taking the city."

As soon as the words were out of his mouth, he knew that his decision to concentrate his army's efforts to the east had been right. Kamose would have disagreed. For Kamose this war was a personal matter and the only enemy face he saw was Apepa's. Driving out the Setiu had meant somehow reaching inside Het-Uart and crushing Apepa himself. All Kamose's campaigns had been nothing more than the clearing of a path to Apepa's palace door. His judgement was flawed, Ahmose thought sadly. He would never have taken the city. I also yearn to see Apepa on his knees before me, but I can wait.

"The northern mound only has two gates," Makhu put in. "One to the Horus Road and one on the west, facing the tributary. Let me drive you into some shade, Majesty. It is going to be a long, hot day." Ramose stepped out of the chariot.

"With your permission, Majesty, I would like to join the fighting," he said. "If the Royal Entrance Gate is also open, I want to be there. I might be useful to General Turi." Ahmose looked down at him. I know why you want to be there, he thought. I don't want to lose you, but I cannot refuse. He nodded brusquely.

"Just do not get yourself killed," he said. "I do not have the time to find another governor for Khemmenu and the Un nome." To Makhu he added, "Very well. Take me to those trees." He pointed. "It is not a good vantage point but it will do until I have a clearer picture of what is happening from the heralds."

Once under the leafy branches of a huge sycamore, Ahmose lowered himself onto the floor of the chariot facing the city and the Followers grouped themselves around him. He could see General Baqet's standard in an ocean of surging bodies, the soldiers of the Division of Thoth already engaged in close fighting with the hordes pouring out of the western gate. To the south-east he could only glimpse the rearguard of the Division of Montu spreading in a mighty curve to mingle with the trailing edge of Baqet's men. There was another gate, hidden from Ahmose's sight. He did not yet know whether it was open or closed. He forced himself to relax the tension gripping his body, uncurling the fists that were clenched against his thighs, unlocking the muscles of his jaw. No purpose would be served by rushing into the fray or even by pacing.

The sun was considerably higher in the sky and Ahmose judged the time to be approximately the middle of the morning before the chariots of the heralds began to carve tracks to him across the beaten earth. The first was from Sebek-khu. "The Division of Montu is engaged in full battle outside the south-eastern gate, Majesty," the man said. "The gate itself was open but is now closed. General Sebek-khu has sent a thousand soldiers to aid General Khety at the northern mound."

"Sebek-khu is confident that he can hold?"

"Yes, Majesty. But he needs the Medjay. He is losing men due to the archers on the wall."

"Order General Hor-Aha to redeploy two of his boats. Bring me word as the situation changes."

The report from the Division of Thoth was similar. "The western gate was closed as soon as the Setiu army came out," the herald told Ahmose. "They have ranged themselves between the outer perimeter of the wall and our soldiers. They are trying to force us into the tributary.

General Baqet is hard pressed although he has generous aid from General Paheri. The ships are somewhat hampered by the ruins of the docks which are under the surface of the tributary and are thus a danger."

"What of the Medjay?"

"They remain in position opposite the western gate and are keeping the archers on top of the wall pinned down."

"Does General Baqet ask for reinforcements?" The herald shook his head.

"Reinforcements would do no good," he said. "There is no room for them. They would only hamper the division's ability to manoeuvre. The Setiu General Pezedkhu is keeping a large contingent of soldiers close around him. General Baqet thinks that he will try to fight his way through our troops to the water." Ahmose was on his feet and facing his herald.

"Pezedkhu? The man himself has left the safety of the city?"

"Yes, Majesty. His troops are an island of discipline in a sea of mayhem. General Baqet believes that his aim is to distract the Medjay and if possible begin to harry our troops from behind so that they are caught between two hostile forces." And he may very well succeed, seeing that I cannot afford to help General Baqet, Ahmose thought furiously. I want word from the Royal Entrance Gate, but most of all from Khety. What is happening to the north?

"If Baqet begins to lose ground, bring me word at once," Ahmose said and dismissed him.

Now he began to pace, fingers gripping each other behind his back, head down, oblivious to the noon heat. Pezedkhu is out. Confront your fear, Ahmose, you coward.

Remember that he cannot win more than a battle. The war is yours. Your impulse is to hurry to the western gate and watch him, fill your eyes with him, let the memories render you impotent. But it is Khety and only Khety who will give you victory or see this day end in the ache of an all-too-familiar impasse. Yet he was unable to shed the sudden mantle of dread that had fallen over him. He knew the feel of it well. Pezedkhu.

When it came, the report from the Royal Entrance Gate was brief. "The gate did not open at all," the herald told Ahmose, "and the wall is empty of archers. Generals Kagemni and Turi urgently desire a decision from you, Majesty, regarding the disposition of the Divisions of Ra and Amun. They took it upon themselves to move their troops from the Royal Entrance Gate to the eastern gate. The flood ditches there are much shallower than on the west and they are no more than knee deep in water. They do not know if that gate opened as there are no Setiu archers or soldiers on that side of the main mound."

"Wait with me," Ahmose ordered him. "I will decide when I have heard from the Division of Horus."

The herald from Khety came at last. He was splashed with mud and limping. There was a bloody gash in his calf. He saluted wearily. "The two gates on the northern mound have remained open, Majesty," he said without preamble. "Foreigners are still pouring out of them and the walls are thick with archers. The fighting is relentless and vicious. General Khety is barely maintaining his position, even with help from General Sebek-khu. He needs more men and he needs the Medjay." Ahmose spoke directly to the herald from the Division of Ra.

"Generals Kagemni and Turi are to take their whole divisions to the relief of General Khety," he snapped. "Go at once." He turned. As Chief Herald it was Khabekhnet's duty to remain beside Ahmose once he had apportioned obligations to those under him and it was to him that Ahmose spoke, thinking aloud as he did so. "I have five thousand Medjay in forty boats," he said slowly. "Two of them, that is two hundred and fifty men, have gone to support Sebek-khu. I cannot leave Baqet entirely at the mercy of the Setiu archers. I will leave him eight boats. Tell General Hor-Aha to take the remaining thirty boats immediately, surround the northern mound, and shoot the men on the walls. He is to command them personally. If the water level in the ditch to the east by the Horus Road Gate has become too shallow for draught, the Medjay are to disembark and fire from the banks. When you have delivered that message, find Kay Abana. If the *North* is anywhere close by, I want to board it."

So now the gaming pieces are in place, he thought, as he watched Khabekhnet's chariot roll away towards the glittering ribbon of water. I can do nothing more at present but pray. Suddenly he was aware that he was very thirsty, and walking back under the shade of the sycamore he beckoned to Harkhuf. "Send someone to Akhtoy for food and drink for all of us," he ordered. "The Followers can stand down for a while. Let them rest." He lowered himself onto a patch of grass beside the patient horses still yoked to his chariot and his bodyguard did the same, laying their weapons on the ground and talking quietly among themselves.

"Majesty, if you will be boarding a vessel, I would like to unhitch the chariot and feed and water the horses," Makhu said. He had been standing in the vehicle ever since he had brought it to a halt with the reins ready in his hands. Ahmose looked up at him with a start.

"I had forgotten you, Prince," he said apologetically. "Take the horses away but send Mesehti back with fresh ones. I may need the chariot again very quickly." A curious peace had enveloped him. He knew that it would not last, but he watched Makhu undo the chariot traces with a calm laziness. The man was talking to his charges softly, his hands sure on their noses and necks, and they were responding with little whickers of appreciation.

I have not misjudged Makhu or Mesehti either, he thought, but neither must I forget that they are indeed Princes with a high lineage. They are accepting the wounding of their pride with a graciousness that pleases me. Perhaps soon I may relent and spread some kind of salve on their dignity. Yet he could not prevent himself from testing Makhu. "Wait and eat with me before you leave," he offered. Makhu shook his head.

"Thank you, Majesty, but no," he replied. "These animals would not understand the delay." He set off through the early afternoon's glare, walking between the horses whose heads kept turning towards him. Ahmose wondered if he treated his wife with the same tenderness.

Akhtoy and a throng of servants arrived, spreading cloths and cushions and laying a cold feast before Ahmose and the Followers. There was pomegranate wine and barley beer, but Ahmose drank copious amounts of water and the bodyguards followed his example.

Towards the end of the meal the heralds began to return and once more Ahmose became aware of the noise of battle that had been so constant and unvarying that his ears had become attuned to it and had shut it out. The sun had begun its downward slip and the afternoon shadows were lengthening. There was no fresh news. Both the Egyptian and the Setiu soldiers were tiring. The Medjay archers had run out of arrows. Khety was achieving a growing advantage thanks to the influx of men with Kagemni and Turi, but the reports from the western side of the city were confusing. Not until Khabekhnet drove up, left his chariot, and saluted did Ahmose hear anything intelligible.

"The *North* is engaged in fierce fighting outside the western gate," Khabekhnet said. "I was unable to approach it. But the *Living in Ptah* is not far away and its captain will be honoured to have you aboard, Majesty." Ahmose thrust a pitcher of water at him and he drained it in several convulsive swallows.

"What of Pezedkhu?" Ahmose asked thickly. Khabekhnet placed the empty ewer at his feet.

"The Setiu General has widened his hold on the area between the gates and the tributary," he said. "His men face north and south and now divide General Baqet's forces. The Medjay are no help, Majesty. Their arrows are gone and since they have been firing at the walls they cannot retrieve any. There is much carnage on the land between tributary and wall. It is almost impossible to tell whether Sebek-khu or Pezedkhu's men are gaining the upper hand."

"Prince Mesehti is coming with your horses, Majesty," Harkhuf broke in quietly. Ahmose nodded.

"He can hitch them and then drive me to the water," he said. "It is time to see for myself what is happening and to let our soldiers see me. Harkhuf, assemble the Followers.

Khabekhnet, be ready to intercept your heralds as they look for me. I will be on the *Living in Ptah*."

The ride to where the ship waited, its ramp run out for him, was not far, but once Ahmose began to cross open ground the noise of battle increased. Screams and curses rose sharply above the almost deafening undertone of thousands of men panting, shuffling, and exchanging blows with axes and swords like some clamorous melody. Dust clouds obscured portions of the conflict, and in the fitful tugging of the wind Ahmose caught the acrid scents of sweat and hot, spilled blood.

The Followers ran ahead while he left the chariot and hurried up the ramp to be greeted by the captain. "I am your servant Qar, Majesty," he said with a bow. "What is your desire?" Ahmose looked about him as the Followers formed a half-circle at his back and the ramp was hauled in. The sailors sat stolidly at their oars but the armed marines crowding the deck bent to him in reverence as his gaze travelled over them.

"Take the eastern ditch and row me past General Sebek-khu, up the eastern side of the city, and then around to the north," Ahmose replied. "I want to survey every arena of battle." Qar nodded doubtfully.

"Then Your Majesty will be returning down the western side," he pointed out. "The fighting is very bad there. I may not be able to get you through."

"All the more reason to let the soldiers see that I am willing to share their danger," Ahmose objected. "And I am, Captain. I have endured greater peril under my brother's command. Let us go." Qar bowed again and left him, shouting instructions to the helmsman. The oarsmen grasped the oars and the *Living in Ptah* slid back into the turgid waters of the tributary.

As they beat around to the east the noise seemed to swell and with it, Ahmose fancied, the heat. Harkhuf spoke quietly and the Followers unslung their bows, drawing closer to Ahmose. He himself had stepped to the railing where he could be easily seen. His eyes found Sebek-khu's standard, the tall pole with its painted symbol of Montu the bull-headed war god waving above the heads of the struggling soldiers. He spotted the General himself, arm raised and mouth wide as he yelled some order to the officer beside him. The man turned away and saw Ahmose. His own arm shot out and even above the cacophony Ahmose heard him cry "The King! It is the King!" The fighting seemed to slow for a moment, the Egyptians taking up the call, then the *Living in Ptah* glided behind one of the two Medjay ships and the scene was lost to view.

"The dead were being rolled into the canal, Majesty," Harkhuf said. "Did you notice? The bodies will rot there and the water will be unfit to drink."

"In another few weeks the canal will be dry and then it will not matter," Ahmose answered him. "The tributary will carry all poison north and empty it into the Great Green." He cupped his hands around his mouth and shouted across to the second Medjay boat, rocking not far ahead. "Captain, what are you doing?" The black braids swung and a black face was turned to him. The Medjay captain bowed.

"No more arrows, Majesty," he shouted back. "Nothing to do but watch." Ahmose slapped the railing in sudden anger.

"Berth your ship on the southern bank, get your men into the water, and carry the wounded across and onto your deck," he bellowed. "How dare you say you have nothing to do!" Qar was calling another command and the *Living in Ptah* began to veer to the left. Sebek-khu and the Medjay were slowly lost to sight. Ahmose found that he was trembling with rage.

"They are simple and biddable, Majesty," Harkhuf reminded him. "They follow their orders but are not good at making decisions for themselves."

"I know," Ahmose replied, biting back a longer tirade. Did Hor-Aha not think past the spending of their arrows? he asked himself. Any Egyptian would have seen the possibility of turning useless archers into almost anything else to aid in the success of the battle. I will have something to say to him when this day is over. The prospect filled him with self-righteous pleasure, but recognizing it as a petty indulgence fed by his deepening dislike of Hor-Aha, he had the grace to feel ashamed. Hor-Aha, like every General, would have his mind and his energies fixed on anticipating the ebb and flow of the bloodshed going on around him. It was the responsibility of senior officers to make such lesser judgements. All the same, Ahmose thought grimly, Hor-Aha must know what sheep his people are. What other duty did he have but to deploy them on my command and see that they did as they were told?

The eastern side of Het-Uart was strangely peaceful, the long shadow of its vaunting wall embracing Ahmose as Qar's ship slid into it. The din from the northern mound and the western edge of the city came to him diminished by a flurry of birdsong in the trees to the right of the canal.

The water heaved and sparkled in the sun. It was very shallow, its level sinking, and the *Living in Ptah* was creeping carefully in the centre between its muddy banks. It inched past the eastern gate. All on board were silent and tense, eyes fixed on the top of the wall, but it remained empty, curving away out of their vision.

Ahmose had expected to see great throngs of Egyptian and Setiu soldiers locked together around the northern mound, but at first he was unable to interpret what he saw when its wall towered above him. The Horus Road Gate stood wide open and men were streaming through it into, not out of, the stronghold. Between wall and canal the bodies lay in untidy heaps. The wall itself was splashed with blood. Beyond it Ahmose could hear the continued clash of weapons and a tumult of yelling. Suddenly he realized what was happening and he gave a triumphant shout. "We are inside the mound!" he cried. "Khety has won it! Qar, put in here for a moment!"

"Majesty, there is still fighting, desperate by the sound of it," Harkhuf warned him. "As the Commander of your Followers it is my duty to request that you do not disembark." Ahmose wanted to hug him. He smiled into the serious young face.

"Draw your sword, Harkhuf," he said. "A King is not of much use on a day like this. There are few things he can do, but perhaps he can sway the final outcome of a battle by his mere presence. Do not worry. Amun is with us!" *Living in Ptah* gave a petulant jerk. The ramp slid into the squelching mud. Harkhuf, shaking his head, ran onto the bank with Ahmose and the Followers behind and they joined the flow of soldiers stumbling wearily through the gate.

All Ahmose's attention was fixed on what he would see ahead so that he was through the high, heavy gates before he was aware of it. Looking back, he could see Qar's ship partially hidden by the throng plodding up the sloping road from the wide cut in the wall and then it struck him. I am inside Apepa's military stronghold, he thought almost giddily. Father, Kamose, I am here or I am dreaming, but no dream could possibly be so real. There is the gate, open, fangless, useless, and I am on the right side of it at last.

He was not given much time to savour the moment, for the troops had recognized him and at once an area of reverence appeared around him and his escort. Faces sagging with exhaustion lit up. Hands numb from their terrible work curled more tightly around the hilts of weapons blunted and soiled with Setiu blood. "Majesty, Majesty," the muttering grew, and became an excited furore.

Harkhuf spotted a junior officer and beckoned him over. His kilt was shredded, he had lost his leather helmet, and one foot was bare. He was holding a short dagger. His scabbard was empty. "Give me a report," Ahmose said. The man looked bewildered.

"Me, Majesty?" he stammered. "Should I not find my superior?"

"No." Ahmose waited. The officer swallowed, stared at the knife clutched in one encrusted hand, then visibly pulled himself together.

"The Setiu forces have retreated back inside the mound," he said. "What is left of them. They tried to close the gate behind them but General Khety was too quick. He rallied the Division of Horus and managed to keep it open. I am of the Division of Amun. My General Turi rushed to support him." He hesitated. "Majesty, I have heard that the other gate, the Port Gate, has also been held open by General Kagemni. He assaulted the enemy in that quarter as soon as you sent him. The slaughter will be great, for where can the Setiu go? Their own walls will hem them in."

"Where is your weapon?" Ahmose enquired. The officer grimaced.

"Forgive me, Majesty. It is still stuck in the body of a soldier I slew. He toppled into the water and his weight forced me to let go the hilt." At once one of the Followers undid his belt and passed it to him, together with his sword. The man glanced at Ahmose apologetically as he reached out for it. Ahmose nodded.

"You need it more than he does," he said. "Now take a message to my generals, beginning with your own. Tell them that all Setiu soldiers are to be killed. I regret the necessity but rumours of this day will inevitably find their way to Rethennu. The Princes of that land must doubt the wisdom of sending any more Setiu armies to die on Egyptian ground. Tell them also that all ordinary citizens must be spared. There are Egyptians living in the north-west quarter of the mound. I have spoken." He smiled and gestured. "Go now. You have done well." The officer smiled back, bowed, and turning he began to run. He was soon lost in the crowd. "We will go back to the ship," Ahmose said to Harkhuf. "I can do nothing here but impede the progress of the victory." Harkhuf's relief showed in the squaring of his shoulders.

"If Your Majesty chose to go forward, the risk of dying would be very great," he commented. "Listen to the uproar! Then who would lead us?"

Who indeed, Ahmose thought as he retraced his steps through the troops still hurrying up a road that was slippery with blood. Ahmose-onkh is too young to rule. Could Aahmes-nefertari subdue the greedy nobles, dominate the generals, and secure the throne for her son? The possibility that she could was not entirely reassuring. Ahmose hurried up the ramp, his sandals heavy with mud, and *Living in Ptah* prepared to continue its journey around Het-Uart. No, it was not reassuring at all, and Ahmose was not certain why.

7

CAREFULLY THE *LIVING IN PTAH* negotiated the
canal between the northern edge of the main
mound and the southern wall of the smaller
military mound. The former bank was deserted, but bodies
lay thinly strewn below the wall that now enclosed the last
resistance of Apepa's Delta army. To Ahmose the scene
held a quality of unreality, perhaps because, although the
battle could be heard beyond, its noise was muted and the
wind rippling the ship's flag and tugging at men's kilts as
they stood on the deck did not reach to the corpses lying
sheltered by the wall. They sprawled mutilated and motionless in the soft late afternoon sunlight like so much
discarded detritus.

Qar shouted an order and the boat slowly tacked left, but
before the northern mound slid out of sight, Ahmose saw
that indeed its other gate, the Port Gate, was wide open and
guarded by several ranks of Egyptian soldiers who saluted
him as he went by. There was no mistaking their grins of
trumph. "All General Kagemni's and General Turi's troops
must now be inside," Harkhuf remarked, and Ahmose
nodded without turning, for the *Living in Ptah* was passing
the northern-most gate of Het-Uart, the Trade Gate, firmly
closed, and beyond it he could see the towers of Apepa's
citadel palace, blunt and solid, rearing above the city wall.

Suddenly they were riding the breast of the main tributary and Ahmose could feel the silent sigh of relief that went through the crew. It was short-lived, however. Looking up, Ahmose saw archers ranged along the top of the wall, each with an arrow already fitted to his bow. Their line ran from the Royal Entrance Gate, also closed, and out of sight around the bend in the island. "Shields up," Harkhuf barked to his men and at once Ahmose found himself under a ceiling of wood. "The foreigners are performing a completely unnecessary duty," the young man said derisively. "We cannot assault the gate and I do not see Apepa wandering up there for us to shoot at." Ahmose peered skyward through a chink in the raised shields, searching illogically for a sight of Tani among the Setiu soldiers. Heartsick, he merely grunted in reply.

Once past the palace, the archers disappeared and the shields were lowered, but Ahmose hardly heard Harkhuf's command for the tumult that had begun to batter at his ears. The western side of Het-Uart ran straight, affording a long view down the tributary to the black skeleton of the ruined docks outside the Civilian Gate and beyond, and it was turbulent with chaos. The water was choked with naval and Medjay vessels. Living men and dead clogged the bank in a congested sea of violent struggle so that for a long time Ahmose could not separate Egyptian from foe. But gradually he was able to identify Baqet's standard far down past the gate. Pezedkhu's red banner of Sutekh was waving on the very edge of the bank and around it Ahmose could see a solid mass of Setiu that boiled back almost to the gate itself and extended in two ragged arms along the water.

The din was colossal. Men slashed at each other waist-deep in water, or were locked clumsily together over the bodies that lay everywhere. Many of Paheri's ships were empty, their ramps resting on the bank, their marines lost somewhere in the fray. The Medjay boats were circling and manoeuvring, the Medjay themselves screaming, weapons raised in black fists. Ahmose scanned the turmoil for Paheri's vessel and saw it side by side with Hor-Aha's, both fully manned. He could make out the familiar face of his chief captain and Hor-Aha's tall figure as he strode up and down, gesticulating. "The Setiu have managed to establish a position on the bank and they are holding it," Harkhuf shouted above the pandemonium. "Where is their General?"

Ahmose signalled to Qar to steer between the other heaving, jockeying vessels, his gaze travelling the bank. He was beginning to make sense of the battle, but he was puzzled. Watching the Setiu carefully, it seemed to him that they were less concerned with widening the circle of victory around them than with strengthening their situation along the water. On the city side they were merely defending themselves, but on the tributary side they were fighting fiercely to sweep away anything standing between them and the water. Why? Ahmose asked himself with growing anxiety. It is not a reasonable strategy. Surely Pezedkhu ought to be trying to wipe out the divisions. After all, he is trapped between wall and water. He cannot get back to the gate without cutting a swathe through Baqet's men and what advantage can there be for him in falling into the tributary? Surely it would be more sensible of him to turn his fronts north and south instead of concentrating westward?

All at once he saw the man himself. Pezedkhu had stepped up onto the remains of the docks and was balanced there coolly, his swarthy chest gleaming with sweat, his bloodied sword held high. Ahmose fought the desire to shrink behind his Followers, to make himself invisible. Pezedkhu leaned down and the face of a Setiu officer standing nearby was turned upward to him. There was something so calm, so controlled about the General's movement in the midst of such hysterical mayhem that Ahmose was momentarily absorbed by it to the exclusion of anything else. He saw the officer nod once. Pezedkhu pointed forward, then back. His broad gesture embraced the whole of the waterfront and Ahmose, following the direction of his muscular arm, stiffened. There were Egyptian boats all along the bank, some with ramps out, some not, most of them empty of men or barely crewed. Pezedkhu, surrounded by his men, stood regarding them with what Ahmose recognized, even at a distance, as speculation. One fist was on his hip and his sword now lay resting on his shoulder. Gods no! Ahmose thought in disbelief even as he turned and was running to the stern, the Followers tumbling after him. He cannot! Such arrogance! Such assurance! But he can, another voice whispered over the sudden panic. He is about to try, and if you do not hurry to thwart him, this battle will almost certainly be lost.

Desperately Ahmose surveyed the rear. Paheri had been joined by the elder Abana. They were consulting over something. *Living in Ptah* was already easing towards their ship as Qar had interpreted the King's need, threading its way through other vessels whose sailors and soldiers, recognizing Ahmose, began to cheer. Ahmose hardly heard them. Gripping the rail in a fever of impatience, he saw the space between himself and his Chief Captain grow narrower. Paheri looked up and saw him. Qar called and the oars were raised. *Living in Ptah* glided forward. "Majesty, I have just sent out a herald to find you," Paheri called. "We do not know what has been happening at the northern mound and we wondered if we should send more ships there." Ahmose waved his words away.

"The mound is taken," he called back urgently. "Look to your boats, Paheri! They are lined up against the bank, empty of soldiers, begging to be fired or taken!" Paheri blanched at Ahmose's tone.

"But, Majesty, the divisions were screaming for our support so I gave the order for the marines to disembark and fight on land," he protested. "More will be despatched if necessary."

"The sailors should have drawn up the ramps and pulled away once the soldiers had left," Ahmose cut in loudly. "Pezedkhu is not fighting to thin our ranks, he is fighting to either gain our ships or burn them. If he is as astute as I believe him to be, he will burn them. If he gains them, he will still have an advantage. He will not be limited to one place. He can carry his men to any point in the conflict, he can engage the rest of the navy. Send a message to your captains if you can. Get the sailors back on board and the ships out into the water. Do it now." He flung around to Qar. "Take me to where the Setiu General is," he ordered. "I want to be as close to him as possible." Paheri had not acknowledged him, but a skiff was pulling quickly away from Paheri's vessel and Ahmose knew that the heralds in it would shout his command through the accompanying din. Qar's oarsmen were bending to their task and already the *Living in Ptah* was drawing near the blackened ribs of the docks. Ahmose reflected briefly what a good thing it was that both sides had expended their arrows long ago.

His precious ships, Kamose's precious ships, built at great cost, lay against the muddy bank, their shadows long and thin over the confusion as the sun sank lower. I will not blame Paheri, Ahmose thought as he anxiously scanned the ships for signs that already his men were retreating to their ramps. No amount of drilling and mock water battles can take the place of real confrontation when nothing is truly predictable and the tables of war can turn on a single unique notion. Pezedkhu is capable of outsmarting us all. I wish that his genius could be put to my use instead of Apepa's. Surely Pezedkhu wearies of serving a King with little personal courage and no judgement!

He raised a hand and the *Living in Ptah* slowly hove to. Behind him were the ships that had not yet been engaged. Before him the struggle beneath the walls went on, a seething tangle of friend and foe, but he no longer had eyes for anything but Pezedkhu and the untidy string of defence-less vessels. The Setiu were responding to some command their General had given. Their rearguard had drawn together, backs to the water, fending off the Egyptian assault, but the rest were spreading out. They had begun to run, and with mingled relief and dismay Ahmose saw them begin to gain the ramps. So Pezedkhu had blundered after all. Either it had not occurred to him to burn the ships or he had weighed both options and chosen to take the riskier one. Arrogance or a slip in the heat of the moment? Ahmose wondered. But perhaps he simply had no time to make a fire.

Paheri's orders had been heard, however, for after the speeding Setiu came the marines, pulling themselves free of the conflict and pounding towards their ships. Some reached their goal and turned to repel the enemy but many, too many Ahmose thought in a paroxysm of alarm, came late and watched the ramps being hurriedly flung into the water so that they could not board. Nevertheless they dashed into the water, clinging to the sides of the ships and attempting to climb. The Setiu were reaching down to lop off hands and arms as their sailors snatched up the oars and their helmsmen scrambled into position.

The Egyptian ships that had been behind Ahmose were now around him, beating towards the foreign crews who were rapidly reversing their prizes away from the bank. But we have no arrows, Ahmose thought feverishly, no means to kill them, and the Medjay are afraid of water. They will not leave their boats to take the leap required to board. He heard Paheri shouting a flurry of commands, his voice clear, calling his captains by name, directing them one by one to block the Setiu's passage. We must board first, Ahmose's thoughts ran on. We must take the initiative. Our men must feel themselves taking back what is theirs. If Pezedkhu's troops jump first, it will seem like an invasion to our soldiers and they will be defending not attacking.

The same threat had obviously occurred to Paheri. He was roaring a string of careful instructions to the ranks of grim-faced men crowding the rails of the Egyptian ships drawing ever closer to the Setiu who had begun to shout insults. Hor-Aha's deep bellow also echoed over the burdened water. "You are warriors of Wawat, not fleas clinging to the hide of a dog!" he was cursing his tribesmen.

"Do not let the Egyptians shame you! Jump, you cowards! Jump!" Ahmose glanced over his shoulder. The Medjay were milling about on their decks under the furious lashing of their captains and Hor-Aha himself was beating his contingent to the rails with a cudgel. Even as Ahmose looked, he picked up one of his men and tossed him bodily over the side. Then to Ahmose's shock he shouted something unintelligible to his captain, placed one bare foot on the rail, and launched himself forward, landing gracefully on the deck of a ship Ahmose suddenly recognized as the *North*.

Kay Abana was running to Hor-Aha who had picked himself up, drawn his sword, and was shaking it at his reluctant men across the gulf he had just spanned. To Ahmose's relief he saw that the *North* was still fully manned with Egyptians ringing its perimeter in precise ranks, waiting quietly for their instructions. All at once Ahmose saw a familiar figure a little shorter than the rest, lips pursed, gloved fingers curled tight about his sword, a frown of determination on his face. It was Kay's cousin, Zaa pen Nekheb. Ahmose found himself breathing a quick prayer for his youngest soldier's safety.

All about him now the Egyptian craft were jockeying to come alongside the stolen vessels. The crunch of splintering oars mingled with the screamed imprecations being exchanged as each side prepared for the encounter. Kay and Hor-Aha were conferring, heads together. They broke apart and Kay pointed. Ahmose's eyes followed the line of his finger. Pezedkhu stood in the prow of a ship that had been steadily and silently easing its way towards the *Living in Ptah* through a narrow channel of water that seemed to have

opened just for him. He was close enough for Ahmose to
make out the man's coarse, almost repugnant yet
compelling features set above a body as thickly compact as
mud brick. His stance was composed, stocky legs apart, gaze
level, watching as he drew nearer to the *Living in Ptah*. With
a kind of resigned fatalism Ahmose realized that the Setiu
General had not only seen him, standing as he was in full
view, but he intended to board Qar's ship and kill him. It
was in his eyes, meeting Ahmose's own over the closing
distance between them. For the moment the cacophony
around him meant nothing, did not exist. Ahmose was his
prey.

Yet Ahmose, searching himself as time ceased to move,
found that Pezedkhu, the fantasy wreathed in the poison of
dread, was gone. Only the Pezedkhu of destiny remained, a
man whose fate had been bound up with the House of Tao
since the stain of Seqenenra's defeat and death and whose
nebulous presence had infused the very atmosphere both
Kamose and Ahmose had breathed ever since. Seeing him
come was like preparing to greet an old friend.

Harkhuf and the Followers hurried to surround him but
Ahmose waved them back. He heard them fitting arrows to
their bows and remembered that a King's bodyguard were
forbidden to waste arrows unless in direct defence of their
charge. In the next second they would fire and Pezedkhu
would fall. Ahmose felt a twinge of regret.

Pezedkhu flicked a finger. It was a tiny gesture, almost
unnoticed, but to Ahmose's horror the General was
suddenly ringed with archers rising from their knees where
they had been hidden, bows straining, arrows already tight
to the string, arrows leaving the string, and before Ahmose

could flinch, someone staggered against him, someone else grunted, someone gave a strangled cough, and he turned on feet gone numb to see his men littering the deck like so many skewered swine. Harkhuf was on all fours, a black shaft protruding from his shoulder, and Ahmose's first dazed thought was: How can I tell Ankhmahor? Qar was running towards him, sailors at his back. Harkhuf began to sway and gasp spasmodically.

"You are a clever man, Ahmose Tao, but not clever enough," Pezedkhu called. "You are no match for me. Did I not kill your father? Did I not haunt your brother to the end of his days? Where are the vaunted Followers now? You are naked before me and I am going to kill you too."

His voice sent shivers down Ahmose's spine. He was no match for this brilliant, brutal man and neither were any of his generals. His mouth had gone dry. He licked his lips, tasting the salt of terror on them, wanting to cower down and close his eyes, but he did not. He felt Harkhuf scrabbling blindly at his ankles in an extremity of pain and he sensed rather than saw Qar lift the man away. Your mother killed to save your life and Kamose died for you, he told himself. So has every other Egyptian fallen this day. This is the moment when you may truly become a King. He stepped forward until the rail was pressing against his waist.

"Your foreign master is not worthy of you, General," he said, surprised at the clarity and evenness of his own voice. "Surely you see that whether you kill me or not, Het-Uart is doomed. It is the last tiny island in a sea of Egyptian power and the waves are about to swamp it forever." Pezedkhu smiled. There was nothing sardonic or patronizing in the wide movement of his mouth. It was warm and affable.

"I have many masters," he replied. "Apepa is but one of them. When his war with you is over, I shall go home to Rethennu, to my wife and my forests and my ocean, until I am needed elsewhere. I like you, Ahmose, and I admired your brother, but what can you offer me compared to all that?" He shook his head and began to unsling his bow. "Besides, your blandishments are hollow. Where are the archers you ought to have held in reserve? You are now dead, and once you are dead your armies will collapse. Apepa will triumph." Pezedkhu selected an arrow and fitted it to his string.

Ahmose waited in frozen impotence. I am taking my last breaths, he thought, but could not accept. How is that possible? The late sun is glinting off the tip of Pezedkhu's arrow as he raises it and takes aim, the tip that will be buried deep within my chest. It is beautiful. Sunlight is life, touching the water and turning it into crystal fragments, warming the curving cedar sides of the boat in which he stands to a polished glow. I should ask him for news of Tani. He will know how she fares. I should fall to the deck and so perhaps deflect his shot and save my life. But he did nothing. He waited, his gaze travelling the length of the arrow, past the gloved hand and rigid, muscled arm forcing tension on the bow to the narrowed brown eyes fixed below his collarbone and the confusion of shapes beyond. Sun sparking briefly on some indistinguishable thing of metal in the shapes beyond …

Something came whistling through the hot air from behind Pezedkhu, gleaming as it revolved, and came to rest with a thud somewhere behind Ahmose. Simultaneously an arrow whipped past him, close enough to stir up a wind, and was lost. Full awareness returned to him in a burst of sound and a blur of motion. The noise of battle buffeted him once more. The smell of freshly spilled blood from the deck filled his nostrils. Dazed, he turned. His bodyguard lay dead around him but for Harkhuf who was sitting slumped at the foot of the mast. Qar squatted beside him, the shaft of a broken arrow in his fist. An axe had buried itself in the wood above Harkhuf's bent head, its long haft still quivering. Ahmose turned back.

Pezedkhu had been thrown off balance. His shot had gone wide. Stumbling to one side he was already recovering, his shoulders hunched, his body swinging around to see from whence the axe had come. The *North* loomed wide and threatening behind him. Its men were launching themselves onto the deck of Pezedkhu's craft and they and Pezedkhu's soldiers were already locked together. Hor-Aha's arm was still raised from the action of throwing. As Ahmose watched, he ran across the deck of the *North* and sprang over the water, landing neatly in the midst of the furore. Zaa pen Nekheb was already across. So was Kay, and he was advancing on Pezedkhu. Ahmose saw him drop his sword and draw a dagger.

Pezedkhu's bodyguard had closed around him, but the soldiers and crew of the *North* were still pouring across. A group of them under Hor-Aha's shouted directions were making straight for the thin cordon of men standing between Pezedkhu and Kay who was circling warily, seeking his chance. At the onslaught the line broke, and heart in mouth Ahmose saw an avenue of vulnerability suddenly appear.

Kay did not hesitate. He rushed forward. Pezedkhu was already recovering from the shock of Hor-Aha's unsuccessful attack but he was encumbered by the tall bow still in his grip. Dropping it and kicking it away, he reached for his sword but he had lost valuable seconds, and before the weapon was half out of its scabbard Kay was on him, elbow tight to his side, dagger poised to thrust into the larger's man's belly. Pezedkhu's arm came up in an instinctive movement of self-defence and Ahmose saw a red gash appear as the knife struck bone and slid down to sever the muscles of the General's forearm. Kay was thrown off balance by the sheer speed of his charge but he did not drop his dagger. He fell forward. Pressing his wounded limb to his chest, Pezedkhu swung his other fist, connecting with Kay's temple. Kay slumped to one knee, waving his weapon wildly to and fro as he fought the dizziness of the blow.

Pezedkhu was struggling to pull his sword free of its scabbard with his one unscathed arm while the other trembled uncontrollably, still hugged against him. Blood was streaming down his body in two dark rivulets and soaking into his linen kilt. He was grimacing with pain. Teeth bared he tugged frantically at the sword hilt, weaving an erratic dance as he tried to avoid Kay's lunges. But as he stepped back, one foot came down on his discarded bow. He stumbled and the bow jerked, tripping him. Pezedkhu went down. Before he could recover, Kay was on him, crawling over the deck, and the blade of the dagger was buried in his throat.

Kay collapsed onto the twitching body, lying prone for a moment in an exhaustion and relief Ahmose could almost feel, then he scrambled up and tugged the weapon free. Feverishly he began sawing at the lifeless wrist, digging and hacking until Pezedkhu's hand came free. Then he rose and turned to Ahmose, holding it gleefully aloft. "I have taken this hand, Majesty!" he shouted. "Pezedkhu's hand! I give thanks to my totem Nekhbet and to your Father Amun of Weset! Apepa is defenceless now! Long life and prosperity to Your Majesty!" Ahmose was forced to cling to the ship's rail for fear his legs would no longer hold him upright. The setting sun's rays were glancing red off the silver ring still encircling one of Pezedkhu's thick, strong fingers. He could even see the deep lines spidering across the General's wide palm.

He is dead, he is dead, he said to himself. So quickly, so easily. He was only human after all, Kamose, a man who fell in battle just like other men. I suppose I imagined some climactic meeting between us when we would come together in single combat with the fate of Egypt at stake but he has been defeated by the ordinary captain of one vessel among many. Regret and compassion overwhelmed him. It is the end of an era, he thought suddenly. Pezedkhu, Seqenenra, Kamose, you wove a sombre garment together, threads of doom and foreboding, of bitterness and terror and murder, and your destinies have been accomplished. Woodenly he turned to find Qar at his elbow. "Send a sailor across to bring me that hand and then take me back to the bank," he said hoarsely. "Khabekhnet must carry it through the ranks. The Setiu must see it. By nightfall the victory will be ours."

He sat on a coil of rope and waited, blind to the uproar around him, until presently Qar bent and placed the hand in his lap. It was no longer bleeding. The fingers curled inward as though reaching for a caress. The nail on the powerful, spatulate thumb was split and the others were rimmed in grime. Ahmose lifted it gently and turned it over. The ring's face was engraved with symbols he did not recognize, foreign symbols, Pezedkhu's name perhaps, or the name of his wife or son inscribed in the language of some obscure Setiu tribe. I knew nothing about him but his skill as a strategist and his great personal authority, he thought sadly. Qar cleared his throat. "Captain Abana humbly begs you to allow him to keep the ring when you have finished with the hand, Majesty," he said. "He wishes to wear it as his rightful booty, but he understands that the Setiu General was no common enemy and you may decide to offer it as a trophy to Amun when you return to Weset." Ahmose nodded, eyes closed. He cradled the hand reverently in both of his as the *Living in Ptah* slowly extricated itself from the last confused clashes still going on and beat its way towards calmer waters.

Khabekhnet and a few of his heralds had seen the vessel emerge. They had paced its progress and were waiting at the place where, hentis ago, it seemed to Ahmose, he had boarded it. The ramp was run out and he walked unsteadily down towards the cluster of mired chariots and weary horses. "This is Pezedkhu's hand," he said, passing it to the Chief Herald. "Impale it on a spear and carry it through the fighting. Call out his death and demand the enemy's surrender. Then bring it back to me." Khabekhnet took it as a flurry of excited murmurs rippled through the other heralds. Ahmose did not wait to receive their bows. Turning away, he strode towards the cluster of tents beneath the sheltering arms of the sycamore.

The noise of the battle slowly dimmed. Other sounds began to take its place, ordinary, comforting sounds, the trilling of birds in the band of growth beside the tributary, the voices of servants as they went about their evening chores, the whinny of a horse from the direction of their enclosure. The flap of Ahmose's tent was folded back and he could see movement inside. As he approached, Akhtoy came out, and at the sight of the man Ahmose felt a great weight of exhaustion descend on him, weakening his limbs and bending his spine. "Pezedkhu is dead," he said huskily. "It is only a matter of time before our victory is declared. My Followers are slain, all but Harkhuf who is wounded. Send my physician to his tent at once." Akhtoy's gaze travelled him swiftly.

"Majesty, are you also hurt?" he asked. Ahmose looked down. His palms were smeared with Pezedkhu's dried blood and below them the blood of his bodyguard was congealing in blotches and long splashes on his kilt and down his calves. He began to strip himself in a sudden fever to be clean, tearing sword belt and linen from his waist and the helmet from his head, pulling off the pectoral, tossing everything onto the earth.

"Bring fresh natron," he said through clenched teeth. "I must wash now, Akhtoy. I must wash." Then he was running for the water, stumbling a little as the bank shelved down, his feet catching in hidden roots, his toes stubbing against small stones, until he felt the cool, flowing resistance of the Nile against his skin. Falling forward he submerged himself, opening his eyes and his mouth to the river's insinuation, rubbing his hands together, forcing his body to remain beneath the surface until he felt the last stains of death soften and dissolve away. Gasping, he broke into the limpid early evening air and saw his body servant waiting with a dish of natron and a towel. Ahmose beck-oned. "Come into the water," he called. The man slung the towel around his neck and waded obediently into the gentle current. "Now scrub me hard," Ahmose ordered, "and when that is done, do it again." The natron in the man's practised fingers grated almost painfully against his skin and Ahmose welcomed the sensation, feeling the horror of the day slough away and a measure of equilibrium return.

Nevertheless when he came to the threshold of his tent with the servant behind him, his body tingling and his mind more calm, he paused for a moment, unwilling to enter a place whose familiarity seemed cramped and old. Akhtoy came forward holding a cap and it was only then that Ahmose realized he had been bareheaded in a public place. "There is food and beer, Majesty," Akhtoy said as he settled the covering on Ahmose's shaved skull. "You have not eaten since early this morning. The physician has gone to tend Prince Harkhuf. Prince Mesehti wishes to know whether or not you will require your chariot again today." The second of dislocation had passed. Ahmose moved forward to the chair drawn up beside his table and lowered himself into it, aware that his legs were aching as well as his head.

"I am not hungry but I suppose that I had better eat," he replied heavily. "It is going to be a long night, Akhtoy. Send to Mesehti and tell him that I want the chariot at once." He drew the cup brimming with dark beer towards him and reached for the bread. "As soon as I have eaten, I will see Harkhuf. Is there any word from Ankhmahor?" Akhtoy shook his head.

"No, Majesty, but he should be returning from Aabtu at any time."

"Very well. Open the shrine and then you can go," Ahmose said. "I want to see Amun." A faint smile, part sympathy, part affection, flitted across the Chief Steward's face.

"Perhaps Your Majesty would like to be dressed before I do so," he suggested and Ahmose realized with a shock that he was still naked, one sturdy bare thigh crossed over the other and between them a nest of curly pubic hair. He rose, disconcerted, all at once filled with a ridiculous urge to burst into tears. Akhtoy nodded at the body servant who went to the rear of the tent and lifted the lid of Ahmose's tiring chest. Akhtoy himself swung the doors to the little shrine quietly open and then backed reverently out.

Decently clad in a fresh kilt, Ahmose ate and drank without conscious appreciation, his eyes and his thoughts on the small golden figure of his god while his servant silently attended to the dishes on the table. He knew that the events since dawn had rendered him numb, that later he would be flooded with gratitude to Amun for the granting of both victory and his life, but for now just the sight of Amun's enigmatic smile under the graceful plumes of his crown brought a certain peace. When he noticed to his surprise that nothing but crumbs remained on the plates the servant was lifting onto a tray, he got up, closed the doors of the shrine, and slipping on a pair of sandals he left the tent.

No Followers came to fill the space around him as he stepped outside, but Mesehti was there holding the reins of the horses harnessed to Ahmose's chariot and he bowed as

Ahmose approached. The sun had just gone down and the shadowless landscape was suffused with a soft golden light tinged with a pink flush that would soon deepen to scarlet as night crept in. Ahmose gestured. Mesehti swung himself up onto the floor of the vehicle and Ahmose followed. "Harkhuf's tent," he said curtly. Mesehti tightened the reins and had opened his mouth to call to the horses when there was a shout. Ahmose turned to see Ankhmahor come running up, his face drawn.

"Majesty, I have only just disembarked," he panted. "The men on the bank are talking of a slaughter of the Followers. Is it true? Are you safe? Where is my son?"

"It is true," Ahmose replied, privately marvelling at the sequence of the Prince's urgent questions. "Get up behind me, Ankhmahor. Harkhuf was wounded. I am on my way to see how he fares." Ankhmahor needed no further invitation. The chariot began to roll. Ahmose felt the man's extreme consternation and said nothing, although he wanted to tell Ankhmahor how relieved he was to have him back. Ankhmahor himself did not speak.

Both men jumped from the chariot as it neared Harkhuf's tent. Ahmose strode inside, Ankhmahor on his heels, and the physician who had been bending over the form on the cot straightened and bowed. "The arrow was barbed and difficult to remove," he said in answer to Ahmose's curt enquiry. "The Prince has suffered much pain, but he will recover in time if no ukhedu develops. I have packed the wound with ground willow and honey and have made up a large amount of poppy infusion which his servant must give him whenever he requires it. I will continue to attend the Prince if Your Majesty so desires."

Ankhmahor had moved to the other side of the cot. Ahmose nodded his thanks to the physician and looked down expecting to see Harkhuf's eyes closed in unconsciousness but the gaze that met his was fully aware although the pupils were huge and hazed with poppy. Sweat beaded on a face grey with agony. The afflicted shoulder was swathed in linen pads. Harkhuf licked his dry lips, and at once Ahmose knelt, lifting the damp head and holding a cup of water from the table beside the cot to the young man's mouth. Harkhuf groaned at the movement but drank briefly.

"Majesty, how goes the battle?" he whispered as Ahmose set his head carefully back on the pillow, and Ahmose realized first that he had not seen Ankhmahor and second that of course he would know nothing of any event after he was shot.

"It is all but won," he said. "I am waiting for a final word of confirmation from my generals. Pezedkhu is dead. Harkhuf, your father is here."

"Here?" Harkhuf's drugged eyes slid away. He smiled as Ankhmahor leaned forward and touched his cheek. "Father, I did my duty," he breathed.

"Of course you did," Ankhmahor reassured him. "The physician says that your wound will heal. You must sleep now, Harkhuf, if you can. I will come back in the morning."

"It hurts," Harkhuf muttered, but his eyelids were drooping and even before Ankhmahor had rejoined Ahmose he had slipped into a restless unconsciousness.

"My physician is a clever man," Ahmose told Ankhmahor as together they walked back to the chariot. "I do not think that Harkhuf is in any real danger. He has acquitted himself well during your absence, Ankhmahor. So did the other officers who died trying to defend me. You will have to recruit new Followers immediately."

"Tell me what has happened while I have been in Aabtu, Majesty," Ankhmahor said. "It is as though the whole world changed while I worshipped in the temple of Osiris. I feel utterly bewildered."

They mounted the chariot and were driven back to Ahmose's tent, but while Ahmose spoke of the opening of the gates and the ensuing battles, his mind was busy with other things. The Followers who were killed must be beautified, he was thinking. Where is the nearest House of the Dead? And what of the hundreds of others we must bury without embalming and trust to the mercy of the gods? Where is Ramose? Have I lost any of my generals? Word should come soon regarding the fighting in the eastern Delta which must be secured if we are to hold onto the great gain we have made today.

Ankhmahor left him outside the tent, for the matter of a new bodyguard was urgent. Ahmose went in to find Akhtoy lighting the lamps and two scrolls lying on the table. Ahmose picked them up. One bore his wife's seal but he did not recognize the imprint pressed deep into the wax of the other. Frowning, he cracked it, but before he could unroll it he heard Khabekhnet's voice requesting entrance. Behind him came Ramose. "It is all over, Majesty," Ramose exclaimed, grinning, his white teeth gleaming out of a mud-grimed face. "The northern mound is yours and most of the Setiu soldiers are slain. When the survivors realized that the hand impaled on Khabekhnet's spear was Pezedkhu's, they began to lay down their weapons." He swept an airy hand down his body. "Give me permission to clean myself," he requested. "I stink." Ahmose smiled back.

"It is the scent of victory," he said. "More seductive than the perfume of Hathor herself. I am glad that you are unscathed, Ramose. Go and rest." Ramose bowed, clapped Khabekhnet heartily on the shoulder, and vanished quickly into the shadows gathering beyond the tent. Ahmose turned to his herald. "The hand?" For answer Khabekhnet laid a leather pouch on the table.

"It is very mangled and has begun to rot, Majesty," he said. "Our men are even now taking the hands of the enemy dead for the tally. Shall I add Pezedkhu's to one of the piles?" Ahmose considered for a moment. There was something distasteful, even disrespectful, in the image of a part of Pezedkhu's strong body being flung onto a heap with hundreds of other hands, all anonymous in their sameness.

"No," he said, making up his mind. "Throw it into the river. Give it to Hapi for an offering. But first remove the ring and deliver it to Kay Abana. He killed the man. It is his trophy."

"The hand is very swollen," Khabekhnet remarked. "I will have to cut off the finger." Ahmose suppressed a surge of groundless irritation. "Then do so," he said shortly. "What of the body itself, Khabekhnet?" The herald shook his head.

"I do not know, Majesty. I have not heard. But I presume that by now it has been added to the other Setiu corpses for burning." I should like to have given him a proper burial, Ahmose thought rather sadly, or at least had him embalmed and sent east to his family. It does not seem in the way of Ma'at to treat the remains of such a formidable enemy as though he was of little account but in the heat of the moment my attention was fixed on my own survival. You will never again see your forests and your ocean, General. I am both glad and full of regret.

"Your heralds have been calling for the city's surrender?" he asked. Khabekhnet nodded.

"They continue to do so but it is too early for a response from the usurper I think," he replied. "The loss of his General and of the battle must first sink below the level of mere shock."

"Very well." Ahmose gestured. "Detail some of your subordinates to tell the officers in every division that when the Scribe of the Army has completed his tally and the burnings begin, all Egyptian soldiers apart from the sentries are to be allowed food and plenty of beer and one day in which to sleep. Remind them also that the wounded must be given whatever the divisions' physicians deem necessary. Try to discover if there are any Houses of the Dead nearby, although I suppose that even if there are, the sem-priests could not possibly beautify every Egyptian corpse." Khabekhnet hesitated.

"Forgive me, Majesty, but such a task is a waste of time. Until now the Delta has belonged to the Setiu blasphemers who do not preserve their dead but allow them to decay under the floors of their houses. Any temples close to us will belong to foreign gods and the only sem-priests nearby reside within Het-Uart itself to serve the Egyptians living on the northern mound. Our soldiers know that if they fall in battle they will be buried without beautification. It is a risk they take for their King. To try to embalm all our dead is not logical."

"You are right," Ahmose said unwillingly after a pause. "It is a foolish quest. You are dismissed, Khabekhnet." The herald bowed at once and retreated and Ahmose blew out his cheeks as he turned to the table. A foolish quest but one that would go a long way towards assuaging my guilt, he thought. Kamose took them from their homes and I have kept them away. Now many of them are dead. They may all be my possessions under the law of Ma'at but I have never regarded them as a vast herd of cattle to be milked or slaughtered according to my whim or the urgency of my need. "I will read the scrolls now," he said to Akhtoy who had been waiting for an order. "Send for Ipi."

Pulling his chair up to the table, he unrolled the thinner papyrus whose seal he had already broken. The penmanship was familiar. It belonged to his wife's new scribe, Khunes, but the signature at the bottom was little more than a large and laborious scrawl. Ahmose made it out with a dawning delight. "Your loving son, the Hawk-in-the-Nest Ahmose-onkh, Prince of the Two Lands," he read. "Akhtoy, this is the first letter I have ever received from Ahmose-onkh and he has signed it himself!" he exclaimed, looking up, but Akhtoy had gone. Eagerly Ahmose's attention returned to the scroll.

"To Uatch-Kheperu Ahmose, Neb-pehti-Ra, Horus, the Horus of Gold, and my esteemed Father, greetings from your loyal son," he read. "I humbly and sadly offer you my sympathy on the death of my sister the Princess Hent-ta-Hent. Khunes told me to say it like that but I really am sorry. I will miss her even though she cried a lot. Khunes is going to show me how to sign my name and titles myself. I hope you are well and have beaten the evil Setiu and will be coming home soon. Your loving son, the Hawk-in-the-Nest ..." Stunned, Ahmose tossed the scroll aside and tore the seal from the other, unrolling it in one savage movement. It had been written throughout in Aahmes-nefertari's own neat, orderly hand.

"My dearest husband," it began. "Forgive me for burdening you with this terrible news when all your energies must be engaged in defeating the enemy, but when would it ever be a good time to tell you something that will cause you grief? Our daughter, Hent-ta-Hent, died yesterday of a fever that Amunmose was unable to exorcise. He tried many incantations but the demon was too strong. She had been fretful for some days before succumbing. Raa and I believed her distress to be caused by teething until the fever took hold with unshakeable force. She died still unconscious. She will, of course, be beautified and correctly mourned and we will place her in a temporary tomb until ours has been finished. She was walking quite steadily until she became ill and had mastered a few simple words which she would say loudly over and over again with such pride! She had begun to try and follow Ahmose-onkh about, a fact that either exasperated or charmed him depending on his mood. He was most distressed when I prevented him from being with her once I realized how the demon had filled her. I miss you so much, and never more than now when the house is in mourning. Send me some word as soon as you are able. Your loving wife and obedient subject, Aahmes-nefertari."

Ahmose let the scroll roll up with a small rustle. For many minutes he sat with the dry papyrus under his motionless fingers, gazing unseeing into the quivering glow of the lamp flame inside its alabaster sphere. Little Hent-ta-Hent, he thought. I remember the feel of her tiny body on my chest as I lay in the garden, the endearing light weight of her, her skin feeding warmth into mine and her sleeping breath making her dark curls stir rhythmically. I can smell her, that wonderful pure smell of freshness and babyhood. Poor Aahmes-nefertari. Of the three children to whom she has given birth only one survives, and though I keenly feel the loss of my little girl, I cannot know the depth of a mother's pain.

Pushing the scrolls aside, he rested his elbows on the table and his chin sank into his palms. It is no accident that this news came to me in the very hour of my triumph, his thoughts ran on. There is a price for everything. Even Kings must pay for what they want. Hent-ta-Hent is the price the gods have exacted for all those who have fallen here today so that I may move ever closer to my goal. Was Kamose also a part of that cost? Even though my destiny to be a King is not so much my own desire as the decree of those same gods who have snatched my daughter in payment and destroyed my brother? A chill shook him, and then all at once the tears that had threatened to overwhelm him earlier came flooding back through his fingers. He heard someone come into the tent behind him, heard Ipi and Akhtoy whispering together in alarm, but he could not move. It is not good for servants to see a god weep, he thought incoherently, but tonight I do not care.

When he was spent, he lifted his head and immediately a square of clean linen was gently presented to him. Taking it, he wiped his face and rose. Ipi bowed and Akhtoy retrieved the linen. "The Princess Hent-ta-Hent is dead,"

Ahmose said tonelessly. "She died of a fever. Take these letters, Ipi. Read and file them. I will dictate replies tomorrow. Stay here. The Scribe of the Army will arrive soon with his report." He turned clumsily to his steward. "Akhtoy, bring wine." Akhtoy bowed low, spreading out his hands in the ancient gesture of pleading or commiseration.

"Majesty, I am so sorry," he said. "Surely the little Princess needs no justification before the gods. Her heart will weigh lighter than the Feather of Ma'at on the scales of the Judgement Hall." His compassion was genuine, Ahmose knew. Akhtoy had daughters himself. But your daughters have not been sacrificed to maintain some sort of cosmic balance, Ahmose spoke to him silently. Surely the gods do not dare to even place Hent-ta-Hent's heart on the scales, for they themselves have willed her death and she is innocent. He was spared a reply. Akhtoy did not wait for one. He backed out of the tent.

Ahmose resumed his seat and looked across at his Chief Scribe, who had retrieved the scrolls and was watching him blankly. "I think," Ahmose said heavily, "that we will be able to go home before long, Ipi." The scribe smiled grimly.

"Indeed, I fervently hope so, Majesty," he agreed.

As Ahmose had predicted, there was no rest for him or any highly placed officer that night. The Scribe of the Army appeared just before midnight, as the depressingly familiar stench of burning bodies had begun to coil throughout the Egyptian tents. A thick sheaf of papyrus was under his arm. He looked more exhausted than Ahmose felt, and gratefully accepted the King's offer to sit. Akhtoy poured him wine, which he drank at once with the greed of true thirst.

"The tally is complete, Majesty," he said, shuffling the sheets of paper and settling deeper into his chair. "Five thousand, four hundred and ninety-one hands were collected and personally counted by me. Of those, two thousand, one hundred were taken from the battlefield by the tributary. The remaining three thousand, three hundred and ninety-one were gathered on the northern mound. It is a terrible loss for Apepa." He glanced up. "The corpses have been fired in twelve locations, well away from the water. Our losses number two thousand dead and five hundred and sixty-three wounded. Of the wounded, some ninety are not expected to live and two hundred and eight have lost either arms or legs to the enemy's swords. When they are able, they should be sent home and pensioned in the usual way. They are of no further use to you." His delivery was brisk and matter-of-fact. No Scribe of the Army, part of whose task was the gruesome necessity of walking from arena to battle arena with his assistants when the fighting was over and sometimes literally wading through mutilated bodies, could afford the indulgence of sentimentality. "The physicians warn me that medical supplies are running low. I have sent to Iunu for more linen for bandages as well as herbs and poppy from the temples there, but it will be a few days before these things arrive."

"Break down our dead and wounded into the divisions and the navy for me," Ahmose requested. The Scribe did so, reading from his seemingly endless lists. Baqet's Division of Thoth had sustained the greatest number of casualties in the desperate attempt to hold off Pezedkhu until Turi and the Division of Amun arrived, and by far the heaviest count of wounded lay with the navy, whose sailors and marines had lost arms and hands while struggling to regain their vessels.

When the figures were firmly fixed in Ahmose's mind, he dismissed the man, asking him to bring regular reports on the rate of attrition among the wounded. He was replaced almost at once by a steady stream of officers from the divisions, come to report on the order slowly being brought out of what had been chaos. The supply of arrows was spent. Swords and spears were lost or broken and soldiers had been detailed to collect discarded Setiu weapons to replace them as soon as it was light. All the officers brought into the tent with them the miasma of smoke and extreme fatigue.

The last to bow his way inside was Ankhtify, Standard Bearer of the Division of Horus. "General Khety sends you his most fervent congratulations, Majesty," the officer said. "Every Setiu soldier on the northern turtleback is now burning outside the walls and their quarters are now occupied by our division. But there is an enclave of Egyptians and foreigners, mostly Keftiu merchants, living on small estates to the north-west of the mound. They are clamouring to be allowed to leave. General Khety is refusing them permission until he has received your command on the matter."

"Those are the estates with irrigation ditches that are usually filled by digging out the wall," Ahmose said. He pursed his lips, considering. "I want to talk to the Keftiu. Tell Khety that I will come and inspect the mound tomorrow. In the meantime he is to detain them all. Have him close both the gates and set sentries inside and outside them. They are to be guarded at all times, particularly the

Horus Road Gate where Khety might be vulnerable to an attack from the east. I have not had any communication from the divisions in the eastern Delta for some time. The risk is small but it must be taken into account. If by some rare chance the northern mound were to be retaken by the Setiu, it would be a disaster. The gates can of course be opened to allow our own troops to come and go during the day. What of the ancient temple to Set?" The man raised his eyebrows.

"Some of the Setiu made a stand within its confines," he told Ahmose, "but they were overcome and slaughtered. The temple itself is not damaged but will require purification. Does Your Majesty wish this to be done tonight? Will you pray there tomorrow?"

"No." Ahmose decided quickly. "The Delta has always belonged to Set but the Setiu took the god and melded him with their own Sutekh. I do not wish to have anyone think that in worshipping Set I am giving my approval to Sutekh also. Let the priests purify the precincts and let the temple remain, but I will not enter it." He rose, a gesture of dismissal. "I will also visit the wounded and drive among the troops," he finished. "Convey my extreme admiration to General Khety for his success today."

When Ankhtify had gone, Ahmose had himself washed, performed his belated evening prayers, offered the customary incense to Amun, and fell onto his cot.

He was about to ask Akhtoy to douse the lamp when yet another shadow darkened the door of the tent. It was Hor-Aha. He came forward swiftly and halted beside the cot, looking down on Ahmose expressionlessly. Ahmose studied the smooth black face on which the only betrayal of tiredness lay in two faint grooves running from the inside corners of those sooty eyes. "The news of the little Princess's death is already spreading throughout the camp," he said without preamble. "I am very sorry, Majesty. What else can I say? The gods' idea of justice does not always conform to our own." Ahmose nodded once and waited. Hor-Aha swallowed. "I have come to give you my shame," he went on. "I am ashamed for the hesitation, nay, the cowardice of the Medjay. I am ashamed at their refusal to obey my orders. I am ashamed at what I hear, that you yourself were compelled to urge them to cross the lesser tributary and carry away the wounded." His deep voice had grown hoarse. "I ask for your permission to punish them." Ahmose searched the smooth, exotically handsome face. There was something different about Hor-Aha, something he could not quite determine.

"I agree that they behaved abominably," he said, "but their fear of water is well known, Hor-Aha. They should have attempted to overcome it and I have no respect for their lack of initiative, but they acquitted themselves well in the early stages of the conflict."

"That may be so," Hor-Aha said gravely, "but now they have made themselves and me objects of scorn among the Egyptian officers. If I was hated before, I am anathema to them now." Ah yes, Ahmose thought. The heart of the problem. Your pride, my old friend, and your secret self-doubt.

"How will you punish them?" he wanted to know.

"I will remove their personal totems," Hor-Aha replied at once, and Ahmose suddenly remembered that each tribesman carried some barbarous fetish or other; a stone from a sacred site, a piece of bone from a wild animal he had slain, even the lock of a vanquished enemy's hair, in the belief that such things had the power to protect him from danger. And will you yourself give up your precious totem, Hor-Aha? Ahmose asked him silently. Will you relinquish the piece of linen stained with my father's blood that you carry on your belt?

"No," Ahmose said emphatically. "No, Hor-Aha. If you do that, they will think themselves so defenceless that their ability to fight will be gone. Then they will be cowards indeed! Leave it alone. Lash them with your tongue, with leather if you like, but do not strike at their spirit." Hor-Aha looked down in reflection for a moment, then his chin rose.

"Your Majesty speaks wisely," he admitted, "but in doing so you heap yet more humiliation upon me. Here." He held out a fistful of something that appeared to Ahmose, in the dim light of the one lamp still burning, like the black fur of a cat with a drooping tail. "I have cut off my hair as an act of extreme mortification." Ahmose watched in astonishment as Hor-Aha laid the two long braids side by side on the white sheet. So that is the difference about him that teased me, Ahmose thought. His chest is bare. I had grown so used to seeing it adorned with those gleaming ropes. Gods! He is giving me his manhood! He looked up and met his General's blank gaze.

"Your men will see," he said slowly. "They will know what you have done, and why." Hor-Aha ran a hand up the back of his naked neck.

"Even so," he replied. "But it is not only for them. It is for me. For my regret. I will do my utmost to see that such

a necessity does not arise again, Majesty. Dismiss me, I beg."
Ahmose did so.

For a while a pregnant silence filled the tent. Ahmose
and Akhtoy met each other's eye. Then Ahmose waved a
finger. "Wrap them up and store them somewhere in the
bottom of one of my tiring boxes," he said to the steward.
"Do it quickly, Akhtoy. I must sleep now or go mad."

But for a little while he could not sleep. Lying on his
back in the dimness, he felt again the languid body of his
baby daughter against his chest and fancied that her warm
breath sighed in his ear. Not until he turned onto his side
did unconsciousness engulf him.

He woke early to a hurried meal and a slow dressing, for
he wished to present himself to his troops in full regal and
military regalia. When Akhtoy had settled the pectoral
around his neck, the golden earring in his lobe, the golden
Chief Commander's bracelets on his wrists and the gold-
shot linen helmet surmounted by the arrogant beak of the
goddess Nekhbet on his head, he strapped on his sword belt
and sandals and emerged into the smoke-hazed morning.
He was greeted by Ipi, who had been waiting armed with
his palette, and a clink of metal and the thud of purposeful
feet as a group of soldiers with Ankhmahor leading them at
once came marching towards him from the direction of the
tributary. They were already livered in the blue and white
of royalty. Coming up to him, they bowed as one then
straightened to watch him expectantly. "Your new
Followers, Majesty," Ankhmahor explained. "I have
selected them from among the Shock Troops of each division. They are eager to serve you." Ahmose welcomed them
briefly before turning to Ankhmahor. Beyond him Makhu

appeared, the wheels of the chariot glinting dully in the clouded atmosphere.

"How is Harkhuf?" Ahmose enquired.

"He has improved slightly and there is as yet no sign of ukhedu in the wound," Ankhmahor replied. "The pain is still intense. He drinks a great deal, both water and poppy."

"Good." Ahmose began to walk to his chariot and the bodyguard fell in promptly around him. "We will make our first stop today at the northern mound."

The vast camp through which he was driven was seething with the bustle of orderly activity and cheerfully noisy. Soldiers laden with dirty linen made their way to the river, pausing to reverence him as he passed. Others sat outside their tents cleaning their weapons or drinking beer. Some lay asleep, oblivious to the happy furore around them, their spare kilts draped over their faces and their spent limbs flaccid on the grass. Many were limping, not from wounds, Ahmose realized, but from muscles stressed with a full day of fighting. A mood of optimism prevailed.

At the canal that snaked from the main tributary around the northern mound and back again, Ahmose dismounted, crossing the dwindling water on a makeshift bridge Khety's soldiers had laid down and walking between the two outflung arms of the Horus Road Gate with a rush of pride. He was met by the General himself and together with Ipi, the Followers and Khety's senior officers, Ahmose spent several hours inspecting his prize. It was an unlovely place, bare of any vegetation except on the roofs of the endless lines of military barracks where the foreign soldiers had managed to grow meagre crops of barley, garlic and vegetables. Khety's men were busy clearing them of everything the hapless Setiu had left, piling pots, garments and even a few unused bows and swords in heaps under the gleam of the morning sunlight.

The wounded were being tended in a large, crumbling mansion close to the temple. Ahmose paced the rows of pallets on which his men lay, his ears assaulted by their groans and cries, which seemed to echo against the high ceilings of the pillared rooms. The physicians moved among them, accompanied by several priests of Set, who were exorcising the fever demons and offering what prayers they could for those already dying. They bowed profoundly to Ahmose as he passed. "I presume that the governor of the mound lived here before Apepa was forced to turn it into a military bivouac to take the overflow of troops coming in from the east," Khety said in answer to Ahmose's query as they regained the open air. "The building itself belongs to your ancestor Osiris-Senwasret's time but the Setiu made some additions of their own, mostly crude mud brick halls. They are not much interested in architecture."

"It is an unsightly shambles," Ahmose admitted, "and of no use to us. When the wounded have gone, you can tear down the Setiu additions and use what is left as your headquarters, Khety. You and the Division of Horus will be stationed here at least until Het-Uart surrenders. How many wells are there?"

"Only four, Majesty. The water supply was of course supplemented by the canal itself, outside the walls."

"Dig more if you need them, and commandeer the gardens of the few estates that exist here. If we continue to hold the eastern Delta, there will be food enough for your men, but we must not presume on our ultimate safety." He turned to Khety and smiled. "You have indeed proved your-self a worthy General and a faithful son of Egypt," he said warmly. "Now I must speak with the inhabitants of those estates."

It was not far to the enclave where the privileged had managed to close themselves off from the stench and noise of the rest of the mound. A rough wall formed a wide semi-circle that joined the main mound's defences at either end. It was interspersed at regular intervals by solid wooden doors, each leading into a small courtyard, the house beyond, and a tiny garden running down to the massive outer wall. The doorkeepers had fled and the doors them-selves stood wide.

In accordance with Ahmose's earlier instructions, the foreign dignitaries had been herded together in the court-yard of the first house. As Ahmose, Khety and the Followers strode through the doorway the babble of excited voices raised in the Keftian tongue abruptly died away. A small sea of dark eyes were turned to him apprehensively before several dozen oiled and ringleted heads descended in submission. Ahmose's gaze flicked over them quickly. There were no women or children present. "Is there a spokesman among you?" he asked. At once the heads were raised. One man came forward, this time kneeling to press his mouth to Ahmose's dusty foot. He wore a kilt as the Egyptians did, but it was heavily and brightly embroidered in a tight pattern of interlocking whorls and the edge that curved up to the woven waistband was thick with red tassels. A red headband encircled his forehead and another held the cascade of oily curls at the nape of his neck. On one wrist he wore a copper bracelet in the likeness of an elongated dolphin whose snout met its tail. Ahmose bade him rise. "Are you all merchants?" he enquired peremptorily. The man understood him at once.

"His Majesty Awoserra Apepa receives his military advisers and all his senior officers from his brothers in Rethennu," he answered, then realizing who he was addressing, he flushed dully under his smooth olive skin. "Oh forgive me, Majesty, I beg you. We are unaccustomed … We concern ourselves only … I did not mean …" Ahmose gestured impatiently.

"Go on!" he urged. The man spread his delicate fingers.

"Thank you. You are gracious. Most of us are indeed traders, here to expedite trading negotiations between Keftiu and Egypt. Some here are architects and artists. His M … Apepa favours the colours and forms of Keftiu and much of his palace in Het-Uart has been decorated by us. I myself am a trader, providing Apepa with ships and olive oil in exchange for papyrus, flax and gold." Obviously encouraged by Ahmose's expression, he smiled. "The loss to your brother of the thirty treasure ships built by Keftians was a mighty blow to Apepa."

"Doubtless." Ahmose looked over the silent throng. "I have no intention of doing you any harm," he said loudly. "Indeed, trade with your country flourished during the reign of my ancestors. We are old partners, you and I. You are to give your names and occupations to General Khety's scribe. Those of you who are architects and artisans will be allowed to return to Keftiu. Egypt has no use for you. This mound is now an Egyptian military base and all your homes are confiscated. Merchants may go back to your island, or if you are enterprising I suggest that you gather up your families and possessions and make your way south to Weset where you should request audience with Queen Aahmes-nefertari who is eager to transfer all trading contracts from the Setiu to what has now become the capital of a united country. I will give you time to obtain permission to do so from whomever rules Keftiu. The gold routes into Wawat are even now being confiscated. Such a shift in your allegiance will be well worthwhile. Ipi, have you made a note of all this?" Cross-legged at his feet, the scribe nodded. Carefully Ahmose gauged their reaction, and seeing nothing but relief and a calculated lust dawning on their faces, he held up a hand. "That is all. You have one month to be gone." A murmured chorus of gratitude followed him as he and his entourage left the courtyard and moved farther along the coarsely erected wall.

"They will hate Weset," Ankhmahor remarked. "Here in the Delta they are close to their beloved Great Green. The desert will suck them dry."

"They will hate my city but love the profit they will make," Ahmose retorted. "Aahmes-nefertari will sort them out and then we too will be all the richer."

The Egyptian merchants, having also been herded into one courtyard, presented Ahmose with a very different demeanour as he confronted them. He could almost feel their hostility, veiled though it was behind their blank stares, and he wasted no civilities on them. "Are there any nobles among you?" he barked, not even bothering to greet them, wanting to shout at them: You are Egyptian, you could have opened the gates long before for Kamose, you could have chosen to spy for us, you are not worthy to live, let alone take up my precious time when hundreds of your brothers lie bleeding and suffering for Egypt's sake. He watched them stealing furtive glances at one another. After some minutes three men stepped forward.

"I am Antefoker, Prince of Iunu," one of them said. "I have an estate at Iunu but I come to my house here so that I may perform my duties as Chief Judge to Apepa once the Inundation has receded. There are always disputes between one landowner and another when the boundary markers have been temporarily washed away. I do not speak of peasant boundaries of course. The local temple officials deal with those." He paused, drew breath, drew another, then finished, "I have not been concerned with the war, Majesty. I am a peaceful man, minding my own business and doing a needful duty."

"Indeed?" Ahmose said mildly. "In other words you have pushed your head into the sand of deliberate ignorance, like some stupid Kushite ostrich, while every true Egyptian has been straining nerve and sinew to free this sacred land." His lip curled in disgust. "You are worse than the traitors who attempted to take my life. At least they were capable of action, no matter how misguided. Seeing that you have concerned yourself with the direction of irrigation canals and crumbling fields, I think I will put a hoe in your hand and give you a shaduf to work. Have you sons?" Antefoker could not answer. His throat worked and his hands clenched. When he did find his voice, it was a croak.

"Majesty, this is not just!" he protested. "I have no love for Apepa, but it was either work for him or become landless! There were many Setiu eager to assume my title and responsibilities if I had refused! Yes, I have sons, and it was for them that I sacrificed my integrity."

"What son respects a father who shrugs off the health of his very soul?" Ahmose cut in acidly. "But perhaps I am unjust. There are many like you still in Egypt, Antefoker, men who perch precariously on the fence and will not touch ground one side or the other. I cannot leave you a judge but I can make you an under-scribe to one of the temple judges in Iunu. I suppose that a noble, no matter how debased, should not be seen with soil under his fingernails. Give the names of your sons to General Khety's scribe. In my army they might learn loyalty. Your estate at Iunu is khato to me. And what of you other two?"

One of them had large holdings in the western Delta where he oversaw the vines that produced Egypt's finest wine. Ahmose entirely selfishly left him in his position after questioning him closely regarding the culture and care of the grapes, but he placed him under the supervision of one of his own agricultural overseers. Once more he made sure that Ipi had scribbled down all the changes. The other rather pathetic nobleman held a minor title and an even lesser post as an under-assistant to the administrator who had governed the mound before the Setiu army had moved in. Obviously he had lost his position and Ahmose left him alone. "The rest of you," he shouted. "I neither know nor care what you were doing here. Take your belongings and leave. Be thankful that I have spared your lives. A less merciful King might have sent you all south into Wawat and you would have perished in the gold mines." He saw a stir to the rear and forestalled the squeak of protest. "One word and I will do it!" he roared. "Khety, Ankhmahor, let us leave. The air in here has a fouler odour than that of burning corpses."

He spent the remainder of the day touring his other divisions, consulting with his exultant generals, having Ipi take down the names of those who had distinguished themselves in the battle and were worthy of rewards, and standing beside the wounded. Towards evening, as he was making his way wearily towards his tent and Makhu was at last driving his equally weary horses back to their stalls, a scout accosted him. "Majesty, I bring messages from the Generals Neferseshemptah, Iymery and Akhethotep," he said. "The eastern Delta is yours. Your divisions have control of the Horus Road and are even now marching on the forts comprising the Wall of Princes. What are your orders?" Overjoyed, Ahmose felt his tiredness slip from him.

"It is not necessary to lose good men in trying to take the forts," he said after a moment's consideration. "It will be enough to hold the Horus Road on their western side. Sooner or later the Setiu inhabiting them will simply concede defeat and walk away and then we can reclaim and hold them. Well done! Tell the generals that if they judge the east to be truly secure I will move to allow the troops to go home in rotation. I will send the details later. Take back to them the news of our victory here."

This time his tent welcomed him with a warm promise of food, drink and a peaceful rest. Akhtoy and his body servant were waiting. There were no scrolls to be read, no immediate decisions to make, only the luxury of hot water and relaxation. He entered happily. Behind him Ankhmahor was giving the orders for the first watch and before him Akhtoy was pouring the wine. Ahmose found himself humming a tune from the nursery of his boyhood as he kicked off his sandals and settled into his chair.

On the following morning Ahmose presided over the funeral rites for the Egyptians who had fallen. The scribes had completed the lists of their names, and the pits into which their bodies had been reverently lowered had been covered over. Ahmose ordered a stela erected over each crater with the names of those beneath inscribed on the stone so that the gods might find them. The funeral itself was a solemn and moving affair with the divisions drawn up in silent ranks behind their standards and the bitter incense pluming skyward in grey columns to mingle with the smoke that still coiled from the fires consuming the dead Setiu.

Afterwards Ahmose kept the soldiers in formation while he mounted a makeshift dais and distributed the awards due to those who had earned them. There were promotions, citations and the promise of the Gold of Valour to certain men who had shown great courage or initiative. It was, of course, impossible to actually present the trophies until Ahmose returned to Weset and had them made.

General Baqet of the Division of Thoth was one of the recipients for his grim determination to hold the line against Pezedkhu's onslaught until the reinforcements arrived, and Kay Abana was another. When Ahmose singled him out for his attack on Pezedkhu, he saw that the young man was already wearing the dead General's ring on a silver chain around his neck. Ahmose had thought long and hard regarding his rash captain. Kay seemed to be impulsive and foolhardy, but Ahmose had come to understand that beneath the swagger that both endeared him to his marines and amused his superiors there was a genuine stoutness of heart and good military judgement. "As well as the Gold of Valour I have decided to place you in charge of my flagship, the *Kha-em-Mennofer*, and give you the title of Admiral," he told a delighted Kay. "As captain of *Shining in Mennofer* you will be responsible for my safety when I am on board her and as Admiral you will direct the course of the navy's strategy during any battle. Your father and Paheri are still the navy's overall administrators." Kay stood looking up at Ahmose and the group of generals who surrounded him.

"Majesty, the honour is too great," he said gravely. "I am overwhelmed. Speech fails me."

"I doubt that," Turi whispered, and Kay obviously heard him. The grin that could soften authority and inspire obedience spread over his face.

"On this occasion you are wrong, General Turi," he called up. "Majesty, I am your servant forever. Thank you." But he could not resist one of the grandiloquent gestures for which he was becoming famous. "As a show of my gratitude and a pledge of my undying loyalty I beg your permission to change my name," he went on with a bow and a flourish. "I am not worthy to do so, but I would like to become Ahmose instead of Kay."

"I am Lord of your life but not of your naming," Ahmose shot back. "Carry my name if you wish, and may it bring you health and prosperity."

"Prosperity depends entirely on you, Great Incarnation," Kay retorted happily. "I thank you yet again."

"He is a good choice in spite of his manner," Turi said as Kay, now Ahmose, stalked back to his place. "He will serve you well and faithfully." Ahmose agreed. Signalling to Khabekhnet to announce the ceremony complete, he bade the generals accompany him to the table set up outside his tent, and left the dais.

The remainder of the day was spent in drawing up plans for the rotation of troops. Ahmose divided the divisions of Horus and Ra so that half the complement of men could go home and sow their crops. The rest of Khety's and Kagemni's hosts he put together on the northern mound so that the full number of soldiers comprising a division, five thousand, were always present. He divided up the other divisions in the same way, providing for half his entire force to continue the siege of Het-Uart. As for the eastern Delta, he sent messages granting his generals the power to give leave to as many fighters as possible while still maintaining the security that had been so hard won. "It is now the beginning of the second week of Tybi," he said. "If the first complement of men go home and sow and then return, leaving their women to tend the new crops, it might be possible to release the rest in time for them to finish their share of the same task. Tybi is followed by Mekhir, the month when most of the sowing is done, and then Phamenoth and Pharmuthi before the season of Shemu when the time of our greatest heat and aridity begins. I do not expect a military offensive from the enemy during Shemu this year. I know that it is traditionally the time for battle, but where will more Setiu troops come from? Not from the east. That flow has been stopped. Not from the northern mound. We have taken that. Het-Uart itself does not support enough soldiers to face us again. It is only a matter of months, I think, before Apepa surrenders."

"I cannot quite grasp the fact that, but for one miserable piece of ground, Egypt is back in the hands of Egyptians," Turi remarked. "After so much misery it seems unreal."

"It will be real enough when the King stands in the palace at Het-Uart before the Horus Throne and gives the order to take it south," Paheri replied. "What of the navy, Majesty?" Ahmose gave him an apologetic smile.

"Many ships have sustained damage during the boarding at the hands of Pezedkhu's men," he answered. "Those ships that need repair, together with their crew, must go back to Nekheb. Kay and you or Baba Abana can go with them. Both of you know shipbuilding. So one of you will be going home while the other stays here. I need the tributary patrolled, even during the lowest ebb of the river. No citizen of the city must be allowed to leave or enter. Cull out those men you do not need and send them to their villages for the spring sowing. I leave those decisions up to the pair of you." Both men nodded sagely. Ahmose stood to signal that the meeting was over and all rose after him. "I must go back to Weset myself with the Medjay," Ahmose finished, "but I will stay here until the middle of Tybi to receive your final reports and I will of course leave heralds with each of you so that we may speak to one another on papyrus."

The truth is that I am strangely reluctant to go home, he said to himself as he watched them wander away in little groups, discussing the situation as they went with an avidity and relief that was apparent in their easy gait. I do not want to arrive there in time for my daughter's funeral when I have already been drained of all pity and regret by the death of my soldiers. I do not want to meet Aahmes-nefertari's new scribe. I do not want to hear of the fine work Prince Sebek-nakht and my wife have been accomplishing together. Life with the army has been robust and simple and I dread a return to the complexities of my household. Or is it just that I dread coming face to face with Aahmes-nefertari for fear that the welter of jealousy and possessiveness I have been able to keep in check will erupt once more?

I have the gloomy feeling that I will be returning to a very different Weset to the one I left six months ago.

Ramose had been standing quietly at his elbow and now interrupted his reverie. "And what of me, Ahmose?" he asked gently. "If you give me a choice I will stay here, you know that." With an effort Ahmose turned to him.

"Yes," he answered. "But I want you to go back to Khemmenu where you belong. Take over the estate and the governorship that is yours. If the siege is not broken by the beginning of Thoth I will be back here, in this same spot, and you with me. Until then, get about some other business and forget the tarnished treasure Het-Uart holds!" He had spoken with a growing irritation, all at once seeing Ramose's constancy as a weak, rather pitiful thing. Ramose looked at him sharply.

"I will obey you, of course," he said simply. "I seem to have annoyed you. I apologize." Ahmose's shoulders slumped.

"No, it is not you," he admitted. "To tell you the truth, Ramose, I am loath to go back to my southern responsibilities myself. I have become someone different these last few months. If I could look forward to some peaceful fishing, a few afternoons at target practice, a jug or two of wine at dinner and then nights without anxiety I might not feel this … this shrinking." Ramose did not reply. He touched his friend briefly on the shoulder, bowed, and was gone.

Ahmose stood for a long while, feet apart, arms folded, eyes on the walls of the city that soared up into the dusky scarlet of an evening sky. The air was soft. Little zephyrs blew around him, stirring the hem of his kilt against his thighs and brushing across his cheek. Between his isolated and guarded tent and those red-tinged defences, his army sprawled, its members weaving patterns of orderliness in the usual apparent chaos. Licks of new flame began to prick the increasing dimness as the cooking fires were kindled.

Hent-ta-Hent is gone, Ahmose thought. Pezedkhu is gone. The Feather of Ma'at quivers and once again the colours and configurations within this living picture that is my life and Egypt's destiny shift into alien shapes to which I must conform. And there sits Het-Uart, enveloped in the sullen silence of a vanquished beast that is mortally wounded but refuses to die. He remained lost in contemplation until the light from the tent behind him became stronger than the fading strength of Ra.

8

AAHMES-NEFERTARI WOKE EARLY, coming to full consciousness with a thrill of anticipation. The scroll still lay on the table beside her couch where she had placed it after reading it for the hundredth time the night before. Today he is coming home, she thought, swinging her feet onto the cold tiled floor. It will not be this morning, but at some hour I will be dictating to Khunes perhaps, or giving the audience to Tetaky that I arranged, or walking beside the water with Ahmose-onkh, and a herald will approach to say that his ship is rounding the bend in the Nile. I will call out the household. We will gather above the watersteps, all of us full of excitement, and there he will be, standing in the prow with the Followers behind. Our eyes will meet. He will be smiling. Oh gods, how wonderful. Ahmose is coming home. I will not be able to settle to anything until I hold him in my arms again.

Calling softly to Senehat, she took up a cloak, went to the window, and rolled up the reed hanging. Cool air flowed over her at once and the drowsy music of the dawn chorus came muted to her ears from the still-shadowed trees of the garden. It was too early even for the gardeners and the dewy expanse of lawn running away below her was empty. Shivering a little, she turned back into the room as her body servant entered and bowed sleepily, her black hair tangled and her shift crumpled. "It is a beautiful morning, Senehat," Aahmes-nefertari smiled. "Go and see if the water is heating in the bath house. Tell Neb-Amun that I want to be shaved as well as massaged after my bath and he is to put lotus essence in the oil. Bring me food while I wait, and send Uni to me as soon as he has dressed."

The girl bowed and departed and Aahmes-nefertari began to pace, trying to keep her mind centred on the tasks of the coming day but unable to see past the familiar delineations of her husband's face. In the months since he had left for the north, after laying such responsibilities on her shoulders that sometimes she despaired of her ability to carry them all, she had often solaced herself with memories. At first her imagination had supplied her with consistently clear pictures, but as the weeks fled by she had found to her distress that her husband's presence became more nebulous, his body, his laugh, his gestures more difficult to conjure. His letters had revived him temporarily, but more and more she had found herself remembering the remembering, two steps removed from experience itself.

Hent-ta-Hent's death had sealed that severing. He had not been there, had not seen the child tossing in a torrent of sweat, had not heard her cries rising above Amunmose's chanting in a room full of the smoke of incense and the intimation of disaster. He had not held those tiny fingers as the warmth of life slowly receded from them, and when Aahmes-nefertari had turned in anguish and loss from the drenched and rumpled cot with its pathetic burden, there had been no strong arms to enfold her pain. No matter what his own feelings might have been when he read her account of his daughter's dying, they could not match her own. She had seen the tiny chest rise and collapse for the last time. He had not. He would be present at the funeral. Hent-ta-Hent's mourning period would not end for another week. But that was not the same.

They had been separated many times before. The years of Kamose's war had been a series of agonizing farewells interspersed with brief periods of reunion tinged with the fear of an uncertain future. But through those years they had each changed little, growing slowly. Kamose's murder and the subsequent purges had shocked them both towards an accelerated maturity that had ripened while they were apart. Ahmose had placed in her left hand a mountain of obligations and in her right the power to discharge them. Together they had created an explosion of fatigue, anxiety, grim willfulness and a burgeoning authority, from which a capable Queen had been born. Aahmes-nefertari was fully aware of what she had become. She doubted if her husband was.

Yet on this morning, this momentous morning, his face was there in all its clarity before her mind's eye as it had not been for many months and with it came a welling-up of love that quickened her heartbeat and reddened her cheeks. She had been lonely and bereaved, one-half of a marvellous whole that would once more be united, and she breathed prayers of gratitude to Amun and Hathor as she measured out the confines of her bedchamber.

It was not Senehat, however, who knocked on her door, but Ahmose-onkh. He came trotting in completely naked, a slab of fresh bread in one hand and a candied date in the other, and made straight for the window, standing on tiptoe to peer over the sill. "Ra has begun to climb in the sky and the gardeners are out there now but they are standing about talking," he said. "They should be setting up the canopies. What if Father comes before we are ready?" Aahmes-nefertari dismissed both the contemplation of her husband and the doubts that lay behind it.

"There is plenty of time," she chided her son. "A herald will arrive first and there will be ceremonies at the watersteps before we feast together. Calm down, Ahmose-onkh, or you will be in tears or trouble before noon. Eat that date, and do not touch anything with your sticky fingers until you have been washed." The child crammed the date into his mouth, chewing furiously, and as he did so both Raa and Uni appeared in the doorway. "Raa, I have told you many times not to allow him to run about naked," Aahmes-nefertari said in exasperation as the nurse took Ahmose-onkh by the wrist after many apologetic bows. "He is too old for that. Dress him formally today and try to keep him clean."

"I am sorry, Majesty," Raa said. "He has an uncanny ability to disappear the moment I turn my back."

"I know." Aahmes-nefertari bent and kissed the top of his shaven head, sliding her fingers through the long rope of hair straggling loose over his right shoulder. "Give him into the care of his guard. He can shoot his little arrows at the trees in the garden. Or see if one of the under-stewards will toss a ball for him. I don't think he will want to sleep this afternoon."

"He is almost ready for a tutor," Raa grumbled. "He needs to put his energy into learning instead of racing about impeding the house servants and bothering the brickmakers."

"I do learn, Raa!" Ahmose-onkh protested as he was led into the passage. "The brickmakers have been showing me how to mix the mud and the straw and scoop it into the moulds."

"You are a Prince. You should not be mixing so readily with commoners." Raa's voice was growing fainter. "I will have a word with your guard who it seems to me enjoys gossiping with the labourers too much …" Aahmes-nefertari sighed and gave her attention to Uni who had been waiting with an impassive patience.

"She is correct, Majesty," he said. "The Prince loves to pat the wet mud and watch the straw being chopped but it is not a suitable pastime for a Hawk-in-the-Nest." Aahmes-nefertari grimaced.

"I know, Uni, but I have been too busy to do more than kiss him good night," she admitted. "I must give the matter some thought. He is an intelligent child. Is it too soon for a tutor?"

"I can ask Yuf to assess his readiness," Uni replied. "Queen Aahotep will not mind. Yuf is to go to Djeb soon to inspect the tomb of her ancestor Queen Sebekemsaf and until then his duties will be light."

"Well, I cannot concern myself with Ahmose-onkh today," Aahmes-nefertari told him. "Speak to Yuf, if you like. It is a good idea. Raa loves her charge but he is continually wriggling out of her grasp and she is becoming exhausted. Come in, Senehat." The girl slipped past the bulk of the steward and began to set the morning meal upon the table. The aroma of freshly baked bread sprinkled with sesame seeds filled the room and all at once Aahmes-nefertari was ravenous. "Send to Emkhu out at the barracks," she went on addressing Uni. "I will speak with him later this morning regarding a parade in the King's honour. Tell Prince Sebek-nakht that no work is to be done on the old palace today and he must hold himself in readiness to greet Ahmose. Summon the Overseer of Grain. I want to talk to him after I have given audience to Tetaky. Send to Amunmose. He is invited to the feast tonight. Neferperet also. I hope that Ahmose approves my appointment of him as Chief Treasurer."

"Majesty, you have worked wonders in the months the King has been away," Uni said, and Aahmes-nefertari knew that the man had sensed the hesitation behind her words. "If His Majesty does not like what you have done, he will change it, but I do not think he will be displeased. Weset is flourishing under your care."

"Under my whip, you mean!" Aahmes-nefertari laughed. "Keep a close watch on the preparations for the festivities, Uni. I want nothing to go wrong. We are celebrating more than the King's return. We acclaim his triumph over the Setiu also." She paused and met his steady gaze. "It has all been like a dream, has it not?" she said quietly. "I look back to the day that insulting letter came to my father, the one in which Apepa complained that the hippopotamuses in our marshes were disturbing his sleep with their coughing. Father was just a southern Prince then, a nothing in the eyes of Egypt's conquerors in spite of his royal lineage. That was not so long ago. Sometimes I expect to wake up and find myself in my old quarters with Tani still asleep in the cot beside me and Father's voice wafting through the window-hanging from the garden outside." She shrugged. "I am overwhelmed by the unreality of what this family has achieved and I cannot believe that I am now the Queen of Egypt."

"There is still Het-Uart," the steward said smoothly. Aahmes-nefertari snorted, and waving him away she moved to the table.

"Trust you to grasp my ankles and pull me back towards the ground!" she responded without malice. "Get about your business, Uni. Senehat, you may serve me now."

After she had eaten, she went to the bath house to be scrubbed and then shaved, plucked and kneaded with perfumed oil. Lying on the wooden bench while the man's sure hands dug into her muscles and the heady scent of the lotus filled her nostrils, she thought of Uni, his perceptiveness, his trustworthiness in spite of his Setiu ancestry, and how she had come to rely on his judgement and quiet support. Akhtoy would be returning with Ahmose and would want to resume his place as Chief Steward. She did not relish the idea. Uni ran the household as she liked it to be run, efficiently and tactfully. He was firm but fair with the servants. He shielded her from unnecessary details. He was an observer. Standing behind her chair while she interviewed those she was considering for various posts, he would make his own assessments of their suitability and they seldom disagreed with her own. She did not always ask his opinion, but when she did, he gave it without dissembling.

I do not want Akhtoy to change all that, she thought, as wrapped in a sheet she made her way back to her quarters and sat down before her cosmetics table. I do not want the two of them glaring at each other over my head as I try to make decisions that will affect the whole of Egypt. But you will no longer be doing that, the other voice, the one she was desperately attempting to restrain, reminded her bleakly. Ahmose will. He delegated his power to you while he was away, but the moment he steps from his ship it reverts to him. You will have to learn co-operation, Queen Aahmes-nefertari! You will have to bite your tongue if his judgement seems less sound than yours.

But why should it? she asked herself as her cosmetician lifted the surface of the table to reveal the compartments full of face paints beneath. We have always been partners, Ahmose and I, keeping no secrets from one another, sharing the making of difficult decisions. What do I really fear? Not the loss of my authority, for Ahmose has always respected my reasoning and listened to my arguments. Perhaps it is merely the suspicion that in the exercise of his own power, male power, not blunted by my presence, he has become arrogant. His letters have been brisk. Almost cold. Because he has been preoccupied and hard-pressed or because he is beginning to resent me?

Or because ... She held her breath against the sharp pain that knifed through her chest. Because I have not given him a healthy male child as I did for Si-Amun? Why should I believe that he is any different from other Kings in needing to guarantee a peaceful succession? As a Prince he did not care about such things and we were utterly united. But as a King, with nothing but a stepson and no daughter now to carry the royal blood, does he see danger and put the blame on me? But I am young yet, and so is he. There will be time for more children, male and female. Oh gods, Aahmes-nefertari, stop thinking. Stop thinking!

"What colour are you wearing today, Majesty?" the cosmetician enquired. He had finished brushing her face with the yellow ochre and was fingering the kohl pots.

"Scarlet," she said impulsively. Yes, scarlet, she told herself, brilliant in the sun, and gold and lapis so that he is dazzled and sees nothing but me.

"Then I will oil your lids and sprinkle them with gold dust and use the black kohl," he decided. "Close your eyes."

When he had finished his work, he handed her the copper mirror and she stared at her burnished reflection carefully. Am I still beautiful? she asked the face that looked back at her so pensively. The full, red-hennaed lips parted in misgiving and the kohl-rimmed dark eyes under the shimmering lids were solemn. Will he still want me? Laying the mirror back in its case, she thanked the man with a nod and dismissed him.

Senehat dressed her in a scarlet sheath that fell in soft, gold-shot folds from her shoulders to her brown ankles. A wide collar of bands of gold, lapis and jasper encircled her neck. Cobras of gold with lapis eyes twisted through her earlobes. The wig she chose was unbraided, a thick fall of black hair resting in three segments, one down her back and one in front of each collarbone, and she surmounted it with a coronet of gold from which a tiny likeness of the vulture goddess Mut, patroness of Queens, hung on her forehead. Senehat pushed bracelets of gold over her wrists and red leather sandals set with lapis beads between the toes of her hennaed feet. Lastly the palms of her hands were painted with red henna before she put on her rings, and as she was doing so Uni came in. "The mayor of Weset has arrived together with your Overseer of Grain," he said. "They are waiting in the reception hall. Khunes has already gone there."

"Good." Aahmes-nefertari lifted her shoulders under the weight of the jewelled collar. "Have my litter ready to take me to the barracks after I have dealt with them," she said. "Where are Mother and Grandmother this morning?"

"Queen Aahotep has gone to the temple with Yuf and Queen Tetisheri is having her canopy erected near the watersteps." A small smile quirked his mouth. "She does not want to miss the King's arrival."

"Very well. Then let us start the day."

She liked Tetaky, the mayor of Weset, and enjoyed his regular reports on the state of the city both he and she loved. They talked easily together while Khunes sat cross-legged at her feet, his palette resting on his bare knees, and noted the salient points of the conversation. When it was over, Aahmes-nefertari spent a few minutes discussing the progress of the spring sowing with the Overseer; then she walked with her scribe into the bright mid-morning sunshine and, getting onto her litter, they were carried to the barracks.

Emkhu, the man she had made Captain of the Household Troops, greeted her reverently, following her into the shade of his room and offering her beer, which she declined. She and her mother often came here to watch the soldiers practise their skill with bow and sword or to sit and pass the time with the officers. Both women felt oddly comfortable in such a masculine preserve, perhaps because they had earned the unqualified admiration of the troops during the desperate days following Kamose's assassination, but also, Aahmes-nefertari privately and amusingly surmised, due to the distinct lack of any bracing male presence in the house. Ahmose-onkh did not count, of course. Neither did the servants, and the soldiers on duty in the passages and outside the doors were not expected to pass the time of day.

For an hour she and her Captain discussed the ranking and performance of the guard that would line the path from the watersteps to the house, escort the King through the garden, and line the walls of the reception hall should he arrive too late to feast outside. Aahmes-nefertari was proud of the net of able soldiers she had created and flung around both the estate and the clamorous city, and she wanted Ahmose to approve. So did Emkhu. Reminding him to have his men in position shortly after the noon meal, she and Khunes were conveyed back through the gate in the rear of the wall surrounding the estate, where she dismissed the litter bearers, told Khunes she would send for him later, and walked slowly through the garden towards the watersteps.

In order to reach the old palace it was no longer necessary to slip through a gap in the crumbling wall that used to divide it from the house. The first task Sebek-nakht had undertaken was its safe demolition under his direction, so that now Aahmes-nefertari could glance to her left as she went and see the ancient building gradually revealed with its towering angles, the heaving stones of its vast courtyard and the maze of scaffolding that clung to it. The front of its façade faced west and was still in deep shadow, the rows of columns flanking the great public entrance managing to project a message of silent warning into the gloom.

Halfway between the columns and the perimeter wall Sebek-nakht had set up his table under a permanent canopy, and it was here that he would confer with his junior architects and Aahmes-nefertari herself, the table littered with plans, while the scaffolding swarmed with sweating workmen and load after load of new bricks was trundled past from the pits near the river where Ahmose-onkh liked to play. The whole arena of industry was empty today on the Queen's orders; nevertheless Aahmes-nefertari's eyes were drawn to it as she passed and she thought of her brothers in an age that had gone, climbing through the forbidden rent in a wall that no longer existed to play their secret games, leaving her alone and envious on the other side.

Briefly she glanced up to the roof where the windcatcher still opened its broken mouth towards the north. There her father, and after him Kamose, had sat looking out over the tops of the shuddering palms and the glint of the Nile in quiet deliberation and there Seqenenra had been brutally clubbed and partially paralyzed by Mersu, the Setiu steward whom he had trusted. Quickly Aahmes-nefertari averted her gaze. It would be good to see the palace come alive again, full of bustle and light, the roof merry with the chatter of women spreading colourful carpets under the stars to escape the heat of Shemu. Perhaps then the forlorn ghosts that hung in the dusty corners and sobbed out their pleas for justice would be satisfied.

Tetisheri was enthroned amid a pile of cushions on the grass at the edge of the path. She too was sumptuously arrayed in a white sheath belted and trimmed with gold ankhs. As Aahmes-nefertari approached, she thought how appropriate it was that the woman should wear the sign for Life, since she was nearing her sixty-seventh birthday and showed few signs of decrepitude. Tetisheri, hearing her come, turned a sour, heavily painted face towards her and waved one thin, gold-weighted arm. "Since the protecting wall around our arouras was heightened and extended, there is no view of the watersteps any more," she grumbled.

"If I want to see the Nile, I must order the guards on this side of the new gates to open them, go through, have them closed by the guards on the other side, and then spend less time by the steps than I would like because the soldiers becomevisibly nervous at my presence. It is a considerable nuisance, my dear."

"I know," Aahmes-nefertari offered, stooping to kiss her grandmother on one wrinkled cheek. "I am sorry, Tetisheri. But I was only following Ahmose's orders. If you wanted to, you could go across the courtyard of the old palace and through the opening in the wall there where the new gates will be hung."

"Humph," Tetisheri grunted. Having made her protest, she was appeased. "New gates. He wants electrum, I suppose, for his fine new residence, if we can ever amass so much silver. The gold in the amalgam is no longer a problem since the Kushites have been cowed; indeed, lately it has been flowing into the treasury and the jewellers' workshops with reassuring frequency. Teti the Handsome has been very quiet."

"So my spies tell me." Aahmes-nefertari lowered herself onto the cushions beside the older woman. "But Kush has never lain quiet for very long, unless my history teacher was wrong. I must confess a secret fascination with that mysterious Prince." Her grandmother sniffed.

"Prince? I would not grace a man with a polluted mix of Egyptian and Kushite blood as such," she said. "It would not surprise me if he also had a lick of the Setiu in his veins. Has he not been a staunch ally of Apepa and his father ever since he assumed the chieftainship of his barbaric tribe? Ahmose will do well to keep a steady watch on him."

Aahmes-nefertari did not reply. It would be pointless to remind Tetisheri that the King had been utterly involved in more important matters than the doings of a self-styled ruler many miles to the south, or even that she and Aahotep had woven a net of scouts who brought regular reports of conditions in both Wawat and Kush. To Tetisheri, Ahmose would always be the rather simple younger brother who needed constant advice and admonition.

For a while the two women sat in silence. Then Tetisheri said, "Next month we celebrate your father's birth. We will go to his tomb and offer food, wine and oil. I hope Ahmose remembers without being told."

"Of course he will," Aahmes-nefertari retorted. "But I warn you, Grandmother, do not push him. In one week we bury Hent-ta-Hent and his attention will be fixed on the loss of his daughter. He will not think of Seqenenra until afterwards." She turned to meet Tetisheri's gaze. The kohled eyes, still sharp with intelligence though nested in a myriad of fine lines and hooded by skin as thin and papery as a dried leaf, met her own.

"I know what you are going to say," Tetisheri forestalled her. "That I have never liked or respected your husband, that I live in the past, that I am full of arrogance and an unyielding pride. It is true, and I am sorry, Aahmes-nefertari. Seqenenra was a King. Kamose I adored. There is nothing left for Ahmose, although you must believe me when I say that I try to overcome my prejudice." She waved a skeletal hand at a fly that was attempting to settle on her neck. "One of the curses of encroaching old age is the return of many youthful memories long forgotten, while the events of the near past seem to melt away. I understand what Ahmose has done. But I cannot help looking behind him to the brilliance and desperation and self-sacrifice of his father and brother, without whom Ahmose would have achieved nothing."

"You are speaking of things that might or might not have been," Aahmes-nefertari said, struggling to contain her anger. "Such thoughts are vain and dangerous. You are the only one, the only one, Tetisheri, who has indulged in the fruitless game of what if. If Father and Kamose had fallen into the trap you step into so willingly and so often, we would have accepted Seqenenra's defeat at Pezedkhu's hands and been separated and gone into exile under Kamose. And if my husband did not possess a more complex mind than Kamose, he would not be coming home today leaving Het-Uart a tiny island in an ocean of Egyptian triumph. Seqenenra began our rebellion. Kamose continued it. Ahmose's task is to complete it. Why can you not see the harmonious weaving of Ma'at in the different destinies of all three precious lives?" She got up and smoothed down her sheath with stiff fingers. "History will pity Seqenenra and vilify Kamose because what he had to do will not be understood. But future generations will worship my husband as Egypt's saviour. What they will say of you I cannot guess. Perhaps that she was beautiful in her youth." An expression of pain twisted the dignified old features and Aahmes-nefertari knew that she had gone too far. Squatting, she took Tetisheri's face in both her hands. "Forgive me, Grandmother," she begged. "That was unfair."

"But probably true." Tetisheri pulled herself out of Aahmes-nefertari's grasp. "I sit here waiting for him so that I can be the first to greet him, so that I can capture his attention, so that he will see me, be conscious of me," she said hoarsely. "I am not stupid, Aahmes-nefertari. I know that he deliberately excluded me from the strategy meetings he held with you and your mother, that in response to my dislike of him he has firmly but politely relegated me to the women's quarters, that in his own gentle but entirely implacable way he has taken away any power I might have exercised. It is my own fault, yet I cannot conjure a warmth for him that is not there."

"Then do not try." Aahmes-nefertari sighed and straightened. "You are his grandmother and as such you have his respect. Do not weaken it by dishonesty. Remember that his blood is yours and he is the King." She looked down at her grandmother's distress. "Kamose recognized his ability to rule," she said harshly. "Kamose knew that he himself would not have made a good King. He was a warrior. He was fated to die by violence and he knew that too. If he had lived, his reign would have been an increasingly ruthless one. He fulfilled his destiny, Tetisheri. It was not the one you would have chosen for him, but your love for him blinded you to his faults, although he saw them clearly. Ahmose was born to restore Egypt to peace and prosperity. Not as glorious a fate as that of a commander who gives his life in the struggle for his country. That is how you see it, is it not?" She paused. Tetisheri was staring expressionlessly at the ground. "You were not born a man and neither was I," she finished in a burst of sudden insight. "We cannot wield the sword or don the Double Crown. Only despair waits for you if you allow the bitterness of your sex to consume you, Grandmother. Ahmose is King. If you will only leave your self-absorption behind you and give thanks for his divinity, you will find in him a kind and forgiving grandson as well."

Turning on her heel, she strode towards the new gate, and seeing her approach the guards swung it wide. I should not blame her for my own private resentment, she thought as she walked through. In berating her I realize that I was castigating myself. Thus I myself am warned. I am not the Son of the Sun. I am not a warrior. Yet I am a Queen, and with that I will be content. Amun forbid that I should end my life swimming in a hot sea of self-pity like Tetisheri!

"Majesty, you should not take the river path unescorted," one of the soldiers called as she set off in the direction of the temple. "The citizens of Weset are already congregating along the bank to see the King arrive. You might be jostled." I might be jostled. Aahmes-nefertari smiled to herself. Not so long ago I might have been the target of an assassin, but today my august person might be jostled. Yet she remembered what Ahmose had said on the last occasion she and he had strolled by the river together, that it was not good for royalty to be so nakedly visible, so approachable to commoners.

"Two of you come with me then," she conceded reluctantly. "I do not intend to go all the way to the temple. I just want to watch the Nile." And to get away from the frenetic preparations going on in the house, she said to herself as the men swung in behind her and she began to tread the beaten track that wound between the high wall of the estate and the spring verdure edging the river. She sensed their disapproval. They think I should be sequestered behind the curtains of my litter, her thoughts ran on. I daresay Senehat would agree with them. My feet will need washing and softening after the dust of the path.

Her sudden desire for seclusion was thwarted, however. As the soldier had predicted, the people of Weset were pouring out of a city that now surrounded the temple and spread in all its tumultuous sprawl to the boundary of the royal precincts. Chattering groups of men, women and children were crowding the path, anxious to be first to take the best positions along the bank, from which they would have a clear view of Ahmose's flotilla when it hove into sight. It was not a gods' feast day, Aahmes-nefertari reflected with resignation, but as if by universal agreement no one seemed to be working.

Seeing her come, the noise gradually faltered and died away only to resume excitedly behind her. Knees were bent, foreheads touched the earth as she passed, and in a wave of affection her name was shouted with none of her titles preceding it, as though she were being hailed by friends.

She was about to turn back in sheer frustration, when she heard a commotion some way ahead and, peering beyond the lattice of shade and sunlight cast by the arching arms of the sycamore and flowering acacia, she saw heads lowered and backs bent but not in her direction. She halted, her heart suddenly jumping into her throat. Figures were coming towards her, dappled by moving shadow, their strides confident, their voices deep and commanding as they talked to each other. Around them a roar of acclamation had broken out. "The King! It is His Majesty! Long life to you, Mighty Horus!" Aahmes-nefertari's heart constricted. Then she was running, past Khabekhnet's imposing height, dodging the dark column that was Hor-Aha, almost colliding with a startled Ipi, until her outstretched arms closed around her husband and his pectoral was pressing into her cheek.

There was a moment when he was taken aback. She could tell by his slight recoil. Then with a chuckle of delight his own arms encircled her, strong masculine arms, crushing her, enfolding her in safety, protection, making her feel tiny and cherished and entirely one with him. For several long seconds she rested against him, unwilling to move, but in the end he moved her away gently, holding her shoulders and smiling down at her. "Majesty, Second Prophet, my own Aahmes-nefertari," he said. "What are you doing out here with no attendants save a couple of soldiers?" She smiled back at him widely, stupidly, drinking in the warmth of his dark eyes, the dearly familiar contours of his face, thinner now, more angular, but the same wide jaw and broad brow under the golden band of his winged headdress.

"Ahmose," she breathed while the men beside him did her reverence. "I could ask the same of you. My household guards are even now lining the garden avenue to salute you as you disembark. Where have you come from? Where are your ships?"

"Oh, I decided to say a quick prayer of thanks to Amun for my victory in the north before I came to the house," he explained. "There will be a full and formal sacrifice made later, of course, but I wanted my first words here to be to the god. It was good to see Amunmose again. As for the ships, my *Shining in Mennofer* is already right behind us and the Medjay not far away." Aahmes-nefertari took one step back, already battling the fume of disappointment and offence rising in her. Am I not dearer to you than the Chief

Priest? she wanted to shout. Do you not know how I have longed to greet you, spent the hours since your letter imagining how you would fly to me with singleminded purpose, your own mind full of nothing but the desire to see me? Have I not impressed you with my scarlet sheath, my new jewels, the message they are intended to convey? Yet you have not really looked at me! With an effort of the will she linked her arm through his.

"The whole household is in a fever of excitement," she said with a forced cheerfulness. "Tetisheri took up her station just inside the gates above the watersteps hours ago. Mother went to the temple early with Yuf so that she would be back by the time you arrived. You should have seen her there. She must have decided to take her litter through the city and re-enter the estate by the servants' entrance. Such a clamour there, too! The kitchen staff began to prepare your feast at dawn!" She found that once she had begun to babble she could not stop. Her mouth opened and closed on words she hardly heard, while inside herself she watched that deadly smoke of resentment gradually thicken. "Hor-Aha," she called to the General's bare spine just ahead. "Where is your hair? Did a Setiu sword lop off your braids?" He gave her a tight smile over his shoulder.

"No, Majesty," he said tonelessly. "I cut them off myself." It was no explanation and all at once Aahmes-nefertari felt like an idiot. The flow of what was almost hysteria in her abruptly dried up. She clenched her teeth.

The press of citizens fell behind them as they neared the watersteps. Aahmes-nefertari saw her husband's gaze lifted wonderingly to the top of the new wall as the remaining gate guards came to attention and saluted. "I hope it has been constructed as you wished, Ahmose," she said. "Its height raised all around our arouras and this gate set in it." She pointed farther along, but Ahmose had halted and was staring through the nearer aperture where the palace gates would one day hang.

"Gods!" he breathed. "Look at this, Hor-Aha! Time has moved more swiftly here than in the north or I have been under some magic spell from which I have only just awoken! The interior wall that used to divide us from the ancient precincts has gone. I can see my garden. The scaffolding … The stacks of bricks …" He seemed bewildered, one hand coming up to tremble slightly on his wife's imprisoned forearm.

"Ahmose, you sent me Sebek-nakht to begin these tasks," Aahmes-nefertari said urgently. "Is it not to your liking? Have we done wrong?" He shook his head.

"No, no!" he exclaimed. "It is wonderful! It is just that my thoughts have been so fully engaged elsewhere, Aahmes-nefertari, and even now I am finding it difficult to drag them away from Het-Uart." He smiled across at her as they moved on, his whole face alight. "I can hardly wait to discuss it all with the Prince. What other miracles is he achieving?"

"There is the new compound for the divisions you intend to quarter here permanently of course," Aahmes-nefertari reminded him, inwardly stung. And what of me? she thought, humiliated. Have I not stood day after day with Sebek-nakht while we thrashed out the plans for your palace, O King? Did I not accord the Prince every courtesy on your orders, seeing to his every comfort, making myself available to him for your sake? I have grown to like and respect him and he in turn has often incorporated my ideas into his vision. There is no room for you. Shocked at the vindictiveness of her unspoken thought, she was relieved to be distracted by the gate guards who ushered them through into the garden and closed the heavy doors behind them.

Emkhu had followed her command. The household troops were now ranked to either side of the path that led through the lawns, past the pond, and disappeared behind the house, their short kilts dazzling in the sunshine, the strong light glinting off the tips of their spears and the bronze buckles of their sword belts. Their leather sandals and helmets gleamed with oil. They were a magnificent sight and Aahmes-nefertari felt a rush of pride as she scanned them. She heard Khabekhnet call the time-honoured warning, "The King approaches! Down on your faces!" and with one accord the men turned, saluting Ahmose with the cry of "Majesty!" while Emkhu himself came forward, knelt, and kissed Ahmose's feet. Without thinking, Aahmes-nefertari bade him rise, saw him hesitate, and heard Ahmose's permission mingle with her own. She bit her lip.

"Majesty, this is Emkhu, our Captain of the Household Guards," she said carefully. "He comes from Birabi, the village on the western bank behind the cliffs. He and his father fought under Seqenenra. His father was killed." Ahmose inclined his head.

"You have an impressive array of soldiery there," he observed kindly. "How many men now guard my house?"

"Thank you, Majesty," Emkhu replied. "At present Her Majesty commands two hundred troops. One hundred patrol the house and grounds, the gates to front and rear, and the outside perimeter of the wall. One hundred stand down. But all two hundred of them are here to do you homage today." Ahmose cast a sidelong glance at his wife.

"She does, does she?" he murmured wryly. "But of course she does. I myself gave her that authority. Carry on, Emkhu." The Captain bowed and shouted and the men turned into the path once more. "They are a fine show, Aahmes-nefertari," he went on. "You have done well with them. You must teach me all their names and individual skills if they rotate their watches inside the house." It was the voice and tone of a younger Ahmose, ingenuous and considerate, and in a rush of gratitude Aahmes-nefertari stood on tiptoe and kissed his warm cheek.

She would have spoken, but Tetisheri had emerged from between the stiff lines of soldiery and was walking quickly towards them in a pool of shadow cast by the sunshade Isis was holding over her head. She was smiling. Coming up to Ahmose, she bowed shortly. "Welcome home, Majesty," she said. "I wanted to be the first member of the family apart from my granddaughter to congratulate you on your great victory over the accursed ones. It will not be long now before Het-Uart throws open its gates and Apepa crawls out to beg for mercy at your feet." She had begun her speech mildly enough, but it had become more animated as it went on, her fingers stabbing the sparkling air, her eyes flashing. Ahmose burst out laughing. Lifting her off the ground, he crushed her in a hug before setting her unsteadily on her feet again.

"In the midst of so much change you at least have remained the same, Grandmother," he beamed. "Egypt should proclaim the Djed Pillar a symbol of your unyielding spine instead of Osiris's. I'm so glad that you can still snarl as fiercely as Sekhmet."

"As long as I do not growl at you, I suppose," she grumbled, not unpleased. She fell in beside him, imprisoning his other arm, not bothering to acknowledge Hor-Aha's presence at all. "I want to know all about the siege and the battles. Everything," she went on, as the three of them progressed along the path between the rigid soldiers. "Come to my quarters this evening, Ahmose, and tell me all about it." Her blatant desire to appropriate him was embarrassing and Aahmes-nefertari felt him withdraw from her imperceptibly.

"Tonight I owe to my wife," he rebuked Tetisheri gently. "But tomorrow I will indeed give you as full an account of my doings in the north as you could wish." You owe me tonight? Aahmes-nefertari thought with renewed depression. How flattering to consider time spent with me as the paying of a debt! What is wrong with you, my husband?

The path ran on beside the house but the small cavalcade turned in towards the row of pillars that marked the great entrance. Here the servants were gathered to reverence him, Kares and Uni among them. He greeted them all with undiluted pleasure, telling them how happy he was to be among them again and dismissing them with the grave politeness he had always brought to his dealings with them. As they scattered, Aahmes-nefertari crooked a finger at Khunes, who had been standing off to one side. "Majesty, this is my personal scribe, Khunes," she offered. "He was trained in the temple of Thoth at Aabtu and I found him working for Amunmose. It was Amunmose who recommended him to me and he has proved himself very able."

Her mouth had gone suddenly dry and she swallowed several times. Why am I justifying my work and my choices to him? she wondered. From whence does this urge to placate him come? It has never been a part of our joining before. Ahmose was studying the young man impassively but deliberately, his gaze almost discourteous. Finally and surprisingly, he sighed.

"You are very handsome, Khunes," he said slowly. "If you perform your duties as favourably as you look, then you must indeed be a paragon of all Thoth's virtues." Khunes was obviously nonplussed. He bowed.

"Thank you, Majesty," he stammered. "As for my physical self I am as the gods saw fit to make me. My skill as a scribe is Her Majesty's to assess." Aahmes-nefertari, watching her husband in puzzlement, saw him open his mouth to say something more. But he closed it again, and passing between the lowering pillars he strode into the reception hall.

Several men were clustered at the far end beneath the dais. They turned as he came in, but between him and them Ahmose-onkh and Aahotep hurried forward. Aahmes-nefertari had expected her son to take the last few steps towards Ahmose at a run, but the boy retained a certain touching dignity, holding his little head high, his expression suitably solemn, his huge dark eyes ringed in kohl fixed soberly on the King. Gold cord had been plaited into his youth lock and a necklet of golden crescent moons and tiny baboons, symbols of Khons the son of Mut and Amun, rested against his childish collarbones. Coming up to Ahmose he halted, raised his hennaed palms, and performed a deep obeisance. "It is good to see you again, Great Horus my father," he said, his high, clear voice ringing out into the dusky expanse. "I trust that you are well and that the Setiu are not?" Off to one side Raa was smiling proudly. Aahmes-nefertari studied his perfect little face with a lump of pride in her throat. Ahmose made no attempt to embrace his stepson and Aahmes-nefertari secretly applauded her husband's tact. Instead he bent down and held out his own hand.

"It is good to see you also, my Hawk-in-the-Nest," he replied. "I am indeed well and the Setiu are not." A grin hovered on Ahmose-onkh's face. Taking Ahmose's fingers, he pressed his mouth to them with a regal flourish then whispered, "Was my letter properly dictated, Father? The bit that I wrote myself—was it correct?"

"It brought me great joy and also much sorrow, Ahmose-onkh," Ahmose answered. "But you realize that from now on, whenever I am away, I shall expect more messages from you." The grin broke into full flower.

"Indeed it will be my privilege," Ahmose-onkh said, and as though the effort of so much formality had exhausted him, he ran to Raa and buried his face in the folds of her sheath.

Aahotep approached him gravely and they embraced without awkwardness, Ahmose closing his eyes and visibly relaxing against her before they broke apart. "You at least have not changed, Mother," he said to her with evident relief. "You are still the loom on which the pattern of our family's life is woven and I have dreaded seeing illness or aging in you after long separations." She smiled faintly, then gave a short laugh.

"Oh, Ahmose, you can be so absurd sometimes!" she chided him. "I appreciate the compliment. You yourself look tired. You need to be here, to rest. I think this is the first time in years that you will be able to do so without facing some crisis or other. Aahmes-nefertari and I have been faithful regents without you. There is nothing here to worry about." She stepped aside, allowing him to cover the remaining stretch of tiled floor to where the group of silent dignitaries waited.

Aahmes-nefertari took a deep breath as the men bowed. "Majesty, when you went north, you placed upon me the responsibility for governing your city and the Uas nome," she began cautiously, speaking directly into his face. "In order to do so it has been necessary to expand the number of administrators in your employ. With peace in the south has come a growing prosperity, and prosperity requires sage management and regulation if it is not to degenerate into a happy chaos." She paused, watching him intently, but there was no indication of anything but interest on his features. "Your mother and I were able to control all the aspects of such development for a while. But with Weset expanding, with gold beginning to come up from Wawat with increasing regularity, with all the building you required, we could no longer find enough hours in the day to oversee everything." He nodded. His gaze had shifted from her to the patient men and he had begun to scrutinize them warily. "For some time I continued to perform my duties as Second Prophet of Amun, command the household troops personally, and assist Aahotep in running our domestic affairs," she went on. "But then Sebek-nakht arrived, the spring sowing was due to begin, I was still attempting to compile the list of suitable men you wanted placed with the Princes of other nomes, and I realized that it was time to discard the notion that I was mistress of a small estate beside a sleepy southern town. That is how it used to be in our father's time. That is how the Setiu saw us." She crooked a finger at one of the men. He came forward smoothly, his long, silver-bordered tunic swirling around his ankles. "This is no longer the estate of a Prince," Aahmes-nefertari pointed out. "It is becoming the court of a King, and with Aahotep's advice I have selected the officials I desperately needed to relieve me, and now you, Majesty, of the need to be actually involved in such matters as assessing grain for the sowing or ensuring that the hundreds of artisans, peasants and masons now under our cloak are organized well and paid correctly. I meet with them every morning here in the reception hall to listen to their reports. Sebek-nakht has designed a row of offices for them and their assistants adjoining the rear of the old palace. At the moment it is not very convenient to have them there, but when we move into the palace they will be close at hand." He was still watching them, eyes narrowed, his body very still. Aahmes-nefertari could not judge what he might be thinking, and all at once she feared him. The emotion was so new to her that she almost gasped aloud. "This is Neferperet, your new Chief Treasurer," she went on, struggling against the urge to shrink away from him as though he had uttered some startling threat. "I have placed Neshi, Kamose's Treasurer, in charge of the temple treasury. Neferperet will now handle the accounting of all our revenues. He can tell you the weight and disposition of every speck of gold dust that has fallen into our hands during the last six months as well as our expenditures. He was in the employ of the mayor of Weset and had control of all the city's wealth. I examined his records myself. He is conscientious and trustworthy." Neferperet bowed again.

Ahmose continued to stare at him, a speculative expression growing on his face. Finally his fingers came up and curled protectively around the pectoral on his breast. "Tell me, Neferperet," he said brightly. "I intend to quarter two of my divisions, Amun and Ra, on permanent alert here at Weset. Ten thousand men to be fed every day. I presume you already know this. Their barracks are being raised on land just south of this house. Am I able to support them and my court," he stumbled over that word, "with grain and vegetables from my own arouras?" Neferperet's eyes took fire. He frowned, chewing his lip, and one hand began to tap absently against his thigh.

"No, Majesty," he said. "Your land will produce enough food for your servants and administrators but not for your soldiers. However, each year I will assess the reports from your Overseer of Granaries, Overseer of Vineyards and Overseer of Cattle, who will in turn receive their reports from Egypt's towns and villages, and I will suggest an appropriate tax based on the level of the flood and the health of the subsequent crops. There is also of course the income that Your Majesty may expect from the renewed trade negotiations with the Keftiu, who have already expressed a desire to send a delegation to Weset, and I believe Her Majesty has also sent your Overseer of Trade to Asi so there may be some fruit from that in the future. As for Wawat and Kush …" Ahmose cut him short.

"My Overseer of Trade," he said heavily. "My Overseer of Granaries and Overseer of Vineyards and Overseer of Cattle." He turned to his wife. "Gods, Aahmes-nefertari, you have been crafting a complete revolution here while I have been slaughtering the Setiu."

"Not a revolution, Ahmose," she responded quickly. "A peaceful flowering. A blooming. The old order was not working any more."

"Well," he sighed. "Bring forward these overseers. They will make a change from conversing with generals."

For another hour, while Khabekhnet, Ipi and the members of the family waited, Ahmose questioned the men Aahmes-nefertari had selected so carefully to form the core of what amounted to a new order for Egypt. A yawning Ahmose-onkh was taken away for his afternoon sleep. Occasionally a servant or herald would appear, consult Aahmes-nefertari in whispers, then disappear again. She herself hardly heard them. Anxiously her attention was fixed on her husband, his gestures, the tone of his voice, the series of expressions that flitted across his face. Once she saw his forefinger creep to the scar behind his ear and she knew that he was either becoming tired or was irritated with whatever Amuniseneb, her Overseer of Granaries, was saying so earnestly.

But at last he dismissed them all with a wave and came striding back. "I am thirsty and my head has begun to ache," he said wryly. "There is much here for a King to try to understand, Aahmes-nefertari, but for now I want to see my own quarters again and lie on the comfort of my own couch in peace and quiet. I presume that the Medjay have arrived by now, seeing that Hor-Aha has gone, and surely my ship is tethered at the watersteps." He graced Aahmes-nefertari with a lopsided grin. "It has been a curious home-coming," was his parting comment. She and Aahotep watched him walk to the door in the far wall beside the dais that led into the bowels of the house, Ipi and Khabekhnet following.

"It is impossible to tell what he was thinking," Aahotep said slowly. "Have we gone too far, Aahmes-nefertari?"

"We had no choice," her daughter answered brusquely. "The load on our shoulders had become insupportable. Sooner or later he will realize that we are creating a hierarchy of government that has not been seen in Egypt for hentis, a full return to the way of Ma'at, but he cannot see it yet. He is still a fighting King even though the need for fighting is almost over."

"He does not want to be here," Aahotep said softly. "He believes that he does, but something in him longs to wander up and down the country with the army and never face the awesome obligations of divinity. In that, he is very like Kamose."

"No." Aahmes-nefertari stared down at the tiny lapis beads on her sandals whose veins of golden pyrite gleamed dully in the dimness of the now-empty hall. "He is not at all like Kamose, but his brother's shadow still lies over him. It will not lift until Apepa yields."

That night, after the feasting that filled the torch-lit garden with laughter and chatter, after the congratulations and songs and light-hearted jokes, Aahmes-nefertari retired to her chambers with a reluctance that dismayed her. Ahmose had received her request to do so with a quizzical lifting of the eyebrows, but then he had patted her knee and told her that of course it had been a long day and she must be tired. He himself had sat on, presiding benignly over the happy turmoil of drunken guests, but she had felt his eyes on her back as she picked her way through the litter of crushed flowers and discarded food to reach the blessed silence of the house.

Senehat was waiting to undress and wash her. Her lamps filled the room with a steady, peaceful glow. The faint scent of lotus wafted to her from her bedsheets, mingling with a whiff of the incense she had offered that morning before her shrine to Hathor, and all at once she was overcome by sadness. She no longer went to the nursery to spend a few moments looking down on Hent-ta-Hent's sleeping face while she whispered the spell that would prevent the demon She-Whose-Face-Is-Turned-Backwards from stealing the baby's breath away. That evil creature had not prevailed. It had been another denizen of the unseen world that had insinuated itself into the little girl's nostrils, her mouth, her tiny ears, and nesting there had lit the fire that had burned Hent-ta-Hent to death.

He did not say one word to me about her, Aahmesnefertari thought, as Senehat's practised hands lifted the wig from her head and slid the scarlet sheath down over her hips into a glimmering heap on the floor. He asked nothing. He offered no sympathy. It was as though our daughter had never lived. What am I to make of such neglect? Is his own wounding so deep that it cannot be expressed or is he simply too honest to cover his indifference?

She sat while her body servant brought hot water and washed the henna from the palms of her hands and the soles of her feet, gently removing the paint from her face and then working the nourishment of honey and castor oil into her skin. Her hair was combed. Woodenly Aahmesnefertari got up so that Senehat could slip the sleeping robe over her head, but when the servant made as if to extinguish the lamps Aahmes-nefertari stopped her. "I am going to my husband's quarters," she said, surprising herself by the impulsive thought. "Bring your pallet in from the passage and sleep by my couch until I return." The hour was late and the summons she had expected had not come. I should just get between my sheets and forget this whole disappointing day, she told herself mutinously, but I would not be able to rest so I might as well swallow my pride and approach him.

Senehat was bending down with a pair of reed sandals in her hand and as Aahmes-nefertari lifted one foot a chilling possibility struck her. Perhaps I have a rival. Perhaps Ahmose's fancy has been taken by some girl presented to him on his way north, a Prince's daughter, a singer or dancer in one of the temples where he stopped to worship. After all, he has been away from my body for six months. He is the King. He can command concubines. He can take more wives if he chooses, and just because our hearts and minds have been in harmony since we were children, it does not mean that it will always be so.

Yes it does, her thoughts ran on. Ahmose has never eyed another woman. He is not devious or deceitful in any area of his life. There is a profound intelligence behind his simplicity but there is no subterfuge. Something else is wrong. Signalling to the guard on her door, she set off along the dim corridors to Ahmose's apartments.

Akhtoy rose from his stool outside the closed double doors as she approached and she greeted him with a smile. "It is good to see you again, steward," she said. "Uni has been keeping abreast of the welfare of your family while you have been away. You must be anxious to see them." He bowed.

"Indeed I am, Majesty, and thank you," he replied. "His Majesty has given me leave to visit them for a few days, now that he has both Uni and Kares to care for him." It was on the tip of Aahmes-nefertari's tongue to retort that Kares was her mother's steward and Uni had his days filled in serving Tetisheri and herself, but she refrained. This is part of the problem between Ahmose and me, she said to herself. The designation of authority.

"Good!" she answered crisply. "Now I wish to see His Majesty. Please announce me." The man hesitated.

"Your pardon, Majesty, but His Majesty is even now preparing for sleep. The feast has tired him. I await his last dismissal before going to my own couch." Aahmes-nefertari restrained a sudden urge to slap him.

"Akhtoy," she said levelly, "do as you are told. Immediately." He bowed at once, nodded, and thrusting open one of the doors he vanished inside. Aahmes-nefertari waited, although she felt affronted at the necessity, study-ing the shaft of yellow light pouring into the passage from the aperture he had left. She heard the steward's voice then her husband's. Akhtoy pulled the door wide and gestured to her, slipping out behind her as she entered the room.

Ahmose was sitting beside his couch, a servant standing behind him in the act of tying the square of linen that covered his shaved scalp. He looked tired. Dark circles shadowed his eyes and Aahmes-nefertari could tell by the way he squinted briefly at her through the lamp's radiance that his head was aching. Nevertheless he smiled at her apologetically as she came forward. "I know I told Tetisheri that I owed you this night, Aahmes-nefertari," he said promptly, "but I am very fatigued. I just want to rest. The feast was excellent. Thank you." She halted, stiffened by anger.

"I have not come to collect a debt," she said bitterly. "Nor is there any need to condescend to me, Ahmose. You could have sent me word." The servant was staring at her and her indignation found a target. "Who are you?" she demanded. The man blinked and came to himself.

"I am Hekayib, body servant to His Majesty," he said amid an explosion of bows.

"Then, Hekayib, you can leave us," Aahmes-nefertari ordered. He glanced at Ahmose who nodded imperceptibly. Still bowing, he found the door and it closed politely behind him.

"I do not recognize him," Aahmes-nefertari said. "I like to know everyone beneath this roof." Ahmose shrugged.

"I sent my previous body servant to tend Ankhmahor's son Harkhuf when he was wounded," he explained. "Then I let him keep him. Why are you so angry, Aahmes-nefertari?" Because you went to the temple first, she wanted to shout. Because you have ignored my grief. Because you obviously do not want to make love to me. There was a time when no amount of exhaustion or indisposition could have prevented you from pulling me onto that couch after you had been away from me.

"I am not angry," she lied. "I have come to tell you that I have asked Amunmose to send priests to stand outside your door every morning at dawn and sing the Hymn of Praise. It is fitting that the ancient custom of greeting the King with the sun should be revived. You also need to know that I meet with my ministers and overseers as soon as the first meal of the day is over. You should be there, Ahmose." She had not moved. She remained where she was, standing in the middle of the room with her fists clenched behind her back.

He regarded her for a long time in silence, eyes narrowed, legs crossed under his sleeping kilt, slowly flexing one naked ankle. Then he said, "You have worked like a slave in the gold mines to establish the foundation of a new mandate for the ruling of Egypt, Aahmes-nefertari. I am in awe of the skill and discernment you have shown. Without you I would have returned to yet another set of monumental tasks and I am grateful. But, my dearest sister, are not these men my ministers and officials, not yours? Am I not Amun's Incarnation and thus the ruler and judge of every Egyptian's fate under the greater laws of Ma'at?" He sighed. "I see that I have injured your pride, but indeed I simply presumed that in leaving everything to you while I was gone we would be continuing to labour for Egypt as one, you here in Weset and I in the north, and that you would require no more thanks for wielding your authority here on my behalf than I would require from you because I fought a significant battle against the Setiu outside Het-Uart. Are we not one mind, one body, Aahmes-nefertari? Have we not always moved in this blessed harmony?"

"Yes," she said tonelessly. "What you say is reasonable, it is true, but, Ahmose, we know each other well. There is insincerity beneath your oh-so-rational words."

"And anger beneath yours," he came back at her swiftly. "I am not forbidding you to be present any more at these meetings. I am telling you that you may know these men but I do not, and if I am to sit at the pinnacle of authority, if I am to rule as well as reign, it is vital that I understand not only who they are but every particular of what they do."

"You do not trust my judgement in engaging them!" she burst out. "They are my choices, not yours, and that irks you, does it not?"

"I come home to more change than has been seen in Weset for hentis!" he shouted. "Walls up, walls down, strange men with strange titles, a wife too preoccupied with building and consulting and dictating to greet her husband with anything other than politeness!"

"I have done nothing but follow your wishes!" she shouted back. "You loaded a sack full of stony responsibilities onto my shoulders before you sailed happily away to cover yourself with a soldier's glory! How dare you accuse me of being too busy to behave like some lazy indolent cat of a woman who must lay aside her sewing and arch her back and purr when her master happens to appear! I have accomplished a miracle here and I have done it at your behest in six months while my daughter died and my husband chased his noble dream!"

"And what have you been chasing?" he shot out. "A handsome scribe and an admiring architect?"

"Ahmose!" She stared at him shaken, feeling the blood drain out of her face. "This is jealousy? You are jealous of Khunes and Sebek-nakht?" His features twisted. He jerked forward then backward on his chair, lacing his fingers tightly together until his knuckles showed white.

"Yes," he said at last, grudgingly. "Of them and all the others. You are not only beautiful, Aahmes-nefertari, but you carry around you a nimbus of power that has not been evident before." His glance at her was almost bashful. "I have been tormented with visions of you and these men who were gathering around you, filling the space I had left while you tested and perfected the authority I delegated to you. Power is a mighty aphrodisiac." He smiled painfully.

"I do not know whether to be complimented or insulted," she said incredulously, her wrath beginning to fade. "You have admitted both that I am not to be trusted and that power has been going to my head." She flung out her arms in bafflement. "They were not visions, Ahmose, they were fantasies. Yes, I am in close accord with my scribe. Of course I am! And yes, I have an understanding with the Prince. How could I work with him if it were not so? But how you were able to translate the necessity for harmony between me and my servants and ministers into a state of mutual sexual attraction I do not know!"

"You've done it again," he retorted. "With the exception of Khunes they are not your servants and ministers. They are mine."

"They are ours," she contradicted him with a heavy deliberation. "I found them, assessed them, formulated the bounds of their responsibilities in my capacity of Queen. Are you frightened of me now, Ahmose? Do you secretly long for a more soothing, biddable female presence? Do you dream of me as I used to be, shy and retiring? Or perhaps you have already found another woman, one more to your old tastes? You have not even kissed me since you returned, let alone shown any desire for my body." He straightened but did not unlock his fingers, squeezing them as though he would fuse bone to bone.

"I am sorry, Aahmes-nefertari," he said softly. "Your letters seemed so capable and cold, so distant, and my days were full of desperation, first in the eastern Delta and then outside Het-Uart. You mentioned men whose names I did not recognize, speaking of them in an off-hand way that indicated an intimacy I could not share. I became afraid, I admit it. Jealous and afraid." He pulled his hands apart and looked down on them resignedly. "There is no other woman. Only you. I confess that I fell in love with you all over again."

What is this? she thought despairingly. Distance and jealousy and the knowledge that you could not be here to take control yourself while I remade your domain, this was translated into passion? Where are you, Ahmose? Where have you gone, that you do not see these things for what they are? Has blood and fire finally blinded you to reality? "Hent-ta-Hent," she said, her voice uneven. "Did her death mean nothing to you? Were you so mired in the phantoms of jealousy and fear that no genuine tragedy could touch you?" He glanced up.

"No," he said simply. "When I read Ahmose-onkh's letter and then your own regarding our loss, I was full of a piercing sorrow, but later that pain was engulfed in a larger, less selfish grief on behalf of the many men who died for me, for Egypt, in the battle. Hent-ta-Hent's passing became simply one of many."

She walked towards him on unsteady feet, and reaching the table she picked up his half-empty wine cup and drained it. Then she pulled a stool towards her and sat down beside him. "You are a fool, Great Horus," she said, "but so am I. I too have been afraid and resentful, not wanting you to come home and undo all my work, not wanting to place the reins of government into your hands when I had delighted in the feel of them." She touched his knee hesitantly. "I still do not want to relinquish the tasks I have begun. Do not shut me out, Ahmose, I beg you." Suddenly he laughed and his hand closed over hers, warm and firm.

"Me shut you out?" he chortled. "When I was in terror of returning to find myself wandering about with nothing to do while my wife ran Egypt? I think that we have both been suffering from subtle delusions, Aahmes-nefertari, why I am not sure. The vestiges of the constant anxiety under which we lived during Kamose's campaigns? The luxury of groundless suspicions now that there has been a lessening of the tension under which we lived for years? It does not matter. I say again, I am sorry and you are right. We have always lived and moved as one. Let us continue to do so. What do you say?"

I say that I still feel the ache of disenfranchisement, she thought to herself, and your present indifference to our daughter's death, no matter what you felt when you received the news, is a betrayal that may dim with time but will never be wholly erased from my heart. She forced herself to look up at him with a smile. "How are we to do that, my husband?" she asked.

"I hear the sting in your voice," he murmured. "We will begin by presiding together at the conference of ministers each morning. You will teach me. I will learn. When I know as much as you, we will listen together and make all decisions together. Agreed?" She sighed inwardly.

"Agreed. I want to show you the new barracks and also the plans for the old palace that Sebek-nakht and I have drawn up," she said. "They are very good, Ahmose. You will approve, I think. If not, I will allow you to change them." His eyebrows rose and for a moment he was nonplussed. Then he beamed, and reaching down he pulled her onto his lap.

"Kiss me," he ordered, closing his eyes. She obeyed, sinking into the familiar feel of his mouth, the taste of him, the odour of his body, the steady pressure of his embrace, seeking the security she had always found in these things. But although they tumbled onto the couch and made love, although she fought to submit to both his desire and her need, a part of her mind remained coolly disengaged. He did not come to me, it whispered. I had to come to him. He did not kiss me. He commanded me to kiss him. Our bodies strive to join but it is more like a struggle than a blending. Even as he enters me, his ka is wandering far away and mine is watching our small child die.

Afterwards they lay side by side gazing up at the flickering of the lamplight on the blue and white painted sky of the ceiling. After some time Aahmes-nefertari stirred. "I forgot to tell you that the one man you did not meet this morning was my chief spy in the south," she said. "He is still in Kush. He has men stationed in Esna, Pi-Hathor, Swenet and in various villages in Wawat."

"You are spying on Wawat? On Hor-Aha's people?" Ahmose said, startled, and she nodded, her tangled hair brushing against his neck.

"Not seriously," she replied. "Aahotep and I do not expect trouble from the Medjay tribes. But they can be volatile, as you know. We like information regarding any offensives Teti-En might decide to make from his stronghold in Kush." Ahmose raised himself on one elbow.

"And why are you still watching Pi-Hathor?" he demanded. "Het-Uy, the mayor, signed a pact with Kamose. He swore that he would not interfere in Kamose's war against Apepa."

"But Kamose is dead," Aahmes-nefertari said. "The Setiu brought prosperity to Pi-Hathor. It was the city that marked the foreigners' southern boundary and it built ships for the Setiu kings. The spies tell me that both Esna and Pi-Hathor are restless. Nekheb has become our centre for the construction and maintenance of vessels, Ahmose. We are ignoring the two towns, although they are also in the Nekhen nome. Do not forget that they are still full of Setiu people." Ahmose grunted.

"So you think that with the death of Kamose they regard the pact as dissolved?" He groaned. "Gods, there is no end to it! No sooner do I gain some control in the north than we are once again threatened from the south! And only two days' sailing away!"

"I do not believe we need to panic," Aahmes-nefertari said carefully. "After all, a large number of our ships have recently gone past both cities on their way to repairs at Nekheb. Esna and Pi-Hathor have seen our strength. They will not act precipitately. Besides, we will be forewarned. The spies will send us word." She smiled faintly up at his worried frown. "Quashing a couple of rebellious townships with a force of Medjay is nothing compared to your victory at Het-Uart. Kay Abana could do it with one vessel!" Ahmose grinned and lay down again.

"He has changed his name to Ahmose Abana," he told her. "The man is incorrigible."

"And what of Ramose?" Aahmes-nefertari wanted to know. "Where is he?"

"I left him at Khemmenu to become acquainted with his duties as governor," Ahmose said. "I am hoping that he will be too busy to spend much time thinking of Tani."

"Is it love or obsession?" Aahmes-nefertari murmured, more to herself than to Ahmose, and realized too late that she had not disguised the moment of envy behind the words. He did not reply. Although their conversation had seemed intimate, a return to the seamless connection that used to bind them, Aahmes-nefertari knew that its fragile weaving had not bridged the gulf between them. The silence lengthened, increasingly fraught with those things that had no present resolution, and she could not break it. At length she ventured a glance at her husband, and seeing that he had fallen asleep she eased herself cautiously over his supine body, gathered up her discarded robe and sandals, and made her way back to the blessed seclusion of her own rooms.

9

SHE WOKE AT DAWN after a troubled sleep in which she dreamed she was holding her copper mirror up to a face so misshapen and grotesque that she did not at first recognize the features as her own, and she came to consciousness sprawled sideways across her couch with the sheet tangled about her legs. The omen of the dream was bad, she knew. As she ate her morning bread and fruit and watched Senehat moving about the chamber, raising the window hangings, laying out a clean sheath, exclaiming softly to herself at a puddle of dried wine on the floor, she pondered its message. I face a completely new and not necessarily comfortable life, she thought. Surely it does not mean that Ahmose will die! But of course not. More powerful omens given by Amun himself support his rise to divinity and his continued position as King in Egypt. A breach has opened between us and the dream reflected it. It cannot endure for long. We love each other too much. It will be healed.

Bathed and dressed and escorted by one of her guards, she made her way to the reception hall, greeting a waiting Khunes as he fell in behind her. Ahmose was already there, seated on the dais in the chair from which for the last six months she had presided, Ipi cross-legged at his feet. She bowed to him as the assembled overseers and ministers reverenced her, swallowing the tide of resentment that she could almost taste and forcing a smile. Another chair had been placed beside his and she mounted the dais and sank into it. "We will not need you today, Khunes," Ahmose said loudly and the scribe, who had already set his palette on his knees and was opening his ink, glanced up at him in surprise.

"Majesty?"

Ahmose waved at him peremptorily. "Ipi is Chief Scribe," he explained brusquely. "I thank you for your service in his absence but now you are free to return to the exclusive business of the Queen." Khunes's eyes fled to Aahmes-nefertari in consternation. She held out a warning hand to him and turned to her husband.

"Forgive me, Majesty," she said cautiously, aware of the many listening ears, "but Khunes has recorded every consultation I have had with these, your officials. He is well informed regarding their ongoing requests and problems. Perhaps today he might be allowed to take the dictation and then spend some time acquainting Ipi with his particular duties here so that Ipi may assume a scribe's responsibilities tomorrow." She saw Ipi nod gravely. The suggestion was, after all, a sensible one. Realizing that Ahmose had spoken impulsively, she leaned close and said in a low voice, "I am not trying to countermand you. Nor do I want to retain control of your court. My concern is for speed and efficiency." He did not look at her.

"It was strange and pleasant to be roused this morning by a priest and his acolytes singing the Hymn of Praise," he murmured. "You have become the very spirit of efficiency yourself, Aahmes-nefertari. Thank you for preventing me from tripping over my own royal toes." He raised his voice. "The Queen speaks wisely," he went on. "Khunes, prepare the papyrus. Ipi, I can do without you for the rest of the day. Closet yourself later with Khunes."

"The scribes' offices and the new archive room are finished, Ipi," Aahmes-nefertari said. "They are ready for you to occupy. Khunes will show you everything."

"Already I wish that I had stayed in bed," Ahmose whispered to her, his flash of irritation gone, and she laughed quietly, her own urge to challenge him swamped in a rush of affection.

"Swear them in, Majesty," she whispered back. "They are very eager to serve you."

For the next few hours the men she had so carefully selected came forward to kiss her husband's feet and hands and vow their loyalty to him and then settled down to a discussion of their current triumphs and worries. Ahmose seemed content to listen, asking few but pertinent questions while Aahmes-nefertari steered the course of the deliberations and Khunes's pen worked away industriously. When it was over and the men had been dismissed, Ahmose rose and stretched. "You have chosen well," he remarked, as they left the hall and emerged into the blinding sunshine of mid-morning. "I am particularly impressed with Amuniseneb. The state of the granaries and the projected abundance of the harvest are of vital importance and he seems to be fully informed regarding both. Do you think that Neferperet as Royal Treasurer will make us rich, Aahmes-nefertari?" She laughed.

"Renewed trade and the increase in taxes that will result from a healthy and peaceful land will make us rich, and

Amun too," she retorted, "but Neferperet will keep us so. I am grateful for your approval, Ahmose. It means a great deal to me." She sighed. "But already the number of scribes and assistants and minor officials is growing under the needs of the ministers and overseers. Our lives will no longer be tranquil."

"Compared to the chattering and scurrying going on around us here a battlefield is a haven of serenity," he said with rueful humour. They had come to the edge of the main path that ran from the watersteps gate to the rear of the estate. The house was behind them, and before them the grass was already beaten down into thin ribbons that snaked in all directions. Men were moving along them singly and in small groups, some with scrolls tucked under their arms, others talking earnestly together.

"When the offices are completed, they will not need to use the garden so much," Aahmes-nefertari remarked. "They will move to and fro between their several doors, all in the shadow of the rear wall beside the servants' quarters. At the moment they work where they can." Sensing a discomfort that was perilously close to bewilderment in him, she took his arm and turned him gently to face her. "Listen to me, Ahmose," she said urgently. "A very short time ago we were princelings living in a southern backwater. Father governed a quiet nome under Apepa's eye. We, his children, fished and swam and played in what seemed to be an endless round of little tasks and pleasures that made up a secure and predictable existence. We had accepted our fate under a perverted Ma'at. All that has changed. Nothing will ever be the same again. Apepa thrust the sword of humiliation into our peaceful nest and Father was forced to counter the insult. From that moment on the die was cast. We cannot go back. Do you know, really know, what has happened in the last year?" She shook his arm and his eyes suddenly lost their vague expression and met hers with sharp concentration. "Egypt has an Egyptian King again. Egypt has begun to sing its ancient song of holiness and fertility. She will be rich. She will be stable and powerful once more. We have emerged from a cocoon and what you see around you is an inevitable flowering as the forces of Ma'at are gathered in. This estate has become the heart of Egypt's administration. You no longer serve the dictates of war, you serve Ma'at and Egypt under Amun. You are a god, my dear brother. You cannot belong to yourself alone any more." She stopped speaking and let him go. He continued to study her face, his own a mixture of understanding and anguish, while the sunshade bearers stood patiently holding the protecting linen over their heads and their guards waited to encircle them when they chose to move on.

At last he nodded slowly. "I know all this," he said, weighing each word. "I have imagined how it would be many times in the long nights when Kamose and I were fighting our way down the Nile and the will of the god was all that kept us going through the terror and misery of those months. But the reality is hard for me to grasp. I see it all but I am almost unable to comprehend it. I wish that I had been here while it was growing." He cast a longing glance towards the closed watersteps gate. "My days will be full from now on, will they not? I would like to take Ahmose-onkh and a skiff and go hunting in the marshes." She shook her head.

"Ahmose-onkh has gone to the temple with one of the we-eb priests," she told him. "He is learning the proper prayers and observances that the god requires of a Prince. Sebek-nakht is expecting you, Majesty. He wishes to show you what he has done." She saw his jaw clench as he turned to look across the garden to where the old palace sat ribbed with scaffolding and shrouded in a murk of dust. The shouts and clatter of the workmen echoed as they swarmed over its rough walls.

"I should be overjoyed," he muttered to himself. "All this is the culmination of everything we have striven for. It is the climax of our struggle, the justification for our honoured dead. Then why do I feel as though I have bitten into a ripe apple only to find it brown with canker inside?" He signalled and immediately the guards sprang to life. He and Aahmes-nefertari stepped onto the springing grass of the lawn. "I loved the old palace when it bore an atmosphere of genteel decay," he said to her as they approached the slight hump that was all that remained of the dividing wall. "It was a sombre place, full of the brooding presence of the past, but it offered privacy and silence."

"Its silence cried out to Father and Kamose for justice," Aahmes-nefertari responded curtly. "Think of it restored, Majesty, full of lamplight, glittering with golden walls and silver doors."

"And what will Treasurer Neferperet say to that expense?" Ahmose shot back. Aahmes-nefertari shrugged good-humouredly but was unable to reply, for Khabekhnet had begun to shout the King's approach and a flurry of excited cries broke out as the workmen shed their tools and loads of bricks and knelt wherever they could.

A group of wigged and white-kilted men turned from the table over which they had been bending and bowed as the pair came to them gingerly over the cracked and heaved paving stones of the vast outer courtyard. Ahmose bade them rise and went forward with a smile.

"Sebek-nakht!" he exclaimed. "It is good to see you again, much sooner than either of us expected. Forgive me for troubling your conscience by preventing you from re-entering Het-Uart to complete the task Apepa set you." The Prince held out his beringed hands palms up, the universal gesture of submission or the acceptance of an unavoidable fate.

"I fulfilled my obligation to my Lord as well as circumstances permitted," he answered, "and I understand that Your Majesty's war could not wait upon the dismantling of mortuary temples." His glance went to Aahmes-nefertari and he smiled. "I am happier building up than tearing down and I thank Your Majesty for the opportunity to do so here in Weset." He indicated the handful of men waiting respectfully behind him. "These are the assistant architects Her Majesty was kind enough to allow me to engage." He introduced them quickly, then smoothed out the curling sheets of papyrus on the table that were rustling softly in the breeze. "I have drawn up tentative plans for the renovation of the palace," he went on, "but the work done so far has been largely cosmetic. The Queen wished me to wait for less easily corrected changes on the edifice itself until Your Majesty returned to give your approval."

"Indeed!" Ahmose said, moving closer to him and looking down at the thin black lines spreading out in a seemingly unintelligible jumble across the papyrus.

Aahmes-nefertari could hear no rancour in his voice. "You had better show me what you have done and tell me the rest, Sebek-nakht, for I can make no sense of these scrawls. If the Queen trusts you, then so will I." He tapped the table, casting a sidelong glance at his wife. "Aahmes-nefertari, you have been out here every day. Have you learned what these patterns mean?" She studied his face, trying to decide whether he was trying to trap her or not, and then berated herself for a coward. If I start to lie now in order to placate him, I will never stop, she thought.

"I have learned some of it," she replied evenly. "I walked the precincts many times with the Prince before we sat in Father's old office and Sebek-nakht explained to me what he would like to do." His indirect scrutiny of her became a full regard and he gave her a half-smile.

"Very well," he said. "Let us walk through the halls of my ancestors, Prince, and I will hear you. How Kamose would have loved to be walking with us!"

He may indeed be here, Aahmes-nefertari thought, as the three of them picked their way through the obstacles of shattered bricks, workmen's tools, discarded pieces of scaffolding and the hunched forms of the peasants themselves, who had laid aside their burdens to prostrate themselves on the dusty stone. I have felt his presence very strongly as Sebek-nakht and I moved through the palace, and once I was sure that I saw him sitting up there on the roof above the women's quarters where he used to go to be alone.

Sebek-nakht had paused before the row of soaring pillars that marked the main entrance.

"There are ten of them, as you know," he was saying. "The palace is of course composed of mud brick, but these are sandstone." He touched one of them. "They are majestic and beautiful even though the painted scenes with which they were no doubt covered have largely been destroyed. Three of them are canting slightly on their foundations, Majesty. They must be taken down and then reset and for that you need skilled masons. May I send to Mennofer for artisans I have worked with before? I will guarantee their competence." Ahmose's gaze travelled up the mighty columns to the deep blue of the sky above.

"Do that," he said. "I trust your judgement, Prince."

They moved inside, crossing from warm sunlight to the sombre dimness of the great audience hall, past the ancient guardroom on the left and the larger room on the right where petitioners, ministers and those who had been summoned waited to be presented to the King. Ahmose halted, drawing in a slow breath. Aahmes-nefertari and Sebek-nakht watched him tensely.

The floor that had once been an ocean of ragged stone wavelets casting pools of tiny irregular shadow had been torn up and replaced. It ran away from the eye, level and even, punctuated by the rows of pillars that marched across its burnished surface. The disintegrating walls in whose holes birds had nested now rose planed and whole to a ceiling that spread high above without rift or sag. The throne dais had been completely refashioned. "This was no work for an architect, Majesty," Sebek-nakht observed. "It required only skilled bricklayers and a knowledgeable foreman from Weset. What you see is naturally the bare bones of a final glory that you must try to imagine."

"I can imagine it," Ahmose said in awe. "Tiles of dark blue lapis covering the floor, the flecks of gold embedded in them catching the torchlight and sparkling like sunshine on water so that the whole room seems alive. Walls sheathed in electrum with images of the gods beaten into them. And a ceiling studded with silver stars." He pointed to the dais, his finger trembling with excitement. "I can see the Horus Throne in the centre, Aahmes-nefertari, and the box containing the sacred Double Crown and the Crook and Flail resting beside it. Where are the shadows that always lurked in the crumbling corners?"

"The ghosts have gone, Ahmose," Aahmes-nefertari said quietly. "They are content, for at last their long sadness is at an end. The palace comes to life again to house a King." She thought she saw tears in his eyes, but if so, they did not spill over. For a long time he stood rooted, looking this way and that, sniffing the air that must seem strange to him, she knew, now that it brought the odour of brick dust and sweat to his nostrils instead of the damp decay that had always hung about the maze of silent rooms. Finally he lifted his shoulders as if to repudiate some unwanted weight.

"Lead on then," he said to the Prince. "I am very pleased."

He was escorted along lesser hallways full of the rubble of reformation, along passages whose roofs had been torn out to expose the ceilings of the stories above, through doorways leading to freshly opened pits and past pits that were being filled in. As he went, Sebek-nakht unfolded his conception of a palace that would emerge from the chrysalis of the old one, its rooms larger and more airy, its passages wider, its stairs more broad. "We cannot go up to the sleeping quarters," he told Ahmose. "Many of the floors up there are not safe and there are dangerous holes where several of the windcatchers have collapsed inward. I have shown you which walls I wish to dismantle entirely so as to enlarge many of the apartments. This will limit the number of people able to inhabit the palace; therefore I request your permission to build two new wings, one reaching out to the north and one joining to your present house to the south. I will design them so that they can easily be adapted to accommodate a larger royal family. I have also designed new servants' quarters of course, and small cells for your governors to inhabit while they are stationed in Weset. I would be honoured to submit those plans to you."

They had come to the foot of the narrow, winding stairs leading to the roof where Seqenenra had been attacked and where Kamose would sit, his back against the remains of the windcatcher, his eyes on the panorama of river and distant cliffs beyond. Ahmose paused.

"These stairs are important to me," he said. "You are a talented architect, Prince, and I congratulate you on the work you have done here so far. I have no criticism, indeed your vision has surpassed my own for this sacred place. But I want these steps left exactly as they are. Are they safe?"

"Yes, Majesty," Sebek-nakht assured him, puzzled. "They have been examined and are sound but I had marked them for demolition and reconstruction. They should be wider and contain only one angle if many women and their burdened servants are to use them."

"Build the women another way to get onto the roof from their quarters," Ahmose said. "I want no one using this stair without permission. Set a door at its foot and another on the roof so that no one comes down it by mistake."

"I can do that," Sebek-nakht agreed. "But surely the stones and other debris that litter it should be cleared away and the steps themselves repaired?"

"No." Ahmose shook his head. "Leave it just as it is, one small part of the ancient structure to remind future kings that without vigilance tragedy may once again fall upon Egypt. I have spoken."

Later, when they had taken their leave of a visibly relieved Sebek-nakht and were almost at the pool in the garden where they would eat the noon meal, Aahmes-nefertari took his arm. "I know why you really want the little stairs left alone," she said. "But is it wise, Ahmose? An unused staircase with doors at the top and the bottom sealing it off, a place where evil went up and pain came down, where Kamose often climbed with his heart full of many strong and secret emotions, surely it is perilous to trap the vestiges of such invisible power. Will it not linger, seep into the rest of the palace, bring melancholy dreams to haunt us and alien memories of a sadness that is not theirs to those who come after us?"

"Perhaps." He lowered himself onto the cushions set ready under the white canopy and at once Akhtoy appeared at the head of a procession of servants bearing trays. "But our destiny was forged on those steps, Aahmes-nefertari, and they are precious to me, both for that reason and as the only portion of the old palace left that will have directly borne the imprint of Father's and Kamose's feet. They will not allow us to be cursed by my decision." She could see that he had made up his mind and would not be swayed. Ahmose-onkh came running from the direction of the watersteps, his guard hurrying behind him.

"Majesty Father, I have been reciting my prayers all morning and I am so hungry!" he was shouting even as he came up to them. "May I eat with you? May I be excused my afternoon sleep today? I want to go to the marshes and see the baby hippopotamus that has just been born."

"Yes and no," Ahmose responded equably as the boy flung himself down between him and Aahmes-nefertari. "We will go together to see the hippopotamuses but not yet. The parents of that baby will be dangerous. Once your aunt, the Princess Tani, was chased for the same reason. She had a love of the hippopotamuses and spent much time watching them." Akhtoy had signalled and the servants were bending one after another to offer the food and beer. Aahmes-nefertari glanced at her husband sharply. Ahmose-onkh was reaching up to take the platter being offered to him.

"I have heard the servants speak of my Aunt Tani but not my family," he said. "Why not? Is she dead? We do not go to her tomb to make offerings during the Beautiful Feast of the Valley. I only have one radish on my dish," he complained to the hovering attendant. "Give me more."

So while they ate, Ahmose told his stepson about the girl who had been full of lighthearted mischief, who had loved to watch the hippopotamuses parting the still water in the marshes as they rose ponderously from the depths, their huge, leathery backs glistening wet, their jutting teeth festooned with green weeds, who had danced and darted through house and grounds and brought laughter to master and servant alike. He spoke of the passion that had flared between her and his friend Ramose, how its flame had settled to a steady glow that still burned in Ramose, and how after Seqenenra's defeat at Qes, Apepa had come to Weset to tear the family apart, condemning each of them to a different exile but taking Tani away as a hostage against any reprisal Kamose might attempt. Ahmose-onkh listened carefully, pushing his favourite vegetable to the edge of his plate to be eaten last. "But my Uncle Kamose the Osiris one did not do as the usurper commanded," he interrupted Ahmose, crunching a stick of celery and waving the remains under his father's nose. "He went to war. What happened to my aunt? Did Apepa kill her there in Het-Uart?" Ahmose shook his head.

"No," he replied gravely. "He may be a usurper, Ahmose-onkh, but he is not a cruel man. She lives there still."

"Oh." The boy began to pop the heap of radishes into his mouth one by one with lusty enjoyment. "Then you will rescue her when you overcome that city, and she will go and live with Ramose?"

"Perhaps."

"I hope so." He was losing interest now that his curiosity had been satisfied and, handing his empty plate up to a servant, he rolled onto his stomach and began to run his hands through the grass where there were insects to feed to the frogs in the pool.

I suppose that he has just received his first history lesson, Aahmes-nefertari thought, watching him with a mixture of affection and sadness. Tani's fate does seem like history now, an ancient story that belongs to another time. Ahmose did not tell him all of it, how Kamose had sent Ramose into the city to pass calculated information to Apepa and his generals, how Apepa granted Ramose a meeting with Tani in exchange for that information, and how Ramose thus discovered that Tani had married Apepa and was known to the Setiu as Queen Tautha. I feel very little pain when I think of my sister now, Aahmes-nefertari mused. What is so badly broken cannot be truly mended. When Ahmose takes Het-Uart, what will he do with her? And will our wounds then be opened afresh? "It is time for your sleep, Ahmose-onkh," she said. "Raa is waiting." He sighed ostentatiously but rose at once.

"Can I swim when I wake up?" he asked. Ahmose gave his youth lock a gentle tug.

"We will go and look at the baby hippopotamus if you like," he said. "An hour or two on the river with you is just what I need." Ahmose-onkh's face lit up.

"Thank you, Majesty Father!" he crowed. "And I can practise with my throwing stick!"

"At ducks, not hippopotamuses," Ahmose said, amused. He watched the boy race away towards the house and turned to his wife. "He has a throwing stick?" Aahmes-nefertari dabbled her fingers in her waterbowl and dried them on the proffered napkin before replying.

"Emkhu had a little one made for him," she said. "He can't hit anything with it yet. Emkhu tells me that the ducks will be quite safe for some years to come." Ahmose did not smile.

"He is almost five years old," he commented. "From now on he will change and grow very rapidly. We must have more children, Aahmes-nefertari, another son, a daughter to legitimize Ahmose-onkh's accession to divinity in his turn. He is all that stands between Egypt's stability and a return to chaos. I would lock him up to preserve him from every vicissitude of life if I could." He had never before spoken so directly of a fear she knew had begun to obsess him and at once she was filled with a sense of failure.

"I know," she murmured. "I am sorry, Ahmose. But perhaps if you are able to stay home for longer than a day or two we might indeed begin to fill those new apartments of which Sebek-nakht spoke." Her attempt to keep her tone light was successful. He laughed and kissed her on the neck.

"We might," he agreed, a glint in his eye. "We must try to do so very hard, my beautiful warrior, in fact tonight ..." He broke off, seeing his mother emerge from the shade at the rear of the house and come walking towards the pool, Kares pacing behind her carrying a stool. "Aahotep!" he called. "You have missed a fine meal!" She waved and soon came to a halt under the protection of the canopy. Beads of sweat stood out on her forehead and one tendril of dark hair was stuck to the moisture on her neck. Bowing shortly to Ahmose, she gestured to her steward, who set down the stool and snapped his fingers at a servant who was holding the beer jug. Aahotep lowered herself onto the seat and drained the cup being held out to her.

"The day is warm for spring," she said. "I was not hungry, Ahmose. I have been with Tetisheri in the vegetable garden. I had it enlarged this year to cope with greater demands. Loads of silt from the flood had to be hauled to it and dug into the sand, and watering it has become a problem, it is now so vast. I want to move it entirely, turn one of the fields to the north from grain to vegetables so that they can be irrigated directly from a canal connecting with the Nile." Kares handed her a square of linen and she wiped her forehead delicately, careful not to smear her kohl. "The days of a few rows of garlic, lettuce and onions is over. I am tired."

"Surely you were not weeding yourself?" Aahmes-nefertari expostulated, and Aahotep gave her a wry smile.

"Certainly not. But I found myself embroiled in an argument with Tetisheri over the cucumbers." Aahmes-nefertari blinked at her, puzzled, and her smile became half-chuckle, half-groan. "Tetisheri does not approve of cucumbers because they first came into Egypt with the Setiu. She does not want us to increase the crop. I told her not to be ridiculous, that cucumbers were cool and juicy to eat and in any case, all permitted food is a gift from the gods. But she was adamant. I was forced to directly over-ride her commands to the garden overseer. She has gone to her quarters to sleep." Aahmes-nefertari did not find the situation funny and neither, obviously, did Ahmose. His expression became thoughtful.

"Although she is aging, she is still in possession of all her faculties," he said. "She should be accorded the reverence and respect due to both and I wish that I could give her some task that would absorb those remarkable energies of hers, but how can I when she continually tries to argue the smallest responsibility into a right to dictate the future of Egypt? I love her as my grandmother. In any other capacity she is an exasperation."

"I want to make the journey to Djeb as soon as Hent-ta-Hent's funeral is over," Aahotep said. "I had intended to send Yuf alone to inspect the tomb of my ancestor Queen Sebekemsaf but I have decided that I need a change of scene." She cast a rueful glance at her son. "I am surely a little bored, Ahmose, when I am reduced to investigating the state of the vegetable garden and quarrelling with another Queen over cucumbers. Let me take Tetisheri with me." She hesitated. "It will be a full progress, two ships, all my staff. She will enjoy it. We will put in at Esna and Pi-Hathor, and Nekheb too of course. We will be fêted and entertained along the way."

"So you believe that Esna and Pi-Hathor need to be reminded that they are now under my permanent rule," Ahmose said. It was a statement rather than a question and Aahmes-nefertari marvelled at her husband's flash of acuity. Like so many others, I am occasionally lulled into thinking Ahmose as straightforward and uncomplicated as he seems, she thought to herself. I ought to have learned the fallacy of that impression a long time ago. Aahotep met her eye.

"The spies tell us that there are always grumblings in those two towns but that the complaints have been growing," she said frankly. "It will do no harm to be seen there. But I do not go south merely to test the public temper. An inspection of the tomb of my ancestor is not an excuse."

"Ask Grandmother if she would like to accompany you, by all means," Ahmose acceded. "Some time spent on the river and in the reception halls of worshipful mayors will divert her, and perhaps she will return in a better humour. How long will you be gone?"

"I am not sure. A month or two, maybe more." Ahmose's eyebrows rose.

"You must indeed be bored, Mother," he said slowly. "Are you unhappy as well?" She bit her lip, a strangely shocking gesture in one so usually composed.

"Ahmose, I am forty-one years old," she admitted. "I have lived through many experiences that rightly belong to the world of men. I have put down a rebellion. I have killed a traitor. It has been difficult for me to return to the mundane chores of household management, in spite of Aahmes-nefertari's kindness in allowing me to share in some of her more important duties. The Gold of Flies sits on the table beside my couch. I sometimes lift it up when I am wakeful at night and remember how you made me go to the temple in the sheath stained with Meketra's blood, the blood I shed, and laid the award around my neck." She put a hand up to her breast as though the three precious golden insects, symbols of her courage, were resting there. "Do not mistake me," she went on more strongly. "I would not go back to that time for all the gold in Kush. I have no desire to be a General. Or an assassin." She smiled at her own small joke. "I am not unhappy but I am restless. A journey upstream will cure me."

"Shall I find another husband for you, Aahotep?" her son enquired impulsively, and now she did laugh, fully and musically.

"Gods no!" she choked. "You would be forced to search beyond the borders of Egypt, for am I not a Queen, wife of one King and mother of another? Besides, to be in Weset as it is transformed is intriguing and to sleep in peace alone is bliss."

Is it? Aahmes-nefertari found herself wondering as she studied her mother's handsome face. You have always been a sensuous woman, Aahotep. It is in your bones, your walk, the grace of your movements. Does your body feel no lack? As if Aahotep had read her mind, her gaze swung to her daughter and in the wide, dark eyes there was a message. Yes I lack, she seemed to be saying, but it is Seqenenra for whom I long, and that yearning cannot be satisfied in this life. I am not happy, but I am teaching myself contentment.

One week later Hent-ta-Hent's tiny coffin was carried across the Nile and Amunmose performed the funeral rites. The day was fine and clear. The sky held nothing but the outspread wings of the hawks gliding languidly on the updraughts of mild spring air. The odour of the river mingled with an almost indefinable essence emanating from the still half-buried crops forcing their way with blind purpose through the wet soil. The proper rituals were observed. The mourners wailed and sprinkled their heads with sand. The sacred adze, the pesesh-kef, was touched to the bandaged corpse to open Hent-ta-Hent's mouth, eyes and ears. Incense billowed about her in streaming clouds.

Yet to Aahmes-nefertari, crying quietly beside her husband, there was something careless and even insincere about the proceeding, a feeling of impatient surprise that the baby should need the full trappings of a funeral at all. She did not live long enough to impress a personality on those around her, Aahmes-nefertari thought. Not even on me and certainly not on Ahmose. He is not weeping. He stands here dry-eyed. No one has mourned her honestly but me. My body carried hers. My breasts nurtured her. I held her close to me day after day, watching her face, rocking her to sleep, seeing her eyes open and her lips smile in recognition when she woke. I soothed her when she cried, her head with its soft covering of down tucked into my neck. The only true anguish is mine.

After the obligatory feast Ahmose dismissed the company but he did not return to the east bank himself. Instead he took a guard and a servant with a sunshade and wandered among the other tombs scattered across the sandy waste like monuments to the inevitability of fate. Aahmes-nefertari, wrapped in grief and unwilling to confront the noisy and commonplace life of the estate for a while, sat under the protection of a canopy and watched him appear and disappear as he wove his mysterious purpose. He paused for some time outside his father's edifice, standing very still, arms at his sides, his blue mourning kilt fluttering in the wind, the sunlight flashing on the gold adorning his brown chest and encircling his wrists.

When he at last moved on to his brother's small courtyard, a grey shape detached itself from the shadow of the stones and came shambling reluctantly towards him. Aahmes-nefertari saw him crouch and fondle the dog's ears before turning and making his way towards her. Coming in under the thin shelter of the canopy, he sank onto the sand by her stool. "What is Behek still doing here?" he asked abruptly. He did not look at her. His gaze, narrowed against the noon glare, was fixed on the stark panorama stretching out before him. Beyond the cluster of tombs the ground ran in an unhurried, slow rise to the funerary temple of Osiris Mentuhotep neb-hapet-Ra that nestled beneath the sharp tiers of the cliff of Gurn, its pale stones almost indistinguishable from the dun rocks behind it.

"He found his own way across the river at the time of Kamose's funeral," Aahmes-nefertari answered. "Don't you remember? There are enough skiffs plying between the banks. He lives at the door to Kamose's tomb. I have appointed a servant to bring him food and water every day, for he will not leave."

Ahmose made no comment. He continued to stare at the silent aridity that seemed to possess its own peculiar sense of exclusive isolation. But presently he stirred and covered her foot with his hand.

"Hent-ta-Hent achieved nothing, became nothing," he said quietly. "She was given no time to emerge from the cocoon of her babyhood. And yet she is here among those who fought and suffered, loved and hated, died of old age on their couches or in the prime of their lives on the point of a spear. When we buried our father and Kamose, we did so in the midst of a turbulence of life that made their deaths seem simply a part of that great agitation. Even Si-Amun, killing himself in guilt and remorse because he betrayed us to Apepa, even his suicide, was stitched into the flow of our living. But Hent-ta-Hent ..." He withdrew his touch and his arms went around his knees. "Her death seems unnatural to me, something unreal, something grotesque and foreign in this time of peace and new prosperity. It does not belong to the common ebb and flow of existence, it does not fit, not like the other losses we have endured." He glanced swiftly up at her and then away. "I am sorry, Aahmes-nefertari. I am expressing this clumsily. I wish I could be more clear, because it is yet another reason why I no longer feel any emotion for our child's death."

"Well at least you are able to admit the lack," she replied thickly.

"I am sorry," he repeated. "It was not for want of memories of her, few though they were, nor for a coldness towards her. She was here. Now she has gone to the gods. I was her father, and that going has indeed left a trail across my ka. But it is a trail of events, not sentiment. Death is no longer intertwined with life as it used to be during our family's struggle. It is something separate, apart."

"It is never separate," she retorted savagely. "If you believe that, you are deceiving yourself, Majesty."

Again there was silence between them, broken only by the scream of a hawk circling somewhere high above and the creak of leather as one of the guards hitched up his belt. Then Ahmose said, "Do you ever miss Si-Amun, Aahmes-nefertari? Do you think about him often? After all, he was Kamose's older twin, your husband before me, Ahmose-onkh's true father. Does he still have a place in your heart?"

"Of course he does!" she burst out. "He was well-meaning and weak and his fate was cruel and dark but I loved him. So did you. As for the love of a wife for her husband, mine belongs now to you and you alone. When I think of Si-Amun it is as though I am peering down a long tunnel to a pinpoint of light at the far end where a man without features stands blurred and indistinct. I do not miss him. If I grieve sometimes, it is for the brutal necessities of the past in which Si-Amun played his part, not for Si-Amun alone." She rose in one agitated motion. "What has come over you today?" He still would not look at her.

"I know that I am causing you to go to the riverbank," he said in a low voice, using the expression that described the plight of women left husbandless and homeless by war. "I am afraid that I am losing your esteem."

A dozen bitter responses sprang to her tongue. Today is for Hent-ta-Hent, not for your self-indulgence. You have treated me without tact or tenderness since you came home. Your insecurity has its roots in a selfish fear, not in love for me. But she swallowed them all with an effort that left her throat parched and her mouth dry. Jerking her chin at her guard and her servant, she walked unsteadily towards the litter that rested at the base of an aged sycamore. The bearers scrambled up at her approach.

"Back to the watersteps," she snapped, and climbing onto the cushions inside she pulled the curtains closed.

With the beginning of the month of Phamenoth the period of growing began. Everywhere along the narrow strip of land bordered on each side of the Nile by desert, the fields were dense with lush crops of wheat, barley and flax, brilliant green carpets whose irregular palm-lined perimeters met the barren sand to east and west in a sharp division between fertility and aridity. Smaller fields held the fronds and traceries of vegetables and herbs. All were patchworked with brimming irrigation canals whose placid surfaces teemed with insect life. Everywhere, the peasants could be seen muddy and barefooted, backs bent over their hoes or standing calf-deep in the thriving profusion of their labours, while the fishermen in their feluccas on the river glided to and fro, the sound of their chanting and the light beat of their finger drums an audible accompaniment to the silent melody Egypt was singing.

Aahotep, Yuf and Tetisheri left for Djeb with a great entourage of servants and guards, boxes, chests, formal gifts for the mayors of the towns where they would put in, Aahotep's personal physician, and private instructions from Aahmes-nefertari to contact the spies in both Esna and Pi-Hathor for whatever news they might have. "I feel uneasy about those cities without quite knowing why," she had said to her mother. "Try to keep Grandmother away from any suspicion of our clandestine activities if you can. She will only confuse things. Use your own intuition, Aahotep, and may the soles of your feet be firm." The whole household had turned out to bid the women farewell. An unusually effusive Tetisheri had embraced Aahmes-nefertari and had tripped up the ramp onto the deck of Aahotep's barge with an uncharacteristic enthusiasm. Her parting shot, though expected, was mild.

"I suppose you will enjoy being rid of me for a while," she had snapped, but the smile that followed had softened the tartness of her words. She is wrong, Aahmes-nefertari thought as she watched the two gaily bedecked craft beat slowly away south, the royal flags of blue and white flapping busily in the breeze off the water and the oars dipping in cascading showers. I will miss her, and Mother too. Mother most of all. She casts a sane presence over the house, although she is so seldom in evidence.

Before she left, Aahotep had approached her priest with the request for a suitable tutor for Ahmose-onkh, and within a week a young man had presented himself at one of the morning conferences where Ahmose had begun to preside with increasing confidence. His name was Pa-she. He was a native of Aabtu. His father was a merchant who also served in the temple of Osiris during the three-month rotation of minor clerics, but Pa-she had an interest in ancient tombs and after qualifying as a scribe had applied for admittance to the temple of Amun at Weset so that he would be close to the City of the Dead on the western bank. He and Yuf had struck up a friend-ship, but Aahmes-nefertari knew that a recommendation to such an important post as Royal Tutor would not be based on friendship alone.

Pa-she entered the audience hall bearing several samples of his writing, a letter from the High Priest, another from his master in Osiris's temple at Aabtu, and a small history of several of the older tombs that he was compiling in his spare time. He waited patiently until the more vital business of the day was concluded and the ministers had scattered to their temporary offices. Then Ahmose beckoned him forward, holding out a hand for his references and reading them quickly before passing them to his wife. Aahmes-nefertari smiled at him encouragingly. "The letters you bring are very complimentary," she said. "But a Royal Tutor must have more than intelligence. He must be able to earn the trust and respect of his pupils. Have you had much to do with children, Pa-she?"

"No, Majesty," Pa-she answered swiftly. "But the opportunity to train a young mind, particularly the mind of one who will rule Egypt one day, is a precious challenge. My father raised me with a firm but gentle hand and I would wish the same blend of kindness and discipline for my pupil."

"Prince Ahmose-onkh needs more discipline than kindness," Ahmose remarked. "His nurse has spoiled him and he has been allowed to do much as he pleases."

"I anticipate a period of mutual adjustment, Majesty," Pa-she replied. "I have heard that the Prince is unruly, but a little wilfulness often denotes a noble and intelligent nature that simply requires direction." Ahmose sat forward.

"It seems you are ready to tame the boy. How will you begin?"

Pa-she's eyes lit up. "The Prince is not yet five," he said eagerly. "I suggest an hour of lessons morning and afternoon for the first six months, during which I will teach him the elements of the simpler hieratic script before attempting the more formal hieroglyphs. The work called Kemyt was compiled seven hundred years ago for just such a purpose. I daresay Your Majesty also began with this ancient text before moving on to the Instructions of Osiris Amenemhat the First and the Hymn to the Nile written by Khety son of Duauf."

"I remember," Ahmose said ruefully. "Every word was accompanied by the threat of a beating. My tutor was a stern taskmaster."

"Beating will be my last resort," Pa-she said indignantly and Aahmes-nefertari laughed.

"You may change your mind before long!" she said. "And if you do, you will have his nurse Raa to contend with. She grumbles about his disobedience but she is very protective." Pa-she hesitated.

"Majesty, I would like you to consider giving me a room next to the Prince," he said. "He must see me as a friend and guardian as well as a teacher. I want to be with him when he eats, swims, says his prayers. Every activity of his will be an opportunity for education."

"It is an irregular request," Ahmose mused, "but I suppose if you want to punish yourself, it can be arranged. Aahmes-nefertari, what do you think?" She studied the scribe's face for a long time before replying.

"It is a peculiar method of teaching," she said slowly. "However, I am willing to accede to Pa-she's request for the time being. Khabekhnet!" The Chief Herald stepped forward from his post at the rear of the hall and bowed. "Find Ahmose-onkh and bring him here. He might as well meet the man at once who will make his life miserable." She returned her gaze to Pa-she. "Never forget that you have a Hawk-in-the-Nest to nurture," she reminded him. "Every word he hears from you will determine his fitness to reign as god when he sits upon the Horus Throne. You will report to me on his progress once a week." Pa-she knelt and then prostrated himself.

"A thousand thanks, Majesties," he said, his nose to the floor. "I will carry this responsibility as Khnum cradled in his divine hands the clay from which man was fashioned on the celestial potter's wheel." Ahmose left his chair.

"You have my permission to laugh occasionally as well, Pa-she," he said dryly. "I wish you good fortune of your charge. Aahmes-nefertari, see to this momentous meeting." And with that he signalled to Ipi and Akhtoy and left the hall.

In the middle of the following month, Pharmuthi, a flotilla of ships arrived from the north bearing the Keftian merchants Ahmose had addressed on Het-Uart's northern mound. There were perhaps fifteen families in all, complete with their goods and servants, and Aahmes-nefertari arranged for their accommodation in Weset through Uni. The task was not easy. All of them wanted choice estates that bordered the Nile, and as Aahmes-nefertari listened to a harried Uni voice their complaints, it was brought home to her how indulgently Apepa had treated them. "We know that the Setiu are enamoured of Keftian goods and art," she told her steward. "The King told me that these people inhabited the choicest property on a mound already crowded. But we must not antagonize them, Uni. They will bring us not only good trade, bronze, gold-chased swords and daggers, vases, lamps, and most importantly, poppy and dye, but also an opportunity to establish political ties with their island. I am also trying to lure Asi traders to Weset. Do your best for them." Uni groaned ostentatiously in a rare show of irritation and acquiesced.

Not long afterwards Aahmes-nefertari received a message that Keftiu had despatched an ambassador to Ahmose's court who would be expected to remain permanently at Weset. It was a triumph for her. She had opened negotiations with the Keftian ruler some months before, reminding him in the most polite and diplomatic terms that his previous ally, Apepa, was now no more than a stingless scorpion with no hope of ever regaining power in Egypt, but that the country's rightful King would graciously welcome a continuation of the traditional relationship between Egypt and Keftiu.

An equally polite acknowledgement of her letter had come, full of courteous but ultimately meaningless words. She had not pressed the issue, but optimistically she had asked Sebek-nakht to add to his already crushing load of work by designing and erecting a series of large houses with gardens for the use of any foreign ambassadors to be lured to the new seat of power. The charming buildings had gone up to the south, between her own estate's protecting outer wall and the now completed barracks that would lodge Ahmose's two permanent divisions. But the Keftian King had obviously taken some time to investigate Apepa's plight, and finding it irremediable had decided to transfer his commitment to a healthier regime. When the ambassador arrived in full pomp with all his household, Ahmose feted him lavishly and spent long hours discussing with him a renewed amity between the two nations, but it was the Queen and Neferperet as Chief Treasurer who hammered out the terms of the trading agreements. Aahmes-nefertari also made sure that one of the kitchen servants and one of the gardeners attached to the ambassador's residence had spent some time in Esna, learning to spy.

Aahmes-nefertari and Ahmose had arrived at an uneasy, unspoken truce, a compromise in the duties and concerns of the administration that extended painfully into their private dealings with each other. Once they had shared every joy and concern, but now they found themselves stepping cautiously around those areas of the soul where aches still throbbed, aware that some hurts were too fresh to be aired. They had begun to make love again but with the same caution they brought to their private conversations and the spending of their passion had become an exercise performed in silence.

Aahmes-nefertari tried not to remember the joyful unselfconsciousness that had imbued their sexual union in the past. Such thoughts would only serve to rub salt into wounds already bleeding. At the end of Pakhons she discovered that she was pregnant once more and she held in her womb not only the new life growing there but also the hope that with its eventual expulsion there might be a purging of every bitterness both she and her husband endured. When she told him her news, he had smiled with obvious delight, kissed and embraced her, and gone to the temple to offer thanks to Amun. But between them lay the deaths of two of her children, Hent-ta-Hent and the first son she had borne to Si-Amun, and her hope was tempered by fear.

Reports from the army and navy still stationed in the Delta arrived regularly. The situation there had not altered. Het-Uart remained closed in upon itself. Ahmose and Aahmes-nefertari read the letters in Seqenenra's office, seated with their backs to the sunshine pouring in between the pillars. Hor-Aha was with them. His hair had grown. It was still too short to fashion into the braids he had worn for as long as Aahmes-nefertari could remember but it was already touching his shoulders in a welter of thick, shining waves which he had taken to smoothing back with one impatient palm.

She had seen little of him since he had returned to Weset. He had divided his time between his Medjay in their village across the Nile and long hunting expeditions out on the desert where he stalked hyena, antelope and lion. Now he folded his fingers around the stem of his wine cup and leaned over the table as Ahmose let the scroll that had just arrived roll up before passing it down to Ipi, sitting at his feet. "How are they surviving, Majesty?" he wondered. "When we left the city, it was full of disease and short of water. It should have capitulated within weeks."

"Plagues have a way of running their course and then withdrawing," Ahmose said. "No doubt many hundreds of citizens died. We saw the smoke from their funeral pyres ourselves. It is a coldly practical assessment, General, but I would presume that their deaths allowed the supply of water from the additional wells the survivors undoubtedly dug to be sufficient. As for food, they garden on the roofs of their hovels. A slim diet but perhaps enough to keep body and ka united."

"They have become like a recurring nightmare," Aahmes-nefertari put in. "Will it ever end?"

"Of course it will," Ahmose assured her. "The divisions in the east are holding the Horus Road and the forts of the Wall of Princes without any effort. It is only a matter of time." He drummed the table briefly. "The troop rotations will be complete by the end of Epophi," he went on. "Then I think you can take the Medjay home to Wawat for a few months, Hor-Aha. They have earned a visit to their families. Abana can bring a portion of the navy here and Turi and Kagemni can move the divisions of Amun and Ra from the Delta into their new quarters south of the estate. We must do our best to ignore Apepa and the remnant of his power until he compels us to do otherwise." Hor-Aha scanned his face thoughtfully.

"It will not be wise to leave the Medjay in their villages for long, Majesty," he said. "They will quickly burrow back into the life of their tribes and ferreting them out and retraining them to Egyptian standards of discipline will be a daunting task. Have you considered bringing their families here? They are creatures of the present. They would happily turn the barracks they inhabit now into a community if their women and children were with them."

"If I do it for the Medjay, I must do it for every soldier in my two Weset divisions," Ahmose objected. "Ten thousand men can be housed without too much trouble or expense but add their wives and children and I create yet another branch of administration." He made a face. "At least, you do," he said, turning to Aahmes-nefertari. His generous acknowledgement of her efforts warmed her.

"But, Ahmose, if you want permanent troops stationed here, you must provide for them to see their families," she reminded him. "Otherwise their morale will gradually be eroded." He tutted, mildly distressed.

"The idea of permanence is still strange to me," he admitted. "My life has been one of movement for the last few years. Yet permanence is taking hold all around me, around us."

"Weset is expanding almost daily," Aahmes-nefertari put in. "People are being drawn here by the prospect of advancement or better commerce or ambition for their children because Weset is becoming the seat of power in Egypt. There is room for many more. Apportion some land for the families of your soldiers. Some may decide not to uproot their relatives, but at least they will then have a choice. I can appoint an Overseer of Army Resettlement if you like, to organize everything. Then rotation will mean a short walk from barracks to town, not a long journey down the Nile to remote villages. Your men will be available to you at all times."

"I suppose you are right," he said reluctantly. "I can do it for the Medjay as well, Hor-Aha. I do not know why these things are causing such quakings in my soul. See to it, Aahmes-nefertari, as you said. I cannot face the prospect." It is the loss of complete control that is afflicting you my husband, Aahmes-nefertari thought as she left the office on his arm. You can no longer be aware of every action your ministers perform and not every order comes from your mouth any more. You are being forced to trust to the intelligence and honesty of others and it is driving you to distraction.

Pakhons slipped into Payni and then Epophi. The summer heat intensified, tightening its grip on man and beast, and the pace of life slowed. Noble and peasant alike slept the long, hot afternoons away, but in the warm nights the streets of Weset were lively as the citizens emerged to conduct their business or simply drink beer and gossip.

For Aahmes-nefertari, plagued by nausea each morning, the hours of soft darkness were an added blessing. At sunset she would go to the bath house to have the sweat and fatigue of the day washed away, then clad in a loose tunic she would mount the stairs to the roof of the house where Senehat had spread rugs and cushions and set out lamps whose flames in the thin alabaster vessels glowed golden against the darkness. There would be bowls of fruit and ewers of water and wine, sennet and Dogs and Jackals to play, blankets to cover her when at last she fell asleep under the forest of white summer stars, but Aahmes-nefertari was lonely. She missed the other women of the household, her mother and grandmother, who in other summers would be up there with her to while away the time in idle feminine chatter.

There had been scrolls from Aahotep and less frequently from Tetisheri. The two of them had been well received in both Esna and Pi-Hathor and had tarried in each town for some days but neither of them had enjoyed their time there. Tetisheri protested that the servants in the mayors' houses were slovenly and inept and the commoners careless in their obeisances when she ventured out. She reminded Aahmes-nefertari that the penis of Osiris had been swallowed by a fish at Esna, "and thus the eating of fish is not allowed by anyone including your mother and me," her letter stated waspishly. "In my opinion it would have been better if the god's penis had been left to wash up on the shore and the fish had decided to feast on the town instead."

But Aahotep wrote of vague undercurrents of unrest in both places. She had spoken briefly with the spies and they had told her of the docks and warehouses lying derelict, the abandoned estates of men who had once grown rich under the Setiu, the atmosphere of uncertainty that pervaded both Esna and Pi-Hathor. "These towns shared the privilege of building, equipping and repairing ships for our invaders," Aahotep had written. "That source of prosperity has now gone to Nekheb. Another source of security for them was the trade route to and from Kush. They are situated halfway between Het-Uart and Kush. But seeing that Weset, a mere twenty-three miles downstream from them, has become the heart of Egypt, their situation is no longer an advantage. All that remains to them is the limestone quarry near Pi-Hathor, and since Ahmose has not yet begun to erect any large monuments, the quarrymen sit idle and hungry. I sense the possibility of a danger to our new stability and I am glad that we devised such a fine web of spies. Tomorrow we move on to Nekheb with great relief. We hope to stay there for at least a month. It will be very hot there, and hotter still as we approach Djeb, but there is health and peace in the air of the southern towns."

Aahmes-nefertari had shown the letters to Ahmose, who had read them and grunted. "Kamose did not trust them either," he had remarked. "But they are impotent, Aahmes-nefertari, caught as they are between Weset and

Nekheb. What can they do but accept their fate? I cannot employ the limestone diggers just to keep them in bread and onions, although I am sorry for them and the ship-builders of Nekheb under Paheri and the Abanas are more reliable than the remnants of the Setiu at Pi-Hathor. At least Kamose did not raze their homes as he did at Dashlut." He had planted a swift kiss on her chin. "You and Mother and your spies!" he had chuckled.

Aahmes-nefertari had been indignant at his unspoken implication that she and Aahotep had been frivolously amusing themselves when they formed their network but she had not challenged him. He was not so contemptuous of the enterprise when we first told him of it, she thought mutinously. In those days he was grateful for any assurance of protection no matter how nebulous. I will not discuss the matter with him again.

Sometimes Ahmose joined her on the roof, and sprawled amid the cushions they talked quietly or played board games or took turns naming the constellations that blazed overhead, but more often he preferred to sit in the shrouded garden drinking beer with Turi, Kagemni, Hor-Aha and others. By the beginning of Mesore the divisions of Amun and Ra were back in Weset and comfortably inhabiting their new barracks, and Paheri and Ahmose Abana had passed through Weset on their way home to Nekheb. Ankh-mahor had also returned with his son Harkhuf, whose wound had left nothing but a steadily whitening ragged scar.

Aahmes-nefertari, sitting high above the hundreds of pinpricks of light that marked the other occupied roofs of the city and listening to the gusts of masculine laughter drifting up from the lawn below, felt as abandoned as a worn-out sandal. The harvest is underway, she thought gloomily. The crops are falling before the scythes of the reapers and the air is full of the flying dust thrown up from the threshing floors. In the vineyards the men and women are singing as they tread the grapes, and the honey from the hives is being poured like thick sunshine into the jars. Gardens are fragrant with the aroma of crushed herbs, coriander and cumin, thyme, and the sharp freshness of the mint. Yet there is no quickening in my womb, no sign that my baby lives. It is too soon, I suppose. In another month it will make its presence known, but for now I feel barren amid a profusion of fertility. Is this how it will be, Ahmose enveloped in a world of men while I struggle to conform myself once more to the trivial world of feminine pursuits? Is this what I have worked for in all the months that he was away?

A flicker of movement caught her eye beyond the palms in whose thin fronds the setting moon was captured and peering over the edge of the roof she saw a skiff go slipping silently by, one oarsman in the stern and the embracing figures of a man and a woman utterly engrossed in each other near the prow. "Senehat," she said dully, and the girl left her perch by the windcatcher and came forward. "I am reminded that I have not yet received an assessment regarding the number of inet-fish to be salted and stored for the Keftian merchants. Keep it in your mind if you can and tell me to deal with it tomorrow." Senehat murmured an assent and melted back into the shadows. Gods, Aahmes-nefertari thought, lying back and closing her eyes. The moon is full, the night's breath is scented with love, and I am reminded of inet-fish. She was too empty to cry.

10

THE WHOLE OF WESET had celebrated the Beautiful Feast of the Valley in the month of Payni, at the day of the full moon, and the Taos had joined the crowds of hundreds streaming across the river with offerings of food, oil and wine for their dead. Ahmose had not forgotten the day of his father's birth in Phamenoth, marking it with the usual prayers and feast as was customary for every family member living or not. Birthdays came round regularly like the various gods' days and were occasions for happy reflection. But the Beautiful Feast of the Valley was an event of universal solemnity and rejoicing while the priests moved from tomb to tomb with incense. When the formalities were over, the relatives of the beautified settled down beside their dead to eat a meal in their presence and speak of them with love.

We have so many dead, Ahmose had thought as he watched the servants lay out the feast within Kamose's little courtyard. Grandmother's husband, Osiris Senakhtenra; Seqenenra, my father; two babies; Osiris Kamose; and Si-Amun, whom we are not allowed to acknowledge on this day. We go from door to sealed door laying our offerings before them, but life is so immediate at this time of the year, an explosion of fruits and grains, the excitement and anxiety of the wait for the harvest and then for Isis to cry, the preparations for the New Year festivities. Only those newly bereaved can mourn. Not that the Feast is intended as a time for grief. It exists for the sanctification of the dead and the conjuring of their memories. Behek is the only one whose loss remains fresh and painful. How much can a mere dog feel? How limited is Behek's power to reason? Does he wait in this arid place for Kamose to come out or does he know that my brother's essence is gone and believe it his duty to guard his long sleep?

Ahmose-onkh was kneeling in the sand with his arms around Behek's neck. His tutor, Pa-she, stood beside him explaining something Ahmose could not hear over the hubbub of the servants' chatter and the clink of utensils. That association is working well, Ahmose's thoughts ran on. There were a few tantrums at first when Ahmose-onkh realized that he could no longer race about the house and grounds with an exasperated Raa in pursuit, but he seems to have not only accepted Pa-she's discipline but be developing a trust in him. Pa-she's weekly reports on his charge's progress do not include that fact, of course, but it is evident in the way the boy's behaviour has improved. Aahmes-nefertari has triumphed in this as in everything else.

He glanced at his wife sitting quietly in her chair a short distance away. A wariness had grown in her of late, a habit of answering him with an abrupt yes or no, a blandness of expression that effectively hid the workings of her mind. To others it might have been interpreted as a return to the shyness of her youth, but Ahmose knew otherwise. She was deeply and constantly angry with him, a rage mingled with disappointment and hurt pride, and though he wished it were not so, he had his own wounded pride to battle. He had tried to bridge the distance between them, joining her on the roof sometimes in the warm nights that were imbued with a sensuous invitation to love, but the words he needed to say had not come and she had rebuffed him with a sharp request not to condescend to her. He would have persevered, desperate to recover the intimacy they had once shared, but his divisions had returned, Ankhmahor and Harkhuf arriving at the same time as Paheri and Ahmose Abana, and he had been forced to turn his attention to his army.

He was careful to admit his relief at the distraction. Sitting in the lamp-hung garden, surrounded by the men with whom he had fought, discussing the future and reliving the Het-Uart siege and battle, he revelled in their robust laughter and frank conversation. He was aware of his wife sitting high above, alone and brooding, but for the first time since he and she had come together as man and wife he was in no hurry to be with her. He wondered if the new pregnancy was exaggerating her mood. He was glad that another child would be born, but he dreaded the accompanying anxiety that would hound him as it grew.

He had gone to the temple in secret to have the omens read, standing a respectful distance from the young priest with the Seeing gift as the man bent over the film of oil on water in the basin, waiting with bated breath for the recitation of the vision. His heart had leaped with fear when the ceremony was complete and he read defeat in the shake of the priest's head. "Seek a message from Amun's oracle as well, Majesty," he had said. "The oil does not always show accurately what will be, but the god's voice is infallible."

"Is it sickness or death?" Ahmose had croaked.

"Both sickness and death for the child," had been the pitiless reply and Ahmose had left the dark room and got onto his litter to be carried home in a fit of hopelessness. Up until then he had simply accepted that children were vulnerable to fevers and diseases. Children died easily. But now he began to wonder whether perhaps there was a disfigurement in Aahmes-nefertari's womb, something invisible but ultimately lethal to the babies she had borne. The possibility increased his anguish. Regardless of their current estrangement, he loved her with a steady liberality that still filled his heart and had never altered.

It occurred to him, the thought creeping into his mind like a snake writhing towards the damp shade under a rock, that some other woman might give him healthy offspring. After all, he was entitled to take other wives. Even concubines. He could not really imagine making love to anyone but Aahmes-nefertari. He knew himself to be the sort of man who cleaves to only one woman and is content. The feel of her skin under his fingers, the odours released by her body during sex, the taste of her mouth beneath his, all meant security and fulfilment to him. Strange flesh could never take the place of those precious things nor be a substitute for the seamless garment of mutual trust and understanding they had woven together. But strange flesh might conjure future Kings and their Queens who would live long enough to reach the age of reason. Horrified, Ahmose tried to put away such uncomfortable deliberations, but the snake, having found a dark and chilly place, curled up and would not be expelled.

Ahmose-onkh had been trying unsuccessfully to entice Behek away from his post. He had given up and at Akhtoy's call he came running in under the protection of his parent's canopy. Pa-she, after a bow in their direction, walked more sedately to join the other members of the household staff where their reed mats and sunshades had been set up just outside the tomb's compound. "Oh it is so hot!" Ahmose-onkh exclaimed, reaching for the jug of water. "Why must this Feast take place in summer?"

"Because during the winter the Inundation makes the river difficult to cross and during the spring everyone is busy with planting and sowing," his mother answered. "It is a fitting time to remember the dead." Ahmose watched with approval as the boy wiggled his fingers in the water-bowl without being told before his servant laid a platter of food across his knees.

"Pa-she has been teaching you good manners," he said. Ahmose-onkh nodded solemnly.

"My tutor knows everything," he pronounced. "Majesty Father, did you know that there are six hundred holy symbols that the mighty god Thoth gave to Ptah so that he could use them to speak everything in the world into being?"

"Yes indeed," Ahmose said gravely. "And we ourselves use them in our formal writing. But surely you are not learning them yet!"

"Not yet." Ahmose-onkh tore a piece of cold roast duck from a bone and bit into it energetically. "I am practising the hieratic script on the bits of clay Pa-she makes me collect myself from the kitchen. I can only form twelve letters so far."

"Twelve!" Aahmes-nefertari exclaimed. "But that is very good, Ahmose-onkh. Will you show me your work soon?"

"I will when I can do them all," he said, licking the salt from a slice of cucumber before putting it in his mouth. Then he looked up at her. "Was that rude, Majesty Mother? I have just learned the admonition of the scribe Ani." He frowned, chewing thoughtfully. "'Remember how your mother brought you into the world and with what embracing care she nurtured you'," he recited haltingly. "'Never give her cause to accuse you and lift up her hands to the god in condemnation of your conduct, and never give the god reason to listen to your mother's complaints.'" He blew out his breath with the effort of his success and beamed. Aahmes-nefertari smiled delightedly across at Ahmose, the first free smile, he thought, that I have received from her since I came home.

"That is excellent," she told Ahmose-onkh. "You have a good memory." Ahmose-onkh clapped gleefully but then destroyed the impression of obedience and erudition he was trying so hard to give by saying, "Which god did the scribe mean, Majesty Mother? We have so many. May I take these bones and scraps to Behek?"

"I am very pleased at the change in him, Aahmes-nefertari," Ahmose commented, his eyes on his stepson's small figure as he crossed the sand. "Pa-she has told us how quickly his pupil grasps and retains what he is taught." Aahmes-nefertari nodded.

"Pa-she asked if he might take him onto the roof some night and show him the constellations," she said. "My first reaction was one of fear, Ahmose. I thought of Father up there above the old palace and then of how Kamose was murdered and you wounded. Isn't it silly? We have never been more secure and yet I still start at shadows."

"So do I sometimes," he admitted. "But the two of them will be quite safe with a guard in attendance." He snapped his fingers at Akhtoy. "It is time to go back to the house," he said. "I want to see Abana and Paheri before they leave for Nekheb. I have given them a month with their wives before they are to go back to the Delta." At once her face became masked.

"I will stay here a little longer," she decided coolly. "I want to leave an offering for Si-Amun and I do not care that it is not allowed."

"Neither do I," he replied softly to her defiant face. "Remember his funeral, Aahmes-nefertari. All of us, Amunmose included, dared to sanctify his body at the same time as we were burying Father." He could not remember whether or not she had honoured Si-Amun at other Beautiful Feasts and he wondered if she was insisting on doing so now as a gesture aimed at his discomfiture. "Akhtoy, fetch the Prince and have the litters brought up," he ordered. "The ceremony is over."

Following Mesore, the first day of the month of Thoth marked the beginning of the new year, the rising of the Sopdet Star, and the start of winter. All Egypt was in festivity, crowding the temples, spreading out along the banks of the Nile where the sweetmeat sellers and those who sold cheap effigies of the gods barked their wares, and flooding the village compounds to dance, drink and gossip. Nobles and the wealthy took to the water in the evening, drifting to the music of drum, pipe and lute while the reflection of their torches rippled in the slow wake of their decorated skiffs and barges.

Ahmose rose before dawn to hear the Hymn of Praise

sung for him in Amun's temple and then officiate himself at the opening of the shrine and the feeding, clothing and censing of the god. He had hoped to find comfort in the faintly smiling face of the divinity who had been venerated by his family for generations and who had been the companion of Kamose's dreams, but the golden features seemed closed to him on this momentous day, breathing an air of self-sufficient mystery into the sanctuary that Ahmose's prayers could not penetrate.

He had told no one of the Seer's damning vision. Nor had he approached Amun's oracle. As long as I do not seek to have the prediction confirmed, I may doubt and thus hope, he said to himself dismally as his body bowed and prostrated itself, his arms lifted and fell, his mouth formed words of praise and supplication with the white-robed men around him. The baby is alive. Aahmes-nefertari felt it move inside her. Taking my hand, she laid it on her belly and I myself felt the tiny flutter of its limbs. All may be well. The Seeing oil may have attracted demons wishing to delude me, poison my love for her and the great promise of the future. Yet he was a truthful man and his rationalizations rang hollow even to himself.

Walking across the outer court of the temple to his litter, scorched and blinded by a sun still unrelentingly fierce, he fought the dejection. I will take her on the river tonight, he vowed. I will sleep with her on the roof. I will make my body an instrument of reassurance for her when my tongue refuses the words I would say. Today the priests begin their watch on the Nile, ready to record the water's rise. Today another year begins with all its unknown joys and terrors and only the gods know how it will end, but surely the regard Aahmes-nefertari and I have for each other is in our own power to preserve or see dribble away like sand through open fingers. Nodding to Ankhmahor and his military escort, he climbed onto the litter and started for home.

Egypt exhaled with relief when the annual flood began. The harvest was safely in, the corresponding taxes set, and Ahmose was becoming reconciled to the daily round of consultations, audiences and small quandaries of which his life was now composed. Sebek-nakht's family arrived in Weset with all their belongings, a signal to Ahmose that the Prince had committed himself finally and completely to his service. Ahmose appointed him Chief Architect and gave him a house next to the houses of the foreign ambassadors who had begun to trickle into the town that was rapidly becoming a city. Ahmose began to look forward to his hour with Sebek-nakht in the old palace. As the level of the Nile continued to swell and then spill over onto the land with its precious burden of silt, the palace also seemed to stir with new life. Ponderously, slowly, it was emerging from its long sleep of neglect, as though the hundreds of bricklayers, masons, artists and junior architects swarming over it were performing the function of sem-priests in the House of the Dead. Gutted and disembowelled, its shell undergoing a restoration to its former glory instead of the preservation of its corpse, it was being beautified for a return to grandeur instead of to a tomb.

Aahmes-nefertari continued to sit with Ahmose through the mornings of audience, but she took little part in the deliberations and her scribe, although also present, did not take notes. Her pregnancy was beginning to show in a certain delicate roundness of her abdomen and the flush of good health on her skin. She spent most afternoons in her own quarters, fulfilling her obligations in the temple as the Second Prophet of Amun, occasionally visiting the household guards' barracks where they were still under the command of Emkhu, and later, resting in the shade of the garden.

Neither she nor Ahmose saw much of Ahmose-onkh. He and Pa-she had formed an army of two. Pa-she accompanied his charge onto the parade ground where the boy had begun his instruction in the use of his tiny bow and miniature sword. They went together into the marshes so that Ahmose-onkh could hurl his throwing stick at the squawking ducks. And Ahmose-onkh held his tutor's hand as Pa-she attended to his own business, moving from his room in the house to the papyrus makers to his forays on the west bank among the dead in order to further his historical study. Ahmose had told Pa-she during one of the weekly reports on Ahmose-onkh's progress that a tutor was not responsible for his pupil outside the hours of instruction but Pa-she had demurred. "Sometimes the most valuable lessons can be learned when the time of formal guidance is over, Majesty," he had pointed out. "The opportunity to instil the good manners, honesty and kindness required by a child of Ma'at does not often arise during the dictating of script or the calculating of the worth of two khar of wheat. When I wish to be alone, I send for Raa and she takes the Prince away. It is as simple as that."

"Raa is getting fat from idleness," Ahmose said, grinning. "And your Prince has become an irritating fount of every kind of half-digested knowledge. Peace!" He held up a hand to forestall Pa-she's indignant response. "I am very pleased with your care of the Hawk-in-the-Nest. See that you do not become weary in your efforts."

One task that Ahmose had been dreading was the long deliberation required to pair each governor of the many nomes he now controlled with a man who would send him trust-worthy accounts of the state of the districts. He had asked Aahmes-nefertari a long time ago to draw up a list of suitable spies, for spies they were in spite of their exalted positions as his representatives. But he had not looked at it. Now he asked her to produce it, partly as a duty lying fallow but mainly as an opportunity to talk with her. She and Khunes came to the office late one afternoon and as a gesture of trust Ahmose dismissed Ipi. Aahmes-nefertari took the chair opposite Ahmose. As Khunes lowered himself to the floor beside her, he passed her a great sheaf of papyrus. Ahmose's heart sank. "There are only twenty-two nomes," he said. "Surely your scribe did not need so many sheets of paper to write them all down!" She smiled at him loftily.

"Of course not," she answered. "But I thought you might want to know how our trading negotiations are proceeding as well. You have officially received ambassadors from Keftiu, Asi, Mitanni and even a few strange and uncouth men from Kush. Neferperet and I have been busy improving the prospects for filling the treasury. After all, the renovations on the old palace have meant the expenditure of vast amounts of grain and vegetables for the peasants and that is only one problem. Feeding the two divisions is another. The fields they are to till have been prepared, but, of course, they cannot be sown until this year's flood recedes." Ahmose leaned forward, intrigued.

"What treaties have you concluded?" he wanted to know. She shuffled the pile of pale beige sheets.

"With Keftiu first, of course. They will send us bronze, poppy and dye in exchange for linen and papyrus. They have other things, vases, cups and so on, but we do not need such luxuries yet." She passed that piece of paper down to Khunes. "With Asi, silver in raw form, not much, for it is rare. We will give them linen, papyrus, leather and grain." Another sheet disappeared into Khunes's grasp. Ahmose could hear its rustle although he could not see the young man. "Mitanni has been difficult. It is far to the east beyond Rethennu and the ambassador is not sure whether he wishes to stay in Weset and waste his time in such a backwater." She smiled. "But several merchants came with him and Neferperet turned his attention to them. Merchants want profit, and these men smell future wealth. They will provide us with spices, precious woods, purple gold, and iron dagger blades, none of which we can make or grow here in Egypt. But for that they want grain and gold."

"The granaries are full, so grain is not a problem," Ahmose interposed. "But gold from Kush and Wawat is not yet fully guaranteed. How will you honour this commitment?" She held up a finger.

"I took the trouble to grant an audience to the men from Kush. They have wandered up to Weset from their tribes in the south seeking assurances that you will leave them alone. They fear Teti-En and the collection of tribes that compose his petty kingdom and they fear you. I told them that so long as they supply us with gold we will endeavour to protect them from Teti-the-Handsome if he should decide to expand the area of his influence."

"Did you indeed!" Ahmose exclaimed. "So I am to provide troops for Kush whenever the troglodytes imagine that their miserable lives are threatened? Have you made it worth my while?"

"I think so," she replied coolly, unperturbed by his outburst. "Kush will keep the gold mines working and also send us ivory, ebony, incense, lapis and exotic animal skins."

"Ah!" Ahmose nodded. "That is very good. So much in exchange for nothing more than a promise of protection. Let us hope that Teti-En remains content with the curious conglomeration of villages he calls his kingdom. I am surprised that he has not sent emissaries to us now that his so-called brother Apepa has been rendered impotent." He sighed. "But, Aahmes-nefertari, I need cedar from Rethennu to build masts for my ships. When will Het-Uart fall?"

There was a moment of silence during which his wife looked across at him, her dark eyebrows raised. She waits for a compliment, he realized suddenly. She has accomplished a great deal on my behalf and I sit here like a selfish idiot. "I am amazed at your efficiency and the success of your efforts," he said at last. "Let us hope that all agreements will bear fruit. Now what of that list of names?" She nodded as though satisfied with his words, and this time instead of reading from the papyrus she slid it across the table.

"Hammering out the trading contracts was as nothing compared to the months I spent preparing this for you," she said crisply. "I searched the archives in the House of Life here in Weset for the lineages of eligible men. After

Khunes came into my employ, I sent him to every House of Life as far as Khemmenu in the north and Swenet in the south, with the same goal. When he returned, I laid out our findings. Age, family history and connections, talents, success or failure in dealing with their own overseers and peasants, behaviour under our father's and Kamose's uprisings; many of my conclusions were a result of a series of hints regarding each candidate that gathered themselves together like grains of sand in a forgotten corner of the house." She jerked her chin towards the list over which he was now frowning. "All the judgement and intuition of which I am capable went into that," she told him. "I am prepared to hold myself responsible for the loyalty of every man I selected."

"Are you?" he said, surprised. "Then you must have been extraordinarily thorough in your research and confident in its outcome." He shook the paper and his face cleared. "I see that you have not only produced a list of names but also which ones will suit which nomes best. I only recognize a few of them." His relief was evident. He had hardly bothered to scan the list. "I confess that it will be a weight lifted from my mind when they are in place and sending me regular communications. I daresay that you and Mother have set those arrangements in place as well?" She made a teasing moue and retrieved the sheet.

"Of course," she said promptly. "I have hired new heralds who are only waiting for your order to summon the men to Weset to swear their allegiance at your feet before scattering to take up their posts." She hesitated. "Ahmose, it might be advantageous to invent a title for them. They will outwardly be advisers to the governors and Princes but knowing themselves to be little more than spies could be offensive to them. I have chosen them for their honesty and reliability, after all." He grunted.

"I told you months ago that never again during my reign would any noble's head be permitted to rise above the level I alone will determine," he said, "and that I would be quite happy to heap titles on them until it took their servants a whole morning to announce them. Titles mean nothing unless accompanied by power, and power I will not give them! Therefore I agree with you." He gazed up at the ceiling and his sandalled foot began to tap against the table's gilded leg. "What shall we call them? Let me see. How about 'Herald of his Lord and King's Son'? The epithet 'Herald' will raise their messages to me above the status of clandestine intercourse, in their own minds at least, and 'King's Son' will make them feel uniquely attached to me. Yes?"

"You are a clever and devious god!" she laughed. "Yes, you have chosen well. Will you give them no power at all, Ahmose?"

"I will not speak of authority to them when they kneel before me," he replied thoughtfully. "But I will be prepared to give them the governorship of any nome that is being mismanaged or whose governor is fomenting unrest."

"The exception is of course Ramose," she pointed out. "You have given him the governorship of the Un nome and full control of Khemmenu, Nefrusi, Hor and Dashlut. I did not place any secondary name against his."

"No. It is not necessary to have Ramose watched. Him I do indeed trust."

"You are losing your caution," she ventured.

"Not entirely," he said. "Sometimes I dream of the Princes' revolt. I was lying unconscious and wounded and did not see it, nor your and Mother's great bravery in putting it down, but the nightmare of it visits me anyway. I want no knife in the back when I am least expecting it, Aahmes-nefertari. Nor do I want to use up my reign in rushing here and there with my divisions putting down insurrections."

"It is not really mistrust any more, is it, my husband?" He met her eyes and saw affection there.

"No, it isn't," he said simply. "You have utterly justified the trust I placed in you, my dearest sister, and that has encouraged me to have faith in the men you have gathered around you in my absence."

"Thank you, Ahmose," she said shakily. "I have needed to hear that. Are you then no longer jealous?" He looked for humour in her face, hoping he would find it, but she was completely serious. He did not want to, but he was forced to answer her with equal sincerity. They had been talking as they used to do in the past when they had made decisions together in perfect accord and he sensed the damage to be done if he spoke with levity.

"Sometimes it still rises up in me, as anger does in you," he admitted huskily. "But I love you, Aahmes-nefertari. I love you as I have always done." To his discomfiture he saw her eyes swim with sudden tears.

"I love you also, my brother," she said. At her side on the floor Khunes stirred.

"Your pardon, Majesty, but I presume that you do not wish a record of the words spoken after 'the men you have gathered around you in my absence'?" Aahmes-nefertari laughed shakily.

"Indeed not!" she agreed. Ahmose watched her, half-expecting her to reach down and pat the scribe on his linen-covered head. Awkwardly he changed the subject, rising as he did so.

"There has been no scroll from Mother or Grandmother for quite some time," he observed. Obediently Aahmes-nefertari also left her chair, but abruptly and unexpectedly she raised her arms above her head, stretched slowly, and yawned, exposing her long, gold-hung throat. The feline quality of the act caught Ahmose by surprise and to his greater surprise he felt himself becoming sexually aroused.

"I am sure that they are safe and in good health," she replied. "In her last letter Mother said that there were indeed repairs to be made on her ancestor's tomb at Djeb and that until they were completed she and Tetisheri were comfortably settled in a house by the river. I think they are enjoying the languid pace of life in the south." He came around the table and slid a hand under her hair. The nape of her neck was hot.

"I will leave the summoning of the men on the list to you," he murmured. "Meanwhile let us go to my quarters, Aahmes-nefertari, or yours, it does not matter. I have missed you in my bed. I want to make love to you." He had swallowed a large portion of his pride in making his request so nakedly and he waited anxiously for her response. For a moment she remained motionless. He was about to withdraw his hand in embarrassment, but at last she turned to him with first suspicion and then a dawning gladness lighting her features. Yes, this time I will be fully present with you, he said to her silently. She must have read the thought behind his eyes, for she bent her head until its crown rested against his chest.

"I am yours to command, Majesty," she whispered. "And you, Khunes, can draft a letter to be carried to the men the King has now approved. I will look it over later."

It was the beginning of a reconciliation of sorts between them, a process which had its share of setbacks and woundings as they struggled to come to terms with the changes that had taken place in each other. It was aided both by the complex but increasingly stable routine of court life with which Ahmose was becoming familiar and Aahmes-nefertari's pregnancy. As the weeks went by she had less desire to be actively involved with the people she had appointed or the policies that she herself had initially instigated, being content to have each day's events and decisions recounted to her by Ahmose in the evenings they had now taken to spending together.

At the beginning of Khoiak, just after the Feast of Hathor, when the river had almost reached its highest level and the air was losing its edge of searing heat, Ahmose Abana arrived. He had tied his skiff to a pole at the watersteps and, preceded by one of the heralds who were always stationed by the gates, he made his way to the garden where Ahmose and his wife with their personal staff were enjoying the last of the sunset. Pa-she and Ahmose-onkh were also present. Aahmes-nefertari's diminishing lap was filled with pieces of clay, for the boy had been proudly showing her the lessons he had so far inscribed on them. Ahmose was watching them both with idle pleasure. The diffused red glow permeating the air and now rapidly fading had enveloped them in its soft light and their voices, his wife's low, his son's strident, echoed in the peculiar auditory hallucination that often accompanied the final glimpse of Ra's disc as he slipped below the horizon.

Mosquitoes trembled above the placid pink surface of the pond and shadows had begun to merge into one dim mass beneath the trees surrounding the lawn. The large lamps hanging from the frame of the canopy had not yet been lit and Ahmose had just signalled to Akhtoy to do so when a herald materialized out of the gloom, another figure behind him, and bowed. "The Admiral Ahmose Abana, Your Majesty," he announced.

"What?" Ahmose waved him aside. "Abana, what are you doing here? It is scarcely six weeks since you ended your month's leave in Nekheb and returned to the Delta. You look terrible. Akhtoy, give the taper to someone else and have food and wine brought."

As the young man came forward and bowed, his shoulders hunched and his normally animated face wooden, a spasm of fear shook Ahmose. The Wall of Princes has been retaken by the enemy, he thought wildly. The Setiu have found more troops and they are even now pouring into the Delta along the Horus Road. The gates of Het-Uart opened and my army could not stand and Apepa is marching on Weset. Taking a deep breath, he forced down the panic and snapped his fingers at Pa-she. "Ahmose-onkh, it is time for you to go to bed," he said. "Don't argue. Gather up your work and put it back in the bag. Kiss me and your mother." With a well-concealed pout of disappointment Ahmose-onkh did as he was told, and taking his hand Pa-she led him away. Ahmose found himself staring after their figures, the tall and the short, both silhouetted against the torches that had begun to shine out from the house, in a kind of stupor. Rousing himself, he looked about. "Ipi, you stay," he ordered. "The rest of you are dismissed." At once the servants reverenced him and scattered, all but Hekayib who was swiftly moving from lamp to lamp with the taper. As he went, he left behind him great circles of strengthening light that threw his shadow out before him on the rough grass. Ahmose watched Abana's features sharpen into full focus as the night was pushed back. The man did indeed look exhausted, his eyes swollen half-shut, his shoulders hunched. Hekayib completed his task, blew out the taper, bowed, and vanished into the pressing darkness.

Ahmose beckoned the Admiral. "You had better sit down before you fall down, Abana," he said. "Are you alone? Did you come in the *Shining in Mennofer*?" Abana sank onto the mat with a groan of relief.

"I came alone in the lightest skiff I could find, Majesty," he answered hoarsely. "I needed speed. It was a mistake not to bring help, for I have had to row against the highest level of the river with the winter winds against me, but I wanted to give you my news in person before it filtered down to Weset through other mouths." He rubbed an eye with one grubby finger and smiled wanly. "Battling the flood, even in a skiff, is no mean feat."

Be calm, Ahmose told himself as his whole body tensed. Why do you presume that his news is bad? How can it be bad when my soldiers are ranged as thickly as rows of grain around Het-Uart?

"I know your skill on water," he said irritably. "You do not need to remind me. Tell me what has happened." Abana looked up at him.

"We have failed you, Majesty," he admitted. "We had a chance to capture Apepa and we blundered. I bring abject apologies from the generals responsible for keeping the city enclosed."

"Capture him?" Aahmes-nefertari put in sharply. "Are you telling us that Het-Uart has fallen?" She was leaning forward, her incredulous expression clear in the yellow lamplight. Abana shook his head.

"May the gods punish us for our sloth," he said bitterly. "I will not excuse us, but I will say that a siege of years is a wearisome thing and men may become inattentive at their posts while still performing their duty." He was stumbling a little over his words, and though Ahmose was desperate to hear what story might unfold, he held up a hand.

"Eat and drink before you go on," he said. "Akhtoy is here." The steward had approached with a servant who laid a dish beside Abana and withdrew. Akhtoy poured wine. Abana snatched it from him and drank deeply before attacking the food. Ahmose waited. At last Abana wiped his mouth on his already stained kilt.

"Forgive me, Majesty ..." he began, and at that Ahmose's patience deserted him.

"Humility before the gods is highly commendable," he roared, "but before a King it is an annoying obstacle best kicked out of the way. You of all men are least given to its exercise, Admiral, therefore stop attempting to master it and deliver your news!"

"Nevertheless, Majesty, my boastful nature has been to some degree reduced by my own idiocy, as you will hear," Abana came back promptly with a spark of his usual impertinence. He crossed his legs, and grasping his knees he began to rock gently to and fro. He is genuinely chastened, Ahmose thought in surprise. This is not a show. "On the twelfth of Athyr we celebrated the last day of the Festival of Hapi," Abana went on. "Of course the whole army took part, but as Hapi is god of the Nile we of the navy observed the rites with especial reverence and joy." He shot Ahmose a quick glance. "When I say the whole army, I mean those men not on duty. And a portion of the navy was continuing its patrol of the canals around Het-Uart, soberly and correctly."

"The rest of you got drunk," Ahmose said dryly. Abana nodded.

"As always on such happy occasions," he agreed. "Paheri had taken command of the navy that night. I and my crew were part of those who, having been relieved, were sitting around the cooking fires with our beer. We were on the east side of the city with water between us and the walls. Suddenly we heard a great commotion coming from the west side where the main tributary snakes beside Het-Uart and where the gate had opened once before. I got up and began to run. When I reached the gate, I saw that a host of Setiu had come out silently under cover of the darkness and were attacking our soldiers. The gate had closed again. Our men were surprised and confused. They had received no warning."

"Of course there had been no warning!" Ahmose protested. "Did the generals expect the Setiu to stand on the wall holding torches and shouting 'get ready, we are coming out'?" Abana's grip tightened on his knees.

"I am s— The city had been very quiet for such a long time, for weeks, Majesty, as though it had died. The foray was completely unexpected. Our soldiers rallied and I saw our ships come round to assist them. I ran back to where the *Shining in Mennofer* was berthed, my crew with me. We were opposite the east side of Het-Uart. We cast off intending to join the fray, but as I stared at the section of the wall across the water from me I saw movement." He clapped a hand to his head. "Fool that I am! I was not on duty. I had been drunk. I was becoming sober but not fast enough. The wall and the sky above were very dark. I could not see well, but my cousin Zaa was beside me and he pointed into the gloom. 'There are men lowering something,' he said. 'I think it is a boat.' Even as he spoke, it struck the water. I was puzzled. If I had not been awash with beer I would have realized sooner that the fighting to the west was nothing but a diversion, but I stood on the deck of my ship without understanding. 'They are lowering another thing,' Zaa said. 'It looks like a big basket. What is happening, Ahmose?' Abana clenched his fists and pounded the ground. "Majesty, I still did not see," he cried out. "If I had let that basket descend to the ground, if I had waited quietly, I would be presenting myself to you this evening in triumph with your vile enemy tied to my mast!"

"Apepa was in the basket," Aahmes-nefertari said tonelessly. "He was trying to escape. What a dishonourable act, to desert his people and sneak away like the weasel that he is. How did you know it was he? Was there anyone else with him?" Tani, Ahmose thought immediately and he groped for his wife's fingers. Finding them cold, he squeezed them gently.

"The steering lamp had been lit on my vessel, Majesty," Abana told her. "I could discern movement in the basket as it slid slowly down the wall. Without thinking, befuddled as I still was, I unslung my bow and fired an arrow at the vague shapes above the rim of the basket. It struck a man who screamed and toppled out, falling to the earth and taking with him a black cloth that had covered those concealed within. There was a shout and the basket was hurriedly drawn up again. I fired once more but the arrow went wide. A face peered down just as the basket was hauled over the lip of the wall. It was Apepa beyond doubt. One of my sailors remembered him from his progress upriver when he came to Weset to destroy your family." The fists unclenched slowly and were offered to Ahmose, palms up. "Now you know why I must beg your forgiveness," Abana said. "The usurper is back inside his stronghold and I am ashamed. I took my ship to the western wall but by then the small battle was over. We lost thirty men but the Setiu were all killed. I took the hand of the man I shot."

He fell silent and Ahmose sat back until his face was in shadow, thinking furiously. Beside him Aahmes-nefertari was breathing quickly and audibly, whether from anger at Abana's ineptitude or a vision of Tani in that basket, he could not tell. No, he would not take Tani away with him, Ahmose said to himself firmly. If he took anyone, it would surely be his oldest son, the second Apepa, and perhaps Kypenpen, his younger son, as well. Queens can be easily made afresh but it is not so simple to create a successor. He cannot spring forth fully mature and healthy from his father's seed. "The man you shot, was he identified?" he asked suddenly. Abana shook his head.

"He was richly dressed in the garb of a steward," he said. "White-haired and bearded in the Setiu fashion."

"His advisers should be executed," Ahmose retorted. "A diversion was the last thing he ought to have decided upon. All it did was alert the whole army and navy, whereas one basket sliding quietly down the wall in the dead of night stood a good chance of being undetected. He has been thwarted. What will he do now?"

Abana snorted. Having told his story without an explosion of rage from the King, he was beginning to recover his natural aplomb. "I think he will try again," he said, "but not soon. His experience will have shaken him. But, Majesty, the situation inside Het-Uart must be very critical if he had decided to abandon the thousands of citizens under his care."

"I am tired of speculating about it," Ahmose sighed. "How much water, how much food, how much disease, how much despair; what does it matter if those gates never open in an acknowledgement of defeat? Get up, Abana." The young man did as he was bid. Facing him, Ahmose could see that both the food and the unburdening of himself had done him good. His face had lost its hunted look. He is not without sensitivity, Ahmose mused. It must have been terrible for him, the frantic journey from the Delta with such a weight on his conscience, not knowing whether or not I would punish him. "If the whole army and navy had been feasting and if you had been drunk while on duty, I would certainly be enraged enough to remove the noses and ears of my commanders and exile them," he said. "But no such undisciplined behaviour occurred. Therefore no reprimand is required, although it seems that the generals' vigilance is waning somewhat. Go with Akhtoy. He will find you a bed and have you bathed." Abana bowed.

"Majesty, you speak truly of your army's conscientiousness," he said. "I thank you for your magnanimity towards me, your eager and remorseful servant." He backed away, still bent low, melting into the blackness between the lights surrounding the trio in the garden and the lamps burning in the house.

"Ipi, did you record all that the Admiral said?" Ahmose asked. The scribe nodded. "Then you also may go." Ipi gathered up his pens, closed his ink, and was gone. "I think it is time for me to return to the Delta," Ahmose said heavily. "The troops need to see me again. Their enthusiasm for an admittedly boring task is fading." He was vitally aware of his wife's fixed profile, the tense immobility of her misshapen body.

"I felt strange when it came to me that Tani might have been in that basket," she said deliberately. "I cared and yet I did not care at all." He put an arm around her stiff shoulders.

"I know," he said simply. "We should go in, Aahmes-nefertari. You are cold." Obediently she rose. He was not sure that she had heard him speak of leaving until shrugging her cloak around her she said, "You will do what you must, go north or stay. As for me, I am imprisoned by this body and must give birth yet again." Her tone was biting, and wisely he did not reply.

Once inside the house she kissed him, and wishing him a peaceful sleep she retired to her own apartments. But Ahmose stood irresolute in the passage just beyond the reception hall, hearing her voice come floating back to him as she paused for a few words with the guard on her door. He could not make out what was said but her tone was warm. She loves the soldiers she has chosen and shepherded, he thought. She knows the names of their wives and children. She knows which ones are standing watch and where. Every week she goes out to their barracks, and if she sees any lack she remedies it at once. The bond was forged during the days I have lost, when I lay unconscious and the fate of Egypt was in her hands. Hers and Aahotep's. A piece of my life is missing forever, but hers went on, and I am eternally excluded from the many maturings that took place around me during that time.

As if in response to his pondering his head began to ache, a subtle pulse warning him that he should go to his couch, but Abana's news had disturbed him. He felt the stirrings of a belated anger, not at the Admiral but at a fate that had teased him with the promise of Apepa's capture only to snatch it away again. Apepa roped to a chariot and driven round the walls of the city for all its inhabitants to see while Khabekhnet called "Your King is taken! Surrender!" It was an intoxicating fantasy, and all the more painful for almost coming true. This struggle has become as stale as water left to stand too long in a ewer, he told himself. Just the thought of it makes me tired.

He walked to his quarters, past the salutes of the soldiers safeguarding the corridors, and as he came up to the door Akhtoy rose from his stool and bowed. Ahmose paused. He knew he should sleep or his headache would intensify but suddenly he could not face being shut up alone with his restlessness. "Send for Prince Ankhmahor," he said. "Tell him to meet me on the watersteps and then you can go to your own couch, Akhtoy. I want to be on the river for a little while tonight."

"The flood has reached its highest level and the current is running very fast," Akhtoy said dubiously. "Is it wise, Majesty?"

"No, it is not," Ahmose replied. "Fetch me a cloak before you go."

Ankhmahor's presence was reassuring. The man had a calm self-possession about him that soothed Ahmose, and as both of them picked up a set of oars and backed away from the watersteps, Ahmose felt his tension and discouragement begin to flow away. The moon was coming up to the full, a misshapen bluish globe whose light was nevertheless bright enough to leave a broken silver trail on the Nile's dark and swollen bosom. The half-drowned trees on either bank made a forest of dim mystery and beyond them on the east bank the city of Weset cast a faint but sinister orange glow against the thick blackness of the night sky. One tiny pinprick of light high above marked the roof of Amun's temple and the reflection of similar lights, hung irregularly along the eastern edge of the flood where the ministers and nobles had their fine new watersteps, shivered and danced. Ahmose made all the quiet beauty his own with a slow intake of breath. "I wish we could fish," he said wistfully. "A King must not offend Hapi, but I miss my favourite pastime."

"Where does your Majesty wish to go?" Ankhmahor asked politely as the current began to tug at their craft. Ahmose shrugged.

"We can drift downstream for a while and then row back," he said. "I need the exercise and besides, I simply cannot sleep yet, Ankhmahor. Het-Uart is driving me mad."

"The situation in the north cannot exist as it is forever," Ankhmahor said reasonably. "If we remain patient, Majesty, the city must eventually fall."

"It could have fallen last month," Ahmose groaned, and while the Prince kept his hand on the helm and they glided in the Nile's blind grasp, he told Ankhmahor all that Abana had recounted. The Prince listened, commented, and before long the pair of them were deep in a conversation that ranged over every stratagem ever conceived for the downfall of Het-Uart. It did Ahmose good, but he was careful to remind himself that nothing new had been said. There was nothing new to say or to be done.

The pull back to the watersteps was hard, leaving little breath for talking, and both men were tired and sweating by the time the skiff was moored and they stood once more before the gates into Ahmose's garden. Bidding the Prince a good night, Ahmose had himself admitted, and skirting the house he entered towards the rear. The bath house was dim and empty, its damp air faintly perfumed with lotus and jasmine. Leaving the outer door open to let in a little moonlight, Ahmose inspected the tall water jars ranged along the walls until he found one full. Taking a handful of natron, he scrubbed himself down and then doused himself in the cold water, gasping and exclaiming as it met his hot skin. The servants had removed all linen to be washed and he found nothing with which to dry himself but he did not mind. A pleasant fatigue had overtaken him. Snatching up his soiled kilt and cloak, he opened the inner door to the house and padded towards his rooms, realizing as he went that his headache had completely disappeared.

As he approached his door, he saw that it was open and

lamplight was streaming out into the passage. Urgent voices were raised within, his wife's and another, and his heart began to pound. Rapid footsteps were coming up from behind. He swung round to see Emkhu hurrying towards him. "Majesty, my men have been looking for you everywhere!" he panted. "Akhtoy said you were on the river but by the time I questioned the gate guards you had returned and disappeared. The Queen needs you." As he finished speaking, Aahmes-nefertari herself called out.

"Is he there, Emkhu? Have you found him?" Ahmose ran through the doorway.

Aahmes-nefertari was clutching the folds of her sleeping shift to her neck and pacing and a man Ahmose had not seen before was standing by the window. He bowed as Ahmose came to a halt, blinking in the flood of lamplight, and Aahmes-nefertari turned on him.

"Where have you been?" she demanded. "Why, Ahmose, you are naked and dripping! Akhtoy said you took a skiff. Did you capsize?" He did not answer at once. She seemed distressed but not ill, so he knew his first fear to be groundless. Walking to his couch he dragged a sheet from it, and only when he had covered himself did he face her.

"I did not capsize," he said evenly. "I went to the bath house and washed myself when Ankhmahor and I returned." His glance went to the man who had stepped away from the window and was regarding him gravely.

"This is Mereruka, the chief of my spies in Esna and Pi-Hathor," Aahmes-nefertari explained. "I have spoken of him to you. He has five men and women under him and he himself lives at Pi-Hathor where he breeds and sells donkeys."

"A useful occupation for a spy," Ahmose commented. Suddenly very weary he sat down in his chair. For a few precious hours I was a Prince again, he thought. Now once more I am a King. "Your news must be important to bring you to Weset in person." Mereruka inclined his head. He was, Ahmose thought, the most nondescript man he had ever seen. Everything about him from his short black hair to his worn reed sandals was anonymous. He had no distinctive features. Even his gestures were unremarkable, being neither too elaborate nor too stilted. Ahmose spared a moment to marvel at his wife's shrewdness in selecting someone who would always be nothing more than a face in a crowd even when he stood alone.

"It is vital, Majesty," Mereruka said. "I have been providing Her Majesty with regular reports, oral of course, on the growing unrest among the citizens of both towns for which I am responsible. I am sure Your Majesty does not need to be told how Esna and Pi-Hathor have suffered. Many Setiu live in those two towns. They used to be prosperous." He may have a face that is easily forgotten but his intellect and manner of speech does not match it, Ahmose thought. Wherever did Aahmes-nefertari find him?

"I know," he broke in impatiently. "Kamose managed to keep them quiet with threats and a pact."

"They are quiet no longer," Mereruka said grimly. "Two days ago the mayor of Pi-Hathor was murdered and his house burned. Yesterday the mayor of Esna was also clubbed to death before a crowd of shouting citizens who had already flung up a barricade across the river and killed one of your heralds coming up from Djeb. They intend to waylay the gold shipments as they appear. They were disorganized and wild in their discontent, but now there are men who are controlling and channelling their dissatisfaction into one coherent force. Only four miles separate the towns. Already there are gangs stationed just north of Pi-Hathor to prevent anyone from leaving the area and warning you. I fear a concerted uprising."

"How did you get here?" Ahmose wanted to know. Mereruka waved away the question.

"I took some of my donkeys towards Esna with my son, left him in charge of them between the towns, and took a raft across the river. I have sent a message to the Queens Aahotep and Tetisheri to stay where they are in Djeb until Your Majesty has resolved this situation."

"Have you indeed?" Ahmose said softly, aware of an irrational irritation. "That was farsighted of you. I presume that you wish to give me your advice?" The man glanced swiftly at Aahmes-nefertari, obviously taken aback by the King's tone. Aahmes-nefertari stepped forward.

"He presumes nothing," she said forcefully. "But we would do well to listen to him, Ahmose." She had tactfully avoided accusing him of an arrogant ingratitude by saying "we," and Ahmose's moment of pique died.

"Yes, we would," he said mildly. "Tell me what I should do, Mereruka. Will the malcontents exhaust themselves after a few violent acts, in which case I may wait and then send judges, or is it necessary to take an army south?"

"Perhaps not an army, Majesty," Mereruka answered carefully. "But in my opinion you have a small rebellion on your hands that will swell into something far more dangerous than it is already if you wait. A thousand men should be enough to quell it." Ahmose got up, casting a longing look at his couch as he did so.

"Thank you," he said. "Will you return to Pi-Hathor tonight?" Mereruka bowed. He was already inching towards the door.

"I must," he said. "I have left my son and the donkeys in a quiet place beside the river, but if he is seen to dally there too long, people who pass by him will begin to wonder why. Am I dismissed?" Ahmose nodded. After another bow, this time in Aahmes-nefertari's direction, Mereruka went out. To Ahmose it seemed that but for his words he had never been there.

"What a remarkable man!" Ahmose commented rather uncomfortably. "Where does he come from?" Aahmes-nefertari had walked to the table and was now facing him, her gown still pulled closed under her chin.

"I heard about him from Uni who heard about him from one of the kitchen servants," she replied. "He was living in Weset with his wife and son and working for a merchant who had hired him to gather information regarding the business dealings of other merchants. It seems that often the largest bribes obtain the richest trade agreements and his master wanted to know what the others of his profession were offering." She smiled coldly. "But what attracted my interest was the fact that although he had become somewhat notorious among the servants of the various households no one could accurately describe his appearance or his habits. Ahmose, what are you going to do?"

"Discipline Esna and Pi-Hathor of course." He shouted for Akhtoy, then turned back to her. "I must teach them a lesson, Aahmes-nefertari. Kamose was uncharacteristically kind to them compared to his treatment of many other towns in Egypt and they have repaid his magnanimity with treachery."

"They are impoverished and wretched," she interposed. He raised his eyebrows.

"Are you defending them? Most of them are Setiu, remember. They could have sent their mayors and delegations here to me to explain their plight and ask for help. I would have done my best for them, Aahmes-nefertari, you know that. But no. Like all Setiu they have behaved in a perfidious and bloody way. Their blithe disregard for any consequence to their actions is an insult to me. I will not have it!" Akhtoy had entered and was waiting impassively. "Get Abana out of his bed and send him to me," he ordered, "and detain the spy. Wake up the kitchen staff. They might as well provide us with hot food. I do not think we will be sleeping tonight."

When Ahmose Abana bowed his way in, seemingly as alert and clear-eyed as ever in spite of his disordered hair and crookedly tied kilt, Ahmose told him what the spy had said. "You are to go south to Nekheb," he commanded. "You should have little trouble as you pass Esna and Pi-Hathor. They are on the west bank of the Nile and Nekheb is on the east. In fact you can travel that far with the spy. I will give you both an escort. Bring three of the ships that were sent down for repairs after the battle outside Het-Uart. That should be enough to deal with the barricade, whatever it is. You can take a look at it as you go. I will march south with a thousand men from the Division of Amun. It will take me no more than a day to reach Pi-Hathor. It is only eighteen miles from Weset. How soon before you can bring the ships?" Abana was calculating, eyes narrowed.

"Eighteen to Pi-Hathor, four to Esna, a further twenty-two to Nekheb," he murmured. "Forty-four miles on foot. Three days if all goes well. Then a further day to round up sailors and such soldiers as will be necessary for this little undertaking." His tone was caustic. "Moving with the current, the river being full and still fast, I should come in sight of Esna in a further day or less."

"Good. Then in five days I will fall upon Pi-Hathor and then meet you somewhere close by. Akhtoy will introduce you to Mereruka." When Abana had left the room, he collapsed into his chair. "Oh damn them, Aahmes-nefertari!" he complained. "I had hoped that the last killing I would have to do would be in Het-Uart!"

"Nevertheless you are glad to be going," she retorted. "You were becoming bored with life here. Admit it, Ahmose." He would not look fully into her flushed face, although he could see her on the edge of his vision.

"Not bored, no." He considered her accusation and then denied it pensively. "But I find that I cannot give myself wholeheartedly to the mundane occupation of Egypt's organization when Het-Uart sits unconquered. A loose thread that spoils the whole beautiful garment we are weaving together." Now he did seek her eyes. "This will be a distraction, a positive action, something to do instead of listening to the faint but constant pulse of frustration coming to me out of the north."

"I had not thought of killing as a distraction," she said waspishly as she moved towards the door. "I am tired and will go to my couch."

"I had not meant it that way!" he called after her. But perhaps I did, he thought to himself a little later as Hekayib was laying the steaming lentil and garlic stew before him and Akhtoy came forward to serve. It will indeed be a welcome detour in the long road to the open gates of Het-Uart and I have less compunction over killing mutinous Setiu than I ought.

In the morning Abana and Mereruka had gone, with twenty men from the Division of Amun. Ahmose summoned Turi and Ankhmahor, warning them that they must be prepared to march in a few days, Turi with troops from his Amun Division and Ankhmahor with the Followers. He had decided not to take any Medjay with him. He did not think that their skill would be needed and besides, they had returned from their villages in Wawat with their wives and children and were still settling into the huts Sebek-nakht had hurriedly provided for them on the edge of the desert with the noise and excited commotion that seemed to accompany everything they did. Hor-Aha had humorously told Ahmose that he had been compelled to take strong measures to prevent whole villages from packing up their meagre belongings and following his archers north into Egypt. Their quarters seemed poor indeed to Ahmose, who had caused a paroxysm of exhilaration among them when he had picked his way through the foetid herds of their cows and goats to welcome them, but Hor-Aha had assured him that they were content.

There were no more letters from his mother and grandmother, but Ahmose did not expect any. Aahotep would make sure that they obeyed Mereruka's request to stay in Djeb for the time being. "Tetisheri would see such a directive, no matter how sensible, as a challenge to her nobility on the part of the peasants of the two towns," Ahmose observed to his wife as they lay side by side in his bedchamber on the eve of his departure. "If she had been born a man, she would be King by now and the Setiu would be nothing but a memory." Aahmes-nefertari drew the blanket up over her breasts, for the night was cool and the fire in the small brazier had burned low.

"She will be intensely curious to know what is happening," she remarked. "Perhaps Abana should have stopped in at Djeb on his way to Nekheb to tell her."

"Just as well I did not suggest it," Ahmose retorted. "She outranks him utterly. She might have demanded to be collected as the ships passed by and he would have had great difficulty in refusing her."

"I wish that I was going with you." Aahmes-nefertari spoke wistfully into the small silence that followed. "You are not the only one who is sometimes bored, Ahmose." He raised his head and kissed her tangled hair.

"I need you here as Queen," he said lightly. "Besides, you are now too big to fit inside my chariot." She did not laugh at his joke.

"You will be back before our baby is born, won't you, Ahmose?" she insisted. He struggled up onto his elbow and looked down on her troubled face.

"This matter will be over in less than a week from tomorrow," he said. "Compared with the major campaigning I have done, it is a mere flick of the sword. The celebration of the Feast of the Coronation of Horus on the first day of Tybi will see me by your side, Aahmes-nefertari, and the baby is not due until the next month. Do not fret."

Her features cleared and she closed her eyes, but he did not move, his own eyes travelling along the pleasant curve of her jaw, the long black lashes lying against her cheek, the thin shadow between her breasts half-hidden by the bedclothes. I will be here, my sister, he thought, but I do not want to be. If you knew how desperately and cravenly I could wish myself a thousand miles from Weset when you give birth, your love for me would turn to contempt in a moment. If the Seer is correct, there is nothing but heart-break for you and despair for me in your distended womb. Amun help me, for I adore you still and would spare you this coming pain if I could.

She had drifted into sleep, her breathing slow and regular, and he rolled onto his back and lay with one arm across his forehead, staring into the red shadows flickering on the ceiling and trying to banish the fantasies creeping into his mind.

11

AFTER BEING FERRIED ACROSS the river to the west bank, Ahmose and his men struck out for the south, past the place of the dead and round the slow curve the Nile took. On their right the run of hummocked sand continued, ending in the serried range of hills that alternately tumbled and rose sharply against a cloudless sky. On their left, beyond the straggling groves of palm trees through which they marched, the marshes clattered softly in the brisk wind, thick with white birds clinging precariously to the stiffly swaying reeds. Here and there Ahmose glimpsed the twin humps of hippopotamus nostrils, and swirls of glittering water told where they had submerged.

The Nile's level was sinking, the sun was bright but without the uncomfortable heat of Shemu, and happily Ahmose inhaled the mingled scents of wet earth and his horses' sweat. Before and behind him his soldiers strode talking aimlessly and cheerfully to one another, the murmur of their conversations a pleasant accompaniment to the creak of his chariot wheels and the dull thud of the Followers' sandalled feet around him. It is like a hunting expedition, he thought contentedly. The men know that they are in no danger from this little routing. Their quarry is already cornered, a rabble of angry townspeople who will present no challenge to their seasoned skill. As for myself, my only obligation is to stand in my chariot and watch Egypt slide by. I am free.

They had started out just before dawn and by noon had covered half the distance to Pi-Hathor. Ahmose called a halt, eating his bread, dried fruit and goat's cheese with his back against a palm trunk while one of the Followers unhitched his horses and led them down to the water to drink. Everywhere in the dappled shade the soldiers were sharing their rations, their swords and bows discarded carelessly beside them. Some had even stripped and were splashing about in the shallows, shouting and laughing. Ahmose did not mind. He was in no hurry to move on, indeed he could have fallen asleep under the crown of fronds whispering dryly high above him. But Turi's voice, brusque and commanding, cut across his somnolence and he rose reluctantly while the soldiers scurried to dress and retrieve their weapons.

Two hours after sunset their one scout came back to tell Ahmose that Pi-Hathor lay a mere mile away. "I think they have been warned of your approach, Majesty," he said. "As far as I could ascertain without actually entering the town, the streets and alleys are still full of people although by now they should be in their houses, eating their evening meal."

"I suppose it was inevitable that word of our coming should have reached them," Ahmose replied. "Now that we are close, we have seen a few peasants watering their oxen. I daresay they also saw us." He thanked the scout and sent him back to keep watch, ordering the rest of his troops to find a place in which to spend the night. They had not brought tents. Each man curled up in his blanket and

Ahmose did the same. Turi appointed sentries as a safe-guard, although Ahmose thought it unlikely that Pi-Hathor would be able to organize a raid, let alone put up any resist-ance to his soldiers the next day.

At dawn, momentarily chilled and stiff, Ahmose left the sandy hollow where he, Turi and Ankhmahor had rested, and after a quick meal they were on the march again. But they had not gone far when the front column halted and someone came running back to Ahmose. It was Mereruka. "You will find Pi-Hathor deserted of men, Majesty," he told Ahmose. "They have all gone to Esna in the night to join the townsmen there. Unless you mean to burn the place do not waste your time with Pi-Hathor. Only women and chil-dren remain."

"They were indeed warned, then," Ahmose said. Mereruka smiled slyly.

"They were. I warned them myself," he announced. "My son has been watching for your arrival. When he told me you were close, I spread the word. It did not take much shouting to persuade the men to hurry to Esna where together they might provide a greater resistance to your troops."

"So now we can strike one blow instead of two and have Abana's assistance to do it," Ahmose said admiringly. "Truly you are a devious man, for a breeder of donkeys. What of my Admiral?"

"We parted company undetected and he continued south," Mereruka declared. "Two of my spies in Esna, reed cutters who must work by the river and thus are never suspected, sent me a message that Admiral Abana had arrived south of Esna last night. Even now he will be prepar-

ing to fall upon the town." Peering down into the man's
face, still indistinct but becoming more clearly defined in
the strengthening light, Ahmose made a mental note to see
that he was rewarded with the Gold of Favours for his
loyalty. And I will need his continued expertise, he thought,
as he dismissed Mereruka and saw him melt away into the
morning's thinning shadows. When all is set to rights in
Egypt, I will make him the Eyes and Ears of the King.
Aahmes-nefertari will be pleased. She has probably already
considered such a promotion for him. With a rueful shake of
his head Ahmose gave the command to form ranks.

It was as the spy had said. The Nile bowed to the east at
Pi-Hathor so that the town was set some way back from the
water and the river path crossed several wide and well-
beaten avenues leading down from the town to the docks.
A silent and apprehensive throng of women and children
stood before the dilapidated warehouses fronting the first
houses, their eyes following the progress of the soldiers as
they passed. A few dogs rushed out to bark and snap at the
strangers from a safe distance but they were the only things
that moved. Even the children were motionless.

Ahmose noted that the docks themselves were falling
into ruin, their planking holed, their supports leaning
drunkenly away from the prevailing north current. There
was no sign of any ships. In spite of his obvious safety
Ahmose's scalp prickled as his chariot rolled past the bizarre
scene. His men had fallen mute. All that could be heard
was the sound of their combined footfalls and the snorting
of the horses echoing off the decaying buildings, but the air
seemed charged with hopelessness and a weight of hostility
that reminded him forcibly of his weeks with Kamose, the

terrible campaign for control of the towns and villages
between Weset and Het-Uart, the killing and burning day
after day until both he and his brother had been half-mad
with the bloodiness and brutality. He was more than glad
when Pi-Hathor disappeared from sight behind him and
the river began to curve back towards the west.

The early sunlight was strong, the air fresh and cool, and
Esna only four miles away. The men soon regained their
good spirits but there was no more idle chatter, for in spite
of the entirely predictable outcome of the imminent
engagement there was still fighting to be done.

They heard the town before they saw it, and the wind
brought to them a sudden gush of hot air and the not
distasteful smell of charring wood. Ahmose commanded
swords to be drawn as he urged his horses past the forward
ranks, Ankh-mahor and the Followers running at his side.
Reaching the front of the column he paused.

Esna's docks were alight, the flames leaping almost
transparently into the brilliant sunshine, the air above
them shaking with their heat. The river around them was
choked with ships and Ahmose realized why there had been
no vessels at Pi-Hathor. The townsmen, all good sailors,
had brought them here and they were clumsily circling
Abana's craft that were easily recognizable by the forest of
bows crowding the decks in disciplined rows. Some of
Abana's men were shooting their arrows into the milling
throng of screaming men on the bank but most were aiming
at targets on the other boats.

Quickly Ahmose assessed the situation. No strategy was
needed here. It was simply a matter of wading at once into
the press of townsmen choking all the ground between river

and buildings and cutting them down. Some were brandishing swords and a few had spears, but most were armed with nothing but knives, quarry implements and tools better served in the construction of ships. Quashing a surge of guilt and pity, Ahmose gave a terse order to Turi and saw him raise cupped hands to his mouth to relay it to his officers. The Followers took up their defensive positions around him, swords at the ready. Eyes scanning the noisy conflict on the water, Ahmose spotted Abana himself. He was standing in the prow of one of the vessels and as Ahmose picked him out, he too saw Ahmose. Bowing briefly, he raised an arm. But Turi's troops were advancing rapidly on the howling mob and Ahmose's attention turned to them.

It was not quite a massacre, for a man had emerged from the crowd and seemed to be a leader of sorts. His voice often rose above the uproar, his words unintelligible but his tone unmistakeably commanding, and obediently the townsmen feinted this way and that, drew into tight groups or ran to take up other positions. Ahmose was reminded of Mereruka's contention that someone was co-ordinating the revolt in both cities. This was obviously the mind upon which all disaffection had centred, the man who had caused it to focus and acquire purpose. Ahmose, watching him attentively, wondered if he had once been a soldier in Seqenenra's army or perhaps even one of Apepa's troops. It was impossible to tell whether he was Setiu or not. He had a sword which he held high and used as a rod to indicate his intention to the men fighting so desperately close by. Every muscle in his body seemed tensed on his task and yet, Ahmose thought rather sadly, for all his effort and courage he must know that his cause was doomed from the start. How I hate this necessity!

For a while soldiers and citizens were inextricably mixed, but gradually out of the clouds of dust stirred up by the to and fro of struggling bodies and shuffling feet the number of citizens began to decline. The pace of the engagement slowed. Bodies littered the ground and the survivors began to flee, casting away their makeshift weapons and running towards their half-drowned fields or plunging into the Nile, where two of their ships, abandoned and on fire, were drifting and listing. Abana's marines had already boarded the others and were hacking at men who were used to handling vessels but not making war on their unstable decks. The screams and groans of the wounded filled the air along with the excited cries of the victors. The clash had lasted perhaps an hour. It was not yet noon, the sun had not quite reached its zenith, and already the battle was over.

The man who had held the rebels together was still shouting. He had jumped from his perch on a rock and was dashing towards the river, not in an attempt to escape, Ahmose surmised, but in an effort to pierce the fog of panic engulfing his men and rally them. A few were heeding him, turning back and pushing their bodies through the churning water. Skidding down the bank he rushed to meet them, wading out until he stood chest deep, the unpredictable movements of the swinging vessels making a choppy wake that broke against him.

He did not see Abana lean over the rail of his ship, evaluate the situation in one swift glance, and launch himself from the deck, landing feet first just behind the man in a great splash that Ahmose could hear. The man swung round but clumsily, impeded by his sword and the resistance of the water. Abana came up crouching and sputtering, flung both arms about his quarry, and unbalanced him. Both men went over, and when they surfaced, Abana had the man's sword wrist in both his hands. He was shaking it viciously, using his jerking elbow and his head to administer whatever blows he could. "Turi!" Ahmose yelled. "Get someone into the water to help him!" The order was unnecessary. Already several soldiers were pounding along the bank to where the two men were struggling. But by the time they had flung themselves into the river, the man's sword had been wrenched from his grasp and was sinking beneath the surface and Abana, one arm around his prisoner's neck and the other tightly gripping his hair, was dragging him to the shore.

His capture marked the last of whatever weak resistance remained. The men still in the river came wading out disconsolately and flung their weapons onto the verge. Turi came up to Ahmose and saluted. "It is all over, Majesty," he said. "What do you want done with those who surrendered?" Ahmose scanned the fiery, crackling ruin of the docks, the jumble of dead bodies sprawled everywhere, the women who had already begun to trickle out of the town and were setting up a chorus of wails.

"Guard them for now," he answered. "Collect the bodies and have them burned. Keep those women out of the way. And I want a count of our dead and wounded as soon as possible."

Leaving his chariot, he walked to where Abana and his prisoner stood, both dripping with water, amid a circle of watchful soldiers who drew back and bowed as he approached. Abana grinned at him, tossing a shower of droplets from his glistening head. "He was no match for the superior training and discipline of an Egyptian Admiral!" he exclaimed. "But he commanded his people well, did he not?" Ahmose nodded and looked the man up and down. He was shivering a little, whether from fear or reaction it was difficult to tell, for his expression remained calm.

"What is your name?" Ahmose asked. The man's eyes dropped.

"Yamu," he said.

"You are Setiu." It was a statement not a question, and the man inclined his head. "Yamu, you have caused much useless bloodshed here today," Ahmose went on. "None of this," he gestured savagely, "was necessary. If the citizens of Pi-Hathor and Esna were dissatisfied, then they should have brought their grievances first to their respective mayors and then to me in Weset. I would rather have appointed a judge to investigate your distress than bring a thousand soldiers to destroy you!" Yamu's head came up and his features were all at once animated by scorn.

"The mayor of Pi-Hathor refused to endanger the cowardly treaty he made with your brother," he said bitingly, "and our mayor here in Esna had much land and cattle and was not eager to risk losing his wealth by complaining of our plight to you, Ahmose Tao. So we cut off their heads."

Ahmose regarded him thoughtfully. There was more than the goad of injustice behind the bitter words, there was a contempt bordering on hatred. You Setiu have always held us in disdain, he mused. You conquered us subtly, without violence, with all the guile and deceit for which you are famous, and because you were able to trick us so easily you looked down on us as innocent and stupid, a people to be used, a country to be raped. You came into Egypt as sheep herders, with permission from the King to graze your flocks in the Delta, and your traders and adventurers followed to take our riches and eventually our freedom away. Now that we dare to raise our poor, simple heads and take back what is ours, you despise us for not being what you believed us to be. No judgement could have appeased this man's rage. Ahmose sighed. "In that case I have no choice but to remove your head," he said. He turned to the division's Standard Bearer who was nearby. "Idu, have the prisoners lined up and our soldiers gathered," he ordered. "I am going to execute this man for treason."

Apprehensively he watched a space being cleared of bodies and his troops hurrying obediently to surround it. The last execution I witnessed was Teti's, he thought, after the battle for the fort at Nefrusi. Teti, who was Mother's cousin and who had seduced Si-Amun into betraying us. He was Apepa's tool and so is this man, however indirectly. Kamose carried out the act himself, drawing his bow in that blood-spattered place. I remember how Teti clung to his son and how Ramose looked when he was forced to push his father away so that Kamose could take a clear shot. Kamose had no choice, but it was terrible nonetheless. Afterwards I heard Ramose weeping in the night and I know that Kamose too lay sleepless, listening to his friend's agony. I had hoped those days were gone.

The soldiers' chatter had begun to die away. The prisoners were being hustled to the front, where they stood uncertainly and fearfully. Eyes turned to Ahmose in the new silence. Kamose let loose an arrow, Ahmose's feverish thoughts ran on, as he stepped out into the sun-drenched space with Turi and Ankhmahor beside him. But I must swing a sword, I must feel the shock of it as it cleaves muscle and bone, I must be prepared to step aside to avoid the spurt of blood, the convulsing of the body. It is one thing to do this in the heat of battle but quite another to be coldly crossing the ground towards a man on his knees with wisps of his drying hair blowing against the neck I am about to sever and water from his saturated loincloth still forming rivulets down his buttocks. Amun help me not to disgrace myself before my people!

Drawing his sword, he addressed the men of Esna and Pi-Hathor. "I have decided in my mercy to let you go back to your homes," he called, his voice carrying clearly in the expectant silence. "You are all guilty of treason, whatever you fancy your justification might have been for this uprising. However, I charge you all to remember this day, both my mercy and the vengeance I am about to exact. Egypt is mine. You belong to me. Forget this again and I will kill every man, woman and child in both accursed towns and raze them to the ground. I have spoken." He heard relief in their murmurs and the aversion he felt for their instant selfishness helped to steady his hands and calm his rapid heartbeat. One of the women began to scream, "Yamu, no! Yamu, no!" Turning to the man, Ahmose gripped the hilt of his sword and raised it to his shoulder.

"Do you want a moment to pray?" he asked, surprised that there was no tremor in his voice.

"Yes," Yamu said, his own voice muffled by the proximity of his mouth to the earth and the luxuriance of the hair hanging to either side of his face. "I pray that you may be cursed forever, you and all your offspring, every Tao until the end of all ages." Ahmose placed his feet apart for balance. He lifted the sword high in both hands, willing them to be an extension of his eyes. The man's neck was straining, the knobbed row of bones exposed. "In the name of my father Amun," Ahmose whispered, and nerving himself he brought the sword slicing down in a glitter of reflected sunlight and the faintest whisper of sound.

He managed to give the order to cast the body onto the fire with the others, to set the head on a stake to rot where it could be seen by anyone going from the town to the river, to walk steadily away from the great pool of blood already being covered with shovelfuls of sand. But when he reached his chariot he sank down beside it, and folding his arms across his stomach he laid his own head on his knees. "Ankhmahor," he croaked. "Send a couple of Followers into the town to find some wine. Any kind. Even palm wine will do." There was a splash of blood across his kilt even though he had been careful to move aside as he pulled his sword free. Raising himself a little, he tore the garment from his waist and flung it into a thorn bush, but with a sick dismay he saw a dark red smear on his inner thigh. Ankhmahor snapped an order at the men behind him and then bent down.

"Majesty, what ails you?" he said. "You have killed before. We all have. You and Osiris Kamose and your father before you, all fighting Kings. The deed was just and necessary. What is wrong?" Ahmose looked up at him.

"There is no end to it," he breathed. His chest felt tight and his shoulders ached with the force of the blow he had delivered. "So many lives laid waste. I had thought ... I had hoped ... Apepa will not surrender. Het-Uart waits for me like some monstrous suppurating wound needing to be cauterized and this," he touched the tip of one finger to the blood still wet on his thigh and held it up, "this is becoming the token of my family. Blood and the Taos. Think of one and you immediately think of the other." Ankhmahor bent lower.

"I will find you clean linen and the Followers will return with wine," he said gently. "Take natron and wash yourself in the Nile, Majesty. There is nothing that requires your attention for the rest of the day. The bodies are being burned and Abana is having the Setiu ships manned for a return to Nekheb. I hear that we have suffered no casualties and no man is so severely wounded that he cannot march back to Weset, but Commander Turi will doubtless bring you an official report later. This punitive expedition was essential, Ahmose, and you know it. Pi-Hathor and Esna could have bred a spreading plague."

"To where? To whom?" Ahmose murmured. He used the rim of the chariot to pull himself up and stood shakily before his Chief Follower. "No Setiu influence remains anywhere in Egypt but the Delta. But you are right as usual, Ankhmahor, and I am almost myself again. I will submit myself to Hapi's cleansing touch as you advise. Send Abana to me when he has finished his business."

It was not the act itself, he thought, as he stood to bathe in the shallows just out of sight of the town. That was not beyond my soul's strength, for I am neither squeamish nor cowardly. No, it was the curse he uttered that caused my soul to cringe, as though he knew of the Seer's intolerable prediction, as though one of his gods, haters of Egypt, spoke through him. It is one thing to accept the will of Amun. It is quite another to know that Amun's enemies gloat over his will and take delight in seeing the misery it brings to his divine family.

By the time he had dried himself and put on the kilt and linen helmet Ankhmahor had provided, he had regained his equilibrium, and sitting on the floor of his chariot he drank thirstily the wine his Follower had found, holding the cup with hands that no longer shook. Turi came to report to him that the debris left by the burned docks had been hauled out of the water so as not to impede shipping, there had been no casualties and few minor wounds, and the rebels' funeral pyres were well alight. The prisoners had been released and had scattered into the town, the women following them. Everything, Ahmose thought grimly, was neatly tidied away. He ordered Turi to rank the men and march them back a little way towards Pi-Hathor where they could rest and spend the night before starting for Weset. Turi left, to be replaced almost at once by Abana, who came swinging along the river path, bowed respectfully, and at Ahmose's bidding, sank onto the grass beside the chariot.

For a while neither man spoke. Not far off, the Followers were talking quietly among themselves. Ankhmahor had taken up a position by the Nile where he could assess everyone coming close to the King. Wordlessly Ahmose passed what remained of the wine down to his Admiral and Abana sipped it slowly. Ahmose watched his leisurely movements. He was becoming rather fond of him. "How old are you, Abana?" he asked impulsively. Abana glanced up at him with mock suspicion.

"I am twenty-three, the same age as you are, Majesty," he replied. "I have accomplished much during my short life I think, but not as much as Your Majesty has achieved. Still, I am proud to possess the new title of Admiral and be captain of the *Kha-em-Mennofer*. I have found favour with you, have I not?"

"Ever the boaster!" Ahmose retorted good-humouredly. "Yet there is much of your father, Baba, in you, his good sense and his ability to win men's trust. Tell me, if you were Lord of this nome what would you do with Esna and Pi-Hathor now?" Abana set the cup before him on the ground and laced his fingers over it, squinting thoughtfully up into the tangled leaves above them.

"You are the Lord of All," he answered after a minute. "It is not for me to decide the fate of these two recalcitrant towns. Yet if their welfare was in my hands, I should search for ways to relieve their discontent. They will not revolt again. The price they have paid is too high. Yet they do not believe even now that they owe you loyalty, Majesty. Not yet." He frowned and pulled at his earlobe. "They are mostly Setiu, accustomed to giving allegiance to anyone who increases their wealth and comfort. So far that has been Apepa. But they are fickle." Once again he looked up at Ahmose sitting cross-legged on the floor of the chariot. "Give them work, put food in their bowls, and they will dance to a different drum. I know them. Nekheb is only twenty-two miles farther south. When I was a child there was much commerce between the three towns. I know them," he repeated.

"And I ask you again," Ahmose persisted mildly. "What would you do with them?"

"Firstly I would replace the mayors with good Egyptians," Abana said hastily. "Secondly I would have the docks rebuilt. Your Majesty's primary shipbuilding facilities are now at Nekheb, but Esna could make rafts for transporting stone and barges to carry goods of all kinds. Remember that the men who work the gold mines in Wawat need more food than can be grown in that arid area. At present the mines are not at full capacity. Apepa relied on the natives to send him gold from wherever they could find it and often that was from the bed of the Nile itself. He did not bother to send miners from Egypt. But you will need much gold for Weset, for trade, for your nobles. You will reopen the mines. I would give Esna and Pi-Hathor the right to bargain for food up and down the river and keep the miners supplied with what they need. If Your Majesty begins to build monuments later, the limestone workers can resume their task in the quarry."

"Ambitious plans," Ahmose said when Abana had drawn breath. "Perhaps they would be viable. Perhaps not. But I have decided to give you the responsibility of trying." Abana scrambled onto his knees and turned in shock. "You have already proven yourself in my service," Ahmose went on, "and in spite of your annoying pomposity you have asked for nothing." He uncrossed his legs and slid from the chariot. "Stand up, Abana. Ankhmahor! Come here!" Ankhmahor came running. "You are my witness to this," Ahmose told him as he halted. "When I get back to Weset, I will have Ipi draw up the correct scroll." Stepping close to Abana, he touched him on the forehead, the breast and his feet. "Ahmose Abana of Nekheb," he said, "I appoint you Governor of the Nekhen nome and I bestow upon you the hereditary title of erpa-ha Prince, you and your sons forever." Taking Abana's sun-warmed shoulders, he kissed him on both cheeks. "Be happy in the favour of your Lord." For once Abana seemed bereft of words.

"But, Your Majesty, I have no sons yet," he stammered, dazed. "I do not ... Does this mean ..."

"I also give you the Gold of Valour yet again," Ahmose cut into the man's stutters. "You are a brave man, my Prince. Appoint whom you will to be your assistant governor. I shall expect monthly reports on the state of my nome." Abana blinked at him.

"My wife Idut is now a Princess?" he queried. "I am a Prince?" The glazed look was clearing from his eyes and they had begun to sparkle. "Majesty, you do me great honour! I will not fail you! I am overwhelmed! I bask in the light of your divine munificence! But what of my *Kha-em-Mennofer*?" he finished in dismay. "Am I to relinquish command of her to another?"

"Certainly not. I need you and my navy in the north, indeed you are to take the ships back to Nekheb, collect your men and your weapons, and return to Het-Uart at once. Your new assistant governor can take the authority here in your place. You are dismissed." Abana took both of Ahmose's hands and pressed them fervently to his lips.

"Thank you, Divine One, thank you!" he breathed, and with many bows he backed away. Then he turned and sped leaping along the path.

"He is a wise choice for governor here, young though he is," Ankhmahor reflected, as both men watched Abana's delirious progress. "He is very capable as well as entirely trustworthy." Ahmose nodded. Young though he is, he repeated rather sadly in his mind. You no longer think of me as young, do you, Ankhmahor? You cannot imagine me leaping and crowing with the lusty health and optimism of my age. Well, neither can I.

"I will lose no sleep over my new Prince," he agreed. "Now have my horses hitched, Ankhmahor. It is time to move on."

Within the hour he and his jubilant force had left Esna behind them. There was much singing and joking around the fires Ahmose allowed to be lit at sunset. Ahmose watched the outline of the western dunes gradually sharpen against a sky that was fading from blue to a delicate pink, and realized that in giving Abana instructions to go north immediately he had unconsciously made up his own mind not to tarry in Weset.

Since Abana had come with the news of Apepa's near escape, the city had never been far out of Ahmose's thoughts and he knew now that he would not be able to wait patiently at home for another two months until Aahmes-nefertari's baby was born. The prospect made him physically agitated, not only because he feared the event itself but also because he had a strong intuition that the wearying situation in the Delta was at last about to change. No omens or dreams told him so, but he had lived for years with the stubbornness of Apepa's city lodged in his gut like the broken haft of a dagger, its ache a constant discomfort. Now that discomfort had changed to moments of intense anxiety made worse by their sourcelessness. He dreaded the coming confrontation with his wife but he feared inaction more.

He was settling for the night as well as he could when he heard a Follower's challenge, and presently Mereruka's face loomed out of the dimness. "My work in Pi-Hathor and Esna is done, Majesty," he said after Ahmose had greeted him. "I will be preparing a report for Queen Aahmes-nefertari, but in the meantime is there anything you desire of me?"

"I am glad you came," Ahmose told him. "Please send another message to Djeb. My mother and grandmother are free to return to Weset whenever they wish, providing it is within the next two months." Aahmes-nefertari would need them, but he did not tell this to the spy. "I have appointed Ahmose Abana as governor of the Nekhen nome," he went on. "You may be useful to his assistant governor, but that is for the Queen to decide. You have provided faithful service, Mereruka, and I am grateful. Does she pay you enough?" Even in the semi-darkness Ahmose could see that the man did not know whether to smile at a joke or be nonplussed at what might seem to be an attempt to subvert his loyalty to his first employer.

"Yes indeed, Majesty." Mereruka answered. "The Queen is generous with goods and I have my donkeys." There was genuine affection for the beasts in the man's words and Ahmose warmed to him.

"Good," he said. "Abana goes south again. Travel with him as far as Nekheb. And do not forget to address him correctly, Mereruka. He is now a Prince." Strange that a peasant should prove himself honest when Princes have died for their perfidy, Ahmose reflected, as he shifted about under his blanket to try and find an adequate spot for sleep on the hummocked ground. A donkey breeder, and a spy as well. An honest spy. He chuckled to himself and closed his eyes.

He was home again by the evening of the following day, dusty and tired. His men disbanded and hurried to their barracks and he himself went to the bath house at once to have the soil of travel sluiced away. Hekayib had just finished drying him and was winding a clean kilt about his waist when Aahmes-nefertari came in, stepping gingerly over the damp stone floor. "I saw Ankhmahor crossing the garden," she said. "I am so glad that you are back safely, and so soon! Are you hungry? Ahmose-onkh and I have not eaten yet." She was dressed in a long, filmy sheath whose white folds glimmered with silver thread. A thin silver band encircled her forehead and her own hair fell waving to her shoulders. Ahmose thought that she had never looked more beautiful. I can't tell her, he said to himself in despair. I can't bear to see that smile vanish from her lips and her eyes darken in anger and disappointment. Going to one of the benches by the wall, he sat so that Hekayib could put on his sandals.

"It was a very easy little foray," he told her. "There is no need to worry about Esna and Pi-Hathor any more. I have made Ahmose Abana a Prince and have given him the governorship of the Nekhen nome." Her eyebrows rose.

"An uncharacteristically hasty decision, my husband! He is fortunate to have earned your trust so quickly." Was there an implied criticism behind her words? Ahmose glanced up at her swiftly but she was continuing to smile at him warmly.

"I am starving," he admitted, rising and giving her his arm. "The evening is still early. Shall we eat in the garden? Then I must dictate some things." She did not ask what things. I assured her that I would be here for the baby's birth, he thought guiltily as her soft hand slid along his forearm and her perfume enveloped him. So she is content.

She does not question me regarding the rout of the towns-men or the business I must conduct with Ipi. All she cares about is having me with her.

Shame made him excessively solicitous of her when they came out into the gentle dusk and paced to her cushions and carpet. He helped her down, drew a short cloak around her shoulders, took the dishes from Uni as they appeared and served her himself. He whisked the few late, lazy flies from her neck and several times reminded Ahmose-onkh, who had leaned across her to empty a platter, not to be so clumsy. She submitted to his care complacently, saying only, "You should go away more often, Ahmose, if missing me makes you so loving when you return!" It was his oppor-tunity to break his news to her, but still his tongue would not form the words.

Ahmose-onkh left them to perch by the pool where the fish were rising to snap at the mosquitoes between the fragrant lotus blooms that floated, blue and white, on the rippling water, and still Ahmose could not speak. Taking his hand suddenly she placed it on her abdomen and held it there and with a flood of distaste, pity, love and dread he felt his child kick vigorously against his palm. "It will not be long now," she said, kissing his ear. "A son this time, do you think, Ahmose? Or better still, a daughter!" He could not answer. Aching with grief he gathered her into his arms.

Later he summoned Ipi and dictated Abana's elevation for the archives and letters to his commanders in the north warning them of his imminent return. The scrolls were to go out with Khabekhnet the next morning. He also sent to Hor-Aha, Turi and Ankhmahor, telling them to be prepared to march in two days. Then he made his way to Aahmes-nefertari's apartments. There were spring flowers in vases all about her bedchamber, pink tamarisk, blue cornflowers, red poppies, the delicate white spears of daisies, spreading a profusion of colour and aroma throughout the room. Lamps burning perfumed oil filled the air with a heavy sensuality. She welcomed him effusively from her couch, arms raised to him, and in spite of his consternation his body responded to her exuberant invitation. "I do not want to hurt you or endanger the baby," he said awkwardly even as he was drawn to the promise of her body, glimpsed tantalizingly through the transparency of her gossamer-sheer linen, and the blatant invitation in her eyes.

"Next month perhaps not," she answered huskily. "But tonight let us put anger aside, my dear brother. We love and need each other, and what could be more important than that?" Het-Uart is more important, he thought as he sank onto the couch beside her. Killing Apepa is more important. Amun help me, how can I make you understand that although you fill my heart and dominate my mind there is a necessity that must temporarily take precedence, consuming me even over my preoccupation with you? He squeezed his eyelids shut and buried his face between her swollen breasts, taut with her pregnancy, as though by hiding in the sweetness of her skin he might become invisible to the world.

"Nothing," he lied, not knowing whether she had heard him or not and presently not caring. "Nothing at all, my dearest."

The storm struck him the next afternoon. Khabekhnet had left for the north, the Division of Amun, the Division

of Ra and the Medjay were collecting their weapons, counting their arrows, and oiling their leather, and Ahmose had
ordered Akhtoy to see to his packing. His travelling cot,
tent, collapsible chair, carpets, and his moveable Amun
shrine were already on board the ship tethered to his watersteps. He had been woken by the Hymn of Praise, held the
usual audience in the reception hall together with Aahmes-
nefertari, and gone with her to inspect the progress Sebek-
nakht was making on the old palace. She had not left her
quarters until the time of audience and was obviously too
preoccupied to notice the flurry of activity in the house or
hear the bustle on the river beyond the gate, and Ahmose
was cravenly glad. They had shared the noon meal, after
which she had gone to her rooms to rest.

Ahmose himself went to the office. There were many
details to be attended to and he had just finished giving
one of the under-scribes the instruction to be alert for any
letter coming up from Aahotep and Tetisheri at Djeb when
the door opened and his wife swept in unannounced. She
was very pale but her eyes in their rims of black kohl
impaled him at once on his own cowardice. "Get out!" she
snapped at the under-scribe. After one horrified glance at
her the man did not wait for Ahmose's dismissal. Snatching
up his palette, he scurried past her and out the door.
Aahmes-nefertari kicked it closed behind him with one
savage movement. "You lied to me," she said evenly, but
there was such an intensity of rage beneath the artificial
calm of her words that Ahmose had to repress the urge to
step backwards.

"No, I did not lie," he began reasonably. "Before
Abana brought his news from Het-Uart, I eagerly intended

to be with you until the baby was born. But he changed everything."

"He did not change what you led me to believe," she cut in glacially. "What was it you said to me only a few days ago? 'I will be at your side on the first day of Tybi when we celebrate the Feast of the Coronation of Horus.' Perhaps you were speaking to Apepa. Or perhaps you were just breaking wind." He put out a hand, desperate to do something to avert the avalanche of pain he knew he deserved, desperate to silence her.

"Aahmes-nefertari, you are right and I am sorry," he offered. "But try to understand why …"

"Why what? Why you played me for a fool? Why everyone in the house but me knew that you are leaving again tomorrow and no one dared to speak the words to me? Why you lacked the courage, let alone the compassion, to tell me that you were leaving? It is not the reasons for your going that have cut me to my soul," she shouted, "it is the lie. The lie!" She came forward clumsily, one arm across her belly and the other reaching for the gilded back of a chair. "Ahmose-onkh burst into my bedchamber wanting to know if he could go with you," she went on furiously. "That was when I knew. You made love to me last night and even on my couch you spewed lies!" She paused for breath and he stepped to her, but she flinched away. "I know what it is," she said hoarsely. "My babies are weak. My babies die. You do not want to be here to see what feeble creature my womb expels and you do not care that I am also afraid, that I am terrified, that I need you with me. You want another wife."

Horrified, he stared at her, aware that she had probed his deepest agony but had not been able to discern the greater truth, that he loved her completely and would only take another woman in the direst dynastic necessity. Nothing I can say will stem the tide of her hurt, he thought. I have brought this on myself. "I am indeed a coward," he ventured. "I did indeed shrink from having to tell you that I must go north at once. Let me try to explain."

"Explain is such a passionless word," she said bitterly. "So cold in its connotation, so damningly reasonable. No, Ahmose. Do not insult me with your explanations. They are phrases of the mind that cannot touch the scorpion stinging my heart."

He would have poured it all out to her then, the Seer's prediction, his own terrible feeling of fatalism, his intense desire to run from her because he could not protect her from what was to come, his intuition that he must stand before the walls of Het-Uart as soon as possible or all would be lost. But the clamour of his thoughts confused him and he could say nothing. Letting go the chair, she turned back to the door. "I do not want to see you before you go," she said. "I do not care if Het-Uart falls or not and neither should you until this baby is born. To Set with you, Ahmose Tao. Do not expect any letter from me while you are gone. I shall be too busy to dictate."

Heartsick, he watched her leave, her head high, her whole body trembling. Once the door had closed he called her name, his throat suddenly released from its paralysis, but she did not come back. "Aahmes-nefertari, you are a Queen now," he said aloud into the stunningly quiet room. "You have crafted a new administration, you have ruled in my absence, surely you understand the sometimes sharp distinctions between you and me as we were, you and me as we would like to be, and you and me now, divinities who carry the weight of a country on our shoulders." But his words melted into the shaft of sunlight gleaming on the surface of the table and were absorbed by the dust motes floating in the air. It is not the divinity you wounded and misled, Ahmose, you fool, he said to himself. It is the woman. And no amount of prayers and prostrations will restore you to her favour.

He had hoped that the venting of her wrath would be enough, that she would be standing on the watersteps to give him her blessing when he and his entourage embarked just after dawn the next day, but though he waited as long as he could, using various pretexts to delay the moment when he must turn and walk up the ramp of his ship, she did not appear. Ahmose-onkh hugged him fiercely. "I have been practising with my bow and my sword," he said as Ahmose swung him high and kissed him before setting him back on his feet. "Are you sure you do not need me, Majesty Father?" Ahmose swallowed past the lump in his throat.

"I need you very much," he answered gravely. "But this time your mother needs you more. Spend some time with her when you are not at your lessons, Ahmose-onkh." He glanced at Pa-she, who nodded his understanding. "Amuse her with board games. Talk to her. She will be lonely until your new brother or sister is born."

"She has become very grumpy," the child muttered. "But I will obey you, Divine One. As the Hawk-in-the-Nest I will take your place and comfort her."

There was little left to say, no other family members to bid farewell. To the accompaniment of Amunmose's chanting and the clicking of the finger cymbals held by the temple dancers, Ahmose finally stepped onto the ramp, Ankhmahor and the Followers behind him. The servants cast off, the captain shouted to the helmsman, and the rowers bent to their task, backing the craft out to where the north-running current would catch it. At the rear came the other vessels bearing Ahmose's staff and the senior officers, Hor-Aha, Turi, Idu, Kagemni, Khnumhotep and Khaemhet. The Medjay and the divisions were already on the march along the edge of the desert under the command of junior men.

Abana will have reached Nekheb and begun his own journey north, Ahmose reflected, but he will continue to be two or three days behind my flotilla. I will put in at Khemmenu and pick up Ramose, but I will still arrive outside Het-Uart before my Admiral. It does not matter. In spite of my feeling for haste I must not presume to find the situation changed when I get there. The thought of seeing Ramose again brightened his spirits, but as he looked back at Ahmose-onkh, a small, rather forlorn figure holding his tutor's hand amid a crowd of tall adults, his guilt returned. He scanned the house anxiously, hoping for a glimpse of his wife at the last moment, but the shadows cast over paths and garden by the early sun remained untenanted. She had meant what she had said.

Through the huge gateless aperture leading to the fore-court of the old palace he saw Sebek-nakht and his architects raise their hands and bow as he slid past. The peasants were already at work, swarming over and around the venerable building. Ahmose could hear the buzz of their cheerful conversations carried to him on the clear morning air. House and palace were receding, swallowed up by the larger picture of palm trees rearing above the thick green vegetation of early spring and between them the roof of the temple. Weset itself was mostly hidden from the river, but present in a continuous susurration of low noise, and the river path was busy. "The renovation of the palace will soon be complete," Ankhmahor remarked. He had come up beside Ahmose and was leaning on the rail, watching the last of the city slide away. "I expect that Your Majesty will want to move into it as soon as you return from the north."

"I suppose so," Ahmose replied unwillingly. As the river curved and his home was lost to sight, his mood suddenly lightened and he did not want to think about Weset anymore.

12

IT WAS THE MIDDLE of Tybi before Ahmose saw the walls of Het-Uart again. The wind had been fitful, not yet coming steadily out of the north to impede the ships' progress as it would in summer, but beginning to be turbulent so that in spite of the northward current some time had been wasted in tacking back and forth. Ahmose had stopped in Khemmenu for longer than he had planned, sleeping for two nights in Ramose's house while he gave audience to the mayor and various other dignitaries and consulted with his friend regarding the city's ongoing reformation. Ramose seemed happy to inhabit once more the pleasant estate that had once belonged to his traitorous father, but Ahmose found himself haunted by a past that waited to ensnare him around every familiar corner of the big house. He had visited his mother's cousin Teti and his wife Nefer-Sakharu many times as a child when Seqenenra had brought Aahotep to Khemmenu to observe Thoth's feast days in his temple there. Teti had been a man who smiled a great deal and had liked to sit in the garden and throw sweetmeats for his and Seqenenra's brood to catch, but Ahmose had been a little afraid of him and his richly decorated wife, although they were always kind to him. Now, of course, he knew why. Teti had proven himself to be a devious and deceitful man hiding behind an affable exterior and he had died for it.

On the third day Ramose had given his assistant governor his last-minute instructions and had joined Ahmose on board his ship. Messages had come from the divisions, who were now little more than a day behind. Paheri and Ahmose Abana were also on their way. Ahmose did not anticipate another halt. Now all I need is for those gates to swing open and my cup of satisfaction will be full, he thought wryly to himself. Perhaps if I petition Shu, he will blow them apart for me. The mental vision of the god of the air with puffed cheeks and bulging eyes attempting to destroy Het-Uart's defences with the force of his wind made him chuckle. "You are happy, Ahmose." Ramose smiled at him from over the rim of his beer mug. "It is good to be on the river again, is it not?"

"Yes, it is," Ahmose agreed, pushing the image of his wife away, as it threatened to come between himself and the glitter of sunlight as the oars made little eddies on the water. He pointed. "Look, Ramose. Over there. A crocodile, just slipping through the papyrus swamp. An auspicious omen, do you think?" The word 'omen' coming out of his own mouth silenced him, and while the sailors ran to the side of the boat to see the beast, exclaiming excitedly, he turned and went into his cabin.

Akhtoy had his tent pitched in exactly the same spot beside the great tributary as it had been the year before, and while his belongings were being carried inside and his cook was setting up a field kitchen, Ahmose got into his chariot with Ankhmahor at the reins and had himself driven as close to Het-Uart as he could get. Then he dismounted and stood staring up at the familiar walls. He had sent Khabekhnet to his generals, summoning them to dine with him that evening. Word of his return had spread quickly among the soldiers who had remained to continue the siege. He could hear their anticipation in the level of noise rising from the vast array of tents spreading out on the plain to his right. But no sound seemed to be coming from Het-Uart.

For some time he and Ankhmahor gazed at the city. Then Ahmose said, "Commander, do you sense that anything has changed since you stood here last?" Ankhmahor hesitated.

"It is a strange question, Majesty," he replied. "I see nothing different, but you are right. It is as though Het-Uart were about to collapse, as though the foundations of its walls were invisibly and quietly crumbling. There is a tension in the air. I thought that it was my imagination."

"I have felt it ever since Abana confessed that Apepa had almost been allowed to escape," Ahmose said. "He has given up the fight, Ankhmahor. He wants to run to the bosom of his brothers in Rethennu and he is frantically trying to find a way to do it without having to personally surrender either himself or his city. Something is about to happen."

"Het-Uart appears dead," Ankhmahor commented. "No smoke is rising from cooking fires or funerals. I hear nothing either." He turned to Ahmose. "Is it possible that the citizens are all dead?"

"No," Ahmose said shortly. "The population is undoubtedly decimated by plague and starvation, but we have yet to see vultures circling above those damnable walls."

A light rain began to fall towards evening, pocking the earth and making the surface of the tributary dance and darken, but by the time the generals drove up, it had ceased and the sky had cleared to reveal a sprinkling of faint stars in the blue-washed sky. Ahmose, wrapped warmly in a woollen cloak, sat at the end of the long table that had been set up outside his tent, with Ramose at his side and Ankhmahor and the Followers behind. Six lamps burned in a row down its centre. Camp stools lined it and the wine jugs stood ready. Akhtoy and his bevy of servants waited to serve simple spring fare: fresh lettuce, cucumber, green onions, radishes, crushed garlic cloves, soft cheese, roasted gazelle meat brought in earlier by hunting soldiers, and bread. No fruit would be available for some months, but dried dates and figs drenched in honey would be offered.

As his men left their chariots and came within reach of the lamplight, Ahmose greeted them, received their obeisances, and invited them to sit. Each face reminded him more vividly of the battle last year and with the memories came a profound contentment. They talked softly amongst themselves as the servants came forward to pour the wine, waiting for the latecomers and passing the time in soldier's gossip, the single gold hoops or jasper coins or turquoise droplets hanging from their earlobes catching the lamps' benign yellow glow, their black, kohl-circled eyes glinting. Some wore cloaks as Ahmose did but some were bare-chested, oil gleaming on their brown skin, the muscles of their broad shoulders tightening and loosening as they moved.

The sheer force of their combined masculinity struck Ahmose like a plunge into cold water. It was bracing and reviving. The men who now served him in Weset, his ministers and officials, were intelligent. Their discussions engaged and challenged him. But their virility was of a different kind, overlaid with the complexities of a life measured out in the sophisticated intricacies of a rapidly developing court. I prefer this, Ahmose thought, as Hor-Aha, the last to appear, bowed and slid onto a stool and Khabekhnet called for silence. For these strategists there are no unspoken objectives, no obsession with details that in the end have little importance. One day soon I suppose I shall have to commit my energies completely to the business of peaceful government, but in the meantime such a commonplace pursuit pales beside my task here, the salvation of Egypt. Signalling to Akhtoy to begin to serve the food, he smilingly surveyed the faces turned to him. "I am happy to be with you all again," he said. "While you eat, you can give me your reports on the state of your divisions one by one. I trust that your soldiers have all enjoyed a proper rotation, that their health is satisfactory, and that they are eager to resume their duties."

"Eager is not the word I would have chosen to describe their state of mind, Majesty," Baqet said. "Resigned might better describe how they feel. The gains we made last year put heart into them and they looked for a corresponding end to the siege. But it did not happen." He leaned back while a servant filled his wine cup. "I am not saying that there are mutinous grumblings among the troops. They have drilled and exercised and practised with their weapons with an admirable willingness. But the talk around the cooking fires is no longer idle soldiers' talk. It is all of the height of the walls, their probable thickness, the strength of the gates, and so on. One mad scheme for breaching the city follows another. We now have the most highly trained army in the world but we are no closer to our goal than Kamose was." There was a murmur of assent around the table.

"My men inside the northern mound talk of standing on its walls and shooting fire over into Het-Uart," Khety put in. "But fire inside the city will not open the gates." Ahmose held up a hand.

"I know," he said firmly. "However, you are wrong, General Baqet, when you say that we have made no progress since the days of my brother. Scrolls were waiting for me from the divisions in the eastern Delta. The whole of that region has been returned to Egypt, the Horus Road is ours, and the forts comprising the Wall of Princes have all been evacuated by the enemy and subsequently occupied by our men. Nothing, nothing remains of the Setiu but that." He pointed towards Het-Uart, bulking vast and high in the gathering gloom. "All we need now is patience and we will have won."

"Patience is one virtue we Egyptians have in abundance," Kagemni said sardonically. Everyone laughed. Ahmose rapped the table.

"Tomorrow the Medjay, the Division of Amun and Division of Ra, and Paheri and Prince Abana with their ships should arrive," he said crisply. "I believe that this will be our last siege season. But I do not want to spend the evening in fruitless speculation or wild schemes. I want to know about my soldiers. Khety, you begin. How has the Division of Horus fared?"

They ate in silence, waited on by the quiet servants, while each stood up in turn and told Ahmose how the months of his absence had been spent. Ipi was busy at his feet noting down any complaints. There were few. A temporary shortage of new kilts for the Osiris Division under General Meryrenefer, a shipment of beer intended for Sebek-khu and his Montu Division that had somehow gone astray. "Food is being rationed at the moment," Sebek-khu had finished. "The flood was ample and the sowing will begin very soon, but as Your Majesty knows, the responsibility for feeding all your thousands of troops is a very heavy one for the Scribes of Distribution. Last summer's crops were good, but you cannot continue to direct most of Egypt's harvest to the north. The Delta has been scoured as you say, but many of the villages are in disarray. It will take time for the peasants to feel safe enough to prepare their fields and orchards. We can look for nothing from them until next year. And please the gods," he said with a shudder, "let us not be here next year."

Once the reports had been delivered and the platters emptied, the men settled down to drink and talk and there was much loud laughter. Ahmose listened contentedly to the hum of the conversations going on all around him, but he did not join in. He felt detached, his mind lazily circling the problem of maintaining a steady supply of food while behind it flowed a river of half-formed thoughts mixed with the sensations the night was bringing to him. The moist Delta air was cool, almost cold, the stars misted by fine streamers of barely visible grey cloud. Behind him Ankhmahor was keeping his watch, so close to Ahmose that he was sure he could feel the heat of the man's body on his upper back. By turning a little on his stool, he could see a lamp shining through the bellied folds of his tent, casting a diffused light on the trunk of the sycamore beneath which it was pitched and being dissipated in the denser blackness of the shrubs beyond. In spite of my frustration I am at peace, he thought. I shall miss the weeks I have spent here keeping vigil beside this obstinate city, this wide tributary.

He left the stool and at once a hush fell. "I am going to my couch," he said. "Leave when you will. Ankhmahor, order my sentries." The men did not stay. Bowing their good nights, they slipped away into the dimness. The servants began to clear the debris they had left and Akhtoy accompanied Ahmose into the tent.

"The city will fall," Akhtoy said suddenly. Startled, Ahmose swung to him. He was pouring scented oil into a basin of water and Hekayib stood by, waiting to wash Ahmose.

"Why did you say that?" Ahmose wanted to know. Akhtoy replaced the stopper on the vial and snapped his fingers at Hekayib who moved at once to remove Ahmose's belt and kilt.

"I dreamed last night on the boat that you were killing a goose, Majesty," he explained. "It is a very favourable omen."

"It is indeed," Ahmose agreed. "So I will kill my enemies. Was the dream vivid, Akhtoy?"

"To the last detail and in the brightest of colours," the steward assured him. "Hekayib, wring out that linen. You are dripping water all over the carpet."

Before noon the next day Paheri and Abana arrived and, after a few words of welcome, Ahmose ordered them to concentrate their ships all along the western edge of the city, covering the Civilians' Gate, the Royal Entrance Gate on the northern tip, and the Traders' Gate. "Will Your Majesty require your flagship?" Abana asked hopefully. Ahmose shook his head.

"Keep the *Kha-em-Mennofer* moored here to the south where I can board her quickly if need be," he replied. "But

I want you to take up a position from which you can direct all our vessels." Paheri shot him a keen glance.

"Does Your Majesty expect a new confrontation with the Setiu?" Ahmose sighed.

"I don't know what I am expecting," he admitted. "Everyone is restless, having dreams and intuitions, swearing that everything has changed when the eye reveals no change at all. But something tells me to be prepared. However, let your sailors sleep on land at night, Paheri. I doubt if we are facing any cataclysm so soon!"

That evening the Amun and Ra divisions with the Medjay straggled into camp. Ahmose gave Hor-Aha instructions through Khabekhnet that in the morning the Medjay were to take five ships and patrol the lesser tributary to the east of the city, concentrating their attention on the one gate in the wall on that side, the Horus Road Gate. The river and consequently the tributaries had regained its banks but would not begin to shrink farther for another month. All Het-Uart's gates led out onto the short plain between wall and water. In the previous year the docks had been destroyed. No one leaving the city would be able to escape without bridge or boat, but still Ahmose was taking no chances.

He had his generals position their troops much as he had done during the last confrontation. Amun and Ra took the western edge, spreading out behind the navy. Thoth, under General Baqet, curved around the southern end, overlapping with the Medjay outside the eastern Civilians' Gate. Sebek-khu's division, Montu, he sent to guard the area in the north-west where the lesser tributary ran between the city and the northern mound, which Egypt had taken and now firmly held. Twenty thousand men, not including the navy and the Medjay, were set to ring Het-Uart on the following day. Each division had makeshift bridges that could be flung across the brimming ditches if the gates should open. Ahmose held the Division of Osiris in reserve.

He knew that his mood of expectancy was probably a delusion, a foolish wish that had somehow been transformed into a magical certainty by his yearning mind, but the soldiers seemed to feel it also. Optimism swept the vast encampment, begun by Ahmose's return with his two divisions but kept alive by rumours that His Majesty had found a secret way into the city, that he intended to bring down the walls at once, or among the more superstitious, that he had been given a spell by Amun's Seer that would ignite the whole of Het-Uart and make it disappear in one enormous ball of flame. The Greatest of Fifty reported these things to the Commanders of a Hundred, who in turn approached the Standard Bearers, and at last Ahmose was brought the news that his whole army was waiting breathlessly for him to perform a miracle.

He laughed, knowing that peasants, even peasants who had become excellent soldiers, were a credulous horde and this spate of wild theories would vanish on the heels of the next wave of intriguing gossip, but he shared their agitation. That night he slept only fitfully, waking often after dreams that he could not remember to lie gazing briefly into the darkness of his tent before drifting into unconsciousness once more.

The following day was no better. Tired and nervous, he managed to dictate a letter to Aahmes-nefertari and one to Ahmose-onkh and make a brief inspection of the chariot horses before retiring to the bank of the tributary where he paced, swam, ate without appetite, and finally decided to while the afternoon away in target practice with his bow. Ankhmahor and Harkhuf joined him, accepting his wager of a gold bracelet and losing.

He was glad when the sky began to fade into evening. He sat in his tent talking to Akhtoy, while outside Khabekhnet and his heralds huddled around a fire and gambled with knucklebones. He had gathered them together in case he needed to send a flurry of orders to the generals, feeling ridiculous as he did so, but determined that he would not be caught unprepared. Both he and Akhtoy were tense. There was a heaviness in the air as though more rain was about to fall. His head was aching mildly but persistently and the scar behind his ear itched.

Shortly after sunset Akhtoy lit the lamps and got out the sennet board. Ahmose did not really want to play but neither did he want to drink or walk outside, so for a further two hours he and his steward tried to concentrate on the game. It had a cosmic significance, even when used to while away a lazy afternoon. Depending on what house a player's cone or spool landed, it could reinforce the luck of the day or attract a negative fate and Ahmose, feeling that his destiny trembled in the balance, was almost afraid to toss the sticks that decided his moves. Beyond the tent the Followers on guard duty paced to and fro, their footfalls muted. Within, the small brazier Akhtoy had lit against the night chill crackled. The rhythmic clatter of the sennet sticks was the only other sound breaking the profound quiet.

Ahmose had just thrown a score that would remove his last piece from the board and give him victory when someone came thudding up to the tent, answering the Follower's challenge breathlessly and pushing his way into the lamplight. He stood panting, his hands on his knees and his head hanging. "Forgive me, Majesty," he gasped. "There were no chariots hitched and I had to run all the way." Ahmose recognized Amun's plumes on the bronze armlet the man wore.

"What does General Turi say?" he rapped out. He was clutching a golden cone so tightly that it was biting into his palm and he let it go.

"Something is happening on the city walls," the officer explained. He was recovering his breath and straightening. "There are men emerging along it, not many, but the night is dark and we cannot see them well. They carry no torches." Akhtoy was already lifting Ahmose's sword belt, bow and quiver of arrows from their chest. Ahmose thrust his feet into his sandals and bent swiftly to tie them.

"Go to the stables and tell Prince Makhu to hitch every chariot," he commanded. "Take one yourself and drive back to General Turi. I am coming at once." The man saluted and rushed out and Ahmose reached for the belt, buckling it on with shaking fingers. "Perhaps your dream spoke true, Akhtoy," he said. The steward held out the quiver and Ahmose ducked his head, drawing the leather strap down onto his chest. "Open the shrine and pray to Amun that it may be so. Het-Uart is finished."

Outside he glanced up at the sky. The Followers were already picking up their spears and Ankhmahor appeared out of the dimness. "The moon is new," Ahmose said to him anxiously. "How can we fight, if we must, in this darkness?"

"If we cannot fight, then neither can the Setiu," Ankh-mahor reminded him. "I do not think we face battle, Majesty. Even Apepa is not that stupid."

"He may be, now that he no longer has Pezedkhu to make his decisions for him," Ahmose retorted. "You are the Commander of the Shock Troops of Amun, Ankhmahor. Get about your business. Send me Harkhuf in your place."

He waited in a fever of impatience for Makhu and his chariot, quelling the urge to flee along the riverbank towards Het-Uart. Shouts echoed in the blackness, followed by the rumble of his awakening troops. A few strides away, through a tangle of bushes, the tributary was little more than a few sullen glints of weak starlight on the fluid obsidian of its surface. The heralds were clustered close by and quickly he dispersed them with orders to bring him whatever information each General had. When his chariot arrived at last, looming suddenly out of the gloom, he signalled to Khabekhnet to get up behind him. "Keep the reins!" he yelled to Makhu. "Take me as close to the city as you can!"

It was not far to the south-western corner of Apepa's mound, but to Ahmose it seemed to take an eternity to get there. At last Makhu brought the horses to a halt and Ahmose jumped to the ground, Khabekhnet following. Before them the lesser tributary, the wide man-made ditch that left the main flow of water and snaked around the eastern side of the city, lay darkly peaceful. To their left the main branch of the Nile ran away into the night.

Ahmose peered up at the wall, cursing the lack of light. There was nothing to see. No shapes moved against the blurred ceiling of stars. The city seemed sunk in sleep. But all along the bank of the canal to Ahmose's right, Baqet's soldiers were hurrying to form ranks and Tchanny, the division's Commander of Shock Troops, came up to Ahmose and bowed. "Majesty, do you want the bridges laid down?" he wanted to know. It was a sensible question. The shock troops of each division were always the first to go into battle and Tchanny needed to be prepared. But after a moment's reflection Ahmose shook his head.

"No, not yet," he said. "I must have word from General Turi before I decide what to do. He is stationed opposite the western gate where the figures were seen. I will send you a runner, Tchanny." The man bowed again and went away just as the Followers, who had been on foot, arrived. Harkhuf's face materialized, pale and tense, at Ahmose's elbow. His sword was drawn.

Minutes passed. Ahmose felt each second with the slow pounding of his heart as he and his bodyguard waited. His eyes were becoming adjusted to the darkness but there was little to see. The night was windless and calm. One of the horses whickered softly and his bronze harness tinkled.

Suddenly a great roar went up, subsiding to a rumble of thousands of voices sharp with excitement. Harkhuf cried out. Ahmose did not move, though his heart gave a jolt that made him feel momentarily nauseous. His face was turned to the west, straining to discern something, anything, but it was from the east that word finally came. One of his heralds was shouting the news even before his form became clear. "The south gate is opening!" he screamed. "Majesty, the south gate!" This is not a fantasy, Ahmose thought in the second before he unfroze. I have won. I know it to the very marrow of my bones. Het-Uart is mine at last.

"Send to Baqet," he said calmly. "The bridges must go down and Tchanny must get his men across the ditch at once." The man had scarcely spun away when a chariot came hurtling across the ground and another herald flung himself from it.

"Majesty, the city has surrendered," he said, his voice broken with exhilaration. "Men on the wall above the western gate have called it and the gate is opening. Generals Turi and Kagemni have ordered the bridges positioned."

"Good. Then they must get their shock troops over the water as soon as they can."

"General Sebek-khu sent a runner to General Turi with the same message," the herald went on. "The Royal Entrance Gate to the north is also wide."

"Then I may presume that the Horus Road Gate and the Traders' Gate are opening too," Ahmose said. He wanted to turn to Harkhuf and embrace him wildly, lift him off his feet, kiss him vigorously. "Go to the northern mound," he instructed the herald. "Tell General Khety that on no account is he to leave it. The Horus Division must stay where it is, with the gates firmly closed. I want no surprise attack on Apepa's part to regain it. I will send to Khety if his men are needed." The man and his chariot sped away. Harkhuf touched Ahmose's arm reverentially.

"Congratulations, Great Horus," he said. "You have triumphed." There was such wonder in the young man's tone that Ahmose laughed.

"It is a marvel after so long, is it not, Prince Harkhuf? But we are not yet inside those damnable walls. It is too soon to be offering me any praise." He walked to his chariot and mounted behind Makhu. "Come," he called. "We will join General Baqet. I want to see our soldiers stream into the south-eastern gate."

Makhu skirted the edge of the canal and soon had to slow for the press of Thoth's soldiers. Five thousand men were waiting to cross the water. They parted at Khabekhnet's warning shouts and Ahmose's chariot rolled through their ranks, but some time before Makhu brought it to a stop by the brink of the ditch where the bridge now lay, its length a span of sturdy planks lashed together but appearing tenuous in the uncertain light, Ahmose knew that something was wrong. Tchanny and his Shock Troops had not moved. Baqet was with them. He bowed as Ahmose alighted and walked up to him, pointing across the water. "What are we to do, Majesty?" he murmured.

The citizens were pouring out of Het-Uart. The gate was clogged with them, a slow-moving mass of humanity that seemed to ooze through the gaping aperture like dark oil and began to spread to either side along the wall. The area between wall and ditch was already choked with them and more were coming. They were almost completely silent, vague faces above huddles of shadowy clothing and bundles of belongings, but for the fractious crying of babies and the sobbing of one nameless woman.

Two thoughts struck Ahmose almost simultaneously. One was that in order to force a way through the tightly packed throng his troops would have to push the people into the water. The second was even more sobering. He knew that he was incapable of giving the order to kill these miserable shuffling creatures. "Apepa is doing this on purpose," he said grimly. "He is using his people to prevent our rapid occupation of the city and perhaps to inspire me with pity for him and for them. Well, I do feel pity. Look at them, Baqet! Have you ever seen such living corpses! I do not think they are a threat to us, do you?" Baqet shook his head.

"I see no soldiers among them, Majesty, but I suppose a few may have weapons concealed beneath their cloaks. The light is very uncertain." Ahmose continued to watch the pathetic exodus. The crowd now extended to right and left out of his sight, a swaying, staggering host that reminded him of paintings he had seen depicting the victims of famine when the Nile failed to rise. But of course they are victims of famine, he thought. Not through lack of a flood but through my siege.

"Open a path through the troops and let them go," he said to Baqet. "It is not in the way of Ma'at to murder those already half-dead from starvation and disease. They can do us no harm. Set men to either side of the bridge to watch them as they cross. Bring torches. Any carrying weapons must be detained." Baqet passed the order to a senior officer beside him who began to shout it in turn. The soldiers clustered by the water began to form themselves into two lines but their movement was misinterpreted by the people on the opposite bank. A flurry of agitation went through them and someone cried out, "Mercy, mercy, men of Egypt! Do not harm us! We are nothing!" They were turning back to the gate in their panic, but the gate was crammed with their fellows trying to get out. Baqet jumped onto the floor of Ahmose's chariot.

"We will not hurt you!" he called, his voice carrying strongly over their shrieks. "The King has decreed that you should leave the city unmolested! Come over! Come over!" He continued to yell until his words pierced their near hysteria. Hesitantly one man, bolder than the rest, stepped onto the bridge and began to edge along it. The herd watched him, their noise dying away. When they saw him walk freely through the soldiers' ranks in the flaring light of the torches, there was a concerted rush to follow him and soon they were streaming across, heads down, eyes darting from side to side at the impassive troops. Most were on foot but occasionally a cart appeared, full of those citizens too old or too sick to walk and hauled by straining men with bent backs. The Egyptians gave these scant attention, afraid of the diseases that lurked beneath the cloaks that swathed the occupants, and already aware that no matter what weapons might be concealed in them there were no longer any men capable of putting up a fight. Baqet rejoined Ahmose. "The donkeys must all have been eaten," he remarked. "This sight is terrible, Majesty. What will you do with them?" Ahmose shrugged, his eyes on the river of dejection spreading out to disappear into the night.

"I don't know," he replied. "They are indeed nothing. The Scribes of Distribution cannot possibly feed them all. They will have to fend for themselves."

"Perhaps they will try to go back to Rethennu," Baqet suggested. Ahmose signalled to Harkhuf and Khabekhnet.

"Rethennu is a foreign country for most of them," he said. "Only the blood of their ancestors ties them to it. Frankly, Baqet, I do not care where they go. As soon as this tide of starvelings abates, get the division across the bridge and through those gates." He made his way to his chariot, turning his back on the forlorn deluge with relief.

He and his escort took up a position where tributary and canal divided and it was not long before the heralds found him. Each one had the same story to tell. Although the gates were open and the bridges laid down, no action could be taken for the press of citizens teeming out of Het-Uart. Ahmose sent them away with the command to let the people go before attempting to enter what would be a deserted city.

That thought troubled him. What was Apepa's true aim? Did he imagine that he would be depriving a bloodthirsty King of the opportunity for a massacre? But it would have been just as easy to slay the people on this side of the walls. Perhaps he wanted to give Ahmose a literally empty victory. Or perhaps, just perhaps, Apepa was dead and his sons had ordered the surrender of the city in a spurt of despair.

Akhtoy and his underlings brought bread, cheese and dried fruit and Ahmose and his guard ate standing, the Followers facing outward where a constant low murmuring filled the darkness. They had barely finished the scanty meal when an officer bearing the insignia of the Osiris Division came up and saluted. "Majesty, the refugees are spreading out through the army's tents," he said. "They are picking up whatever food they can find. Our Scribe of Distribution is afraid that he will not be able to protect the stores of grain."

"Tell General Meryrenefer to form a detail to guard the granaries," Ahmose decided. "Also as many men as it takes to keep the people moving. They must be allowed to scavenge whatever scraps are readily available, but they must not linger or steal tents, clothing or weapons. Any that do so will be killed." He wondered how the navy was faring, whether any of the citizens would be sufficiently strong or crafty to try stealing a boat in the confusion. After all, the bridge from the western gate would lead them straight through Abana's ships strung out along the tributary. Oh surely not, he told himself impatiently. I am being foolish. These scarecrows are no match for armed marines.

In another hour the muted sounds of the flight had lessened and Ramose appeared out of the dense blackness. He bowed and then stood with his arms folded tightly across his chest, his face turned towards the city. "I crossed the bridge and managed to walk all around the outer perimeter of the wall," he said. "It has taken me a long time. Every gate is spewing out its filth." His tone was bitter. "I questioned the citizens as I went, hoping to hear that Apepa was dead, but I was assured that he still lives, shut up in his palace. I will see Tani again this night. I know it." Ahmose experienced a second of pure shock. He had completely forgotten about his sister.

"It has been some time since you entered Het-Uart as a spy for Kamose," he said cautiously. "Remember your pain, Ramose, when you were allowed to confront her and discovered that she had married Apepa. She may not greet you with any joy. She may even be dead. There has been plague and starvation in the city." Now Ramose turned at last. His teeth were bared, a gleam of ivory in the dimness.

"If there is any justice under the Feather of Ma'at she will be alive and Apepa dead," he hissed. Ahmose had seen his friend in distress, even angry, but he had not known that Ramose was nursing such corrosive hate.

"Do you still love her?" he half-whispered so that his attendants could not hear. Ramose looked away.

"I do not know," he answered stiffly. "But she is mine by right. The contract of promise lies in Seqenenra's archives at Weset and I will have her, come what may." Is it not enough that I have made you governor of the Un nome and bestowed a title on you? Ahmose wondered rather sadly. You are master of Khemmenu, you inhabit your family's estates once more, you have my total trust and favour, but it seems that the only compensation you truly desire for the wrongs you have suffered is the reanimation of a corpse.

"We cannot re-enter the past, any of us," he said aloud. "I want my father back. I want Kamose here at my side with all his harshness and his unshakeable integrity. If it were possible, I would wish my daughter alive and well and happy. We have all suffered, Ramose."

"Seqenenra and Kamose and Hent-ta-Hent are dead," Ramose retorted. "You cannot claim them. Tani lives. That is the difference." But, my dear Ramose, there is no difference, Ahmose wanted to tell him. The Tani you knew is most decidedly dead. The girl you loved has drowned in the ocean of time and you will never find her again. Wisely he kept his counsel.

He had not expected to be summoned before dawn, but not long after Ramose had left him to go and sit huddled by the water, a herald came. "General Baqet is about to cross the bridge, Majesty," he said. "He wishes to know if you will join him."

"At once," Ahmose replied. "Harkhuf, have the Followers fall in. Khabekhnet, go and rouse Prince Ramose. Makhu, turn the horses." A thrill took him, a shudder of anticipation mixed with dread, but he hid it, springing into the chariot. Ramose was scrambling to his feet and he and the Chief Herald came running to step up behind him.

It was not far to the bridge where Baqet waited with his own guard and some twenty soldiers holding torches. He saluted gravely, but Ahmose could see his own excitement mirrored in the other man's flame-lit eyes.

"The Shock Troops under Pepynakht have already gone in, Majesty," Baqet told him. "Also three Commanders of a Hundred with their men. The standard is with them." Ahmose nodded.

"Makhu, get down and lead the horses over the bridge," he said. "They will not want to go, otherwise." Makhu did as he was bid. The horses were skittish but responded to his gentle urging and presently Ahmose found himself before the mighty bronze-studded cedar Civilians' Gate. His gaze travelled along its two thick doors, now laid open. Beyond them there appeared to be a wide street cut through the surprising width of the walls and sloping gently upward into dimness.

"This is the way I entered before," Ramose remarked, his voice thin with emotion. "The avenue will rapidly narrow until it meets the road to the palace." Ahmose did not respond. He tapped Makhu on the shoulder and the chariot began to roll, past the gates and on up the mildly graded thoroughfare.

The torchbearers had quickly passed him and were moving ahead so as to illumine his way, and by the rods blazing in their hands Ahmose could see the black holes of alcoves to either side for the gate wardens. The street beyond was wide, but as Ramose had said it soon shrank to a width little more than his chariot's axle. Buildings hemmed him in, uneven grey mud brick houses that leaned against one another in a suffocating jumble. Alleys almost too narrow for the passage of a donkey led off to right and left at irregular intervals, opening small, dark mouths whose throats could not be penetrated by the light of the torches.

The silence was eerie. No bleat of goat or sheep, no barking of dogs, no human cry pierced it. The sound of the soldiers' sandals and the soft rumble of the chariot's rims over the packed ground seemed almost too loud to Ahmose, as though they were desecrating a tomb. Bones lay scattered here and there. At first Ahmose thought, with a spasm of sheer revulsion, that they were human. He remembered Sebek-nakht relating that the Setiu in Het-Uart were being forced through lack of space to bury their dead under the floors of their houses and he had a sudden and lurid vision of hungry citizens digging up and eating their freshly buried relatives, but then he recognized the desiccated skin of a goat clinging to what was obviously the remains of its spine and he realized that the bones were animal. Everything—rats, dogs, goats and cats—had been consumed. He looked up to where there might have been some evidence of the grains and vegetables grown on the roofs but not a tuft was visible. Khabekhnet snorted. "Majesty, the stench! Death and plague and disease!" he mumbled and Ahmose, half-turning, saw that the man had a corner of his kilt held over his nose. Het-Uart did indeed stink, an almost overpowering brew of human excrement, rotting bodies and boiled offal.

Presently the chaotic tumble of common houses drew back and the cavalcade began to pass sheltering walls broken here and there by slightly wider alleys and occasionally sycamore trees whose sad, almost leafless branches drooped towards the gaping apertures of wells dug at their feet. Many of the doors set into the walls stood open and Ahmose, glancing apprehensively through them, saw the ruins of what once had been small but beautiful gardens, now nothing more than patches of hummocked dirt. Several had been entirely dug up, for burials Ahmose assumed.

Ramose had left the chariot and was now walking beside it, one hand resting on the rim of its frame as though for security. "These were the homes of the rich," he said wonderingly. "Nothing is left, Ahmose. Even the wealthy have eaten their own grass. Oh gods, look there!" A shrine had appeared, little more than a low granite pillar support-ing an image of one of the Setiu's barbaric gods, Anath perhaps, judging by its crudely fashioned breasts, but the pedestal had tilted over the edge of a pit that extended into the road. An almost unbearable odour rose from it, and as Makhu eased the horses gingerly around its lip, Ahmose caught a glimpse of white limbs protruding from a meagre scattering of earth. Fighting an urge to vomit, he fixed his gaze on the brown flanks of the animals ahead of him. "They are all dead or gone," Ramose breathed. "I am afraid of what we may find in the palace, Majesty." So am I, Ahmose thought. But as long as Apepa still crouches there like a spider in a disintegrated web, I will allow sheer happi-ness to overcome my apprehension.

A slight breeze freshened the air and Ahmose inhaled it with relief. The ominous silence was also gradually left behind as the sounds of the army flowing into Het-Uart through the other gates grew louder. The crossroads of which Ramose had spoken were crowded with troops from several divisions mingling noisily, and Makhu pulled the horses to a halt. Turi and Kagemni had found each other. They saluted Ahmose and came hurrying over to him. "This is a terrible place!" Turi exclaimed. "Even before the plagues and the siege it must have stunk with so many people jammed into it! How could they live like this?"

"They are not like us, that is how," Kagemni said. "When they ate the rats, they were eating their own kinsmen." He graced Ahmose with one of his rare grins. "Majesty, it is over," he said warmly. "Egypt is whole once more."

"Have you encountered any Setiu soldiers?" Ahmose wanted to know. He was looking over their heads to where the temple to Sutekh reared its pillars away to the right and next to it the walls of what he knew to be a barracks. Turi followed his gaze.

"The temple had been invaded, by the sick I think," he said. "Its courts and anterooms are still full of their detritus: pallets, bowls, animal bones, physicians' pestles. There are even a few decomposing bodies. As for soldiers, no. We entered their compound and found none. Perhaps they were all expended during the battle last year. The men are disappointed." He laughed. "They feel cheated of a proper victory."

"Keep them away from the temple!" Ahmose said urgently. "The pestilence may still linger there. Set guards outside it. Have your troops search the city for anyone left, but they must do so very carefully. I want no illness spreading in my army." Now at last he looked to where the palace walls loomed just beyond the soldiers' quarters. "I shall be in there," he told them, jerking his chin in its direction. "Bring me reports when you are ready. General Baqet, you may also deploy your men throughout these miserable streets." O Amun, Greatest of Greatest, he prayed as his commanders saluted and melted back into the press of their men, let Apepa be alive and waiting for me. Let this night be remembered as the mightiest vindication in Egypt's history.

It was not far to the tall cedar doors set into the palace's protecting wall. Ramose had relinquished his hold on the chariot and now walked with his arms folded and his head down. Khabekhnet jumped from the vehicle and together with Ankhmahor and half the Followers, who had taken the torches from Baqet's escort of Shock Troops, ran to precede the horses. Ahmose did not believe that he would need their shield. There was no danger here. Het-Uart was dead, its diseased heart pulsing out the last of its life somewhere within the maze of corridors and courtyards Ramose had described after his return. Ahmose spared a glance at his friend as Makhu slowed the chariot but could not see his face in the dimness. He looked up at the sky. He had no idea how long it had been since he had received the news that the gates were opening but there was no hint of dawn yet. The stars still flared white in a velvety blackness. More torches could be glimpsed through the palace entrance, moving to and fro across Ahmose's vision like flames that had escaped from a fire. He stepped down, and bidding Makhu wait, he followed his defenders into Apepa's precinct.

The space he entered was full of his own soldiers. In front of him, right in the centre of the imposing path that led to the shadowy bulk of the building beyond, the standard of Montu had been planted and beside it his own royal flag, its blue almost inky and its white greyish in the uncertain light of the one torch that had been set before it. Statues lined the avenue, strange figures holding staffs or emblems unfamiliar to Ahmose, most of them bearded and horned, their solemn features seeming to twitch and stir in the flickering torchlight. To right and left he received the impression of vast, shrouded gardens. The scent of orchard blossoms came to him faintly and he heard leaves rustling. But the ground was barren, a carpet of brittle, dead grass interspersed with patches of bald earth. No water, he thought. Apepa could not water his precious lawns and flowerbeds and rain was not enough.

Sebek-khu was coming towards him with Tchanny, who was holding a torch. They bowed. Both were smiling. "My division came in by the Royal Entrance Gate, Majesty," Sebek-khu said. "It is very close by, through the ancient citadel fortification and Apepa's orchard and then down at once to the tributary. I was surprised to meet no resistance at the palace walls. I entered the palace with a small force intending to battle whatever remnant of Apepa's soldiers remained but there are only a few courtiers left." Ahmose felt a wave of despair settle over him like a well-worn cloak.

"Apepa is not here?"

Sebek-khu shook his head, his smile fading. "No, Majesty, not unless he is hiding somewhere. I have made a cursory examination of the building but it is vast and complex and I and my men have not been in possession long. However, his vizier is waiting for you. I have detained him in a small room close by. He wanted to greet you in the reception hall but it would have taken many soldiers to watch him there. I am afraid I have insulted his dignity."

"To Set with his dignity!" Ahmose responded loudly, a dull fume of disappointment rising in him. Are we to be thwarted of our vengeance, Kamose? All this, the desperation, the killings, the uncertainty and the pain, ours and the citizens of this accursed place, is it all to be for naught? If Apepa has gone, I will cast soil upon my head and howl like a wounded dog. "Take me to him," he finished irascibly. He was suddenly aware of an extreme fatigue. Excitement had carried him this far but now he wanted to turn aside, go down and out those deceitful gates, get onto his couch and draw clean sheets up over himself. Het-Uart was a ruined void.

He set off behind his General, pacing between those peculiar statues whose foreignness made his scalp prickle, Khabekhnet and Ramose to either side, the Followers now at his rear. Directly ahead, a row of tall pillars marked what Ahmose supposed was the main entrance. No lights showed between their frowning girth; indeed, the darkness beyond them was deeper than the night outside. Sebek-khu did not approach them. He veered left, skirting the edge of the palace and stopping outside a small door set into the western wall. Ramose gave an exclamation. "I have been here before," he said. "This is where I was brought." Ahmose held up a hand.

"Khabekhnet," he said. "Go in and call my titles." Sebek-khu opened the door and the herald stepped through.

"Down on your face before Uatch-Kheperu Ahmose, Son of the Sun, Horus, the Horus of Gold, he of the Two Ladies, he of the Sedge and Bee." Khabekhnet had of his own volition added the two titles Ahmose had refused to accept at his first coronation because he was not yet King over both Upper and Lower Egypt. Now he heard them ringing out in his Chief Herald's authoritative voice and a lump came into his throat as he followed. It was a magnificent thing for Khabekhnet to do.

Candlelight met him, soft and diffuse, making him blink after the limited range of the torch Tchanny had borne. He found himself in a pleasant room with low, gilded chairs and one elegant table holding a cluster of fat candles. Cushions of hectic colours and busy patterns lay piled here and there. Three tall alabaster lamps should have illumined the space, but they were not lit. The walls were of a dull yellow ochre and just beneath the ceiling there ran a giddy frieze of black-painted repeated whorls. A closed golden shrine stood in one corner.

The floor was carpeted and in its centre a man was kneeling, forehead touching it, one hand clutching a blue-and-white staff of office. Ahmose looked down on him for a moment before bidding him rise. The soldiers around him had reverenced Ahmose and now stood watching their charge carefully. "Get up and give me that staff," Ahmose commanded. The man struggled to his feet. He was in middle age with a lined face dominated by both a hooked nose as curved as a hawk's beak and a braided beard. His black hair was very short. His long, plain white gown was belted in silver. Obediently, his kohled eyes fixed on Ahmose, he did as he had been told. With one savage gesture Ahmose broke the staff in two across his knee and threw the pieces into a corner. "Who are you?" he rapped. The man cleared his throat.

"I am Vizier and Keeper of the Royal Seal Peremuah," he said steadily. "It is my duty to officially surrender the city of

Het-Uart to you on behalf of my Lord, His Majesty King Awoserra Apepa."

"And where is His Majesty?" Ahmose demanded. He knew it was not worthy of him, but he was unable to keep the sneer out of his voice. The man flushed.

"He has relinquished his city and gone to join his brothers in Rethennu. I have his authority to render to you my charge, the Royal Seal, in token of his acknowledgement that Egypt is now yours."

"It always was," Ahmose replied automatically but he was perplexed. "How can Apepa have escaped, with Het-Uart girdled by my soldiers for so many months? How long has he been gone?" he asked Peremuah. The vizier's eyes became hooded. He stared at his silver-sandalled feet and said nothing.

All at once the answer came to Ahmose and he rounded on Khabekhnet. "Take my chariot at once," he ordered. "Ride out through the Royal Entrance Gate as quickly as you can and find Prince Abana. He should be somewhere close by. Detain every citizen and cart that has not disappeared. I want them all searched, regardless of their condition. How long?" he shouted at Peremuah as Khabekhnet ran out. "And where in Rethennu was he going?" Peremuah sucked in his lips and raised his head. His expression was obstinate.

"I was instructed to tell you only that His Majesty had gone and to give you the Seal," he persisted. "I am sorry."

"Are you?" Ahmose said furiously, though his anger had been sparked by frustration, not by Peremuah's demeanour. The man was only doing his ministerial duty. "Give it to me then!" Peremuah pulled open a drawstringed bag hanging from his belt and withdrew the Royal Seal, passing it to Ahmose with a short bow. It was a small clay cylinder. Ahmose looked down at it as it lay on his palm. He rubbed the raised characters of Apepa's name and titles with one tentative thumb, knowing that he held in his hand the last agent of all Setiu power in Egypt, then he dropped it to the carpet and ground it contemptuously under his heel, feeling it break and crumble. "So ends Apepa's reign," he said, scuffing the grey grit. "Peremuah, you are to be held here until I find someone who will tell me where Apepa has gone. Afterwards you may leave Egypt." The man recoiled in shock.

"But, M … Majesty am I not to die?" he stammered, unconsciously giving Ahmose his title, and Ahmose snorted.

"Don't be ridiculous!" he snapped. "You are neither a soldier nor a traitor to your master and I am not a demon. Stay in this pesthole or hurry home to Rethennu, I do not care which. Sebek-khu, see to it. And now, where are the remaining courtiers?"

"I had them herded into Apepa's quarters," Sebek-khu told him before flinging an order at Peremuah's guardians and indicating an inner door. "They are mostly women." He cast a sidelong glance at Ahmose as they emerged into a deserted passage, Ramose and the Followers coming after, and instantly the vizier vanished from Ahmose's mind. He knows that Tani might be among them, he thought anxiously. He has never seen her but everyone is aware of my family's tragedy. What shall I do if she has also gone?

He trudged after his General and was soon lost in a maze of narrow intersecting corridors and halls that seemed to fold one into another like a child's nightmare of endless ochre walls and echoing unlit spaces. Sebek-khu and several of the Followers had snatched up candles that cast a flickering light around the company but outside their flames the darkness was unrelieved. To Ahmose its quality was both desolate and eerie, as though the thousands who had thronged the palace and then fled had left fading traces of themselves behind to fill the hollow rooms with a whispering panic. Sebek-khu, although he had an almost infallible sense of direction, often hesitated before a branching black void. There were brackets for torches at regular intervals, usually on the walls beside the many closed doors that Ahmose had no desire to see open, but they were empty. Often he found himself crossing tiny courtyards that were open to the sky, with fountains that no longer spewed water into their basins and stone paving littered with all the evidences of a hurried abandonment. At such times he looked up and took comfort from the squarely delineated pattern of white stars above him.

But eventually there was a glow of light at the end of a narrow passage, and Ahmose came to a halt before two imposing doors. The soldiers to either side stiffened and saluted him, and at a word from Sebek-khu they pulled the doors open. Ahmose walked through. One swift glance at the wary faces turning quickly in his direction told him that Apepa was not among them. He had clung to a far-fetched hope that the man might have disguised himself and not yet slunk out under cover of the vast flow of his citizens in spite of what the vizier had said. These people were mostly of the right age but none of the four or five men resembled him. I suppose the younger courtiers were adventurous enough to join the commoners, Ahmose thought, but age brings caution and an increasing fear of the unknown. Tani is not here either.

He spared a moment to absorb the impressions the large room was forcing on him. The walls were hung with mats woven in the same hectic colours and whirling patterns he had noticed on the cushions in the place he had first entered, and where they ceased there were scenes of white-tipped mountains thrusting above a blue ocean dotted with ships. The water itself teemed with exotic sea creatures Ahmose could not identify. There were two inner doors, both of painted wood. On the surface of the left-hand one a hump-backed bull with golden horns and flaring nostrils glared at him and on the right the Setiu sea-god Baal-Yam with his plaited beard lifted his naked torso from the frothing water. Unlit lamps curved and frilled like seashells were placed at random.

What Ahmose could see of the few unoccupied chairs showed him legs made in the likeness of full-breasted girls with short skirts and ribboned ringlets holding up gilded seats whose backrests were ivory dolphins, and more dolphins, silver this time, smiled at him benignly from the bases of the many wine cups cluttering the low tables. The sheer foreignness of his surroundings made Ahmose cringe. It is one thing to trade with Keftiu for exotic objects, he thought. Many of them are pretty. But there is nothing Egyptian here at all, no evidence that our conquerors had anything but disinterest for our art or our gods.

He turned his attention reluctantly to the silent throng regarding him with a palpable fear. The women were unpainted and dishevelled, their hair undone, their long woollen skirts haphazardly tied. A pile of tasselled cloaks lay on the carpeted floor beside an unlit brazier. The room was warm with the press of bodies and smelled faintly of sweat and perfumes. "Are you all drunk?" Ahmose enquired. One of the men detached himself and came forward.

"We have been finishing our Lord's supply of wine," he said simply, "but we have not been able to shut out the disaster around us. What Egyptian are you?" Ahmose was nonplussed. He had never been asked that question before, and he realized that in dressing and leaving his tent so hurriedly he had neglected to snatch up any emblem of his position. Even his linen headdress was plain. Sebek-khu answered for him.

"You are addressing His Majesty Uatch-Kheperu Ahmose. Do him reverence," he barked. The man bowed, obviously confused, and the rest followed suit awkwardly.

"Forgive me, Majesty. I am Semken, mayor of Het-Uart. I could not leave my city."

"You speak straight to the point, I see," Ahmose commented. "Now tell me, where has Apepa gone?" Semken shook his head.

"I swear I do not know. I am only a mayor, Great One, not a courtier. I was summoned to the palace three days ago and given instructions by Vizier Peremuah to prepare the citizens for the evacuation that took place this night. But when it was time for me to go, I could not bring myself to do it, although I made sure that my family left. Instead I came here. Perhaps the vizier can tell you our Lord's whereabouts."

"He could, but he refuses." Ahmose lifted his gaze to the huddle beyond. "Do any of you know where he has gone?"

he said loudly. No one stirred, but suddenly there was a cry and a young woman broke away from the rest. She was pointing at Ramose.

"You!" she shouted. "I know you! In the bath house here at Het-Uart! You were washing beside me and you had a guard with you. He tried to stop me talking to you because you were Apepa's southern prisoner and you asked about a Princess Tani." She stood in the middle of the floor, clicking her fingers in exasperation. "Your name … Your name …" Then her face lit up. "You are Ramose!" Ahmose turned to his friend. He was staring at the girl and frowning, struggling to recollect her.

"Yes," he said slowly. "And you are Hat-Anath, daughter of an assistant scribe to one of Apepa's Overseers of Cattle. I remember you now." A tiny smile came and went on his mouth. "I must apologize for not honouring the invitation you extended to me at that time, to visit you in your quarters."

"It is still open," she replied promptly, smiling back at him, not the least embarrassed by her disorderly appearance. "Unless you found your Princess, of course."

"I found her," Ramose said quietly, "but I lost her again."

"Where is your father?" Ahmose interposed sharply. Hat-Anath gestured behind her.

"Here, and my mother also. Since the siege began in earnest, my father has been unable to carry out his duties." She peered searchingly into Ahmose's eyes. "They say that you have slaughtered all the Delta cattle as your brother did and you will kill us too," she said. "It is not true, is it?"

"No," Ahmose answered soberly. "But I intend to burn down this palace, so I suggest that all of you leave the wine jugs behind, gather up what you can, and hurry away. My men will not accost you."

"But where can we go, Majesty?" Hat-Anath spread out her hands. "I am an Egyptian. I was born here in Het-Uart. So was my father, though my grandfather was Setiu. The Delta is all I have known!" Ahmose sighed inwardly. We have fought a dirty war, you and I, Kamose, he thought sadly. But what civil war is not dirty? We have been forced to destroy the innocent along with the guilty in our bid for freedom and you, Hat-Anath, are just another casualty.

"I am sorry," he said aloud. "But the problem is not mine. If your father still has family beyond Egypt's borders, then you must go to them. But I warn you all." He had raised his voice. "Get out of the palace." She would have made another protest but Ahmose lifted one admonitory finger. "No," he said. "I have spoken." He turned once more to Ramose whose expression was unreadable. He was still staring at Hat-Anath. "Ramose, do you want her?" he asked with inspiration. Ramose started.

"Want her, Ahmose?" he repeated. "For what purpose?" Ahmose surrendered.

"For no purpose," he said wearily. "Sebek-khu, let us go." He had expected an outburst of consternation when he turned his back on the courtiers but there was none, and he was followed through the doors by a resigned quiet.

He and the others had barely reached the end of the passage when they were approached by Sebek-khu's Commander of Shock Troops. He was carrying a torch and in its glare his face betrayed an anxiety that vanished when he saw them. He bowed.

"Majesty, I am glad that I have found you. I presume that you have just spoken with the people in Apepa's quarters. There is a woman who refused to join them. She insisted on remaining in her own rooms. She says she is a Queen, therefore I hesitated to compel her. She has asked that you be brought to her." His tone betrayed his annoyance at such impudence. Ahmose felt his blood begin to race and beside him Ramose drew in a quick breath.

"You will lead me there," Ahmose managed to say. "Ankhmahor, take the Followers and go with Sebek-khu. Find the throne room. I expect it is just beyond the main entrance. Wrap the Horus Throne and the box containing the Royal Regalia in whatever clean linen you can find and escort them to my tent. Have them well guarded. Ramose, come with me." It was Tani who waited for him. It had to be, and he did not want to greet her in the presence of any avid ears. I shrink from greeting her at all, he thought. What can I say to her? How can mere words bridge the gulf between us after so long? Do I love or despise her?

"So she is still alive!" Ramose whispered with such wonder and anticipation that Ahmose was ashamed of his instinctive need to recoil from this reunion. He nodded curtly at the officer.

"Let us move on, then," he said.

13

IT WAS NOT FAR to the women's quarters. They were of course situated close to Apepa's own private rooms and Ahmose found himself standing outside yet another set of sturdy double doors long before he was ready. The guards who had been leaning against the passage wall and talking desultorily sprang to attention as he came up to them, saluted, and at his reluctant invitation, opened the doors for him. He felt as though his feet were encased in Nile mud but he forced them to carry him forward, Ramose behind him. The doors closed.

The first thing that impressed itself upon him was the light. Two golden lampstands holding alabaster cups were feeding a mellow glow into a charming room of soft rugs, silver-chased cedar chairs, a low ebony table topped with ivory squares for the playing of board games, and in one corner a delicate little shrine. "You have oil!" he blurted. The woman standing by the table did not smile. She was swathed in a thick woollen cloak patchworked in red, blue and green, her small feet encased in short leather boots, her long black hair bound to her forehead by a single fillet of gold. Lapis hung from her ears and encircled both wrists, and rings shone on every finger of her trembling hands. She was fully painted, her eyelids glittering with sooty shadow in which gold dust had been mingled, her eyes kohled, her mouth orange with henna. Here at least was someone with enough dignity to refuse the numbing escape of wine in the face of dissolution. Ahmose stared at her, his own mouth so dry that he could not swallow, his heart thrumming with such force that he thought he might faint.

"Of course," she said, and it was Tani's voice, a little deeper than the girlish treble he remembered, a little more deliberate, and with a courtier's clear accent. "And fuel for my brazier too. Being a Queen has its advantages, Ahmose, particularly during a siege. It is good to see you again."

He could not answer. This familiar yet utterly alien creature gazing at him so calmly had rendered him wordless. He stood there stupidly, woodenly, and watched those huge gazelle's eyes suddenly become liquid. "It is good to see you again!" she cried out, and all at once she was speeding across the floor, the cloak falling away from her. His arms opened and then he was embracing her, his body instantly recognizing the vitality that had always imbued her bones, her cheek tight against his neck, her tears warming his jaw.

"Tani," he choked. "Tani. Tani. You have grown up. I hardly knew you. How beautiful you have become!" She was laughing and crying, hugging him, patting his back, babbling unintelligibly, but he was still incapable of speech, so full was his heart. For a long time they clung together. When finally he set her away, she turned to Ramose. He had been waiting stiffly, arms at his sides, but now she lifted them gently by the wrists, looking into his tense face.

"And you, Ramose. You lived. You lived! After you left here, there was no more news of you. I was forced to presume that Kethuna had put you in the forefront of the battle and you were dead." He twisted his hands, and taking hers he kissed them before letting them drop.

"He intended me to die but he was thwarted," he replied huskily. "Kethuna perished."

"I am so glad." She was reaching for her brother again, her fingers brushing his and then closing around them. "Tell me everything, Ahmose. How is Mother? Is Grandmother still alive? And Kamose? Is he here in the palace with you or down by the river with the troops?"

She knows nothing, he realized as he allowed her to lead him to a chair. We at least knew that she had survived and indeed been treated with every courtesy, but what must it have been like for her, with only the phantasms of her imagination for a herald? He sat and she lowered herself opposite him. "Ramose, come here beside me," she called. Obediently he pulled up another chair and joined her, but her attention had returned to Ahmose. "So Kamose is the Horus of Gold, the champion of Ma'at," she went on, the catch of a sob in her throat. "He is the victor. No one in Het-Uart believed it was possible."

He found his voice then, and with her eyes fixed on him in an eagerness that quickly became horror he told her of the rebellion of the Princes, his wounding and Kamose's murder, the death of his and Aahmes-nefertari's children. He did not speak of his campaigns, the planning of the sieges, Pezedkhu's defeat at Abana's hands. She had been an observer of those things, although from a very different view. When he had finished, she sat bowed in her chair as though threatened, her body straining away from the shock of his words. "The Princes conceived that evil plot, Ahmose, not Apepa. Not him!" she insisted, her voice breaking. "He would have encouraged insurrection but not murder! Oh, Kamose, beloved!"

"Why not?" Ahmose snapped, unimpressed by her grief, his former sympathy evaporating. "He commanded the attack that left our father half-mute and paralyzed. Why stop there?" Tani straightened. Her face was flushed. She clapped softly and a servant appeared from the inner room and bowed. "Heket!" Ahmose exclaimed. "So you are still attending my sister."

"I am," the woman said promptly. "And I hope you can persuade her to go home now, Prince. I miss the desert and my family." She knows nothing either, Ahmose told himself with a fleeting sense of impotence. Both of them have been existing in the bubble of time Apepa created here in Het-Uart while outside the whole of Egypt has changed.

"Of course she will go home now!" Ramose cut in loudly. "It is all over. She is no longer a hostage. She is free." But Tani was shaking her head, her eyes bright with unshed tears.

"Bring wine and cups, Heket," she ordered. "There should be a flagon left, on the table by my couch. No, Ramose," she went on miserably. "It is not so. I made a promise to my husband."

"What do you mean?" he demanded. "What promise? Tani, the usurper has gone. All you need to do is have Heket pack up your belongings, get on a ship, and sail upstream to Weset! Or better still, to Khemmenu, where we will sign a marriage contract and you will enter my house as my wife at last!" His voice had risen. He was clenching his fists against his knees and leaning over them as though in pain. Ahmose made a motion to stop his flow of increasingly vehement words.

"What is it, Tani?" he said sharply. Her lips had begun to quiver.

"He wanted me to go with him," she half-whispered. "Uazet, His Chief Wife, and his sons, and several of his other wives, they all went. But I begged to be allowed to stay in the city so that I might see you again, Ahmose, and Kamose. He gave in, but he made me swear an oath before my Amun shrine that I would not tell you where he has gone. As for marriage ..." She swung round to Ramose, her mouth working so uncontrollably that her words became slurred. "I am already married. I have a husband. I signed a contract with him." Ramose sprang from his chair and stood before her, hands on his hips. He too was shaking, but Ahmose, watching him, had the immediate intuition that the anger consuming him owed nothing to love or bewilderment. It was the pure rage of frustration.

"You are under no obligation to that man!" he shouted. "He tore your family apart! He made you a prisoner here! He seduced you in order to cause Kamose the greatest possible agony! You do not belong to him by any law of decency Ma'at decrees! You belong to me!" She put her face in her hands and began to rock back and forth.

"I am his wife!" she sobbed. "He is my husband! He has dealt honourably with me! I cannot desert him now that he has lost everything!" Ahmose, horrified, put a hand on her hot spine. His touch immediately stilled her and she looked up. "Ramose, I cannot marry you," she said almost incoherently, stumbling over her words. "I was not forced to sign that contract. I was not threatened. I set down my name and title of my own volition." He bent slowly until his face came level with her own. For a long moment he searched her eyes, then he straightened up.

"You love him," he said dully. "I can see it but I cannot believe it. You love that abomination. Then curse you, Queen Tautha. You deserve each other." He spun on his heel, strode to the doors, wrenched them open, and was gone.

Tani drew a shuddering breath. Heket, who had been waiting dumbfounded, came forward, setting out the cups and pouring wine. Tani lifted hers and drank quickly, both hands around the stem of the goblet. Ahmose did not move. "Is it true?" he asked her tonelessly. She nodded.

"Yes. Oh forgive me, Ahmose, and try to understand! I came to Het-Uart as little more than a child, terrified and alone, adoring Ramose, missing my family, and when I heard that Kamose had begun a new revolt I was sure that Apepa would execute me for his disobedience. But I was wrong." She took another gulp of the wine then put it on the low table and pushed the cup away. "He was gentle and kind. He talked to me, gave me gifts, told me that he admired the Taos for their courage even though he was forced to fight them for their treason. He knew my confusion. He was so patient." She rubbed both wet cheeks, then sat staring at her hands. She would not look at Ahmose. "I did not fall in love with him as I did with Ramose," she went on in a low voice. "That love was fierce and all-consuming and when it died, as first love often does, it left an echo that brings me a small ache even now." She smiled wanly. "My love for Apepa grew slowly. It is a solid and lasting emotion, Ahmose. I will not excuse it."

"We expected the child who left us to return a child," Ahmose responded woodenly. "It was a cruel and unreal hope. Perhaps you are not to blame. We have both loved and hated you since the news that you had married our enemy, but I see now that you did not deserve our hate. You managed to do more than just survive here and for that I am proud of you." She turned to him and he took her face between his palms. "Ramose does not know it yet but he does not really love you any more," he went on carefully. "He turned his love into a continuing fantasy so that he could retain his sanity through the dreadful bereavements he has had to endure. Now perhaps he will taste true freedom for the first time since Father agreed to let him court you officially. And you, Tani, are also free. You can go home." She pulled away from him.

"No," she said more strongly. "No, Ahmose. I do not want to see Weset again. I want to go to my husband."

"Where is he?"

"I already said I cannot tell you. I made a vow." Ahmose got out of the chair.

"Tani, I must find him, surely you see that!" he protested. "He cannot be left to raise a new army and try to recapture the Delta! I will never sleep soundly again if he is left to roam Rethennu!" An expression of obstinacy crossed her features. Ahmose recognized it from her younger days and it gave him a pang of almost unbearable loss.

"What would you think if Aahmes-nefertari betrayed you in such a manner?" she asked. "Especially if she had sworn to you that she would not."

"But, Tani, your silence is traitorous, can't you see that?" he urged. "Apepa is an enemy of Egypt and if you aid him in this way, even indirectly by your silence, you are guilty of treason."

"Then you will have to execute me," she said resolutely. She rose also, folding her arms. "Not only did I give my word but I swore by Amun. It is a binding vow. If I break it, I am in danger of an unfavourable weighing when my ka enters the Judgement Hall and stands before the scales." Her stubborn chin came up. "You must do with me what you will." He pursed his lips and surveyed her.

"You don't want to tell me, do you?" he said. "You really do love him." She did not respond. He shrugged his shoulders, a gesture of futility. "I cannot release you to wander off alone in the direction of Rethennu, although I suppose I could have you followed," he said, half-talking to himself. "Nor can you stay here. All I can do is put you in my tent and have you guarded so that you do not run away. Oh, Tani," he finished bitterly. "You would run away, wouldn't you?" She pursed her lips and her head sank. Ahmose deliberated for a moment before turning to the servant. "Heket!" he ordered. "Gather your mistress's possessions together and I will send someone to take them down to my camp. Tani, come with me." Without another word she walked to her cloak, picked it up, and wrapping it once more around her shoulders she went to the door.

Outside Ahmose collected the two soldiers and with Tani leading the way they made their way through the empty palace. Tani remained silent and Ahmose, his eyes on the coloured tassels of her cloak dragging along the floor at her heels as he paced behind her, wondered what she was thinking. He had become lost at once, but she strode on confidently through the dark, tortuous corridors, one hand brushing a wall, her leather boots making no sound.

Some time later Ahmose glimpsed light ahead and almost at once Tani moved to one side. Sebek-khu, Ankhmahor and the Followers were coming, haloed in the harsh glare of a torch. Ankhmahor was carrying a large box. Bowing briefly, Sebek-khu wasted no words. "The Horus Throne has gone, Majesty," he said. "Also the Royal Regalia. We have searched for them as well as we could but found nothing." Tani stepped forward.

"You will seek in vain," she said. "My husband has taken the Throne and the Regalia with him, disguised in one of the carts. It is a small revenge, I think."

"A small revenge?" Ahmose spat. "The seat of the Divine and the symbols of his power and mercy? What in Amun's name is wrong with you, Tani?" He made himself become calm. "General, Prince, this is my sister, the Queen Tautha, wife to Apepa." Their eyes widened in astonishment and then a swift, commiserating pity as he had known they would. He felt sick, and dirty to the marrow of his soul. "Ankhmahor, what do you have there?" he enquired through clenched teeth. Ankhmahor passed him the box.

"It was sitting on the dais in the great reception hall where I presume the Horus Throne had been placed," Ankhmahor told him. He lifted the lid.

It was a bulbous headdress of starched deep blue linen that swept out in two flanges above the ears and was covered in small golden discs. Ahmose pulled it up into the light. Two ribbons, also blue, trailed from its rear. In the centre of the supporting band of gold that would rest on the forehead there was an empty notch. Ahmose fingered it cautiously. "What is this?" he said.

"It is a Setiu crown," Tani answered him. "Apepa wore it often. He left it for you as a tribute to your victory over him." Ahmose at once tossed it back in its chest. He wanted to rip it apart and grind its tatters under his feet as he had done to Apepa's seal, but he knew that he must not lose the last shreds of his self-control. The desire to start mindlessly killing would then become too strong.

"It is no tribute," he said thickly. "It is an insult. He takes the hedjet, the deshret, the heka and the nekhaka, Egypt's most sacred royal possessions, and substitutes a piece of Setiu blasphemy. I suppose that he set the Holy Uraeus in the notch whenever he pleased, but of course that belongs with the Double Crown. He would not leave that behind." He thrust the box back at Ankhmahor. "Take it down to my tent, and Queen Tautha too," he commanded. "Detail some of the Followers to guard her. She is not to leave it. Tell Akhtoy to set up a couch for her." Tani put a tentative hand on his arm but he shook it off. "I will find him if it takes me the rest of my life," he said bitterly. "The thief must be made to return the valuables he took before I punish him." Ankhmahor bowed and hesitated and Tani correctly interpreted his look. Before he could touch her, she pushed past him, and he and his men followed her into the dimness.

"We are close to the throne room, Majesty," Sebek-khu said. "Come and rest for a while."

I feel as though I have never slept and will not do so again, Ahmose thought as he allowed his General to lead the way. How can such a triumph be mingled with such grief?

A few soldiers with candles in their hands were wandering about the room as Ahmose entered, their voices echoing against the unseen ceiling high above. But Ahmose's gaze was drawn to the naked dais and the row of pillars beyond it where the sky could be seen. The stars were beginning to pale. He went to the steps leading up to the platform and lowered himself, letting his muscles relax. "What a night it has been, Majesty!" Sebek-khu commented. "I still cannot quite believe that the siege is over."

"I had hoped that it would all be over, everything neatly tied," Ahmose murmured. "But it is not so. Must I mount a full invasion of Rethennu to put an end to this whole unhappy story, Sebek-khu? What does Amun desire? I wish I knew."

He heard the commotion before he saw its cause, a din of excited voices coming nearer and finally bursting through the doorway in a blaze of lighted torches. Abana came striding over the tiled floor, Pezedkhu's ring glinting on the gold chain about his neck, his cousin Zaa trotting beside him and a gaggle of sailors behind them, who were surrounding a man and three women. Their hands were tied before them. The youngest woman looked terrified. She was panting and crying.

"Majesty, I have news!" Abana was shouting even before he had come up to Ahmose and made his reverence. "These Setiu are my prisoners!" Ahmose remembered his order to have any Setiu still in the vicinity of the city detained, but one glance showed him that the man with the untidy beard and sullen expression was not Apepa. Prince Abana's eyes were dancing in the orange flames held by his subordinates. Ahmose did not get up.

"Tell me then," he said.

"You had sent for me," Abana began with a flourish. "And I had received the command your Chief Herald was passing to every officer. Thus I deduced that Apepa was not to be found in the palace. But before I could answer your summons, I was forced to deal with a matter of some confusion. My sailors had been sleeping ashore, as you had so graciously permitted, and the ships were unmanned save for two sentries on each. We were unprepared for the sudden opening of the gates and the flood of humanity that followed. I confess that for once I and my men were taken by surprise." He paused, looking suitably but entirely falsely crestfallen. "The *North* under Captain Qar had been berthed almost exactly opposite the Royal Entrance Gate and I myself was not far away. Both Qar and I were sleeping on the northern bank of the tributary. By the time I woke, the first mighty wave of citizens had flowed across the bridge the men of Montu had flung down and was spreading out beside the water, in reach of the ships' ramps."

"Admiral, you have missed your calling," Ahmose broke in, amused in spite of himself. "You should have been a village storyteller."

"Majesty, you offend me," Abana rejoined airily. "It is necessary to set the scene for you. May I continue?"

"If you must." Ahmose had begun to smile.

"There was such a press of running, weeping people that neither Qar nor I nor any of your captains could see at first what was happening. You had decreed that the Setiu should be allowed to go away unmolested. They did not seem interested in the vessels. They were disappearing into the fields and orchards. But by the time their ranks had thinned, Qar realized that the *North* had gone." Ahmose sat up, suddenly alert. "The bodies of the two men left on watch had floated to the bank. There was no sign of the *North* anywhere. Qar is not to blame," Abana insisted earnestly. "There was so much chaos, and it was very dark. I realized at once what had happened. Apepa and his guards and perhaps his family had disguised themselves as peasants, slipped onto the *North,* and rowed away under cover of the exodus Apepa himself had engineered." His voice held genuine admiration. "It was a bold scheme."

"Certainly, if it is true." Ahmose had risen, all weariness falling from him.

"Oh it is true," Abana assured him proudly. "At that time the word to detain the Setiu had come. Zaa and I caught these three suspicious fish. One look at their soft hands and pale skin convinced me that they were no more peasants than I am. Furthermore, they are very bad liars. This man," he reached behind him and pulled his prisoner forward by the rope around his wrists, "this man tried to pretend that he was a merchant but he had traces of henna on his palms. Zaa and I took them aboard the *Kha-em-Mennofer.* We upturned the pretty little one and hung her over the side. Zaa took one leg and I took the other. It was quite a view!" He grinned. "By the time she had finished screaming and her sister and mother had finished begging us not to drown her, her father had told us everything." He bowed. "Majesty, behold Yamusa, Herald to Apepa. His Master is on his way to the city fort of Sharuhen in Rethennu, together with Chief Wife Uazet, Chief Scribe Yku-didi, royal sons Apepa and Kypenpen, and others of the royal brood. Unfortunately I think it is too late to catch them before they reach their destination. They will have headed straight out into the Great Green, turned east along the coast, and I believe that Sharuhen is a very short way inland." Ahmose walked straight up to him and briefly pulled him close.

"Abana, you are able to constantly amaze and delight me," he said. "Well done. You have opened my path before me." The men who had been surveying the hall had been drawn to the group at the foot of the dais and had listened to Abana's tale with rapt attention. Now, seeing the King embrace his Admiral, a murmur of approval ran through them. Abana dropped to one knee.

"Majesty, your touch is the greatest privilege that could be bestowed upon your subjects!" he exclaimed. "I am truly honoured!"

"Get up," Ahmose said. He was scanning the four prisoners without much interest. "I have already given you enough gold to keep you in lentils for the rest of your life, Abana. Would you like to keep these Setiu?" Yamusa cried out and his wife burst into tears. "Be silent!" Ahmose roared, the sound striking the walls and returning magnified by the void all around. "There was no word for 'slave' in our language until your ancestors brought it in! Abana?" The Prince was looking doubtful.

"Courtiers are no good for physical labour, Majesty," he commented. "And it might be foolish to place foreigners in positions of responsibility. The two girls could be trained to perform domestic chores or even as body servants, but Yamusa is a herald. Perhaps he can learn to call the tally to my Overseer of Grain while the harvest is being piled in my granary." He turned a sober eye on their agitation. "Oh, do not worry," he said scornfully. "We who live under the mantle of Ma'at are not wantonly cruel. We treat our servants well. Thank you, Majesty. I will take them." He snapped his fingers and his sailors ushered them out. The woman was still weeping. "Now!" Abana went on. "When do we leave for Sharuhen?"

"As soon as we may," Ahmose replied. "You have my gratitude, Prince. You are dismissed." Sebek-khu had come up beside him. "Make sure the palace is empty and then set fire to it," he ordered the General. "Every piece of furniture, every hanging, every couch and piece of cloth. There is to be no looting. Not one silver cup is to leave the building. Burn it all and then raze whatever is left. But the northern wall beyond the grounds was erected by my ancestor Osiris Senwasret. See that it remains standing."

"What of the city itself?" Sebek-khu wanted to know. Ahmose hesitated. He would have liked to command its complete destruction but that would take much unnecessary time and effort.

"It is a festering slum," he admitted, "and I suppose it ought to be levelled. However, it is very advantageously placed for any trade coming into the Delta from the Great Green. I will give some thought to having it repopulated. The defences here and on the northern mound must go. Your division and the Division of Horus under Khety can see to it. Ten thousand men should be enough to tear them down."

He and the remaining Followers left the throne room then, and guided by one of Sebek-khu's officers he made his way outside. Night was gradually giving way to a faint thinning and the stars were paling. Ahmose took a deep breath. The air smelled stale and was very still. Ra was not yet breathing, although he was nearing the moment of his birth. Dismissing the man and telling him that the mayor Semken could be released, Ahmose strode quickly across the desiccated ruin of Apepa's lawns and out through the towering gates. Here he encountered Turi, and Makhu had returned with the chariot, but Ahmose lingered. "I want to see the sun rise from here, from the centre of Het-Uart," he told his friend. "It will not be long. Walk with me, Turi. The dawn is very chilly."

For some time they strolled around the area before the wall. Soldiers streamed in and out of the gates. The horses stood patiently, heads lowered, blowing softly out of their nostrils. Makhu was sitting on the floor of the chariot, the reins slung over his shoulder. Beyond the city a mist hung about the feathered tips of the motionless palms and the horizon to the east was still lost in a soft, pearly greyness.

All at once Turi stumbled, and bending swiftly he retrieved the thing that had caught in his sandal. Brushing the soil from it, he examined it casually and then more closely. It was a charm or part of an amulet approximately the length of his palm and as he studied it an expression of disgust grew on his face. "Majesty, look at this," he said, passing it to Ahmose.

At first glance it appeared to be the work of an artist with no ability, a kneeling figure whose head was too large, its torso too short and undefined, and its lower portion reversed so that its trousered buttocks were presented. But as Ahmose stared at it, he saw that in fact there were two figures. The one above had two large slanting eyes without pupils above a thin nose and a widely grinning mouth. In spite of the clever caricature the features were undeniably Setiu. Its face was canted slightly downward, giving it a gloating, predatory effect. It wore a ribbed and pleated headdress and from its forehead the crude likeness of a snake curled back.

Beneath the lappets of the headdress two extended arms ended in bony, clawed fingers curved about the imprisoned elbows of the second figure who was kneeling before it, head lost in the shadow of its neck, knees bent and spread, its lower back sunk and straining under the pain of its position. "Look closely at the feet," Turi said tersely. Ahmose did so, not sure what he was supposed to see. Puzzled, he glanced at Turi. "The Egyptian's leg has been broken," Turi showed him. "One foot is turned up in the natural way, revealing its underside. But the other is flat. You cannot see the arch. He has been tortured. There is pure hate in that little carving." Ahmose wanted to fling it away but he found himself still holding it.

"It has been made from a mould," he said. "There might be dozens, hundreds of them scattered about Het-Uart. This is not just contempt for us, Turi, this is indeed pure hatred." His own fingers closed around it as though his flesh could insulate him from its invisible fume of corruption. At that moment a faint breeze brushed his cheek. He lifted his head. The whole eastern horizon was now flushed with scarlet and in the centre of his gaze the sky was shimmering. Even as he watched, Ra lipped the edge of the earth, rising triumphant over a free and united Egypt for the first time in many hentis, and Ahmose stood there with unfelt tears on his cheeks and the symbol of all he had won held tightly in his hand.

Tani was deeply asleep when he entered his tent, the chests containing her belongings piled neatly against one wall and Heket, equally lost in slumber, sprawled on a mat on the carpet beside her. Ahmose was hungry, but he needed rest. Warning Akhtoy to wake him at noon, he quickly shed his sandals, pulled off his limp kilt and helmet, and fell onto his own cot and into his dreams almost simultaneously. When he woke to find the steward bending over him and the aroma of freshly baked bread filling the tent, he was still clutching the Setiu charm. Akhtoy took it from him, grimaced briefly as he saw what it was, and tossed it into Ahmose's jewellery box. "Your sister is walking by the water in the company of Heket and a guard," he said in answer to Ahmose's question. "She ate very little when she woke, Majesty. She seemed pleased to see me again, as I was to see her." He hesitated, the agony of polite indecision written all over his face. "Forgive me, Majesty, but how am I to address her and in what way is she to be served? An army camp is no place for a Princess." Ahmose had sat up and was surveying the contents of the tray Akhtoy had set before him. In the background Hekayib was moving quietly around a basin of steaming water, a razor in one hand and clean linen draped across his arm. Ahmose sighed gustily.

"I know," he said. "I want to send her back to Weset but I fear she will not go. You must call her Queen Tautha, Akhtoy, and accord her the deference due to her title. I suppose she has become my prisoner," he went on gloomily. "Go to the Scribe of Distribution of Turi's division and ask him for an officer's tent for her. When you have done that, send Ipi and Khabekhnet to me. And keep her out of here until I have been washed and shaved."

He ate and drank with pleasure, sat quietly while Hekayib shaved his face and skull, and allowed himself to be dressed, enjoying every moment of his liberation. For that was what it was. Liberation. His determination to pursue Apepa had been reinforced by the sight of that profane little carving, but mounting a campaign in Rethennu would not be the same as taking Het-Uart. He would be leaving an unpolluted Egypt from which the last vestiges of foreign occupation had been purged. Rethennu had poured an ocean of soldiers into the Delta over the last few years. The Princes there had denuded themselves of men in order to shore up Apepa's weakening hold on the country. Ahmose did not anticipate any great struggle to reach Sharuhen. It was time to send out scouts who would describe the fortress.

Hekayib had just tied Ahmose's sandals and was tidying away his cosmetics table when Tani returned. She entered the tent diffidently, almost shyly, the multi-coloured cloak enveloping her, her own colour high from the brisk morning air. Ahmose greeted her and invited her to sit. She did so cautiously, perching on the edge of the stool and watching him somewhat warily. He felt irritated by her and angry at his own pettiness. This was his sister, his blood, sacrificed by Kamose and now returned to him whole and sane. I ought to be overjoyed to see her here, he thought, but all I want to do is punish her. Perhaps I am angry because I do not like to imagine Apepa as having any kindness or mercy in his character. I want to slaughter a monster, not kill a man. "Akhtoy has not changed at all," she began. "He is exactly the same. He is finding me my own tent."

"Yes."

"It is really not necessary to have me watched all the time, Ahmose. Even if I wanted to run away, I do not think

that Heket and I would get very far on our own, do you?"
He scrutinized her carefully.

"I don't know," he answered warily. "I don't know you
any more, Tani. Perhaps you are entirely capable of
trekking all the way to Sharuhen. That is what you want,
isn't it?" Her eyes became clouded and she leaned forward.

"Yes, more than anything!" she said. "Please don't send
me to Weset, Ahmose! It is not my home any more. If you
do, I shall simply leave as soon as I can slip away. Apepa is
my home. He needs me."

"Spare me the speech you have given me already," he
cut in brusquely. "Apepa is almost twice my age and you
are three years younger. I can understand his salacious
desire to have you in his bed but don't insult me by
pretending that you harbour any affection for him." Her
features twisted.

"But I do," she cried out. "Oh what is the use! Chain me
and send me back to my mother whose forgiveness and
gentleness will burn me like the hot coals of a brazier! And
my grandmother, who will not trouble to disguise her
contempt for me! And my sister, who is now herself a Queen
and will not miss an opportunity to remind me that it is far
better to be a Queen of Egypt than the wife of a fugitive
chieftain!"

Ahmose swallowed uncomfortably. Her outburst came
far nearer to the truth than he wanted to admit. He did not
remember her as being so astute. Perhaps she is right, he
thought, and the thought surprised him. Perhaps she will
never really be welcome any more in Egypt, with the taint
of Setiu on her. What could she be at court in Weset other
than a curiosity?

"An army on the march is no place for you," he said. "We have no litters. You cannot stand in a chariot for hours on end."

"But I could sit in one!" she broke in eagerly, sensing victory. "I could curl up at your feet, behind your charioteer! Armies do not speed, Ahmose. Will you take me with you?"

"I intend to kill him, and his sons too," Ahmose said heavily. "His line must be extinguished so that no threat to Egypt remains. No plea will sway me when I face him, Tani. There is too much at stake for me to care about your misguided loyalties."

"I know. I will not think of that now. Will you take me, Ahmose? In memory of the love we all once had for each other?"

"We still love you, Tani," he said but he was lying and she knew it. "Yes, I will take you to Sharuhen. And may you have joy of the journey."

They were interrupted by both Ipi and Khabekhnet, and gratefully Ahmose turned to more welcome considerations. He wished that she would leave while he gave his instructions but he could hardly expect her to hover outside while he did so. "Ipi, take down these orders for Khabekhnet to carry," he said. Ipi had already sunk cross-legged to the floor and was readying his palette. "The scouts of the following divisions are to leave for Sharuhen at once. Amun, Ra, Ptah, Thoth and Osiris. They must take the Horus Road, contacting Generals Iymery and Neferseshemptah on the way. Those two divisions, Khonsu and Anubis, will remain in the Delta for now. Then the scouts may pass on to the Wall of Princes and thus into Rethennu. I will follow almost at once and will expect their reports as soon as possible. Make six copies, one for each scout and one for your files. Khabekhnet, when you have delivered them, appoint heralds to take the news of Het-Uart's fall to the whole country. Have it called in every village, but designate one to go straight to Weset with a scroll for the Queen which I shall dictate as soon as Ipi has prepared the commands for the scouts. Am I understood?" Khabekhnet nodded. "And tell General Hor-Aha and Prince Abana that ten ships full of Medjay will be required to take the tributary right out to the Great Green and so cut off any aid to Sharuhen from the sea. That should be challenge enough for my impulsive Admiral. That is all." They made their obeisances and left. Tani stirred.

"Five divisions," she said. "Twenty-five thousand men. Do you think you can take Sharuhen with so few, Ahmose?"

"I do not anticipate any resistance on the way. Rethennu is exhausted," he replied testily. "If I do encounter trouble, I can bring up the two divisions in the eastern Delta very quickly. I ..." He stopped speaking, suddenly aware that he was about to discuss his strategy with an enemy. What if Tani escaped his vigilance somewhere close to Sharuhen and ran ahead to warn her husband that the Egyptian army was coming? Would she do such a thing? Would her betrayal extend to an active treason? She was waiting for him to continue, her expression alert, her eyes sharp with concentration, but he could see nothing furtive in her face. It was as open as it had ever been. Tani had never been able to hide her thoughts. "Further than that I cannot see," he finished lamely. "The scouts will describe Sharuhen."

"It is a mighty fortress," she said unexpectedly. "A walled city like Het-Uart but with the advantage of the ocean to protect its western flank. Pezedkhu told me. It will not be an easy conquest, Ahmose." At once he was ashamed of his accusatory thoughts.

"Yet conquer it I will," he said emphatically to hide his discomfiture.

There was an exchange of voices outside and almost at once the tent flap was raised. Ahmose had expected to see Ankh-mahor but it was Ramose who came forward. He bowed reverently to them both, something he often forgot to do and for which Ahmose forgave him. Obviously he had something weighty on his mind. "Majesty, I would like to speak to you privately," he said. He did not look at Tani. She rose at once and shrugged the heavy cloak around her shoulders.

"I will go and see if my tent is ready," she said. On passing Ramose she paused, but he kept his gaze on her brother and with a scarcely audible sigh she went out.

"Sit down," Ahmose offered. "I am very sorry that your hopes have been withered, Ramose. You must feel as though your soul has been drenched in acid." Ramose took the stool Tani had left. He did not respond to Ahmose's implied invitation to unburden himself. Instead he spoke.

"You will be marching on Sharuhen within the week, Ahmose." It was a statement. Ahmose nodded.

"Then I have a request. No, a petition." He ran a hand through his hair. "I pray that you will not consider me faithless to you or fickle to Tani when you have heard it. The gods know that I have carried my love for her like a child in the womb for years but now that love is stillborn." He glanced across at Ahmose. "The part of me where my memories live will always love her but I am sick to death of the past." He drew one finger across his eyelid and Ahmose realized how tired he was. "Forgive me," he went on. "I have spent the better part of the night in my tent thinking, and this morning in the palace. The fires have been set. It is beginning to burn."

Ahmose waited. There was a silence while his friend took a breath, pursed his lips, frowned, and finally flung up his hands. "I ask you to let me go home to Khemennu," he burst out. "If Tani had gone with Apepa to Sharuhen, I would want to come with you, but it is pointless now. I am not one of your generals. I accompany you as your friend. But you do not need me by your side any more. I would like to take up my governorship immediately." Ahmose felt his heart sink.

"You have been my defence against the loss of Kamose," he said slowly. "Indeed, you have often taken his place. But if you wish to go home, you have my permission. And my blessing." However, Ramose's expression of distress did not change.

"There is more," he admitted. "I would like to take Hat-Anath and her parents with me."

For a moment the name meant nothing to Ahmose, but then he remembered the girl in Apepa's apartments, dishevelled and defiant, and with her face two others came into his mind, sketched in a terrible clarity. Ramose's father, Teti, and his wife, Nefer-Sakharu, both tools of the Setiu, both executed for treason. Ahmose remembered the many tragedies Ramose had endured at the hands of himself and Kamose. Had Tani's defection been the last stone laid upon his friend's back, the one that had broken him at last? This is a test for you, King of Egypt, his mind whispered. Will you live with your feet continually bogged down in the morass of mistrust or will you choose this moment to pull yourself free?

"For what purpose?" he managed. "Do you want more servants on your estate? And what of Senehat?"

"No." Ramose said decisively. "I like Hat-Anath. She is gently bred and she has spirit. She reminds me a little of Tani, or perhaps Tani as she might have been if fate had not dealt so cruelly with us. She will make a good governor's wife and I, dear Ahmose, I will make a good governor. As for Senehat, I am very fond of her. She was a diligent servant and a gentle presence in my bed in Weset when I most needed a woman's comfort. If she wishes to come to Khemmenu, it will not be as an underling. I will find her an honest husband." He was looking directly into Ahmose's eyes as he said this. You are not a fool, are you? Ahmose thought. He got up.

"Go home, my friend," he said warmly. "Take the girl with you and teach her how fortunate she is to be married to an Egyptian. I shall miss you very much." The speech had cost him a great deal. I don't want you to go, he shouted silently. I don't want anything to change between us. I don't want these turbulent days to warp and twist what we have, as they have driven Aahmes-nefertari and me apart.

"Thank you, Ahmose," Ramose said with a touching dignity. "I am grateful for all the evidences of your favour. May Thoth continue to grant you wisdom, as I will continue to love and serve you."

The tent seemed smaller and darker when he had gone.
I hate change, Ahmose mused as he sat motionless in the
chair, which is odd because I have spent the better part of
my short life fighting to achieve it. But there is the change
one wreaks oneself and the change that occurs outside the
bounds of one's control, and it is the latter that causes me
such distress. Be happy, Ramose. It is time the gods deigned
to smile on you. Be at peace.

He was relieved when Ipi bowed his way in and settled
down to take the letter that must be dictated to Aahmes-
nefertari. A longing for her overcame him as he searched
for the right words to say. There had still been no communication from her. Ipi had applied his papyrus burnisher
with his usual vigour and skill. His pen was poised above
the blank scroll and he was waiting patiently. At last
Ahmose cleared his throat and began. "To the Queen of
Egypt, the Second Prophet of Amun, greetings," he said.
"My dearest Aahmes-nefertari, you will be overjoyed to
know that Het-Uart is in my hands and even now its walls
are being razed. However, Apepa has fled to Rethennu and
I trust you will understand that I must pursue him for the
future security of this land. So it will be some time before I
can kiss you and assure myself of your good health. Our
child will be born very soon. Forgive me for asking you
once more to walk that path alone. I know your anger and
your loneliness and I beg you not to think of me with
condemnation, for I love you truly. I must speak now of
Tani ..." His voice sounded thin and prating in his ears
and Ipi's rapid breathing very loud. He had a sudden thirst
for wine.

14

IT WAS A FULL WEEK before Ahmose and his five divisions uncoiled from the outskirts of Het-Uart and began their march east along the Horus Road. In that time the interior of the palace had been reduced to smouldering rubble and gangs of soldiers from the remaining divisions had begun to demolish its thick walls. A few civilians were trickling back to the city, apprehensive but determined to sleep under their own roofs after wandering aimlessly on either side of the tributary, and Ahmose gave permission for them to return. They were mostly the poor who had nowhere else to go and thus were no threat to the troops who cursed and sweated as they fought to bring down Het-Uart's defences. Ahmose had no food to offer them, but the Delta was now open and they were free to scrabble about for whatever edible vegetation or unwary animals they could find at that time of the year.

The major sowing of crops would not take place until the following month, but the river had receded to its spring level and the flood plains were already mostly dry. The Horus Road ran east on whatever elevated ground there was, weaving in great curves around the many permanent lakes and tiny waterholes that would not empty. Morale was high among the men. They sang as they strode along beneath the trees, spears canted on their shoulders, axes and swords clattering against their thighs. Ahmose rose at the head of the column that snaked away behind him to be lost in the cold mist of early morning. In front were Ankhmahor and the Shock Troops of Amun and directly behind him rolled the chariot carrying Tani and Heket, a sunshade fixed to its frame, Makhu guiding the horses. His own chariot was being handled by Mesehti.

They covered only twenty-five miles that first day, less than Ahmose would have wished, but in places the Horus Road itself was still soft and the troops needed toughening after their long sojourn outside Het-Uart.

By the second night out the verdant growth of the Delta had begun to thin and they rested on the edge of the Sea of Reeds, a wide marshy area choked with birds, frogs and clouds of mosquitoes and gnats that greedily descended on the army and made the hours until dawn a misery. The road ran straight through its centre, dry enough for chariots in the summer but hard work for horses to pull the little vehicles through the crusting mud at this time of the year until the sun had baked it firm. Ahmose ordered all riders to walk beside their chariots and Tani also got down and paced behind Makhu in her leather boots. She had joined Ahmose and his generals around the fires that were lit in the evening but had said little, sitting on the ground with her chin on her knees, her whole body swaddled in the tasselled cloak. She seemed content and was not suffering any physical discomfort, and Ahmose left her alone.

Towards the end of the fourth day Ahmose began to smell the ocean. The ranks had emerged with relief from the rustling density of the reeds into a rough desert country of sand and gravel and in leaving the watery lushness behind they had also left its varied odours of wet vegetation. The drier air that now filled their lungs carried nothing but the strong tang of brine borne on a stiff, prevailing west wind straight off the sea. Ahmose, who had never even seen the Great Green, tried to analyze what his nostrils were drawing in with equal measures of delight and distaste, and gave up. The scent was beyond anything he knew, but the wind brought salt that coated his lips and made them burn.

At about noon of that day he had sighted portions of the Wall of Princes, the series of small forts his ancestors had built to guard Egypt's north-eastern border. They were strung out north to south across the Horus Road, straggling from the Great Green to disappear in the desert. There had been shouted greetings exchanged between the sentries on the walls and the Standard Bearers of the Divisions but Ahmose had not halted, though he had noted that several of the forts were in need of repair. And why should the Setiu have bothered to restore them? he thought sarcastically. There were no invaders to threaten their hold on Egypt from the east. Their true enemies were in the south, in Egypt herself.

That night the wind still blew and a squall of rain hit the camp, icy and penetrating. The men lay huddled around their fires in cloaks and blankets, too cold to sleep. Only Tani seemed at peace, lying on her rug under the protection of the unyoked chariot, the tight weave of her heavy Setiu cloak keeping her snug while thousands of soldiers shivered under the lighter Egyptian wool. Ahmose, equally uncomfortable, realized that in passing through the Wall of Princes the Horus Road had ended and he had left the security of Egypt. The rain and dropping temperatures were a fitting welcome to a part of the world he had always hated and feared, although he knew little of it. Most threats to Egypt have come from the east, he reflected, listening to the drenched sentries coughing as they walked the perimeter. My country lies warm and safe under the spells of beneficent gods but they have no interest in anything beyond. Here cold and darkness reign.

But by morning the sky had cleared, although its pastel grey-blue colour seemed to add an extra dimension to the quality of frigidity in the air. The camp was subdued as it broke up, the men saying little and preparing to set out again with their sopping blankets draped around their shoulders to dry. Ahmose anxiously scanned the view ahead. There was a track winding across the pebbled sand but did it lead to Sharuhen or wander away to be lost in some lonely desert waste? He decided to follow it as long as the sun was fairly low in the east and then when noon came to wait for the arrival of the scouts. The thought of leading twenty thousand men astray was not a pleasant one, but a march of a few hours would warm their blood and improve their dispositions.

He had just called a halt and the men had fallen out to squat in the sand and eat their bread and onions when his vanguard spotted a moving dot on the horizon. At Ahmose's urging Mesehti drove the chariot ahead of the Shock Troops who had sprung to their feet and were reaching for their weapons. He got down and stood shading his eyes. The dot soon separated into a group of six men coming steadily towards him. Ahmose sent one of the Followers to bring up food and beer and by the time he returned the six scouts were wiping the sweat from their brows and two soldiers were erecting the canopy Ahmose had ordered set up. The wind was still brisk, with an edge to it, but the sun was high and dazzling.

Khabekhnet summoned the generals and Turi, Kagemni, Akhethotep, Baqet and Meryrenefer settled themselves in the sand to hear the report. Ahmose, listening to their idle comments in the moment before he spoke, suddenly missed Hor-Aha. He had, of course, gone with the Medjay and Abana, the ships leaving Het-Uart at the same time Ahmose pulled himself up into his chariot and gave the order to march. Few councils of war have been held without him, Ahmose thought rather sadly. His words were few but always cogent. I would like to see his black skin gleaming beside me and this strange-smelling breeze tugging at his braids. Perhaps I shall give him a princedom after all. He broke into the chatter with a wave of his hand. The scouts had finished their meal and were waiting for his permission to speak. It was the scout from Amun's Division who gave the report.

"You are three, perhaps four days away from Sharuhen, Majesty," he began. "This track leads straight to it. You have been proceeding due east until now, but tomorrow it will veer north and take you through a country of vast sand dunes. Slow marching, and very cold at night. The dunes end about two miles from Sharuhen where this kind of desert begins again." He indicated the glaring expanse of stone-littered sand all around them. "Two miles to the west of the fort, on the ocean side, the dunes begin again. They fill all the ten miles between the fort and the Great Green. There is room enough for you to surround Sharuhen

completely. But it is as big as Het-Uart, and built of stone."
A murmur of dismay ran through the company and
Ahmose's heart sank. Stone. He was facing another siege
unless the gods intervened, and Sharuhen would not fall
easily, if at all. Its inhabitants were well-fed and strong, not
yet worn down by the months of deprivation a siege
produced. "There is a wide road through the dunes from the
city to the water," the scout continued. "Ten miles, but it is
well travelled by merchants bearing goods to Sharuhen.
Donkeys are available in the small village by the coast and
also outside the fort's western gate. We decided to steal one
and make the journey to the Great Green. We understood
that Prince Abana would be attempting a blockade from
the sea. Nothing is there but the ramshackle village, as I
said, some five or six craft of Keftian design anchored
offshore, and the *North*." He grinned at Ahmose's expression. "There is no longer any doubt that Apepa is within
the city."

"What of gates?" Ahmose asked tersely.

"There are four: north, south, east and west. They are
similar to the gates of Het-Uart, very thick cedar and
studded with bronze reinforcements. Many soldiers walk
the walls above them."

"And outside?" The scout shook his head.

"It seemed to us that Sharuhen, being so powerful and
isolated, has no need of troops outside its walls. Indeed,
Majesty, we saw few people on our journey beyond the
Horus Road and they were mostly women, children and old
men. We questioned some of them. They belong to the
tribe of barbarians that holds all the southern coastal
region. Apparently another tribe controls the north and yet

more inhabit the high hills far to the east. You will see them in the distance before long. But the hill tribes simply fight each other. They did not even answer the call put out by Apepa's brothers to come to his defence. I believe, as you do, that most of Rethennu is denuded of able-bodied men. We killed them all in the Delta." A ripple of laughter greeted his words but it quickly died. Ahmose could see that the generals were thinking of stone walls and mighty gates, even as he was.

"Thank you for your report," he said to the scouts. "It was clear and you were thorough in your duty. Return to your divisions."

After they had snatched up the remnants of their meal, the scouts departed. There were a few long minutes of gloomy silence. Then Kagemni spoke for all of them.

"We face another siege, in a country we do not know, far from the source of our food and supplies," he said heavily. "The route from Egypt will have to be patrolled against attack all the time, in spite of the present emptiness of the land through which we have passed. Is it worthwhile, Majesty? Why not simply reinforce the Wall of Princes, make it an impregnable barrier to all foreigners, and retire behind it?"

"After all, Egypt is now one," Meryrenefer added. "Apepa is back in the land of his ancestors. Het-Uart belongs to you. Your long struggle is over."

Ahmose found his eyes wandering to Tani. She had climbed a small hummock of land some way away from the noise of the resting army and was sitting shrouded in her cloak with her back to them all. Heket was holding a sunshade over her. Why not go home? he thought pensively. I could send Tani ahead with a suitable escort and turn my army around and leave Apepa to whatever end fate has in store for him. But there are his sons …

"It would seem sensible to take your advice," he said carefully, "but I must consider the future, not just our present dilemma. If I return to Egypt, I leave behind a man who has ruled Egypt, and also his heirs. I leave threats to whoever will come after me, men who may raise a unifying flag for any new attempt by foreigners to invade us again, by force or guile, it does not matter. I must at least try to remove any possibility of a claim being made to the throne of Egypt in years to come."

"But, Majesty, a stone city!" Baqet expostulated. "We are utterly impotent against Sharuhen! A long siege is inevitable, this time with the need to defend our forces from the Great Green and all the surrounding tribes as well as watching the gates! Have we the heart to do this?"

"The soldiers will not lose heart if they are allowed regular visits to their home villages," Ahmose answered. "Believe me, Baqet, my heart sinks to my belly at the prospect, but I must see this matter through to its end. That is all. Prepare to march." Reluctantly they got up and left the protection of the canopy which was quickly dismantled.

Ahmose sent a runner to warn Tani. He was angry and depressed. Twice we had an opportunity to capture Apepa and effect a conclusion to this miserable, endless business, he said to himself as he walked to his chariot. Twice we failed. So for our punishment we must go on. I am beginning to feel like a soul condemned to swim forever in the lake of the Underworld while Kamose and my father sail past me in the Celestial Barque, their battles won. Amun, give me the courage necessary to look upon Sharuhen and not despair.

It was as the scout had said. Next day the track turned north, entering a vast waste of rolling dunes whose crests bled in the constant wind. For three days the soldiers trudged with heads down. Sand blew across their path with a constant dry whisper, insinuating itself into nostrils and between parted lips, grinding against teeth, clogging chariot wheels, and settling into seamed flesh. Far to the east Ahmose thought he could discern a thin line of green at the foot of the mountains that had begun to be sighted on the second day and he remarked grimly to Mesehti how it was not surprising that the Setiu had been so desperate to gain permission to graze their flocks and herds in the glorious fertility of the Delta so many hentis ago. "Your ancestors erred out of pity and generosity in letting them in, Majesty," was the Prince's curt reply. "Such a decision was in the way of Ma'at but disastrous for Egypt." Ahmose silently agreed.

At night the wind lessened, but a cold came down to disturb the soldiers' sleep and rime their blankets with frost. If we are here through summer to winter and another spring, I must find warmer clothing for the troops, Ahmose noted to himself as he lay shivering beside the remains of the fire Mesehti had lit for him earlier. Woollen tunics perhaps, with sleeves. More blankets certainly. Oh, Amun, are you here with me in this accursed place so far from your temple and Amunmose, your High Priest, and Aahmes-nefertari, your Second Prophet? He had intended to try and pray but the vision of his wife's face rose before his inner eye and the words of praise and pleading died. He gave himself up to a troubled half-sleep.

Just after noon on the fourth day, their eighth out from Het-Uart, they sighted Sharuhen. Five miles away, it rose out of the gravelled desert around it like a piece of the mountains to the east that had been lopped off, smoothed, and rammed into the earth by a giant hand. Its air of permanence and invulnerability was daunting. They approached it cautiously, relieved to have left the dunes behind, watching as its towering bulk gained definition in the shimmer of the afternoon light.

Ahmose called a halt just out of range of any archers on the walls and at once deployed his divisions, four to encircle the fort and one to form a perimeter around them to guard against outside attack. There was no shelter anywhere on the plain. A few stunted and thorny bushes clung tenaciously to life and there was some evidence of hardy desert flowers that would bloom briefly under winter rains but it was a desolate arena for a siege.

Ahmose had his tent pitched close to Turi's. Everywhere he looked his men's own little shelters were mushrooming white all over the stony ground. Chariots were racing to and fro, officers were shouting, the wagons full of food and supplies were being unloaded, but the noises of preparation were eclipsed by the sudden wild clamour coming from the walls of the city. Ahmose could see men up there running about, pointing and yelling, a mad stridency of surprise, but there was no terror in the voices. They know they have no need to fear an immediate death at our hands, he thought dismally. Our swords cannot reach them. Not yet. Not until they are starving. And this place is big enough to hold many fine gardens and wells within its stone enclosure. There are none outside. Sharuhen is going to defeat me. I feel it. He turned to Khabekhnet, waiting dutifully at his elbow. "Send a runner with guards to the coast," he ordered. "He can take a chariot. I want to know if Abana and Hor-Aha have arrived and what they have done so far. If all is well with them, have them brought back here together with the Medjay and then summon the generals to a council this evening." Khabekhnet bowed and went away, bowing again to Tani who was picking her way towards Ahmose.

"You have commanded Akhtoy to erect my tent beside yours," she said without preamble. "But I will not be needing it, Ahmose. I wish to go into the city at once." Her chin was up and her eyes were defiant. He scanned her face, weighing the advisability of keeping her with him through the strategy discussions he was about to hold.

"I would like to issue a formal request for Apepa's surrender before I say farewell to you," he answered her. "That will be done in the morning. I beg you to endure my company for two more days, Tani." Her expression softened.

"I am sorry," she said contritely. "I am torn in two between my love for my husband and my loyalty to you, my brother. I will stay. This is an unforgiving site, is it not?"

"Yes, it is. Change your mind and let me send you home!" he urged without much hope. "What is there for you to look forward to but exile among foreigners here or in similar places for the rest of your life! And if your husband dies, you will be nothing, the minor wife of a fugitive chieftain. Do you not sometimes miss your little room on the estate at Weset, the lily pond and the hippopotamuses, your mother's voice and the desert at sunset?"

"Yes, I miss those things," she said quietly. "It makes no difference, Ahmose. If my tent is ready I will go and rest."

Ahmose held his conference inside his own tent at dusk to escape the first chill of evening. The space was crowded with his men but they were subdued, sipping their wine soberly and talking mildly, without enthusiasm. Six Keftian captains had come with Abana and now sat cross-legged on the floor around him, their tight leather caps reflecting the lamplight, their dark eyes wary and their thin, aquiline noses poised to sniff the way this new wind would blow.

The furore on the walls of the city had died down but citizens still thronged up there, looking out curiously upon the Egyptian host. Ahmose had forbidden the arriving Medjay to shoot at them. There was no point yet in killing anyone.

"I have given much thought to our situation," he began, and at once all conversation ceased. "I do not need to tell you all that we are in an untenable situation. Not with regard to a siege, of course. We have become experts at that particular military necessity. I am referring to the need to feed and water twenty-five thousand soldiers." No one moved and no one had laughed at his bitter joke. "This afternoon I have set up a series of stages back along the route we have come, with runners and a handful of soldiers to carry news quickly to and from the Delta. But the distance is too great for the continual transportation of water and difficult even for food. I could send an expedition into the mountains where there must be streams and springs to nourish the tribesmen who inhabit that region but I am loath to approach them. They gave no aid to Apepa in Egypt. I presume that they will not care to help us and even if they did agree, the supply would be dependent upon both their goodwill and whatever we were willing to pay them, and thus unreliable. I cannot take the chance of seeing my army die of thirst at the mercy of Rethennu's goatherders." He swivelled in his chair and fixed his eyes on the Keftians. "Are you aware that your ruler has concluded treaties with my court at Weset?" he asked. They nodded and one scrambled to his feet.

"We know of this, Majesty," he said. "Already an exchange of goods is passing between Keftiu and Weset. Trade between our countries has always been peaceful and profitable and you will please forgive me if I say that we have not cared who sat on the Horus Throne so long as we could embark from Egypt with linen and papyrus in our holds. The Setiu no longer control the Delta; therefore we are disposed to help you as we are able."

"You have six ships anchored off the coast," Ahmose stated.

"Yes. We had unloaded urns of oil for Sharuhen and were preparing to sail home."

"They are large ocean-going vessels, Majesty," Abana broke in. "We have nothing like them. They would do very well." He had obviously caught the drift of Ahmose's thought. Ahmose smiled at him wryly then turned his attention back to the Keftian.

"If you will agree to ferry food but particularly water from the Delta to my army here, I will pay you with gold," he told him. "And of course you would accrue a store of goodwill in Egypt that Keftiu might wish to call upon in the future."

The captain hesitated. He adjusted the wide woven belt around his waist and pulled at the wrap of his black-and-white patterned skirt. Then he folded his arms. "Keftiu is continuing to trade with Rethennu, Majesty," he pointed out cautiously. "They supply us with cedar and other things we value. If I and my fellow captains help you, we are in danger of provoking Rethennu into cutting off trade with us."

"I have no quarrel with Rethennu," Ahmose said emphatically. "I fought Setiu soldiers who were sent into the Delta, into Egypt, to bolster Apepa. I am here because I want Apepa, not because I plan to invade and subjugate Rethennu. When I have him, I will go home. This incursion will not extend beyond Sharuhen." The captain still looked doubtful. His compatriots were studying the carpet.

"I must send to my merchant on Keftiu and he will approach our ruler," he said. "I do not want to inadvertently make an enemy of either Rethennu or Egypt." He was clearly becoming distressed.

"Send then," Ahmose said heavily. "And if you receive permission, ask for more of Keftiu's ships. Six will not be enough. I will dictate a letter to your ruler asking for his brotherly help. But while you are waiting for a reply, will you work with Prince Abana in bringing us water? For gold?" The captain gave in. His arms loosened.

"Very well," he agreed, and sank to the floor.

"Thank you. If you will go with the Commander of my Followers who is outside, he will find you a meal, and my Admiral and his marines will see you safely back to your ships." Abana rose at once and while the Keftians were filing out he came over to Ahmose.

"Their ships are interesting, Majesty," he said in a low voice. "I and my captains can learn much about their construction and handling. Later we will need such craft of our own if we are to extend Egypt's trade."

"Treat them courteously, Abana," Ahmose replied in the same tone. "Praise their seamanship. Let our sailors mingle with theirs. I have no doubt that the ruler of Keftiu will see the wisdom in giving us aid, but in the meantime I need that water!" Abana bowed and smiled.

"I understand perfectly, Majesty. Rest assured that tomorrow morning they will be on their way to the Delta escorted by the *Kha-em-Mennofer*. I expect to return with water in six days. I will instruct Paheri to dispatch more ships from here in three days. Thus a constant if meagre supply will be ensured until more ships arrive from Keftiu." He went out and the remaining men exchanged glances.

"A brilliant move, Majesty," General Akhethotep purred. "Keftiu has more to lose in the long run by refusing us support than by choosing to side with Rethennu. Now what shall we do about Sharuhen?" No one answered him.

Ahmose slept well that night in spite of the fruitless discussion in which he and his generals had become mired. Sieging was simple. Protecting the outer flanks of the army was simple. Only entering Sharuhen was impossible, and after several hours of useless wrangling and ever more unrealistic plans Ahmose sent them back to their quarters. Hor-Aha had made the only solid suggestion, that when one of the gates opened to admit Tani it might be stormed. It was a valid though slim idea and Hor-Aha was disappointed when Ahmose refused it. "It would make my sister seem to be a traitor to her husband," he had told them. "Apepa and the chieftain of Sharuhen would believe that she had betrayed her honour. Desperate as I am to put an end to this protracted war, I will not do Tani this disservice."

"Majesty, your familial loyalty does you credit," Iymery had said. Daringly he went on, "But your main objective should be taking the city, not preserving your sister's good name." A mutter of assent mingled with apprehension went through the men. They were expecting a display of royal anger from Ahmose but it did not come.

"I appreciate your honesty, General," Ahmose had responded equably. "I believe that I promised all of you the liberty of speaking your thoughts freely to me when we first began to craft this army. Besides, Tani herself would see what we were about to do and she would refuse to approach the gate. My mind is made up against this. I have spoken." Baqet had grimaced ruefully.

"I suppose she would not," he had put in. "Your sister may now be Queen Tautha and her allegiance misplaced but she is still a Tao, possessed of that same fierce sense of principle that propelled us all towards the recovery of Egypt's sovereignty. Such singlemindedness may yet wear down Sharuhen's obstinacy. Stranger things have happened if the will of the gods is bent in our favour."

Ahmose had thought that their mute disapproval would rankle and prevent him from relaxing as he lay on his cot in the dark. It was the first time any disagreement had come between him and his comrades-in-arms. But he realized with a rush of humility that they not only revered him as their King but also held an affection for him as himself, a man, and he slid into unconsciousness on a tide of gladness.

The morning was not quite as cold as mornings had been since the army left the Horus Road. No frost had formed, the sky was a friendly hue, and the sun shone with a welcome warmth. Word came to Ahmose as he was being dressed that the scroll he had dictated the night before to the Keftian ruler was on its way with a herald and one of the foreign captains, and that the rest, together with Abana in the navy's flagship, had set out for the Delta. Morale among the troops had risen now that they were settled into permanent positions, and the Medjay, having been prostrated by seasickness on the journey from Het-Uart, had recovered and were out behind the Division of Amun, shooting at targets with many shrieks and spirited laughter.

A siege creates a strange city, Ahmose reflected as he stepped out into the sparkling sunlight. No women or children, tents instead of mud houses and shops, but all else resembles a vast town with its streets, its grain stores, its shrines, its throngs of people, the smells of cooking and the braying of donkeys. There was no sign of Tani or her guard, although her tent flap had been folded back. Ahmose was guiltily relieved. Sending for Khabekhnet and his chariot, he surveyed Sharuhen while he waited. Once again the top of its walls were crowded with sightseers, both men and women, their hair and clothing whipped about by the stiff breeze, their faces indistinguishable but their gestures and the swell of their blended conversations betraying a high excitement. "They could be celebrating a festival judging by their noise," Ankhmahor commented. He and the Followers were close by, as always. "I would not be surprised to see them rain flowers down upon us, Majesty."

"Not flowers I think. There is an overtone of arrogance in their babel," Ahmose remarked. "They know themselves to be inviolate. Well, we shall see if we can shake their attitude of invincibility a little." Khabekhnet had come up and saluted and Ahmose turned to him. "You will come with me and shout this message at every gate," he said. " 'To the commander of the fort of Sharuhen, greetings from Uatch-Kheperu Ahmose, Son of the Sun, the Horus of Gold, he of the Sedge and the Bee. I, King of Egypt, swear by the Divine Amun that if you deliver to me the Setiu Apepa and all his family, together with the Horus Throne and the Royal Regalia he so deceitfully stole, the inhabitants of your city will be spared. If you refuse, I will put every man, woman and child to the sword. You have until tomorrow morning to make an answer.' Repeat it to me, Khabekhnet." The Chief Herald did so. "Good," Ahmose said briskly. "Ankhmahor, bring the Followers and the royal flag planted outside my tent. Here is Mesehti with my chariot. We will begin with the south gate, seeing that it is the closest."

He had made sure that Hekayib attired him as sumptuously as possible, in a kilt shot through with gold thread that would catch the sunlight and a starched linen helmet of blue and white, also glittering with gold. The massive pectoral that Kamose had commissioned and that Ahmose had adapted for himself covered his breast, alive with turquoise and jasper and the sacred lapis. Golden ankhs swung from his earlobes. Moonstone and carnelian rings encircled his hennaed fingers and lapis scarabs set in gold adorned his wrists and arms. He mounted the chariot, Khabekhnet beside him, Ankhmahor carrying the flag behind, and at a word Mesehti shook the reins. "Majesty, it is a grave risk to drive too close to the gate," Ankhmahor warned him as they picked up speed. "You will be within range of their archers."

"I know," Ahmose shouted back at him against the rushing wind of their passage. "But it is a chance I must take. If I do not appear with Khabekhnet, the ultimatum will not be taken seriously and anyway, I will seem to be a coward."

It did not take long to cross the mile of gravelled sand between his camp and the fort. The space was full of soldiers bent on their errands, who paused to reverence the sun-fired figure flashing by them, one jewelled hand raised in acknowledgement, the symbol of his authority fluttering audibly above him. Ahmose noted their respect absently. All his attention was fixed on those massive stone walls drawing nearer and beginning to loom over him.

The motley crowd of people on their summit set up a concerted roar when they saw him come. It did not abate until Mesehti had brought the vehicle to a halt before the tall gate. Ahmose waited, looking up calmly. Gradually an expectant silence fell. Khabekhnet drew in a deep breath. "To the commander of the fort of Sharuhen, greetings from Uatch-Kheperu Ahmose, Son of the Sun," he began, his well-trained herald's voice ringing out clearly and forcefully on the limpid morning air. No sound from above disturbed the remainder of the challenge, but the moment the listeners realized that he had finished, a chorus of jeers and insults went up.

"Go home to Egypt, scum of the Nile!"

"Die of boredom, desert rats!"

"Baal-Reshep hates you, murderers!"

At a curt word from Ahmose, Mesehti wheeled the chariot and began to traverse the long curve that would take them to the eastern gate, several miles distant. "Savages and vermin!" Khabekhnet growled. "I hope our soldiers heard their taunts. Then they will be more than willing to slit a few throats when we finally breach these accursed defences." Such an outburst was unusual for the Chief Herald. Ahmose agreed with him. He himself was seething with rage, but he pressed his lips together and gazed grimly ahead as the huge chunks of stone flitted by.

It was noon before they drew up before the fourth gate, having endured the same taunts and ridicule at the eastern and northern portals. The Followers who had run beside the chariot were panting and pouring sweat. Ahmose himself was damp and tired and Khabekhnet surreptitiously tested the strength of his throat before looking up, squaring his shoulders, and delivering the last call. Behind the chariot the road to the ocean lay white and empty. The sun stood at its zenith, almost blinding Ahmose as he followed the direction of his Chief Herald's gaze.

He squinted into its glare and saw that here the crest of the wall was naked save for three men who stood limned against the bright sky, listening impassively. They were bearded and hawk-faced, their heads encircled by decorated and tasselled cloth bands, their bodies hidden under thick calf-length tunics bearing many-coloured geometric patterns with fringed necks and hems. All held spears and the one in the centre also had a huge axe resting by his ankle with the haft against his palm.

Khabekhnet ended his delivery. Ahmose waited for some response from those motionless sentinels, some indication that they had heard and understood the message, but they continued to stare down at him with seeming indifference and before he could be made to feel foolish he tapped Mesehti on his moist spine. The weary horses turned away. "I wonder who they were," Khabekhnet said as the chariot neared Ahmose's tent and stopped. "The commander's personal guard perhaps." He stepped down stiffly and Ahmose followed. His head was pounding after a morning in the sun and wind.

"I have a feeling that the man in the middle was the commander himself," Ahmose replied. "There was plenty of time for him to be told that we were circling the city with our challenge and he climbed up above the western gate to hear it for himself. I fear it was an act of hollow bluster on our part, Khabekhnet, but it had to be done." Khabekhnet set the flag back in its place, bowed, and strode away.

Ahmose dismissed Mesehti and entered his quarters. "My head is splitting," he said to Akhtoy as he dragged off his kilt and helmet and slumped onto the couch. "Go to my physician and get me poppy." He lay with eyes squeezed shut and fingers pressed against the pain throbbing in his temples. Outside, Ankhmahor was releasing some of the Followers and giving the rest their instructions for the afternoon, his familiar tones bringing a sense of security to Ahmose as he waited tensely for the relief the drug would bring.

You did this to me, he spoke to Apepa in his mind. It was your hand that guided the assassin who murdered Kamose and left me with this demon in my skull. If it swallows up the rest of my life, I will siege Sharuhen until you give in. Akhtoy returned with Hekayib and together they helped him to sit. Carefully Akhtoy spooned the milky liquid into his mouth and lowered him back onto his pillow then Hekayib bathed him gently. Ahmose began to doze under the body servant's soothing touch. "Where is Tani?" he asked drowsily.

"Her Majesty has gone to see the Great Green with Heket and her guards," Akhtoy answered from across the tent.

"She is avoiding me," Ahmose commented, already almost asleep. He did not hear his steward's murmured reply.

He woke to eat at sunset with the pulse in his head reduced to a dull ache, then slept again. There was nothing to do, no orders to give, no change in his army's deployment. Akhtoy told him the next morning that Tani had come to his tent, been told that he was not well, and had gone away again. Ahmose was glad that he had been unconscious at the time. He did not want to talk to his sister any more, to sit with her in an atmosphere of awkwardness and hidden anger, to see her eyes slide away from his at the introduction of any remark other than the lightest observation. The poppy had left him with a slight nausea. He refused the first meal but drank some beer, had Hekayib dress him in the same sumptuous clothes he had worn the day before, and ventured out into the freshness of the early air.

Khabekhnet and Ankhmahor were squatting on the ground deep in conversation and Mesehti was sitting on the edge of Ahmose's chariot, legs swinging, face turned into the morning breeze. All three straightened at his approach. "We will take up our station beneath the southern gate and we will stay there until Ra stands overhead or Sharuhen gives us an answer," he told them as he stepped into the vehicle. He nodded at Khabekhnet who climbed in behind him, and once more they rolled towards the fort, coming to a halt almost at the gate. This time the wall was deserted. The citizens have been ordered to stay away from the summit, Ahmose surmised. Not to spare us the indignity of hours of abuse but to lengthen every minute we wait here in heat and silence. They will make no counter until the afternoon comes. Someone is watching us although we cannot see him, a sentry directed to record every bead of sweat, every shift of weight from one weary foot to the other, every sigh, until the commander deigns to appear. He settled his hip against the wicker frame of the chariot and closed his eyes, deliberately imagining himself sitting on his watersteps at Weset with the Nile running cool and shaded before him and the fishing skiff of his boyhood tugging invitingly at the pole to which it was moored.

As he had thought, the sun had travelled half the sky before there was movement on the wall above the gate. At first Ahmose and his men had talked sporadically, but before long all conversation had been sacrificed to the need to remain upright and still. Ahmose, having exhausted all visions of his home, had fallen into a grim trance when Khabekhnet leaned forward and whispered, "They are here, Majesty." Ahmose lifted his head. The same three men had come out and were bending over the waist-high lip of stone that ran around the battlements, but this time the figure in the middle had a tall bird's feather stuck in his headband and the one to his right lifted a horn to his mouth. The tone, when it came, was shockingly harsh and Ahmose felt his exhaustion blow away with its strident blast.

"Ahmose Tao, self-styled King of Egypt," the man in the centre called down. "I am the hik-khase of this fortress city. My word is the law. You insolently demand the surrender of Awoserra Apepa, true ruler of Egypt whom you hounded from his country like the desert dog you are. He is here under my protection and so he will remain. I laugh at your presumption and I mock your boastful threats. Take your toy soldiers and go back to the hovel from which you came. Sharuhen will never open to such as you." Then he was gone as quickly and quietly as he had come and Ahmose found himself staring at nothing but the rim of the wall.

"He did not even bother to tell us his name, Majesty," Ankhmahor said in a strangled voice. "We are certainly in a country without Ma'at when the lord of a city, even an enemy, treats with another lord in so rude a fashion."

At that moment something struck Khabekhnet on the side of the head. He cried out and raised a hand and as he did so the whole top of the wall came alive with people screaming, shouting and throwing missiles that Mesehti, bending to retrieve one that had fallen with a soft thud into the chariot, identified with a spasm of disgust.

"It is donkey dung!" he exclaimed, flinging it away and rubbing his palm on his kilt. "They are pelting us with animal excrement, Majesty!" Tightening the reins, he jerked the horses savagely around. Several Followers jumped into the chariot to shield Ahmose from the barrage and with Ankhmahor and the remainder of Ahmose's guard they dashed out of range of the hysterical crowd.

Once safely dismounted by his tent, Ahmose told Mesehti to wait. Taking up a handful of waste he walked unsteadily to where Tani's small tent had been pitched and wrenching up the flap he strode inside. She was standing by her cot in a loose robe, her hair falling down her back, obviously about to take her afternoon rest. Ahmose came right up to her and thrust the offending matter under her nose. "This is donkey dung, scraped off the streets of Sharuhen and showered on me when I was placed before the gate to hear the answer to my ultimatum!" he ground out. "This is the insult your fine husband and his Setiu brother commanded to be heaped on me and my nobles! These are the brutes you have chosen above your own family, above Ramose, an honourable man who loved you!" He tossed it onto the carpet at her feet. "Have Heket pack up your belongs and leave this camp at once. Mesehti will drive you to the gate. I do not want to see you any more, Tani. Your presence is an affront to every loyal Egyptian here." She had gone pale and was beginning to tremble at this furious outpouring of his wrath. Tears slipped down her cheeks and Ahmose was too enraged to care whether they were from fear of him or shame for her husband's race.

"Ahmose, I am so sorry …" she stammered, but a wail from Heket, cowering in a corner, cut her off.

"Majesty, I do not want to go to the Setiu! I want to go home to Weset!" she cried. Running to Tani she flung herself down. "Release me from your service, I beseech you!" She twisted towards Ahmose. "Divine One, have pity on me," she sobbed. "I am not a slave. I have been faithful to your family, even within the stinking confines of Het-Uart. Please, let me go!" Ahmose answered before Tani could speak.

"I would not order the scruffiest cur that scavenged for food by the docks at Weset to enter that accursed place," he said. It was a deliberate affront to his sister and she gave a strangled whimper. "Put your mistress's possessions in order and then you are free. I will arrange passage for you on the next ship sailing to the Delta." He stepped away from the grateful mouth that was seeking his foot. "As for you, Tani,

I do not think that I wish to kiss you goodbye."

"Ahmose, please … For the sake of our youth together …" She was weeping openly now, her neck and the front of her robe already soaked with her tears. "We must not part like this. If you send me forth without your blessing, I will be walking unprotected under the eyes of foreign gods. You may regret such withholding in the days to come." He spun on his heel and stalked to the tent opening, his heart so full of pain, anger and sadness that he felt it would choke him.

"My only regret is that Ramose did not strangle you when he saw what you had become," he snarled, and pushed his way out into the warm afternoon.

He did not see her go. After a brusque word to Mesehti he shut himself up in his tent. His eyes burned, and although he washed his hands, he fancied that the stench of the donkey excrement still clung to his skin and fouled the air around him. He sat in his chair, and after a long time he heard his chariot's harness rattle as Mesehti drove her away. He was still sprawled in the same position when his charioteer returned to tell him that the gate had opened for her and a small contingent of soldiers had hurried out to pick up her belongings and usher her quickly inside.

The evening was warm and Ahmose was eating his meal just beyond the door to his tent so that he could enjoy its unusual softness when Ipi came up to him and bowed. The Chief Scribe had a scroll in his hand. "From Weset, Majesty," he said. "The herald saw me as he was crossing to you. He will rest and then present himself to you for a reply." Ahmose nodded and pushed his plate away.

"Read it to me," he ordered. Ipi sank to the earth at once and broke the seal.

"It is from your esteemed mother," he said, unrolling it and peering at the characters in the fading light. "'My greetings to you, Ahmose, Lord of All Life. Know that on the twelfth day of Mekhir your wife gave birth to a daughter. Aahmes-nefertari has recovered well but the baby is thin. She vomits back her nurse's milk and cries a great deal. I have obtained goat's milk for her which she seems able to retain a little longer than the other but the physician's prediction for her survival is not good. Neither is the name chosen for her by the astrologers. I have waited to dictate this to you so that I could include it. Also I had hoped that Aahmes-nefertari would give you this news herself but she refuses to communicate with you. She has seemed very melancholy since Tetisheri and I returned from Djeb and I fear for her health also.

"'The astrologers insist that the baby be called Sat-Kamose. Aahmes-nefertari received their decision with an apathy that is quite unlike her, but I and your grandmother were angry. We sent the men back to the temple to cast the horoscope again and I questioned High Priest Amunmose regarding their qualifications, all to no avail. The astrologers are knowledgeable, seasoned priests. They did recast the baby's horoscope but they refuse to seek another name. I believe that your distress at this tragedy will be as deep as mine. If it is, I entreat you to come home. I gather from your last missive that you have settled into yet another siege; therefore it should be possible for you to leave your generals in charge of the army for a while. If you cannot leave Sharuhen for your daughter, perhaps you should do so for your wife.'" Ipi looked up. "That is all, Your Majesty. Apart from the Queen's titles and signature of course." Ahmose met his eye. Sympathy and concern were there behind the good servant's expression of politeness.

"Thank you, Ipi," he managed. "I will send a reply tomorrow." His tone was dismissive. Ipi retrieved his palette from beside his knee, got up, bowed, and disappeared into the gathering dusk. "Clear away this mess and then leave me," Ahmose said to Akhtoy, and rising himself on legs gone suddenly weak he took the few steps back into his tent, pulling the flap closed behind him.

Hekayib had lit a lamp while Ahmose was eating. Ahmose stood staring into its alabaster radiance, unable to go any further. Oh gods, poor child, poor Aahmes-nefertari, he thought incoherently. The Seer warned me, he was emphatic, "death" he said, but somehow I had hoped that this time there would be a reprieve. Sat Kamose. The two words rang through his brain and reverberated in his heart like a funeral dirge. Sat Kamose, one a name that belonged to a murdered man, the other owned by a goddess who stood at the portal to the Underworld and poured the water of purification over the deceased. She was doomed even before her birth, his thoughts ran on. Marked for Osiris in her mother's womb. And what of Aahmes-nefertari?

He moved woodenly to his Amun shrine, opened its doors, and sank to the floor before the delicate golden image of Weset's totem, but he found that he could not pray. His mind was too fractured. Aahotep's letter had held a note of criticism as well as concern, he realized. "Should" and "entreat" she had said. It was true that nothing would be gained by his presence here. The monotonous routine of the siege would continue without him. Heralds would keep him informed of any changes in the situation. He did not anticipate a swift conclusion to the problem of Sharuhen. But terrible changes were taking place at home without him, events that would slide into the past weeks before their pain struck at him. This time you must be by Aahmes-nefertari's side when that baby dies, his heart whispered. This time you must not fail her, for if you do, she will be lost to you for ever. At last he was able to get up onto his knees. Closing his eyes and raising his hands, he begged his god to stand between Sat-Kamose and the Judgement Hall until he was able to hold her just once as a living child.

Summoning Akhtoy, he gave orders that his chests should be packed. He sent to Mesehti at the stables to have his chariot ready just after dawn and he told Ankhmahor to prepare the Followers to leave for Weset. Ipi and Khabekhnet were also warned. The herald who had brought Aahotep's scroll was dispatched at once to the Delta with a request to Paheri to have a swift ship waiting with double the usual complement of rowers so that there would be no need to stop anywhere along the Nile. When Akhtoy had closed up the last chest, Ahmose went to bed, lying on his cot in the denuded tent while the need for haste continued to grow in him, a lump of stone more forbidding than the blocks that kept him from Apepa.

By the time the sun rose, he was fed and dressed. Leaving the horse-drawn carts containing his servants and his goods, he had Mesehti drive him to where the Division of Amun was already drilling, the soldiers' kilts swirling as they marched, the tips of their spears glinting red, the brisk commands of the officers carrying clearly in the cold, early morning air. Turi was watching critically from the small dais that had been set up beside the parade ground. When he saw Ahmose dismount and come towards him, he jumped down and bowed. "Majesty, I did not expect to see you today!" he exclaimed. "Have you come to personally put the division through its paces?" Ahmose shook his head.

"No. I have received word that my daughter is born but she is dying. I must go home." Turi put out a gloved hand.

"Oh, Ahmose, I am sorry," he said. "Tell Aahmes-nefertari how sorry I am." There was no formality in Turi's words. He had known the family for a long time. Ahmose smiled briefly.

"I am Commander-in-Chief but you are the General commanding my pre-eminent division," he said. "I want you to take my place while I am gone. You have my authority to make whatever decisions are necessary regarding the efficiency and well-being of the army, Turi. The water supply has been dealt with. Consult often with Abana. Give the Keftians anything they desire within reason. I expect regular reports, but I don't suppose they will contain anything new. Detail soldiers to hunt at the foot of the mountains. They might as well occupy themselves in providing whatever fresh meat they can find. But impress on them the need to stay away from the tribes. I want no battle front opening on our eastern flank." He took a deep breath. "I will return when I may, but not until I am sure that Aahmes-nefertari does not need me."

"I understand. How will you travel?"

"By chariot as far as Het-Uart and then by boat. It might be faster to board one of the water carriers at the Great Green, but I should inspect the runners I have positioned along the land route into Egypt as I go. Meet with the other generals every week, Turi. The mood of a besieging army can become downcast very quickly. I think that is all, unless you have a query." On impulse he embraced his friend. Turi hugged him unselfconsciously before bending to kiss his hand.

"May the soles of your feet be firm, Majesty," he said. "Do not worry about Sharuhen. Greet your mother for me." There was nothing left to say, but Ahmose was suddenly reluctant to go. For a moment he scanned the wheeling ranks of his troops, now brilliantly lit under a fully risen sun. You would be proud to see how these peasants have been transformed into soldiers, Kamose, he thought, and mounting his chariot he spoke a word to Mesehti and began the long journey back into Egypt.

15

AHMOSE REACHED HET-UART in eight days, having satisfied himself that the stations of runners he had positioned along the land route into Egypt were secure and efficient. He paused briefly to consult with Generals Iymery and Neferseshemptah whose troops were manning the Wall of Princes and patrolling the eastern Delta, pleased to see peace and order growing everywhere in the newly sown fields and dense orchards surrounding the villages. Het-Uart itself was a hive of industry. The walls of both mounds already resembled the crumbled ruins of some ancient monument, although they would not be completely demolished for several months, and of the palace there was scarcely any sign save for a huge area of scorched red earth, a few blackened trees and the wall built by Ahmose's ancestor Senwasret, standing proudly and now pointlessly between the vanished building and the road to the Royal Entrance Gate.

Many citizens had crept back, but the majority of mud houses were occupied by the soldiers of the Montu Division. Khety's Horus troops had similarly drifted into abandoned homes on the northern mound. Ahmose noted the strategic advantage of the city for both trade and as a military base for any incursion he might choose to make into Rethennu in the future. *I shall build a new, fortified* palace on the site of the old one, he decided. Not as my capital of course. Weset will remain the centre of Egyptian administrative power. But Het-Uart will serve as my northern bastion.

Three ships were waiting to take him and his entourage south and it was with a feeling of both apprehension and relief that he boarded the *North*, Abana's old command, with Ankhmahor, Ipi and Khabekhnet, greeted captain Qar, and leaned on the rail to watch the other two craft being loaded. He had spoken to Paheri and Baba Abana, who were engaged in co-ordinating the convoys of water for the troops at Sharuhen from the Delta end. He had made a brief inspection of both his naval and divisional officers. There was nothing left to do but wait for Qar to shout the order to cast off.

The journey to Weset that ordinarily would have taken at least a month was accomplished in a little over half that time. Paheri had provided two teams of rowers and, while Ahmose slept, the *North* continued to beat its way slowly south. Khemmenu was approximately halfway between Het-Uart and Weset and Ahmose was tempted to put in there. He missed Ramose and he was curious to see the Setiu girl, Hat-Anath, framed against the setting of Teti's old house, but overriding his inquisitiveness was a growing sense of urgency and he resisted the temptation.

In the middle of a bright late spring morning the *North* rounded the long, sweeping curve that heralded the approach to Weset, and with a mixture of excitement and inner cringing Ahmose saw the familiar sprawl of closely packed houses along the bank beyond the river path dappled in the shade of the palms and sycamores that meandered throughout his town. Amun's temple rose warmly beige above its own sheltering trees. As the ship beat ponderously towards the eastern bank, his watersteps drew nearer, with the old palace bulking grey above the high new wall encircling the whole estate and a little farther along, the closed and guarded gate to his garden. Qar issued a flurry of orders. The oars were lifted in unison from the water and the *North* drifted gracefully to bump gently against its mooring poles. Sailors picked up the ramp and prepared to run it out. Ahmose was home.

The soldiers at either side of the gate had straightened at the sight of the royal flag flapping from the *North*'s tall mast. They had been peering warily at the trio of men waiting to disembark, their attention veering between the *North* and the two craft behind it, but as the ship came closer their expressions cleared. "It is His Majesty!" one of them exclaimed. "The flag spoke true!" They dropped their spears and rushed to steady the ramp. The gate behind them was opening. Faces appeared, then the gate was flung wide. Ankhmahor and the Followers walked down the ramp and Ahmose followed. He gave no orders. The Followers fanned out around him as he passed quickly through into his own domain, the scent of blooms and wet grass rising to meet him, the morning shadow of the house casting remembered shapes upon the glistening lawn, and farther away, the smudges of unfolded white and blue lotuses rocking almost imperceptibly on the glittering surface of the pond.

A canopy had been erected there and two figures sat side by side under it in a welter of scrolls. Alerted by the commotion, they looked up, then Ahmose-onkh detached himself and came racing along the path. Halfway to Ahmose he slowed to a dignified walk, but Ahmose could see his body tight with the effort the boy was making to control it. He came up, halted, and performed a deep bow. "I am overjoyed to see you so unexpectedly, my Father," he said.

"And I you, my little Hawk-in-the-Nest," Ahmose replied. He reached down and straightened the youth lock that lay in a glistening braid over one narrow shoulder. "Are you perhaps too grown-up now to allow me to embrace you?"

"No, indeed," the child said gravely, then a smile split his face and he flung himself on Ahmose. For a moment he hung on Ahmose's chest, all arms and legs, before Ahmose set him back on his feet. "We know that the impostor ran away to a fort called Sharuhen," he remarked. "Have you captured him yet, Majesty?"

Ahmose studied the solemn little features. They had changed just since he had been away. The eyes were larger, the jawline wider, the cheeks thinner. He is beginning to leave his babyhood behind, Ahmose thought with a pang of love and pride. He will soon be a handsome youth. "Pa-she and I have been studying Rethennu," Ahmose-onkh was saying. "Just beyond Sharuhen there is grassland and forests and mountains that sometimes shake, and locusts come and eat the crops. It sounds like a horrible place. Have you seen the mountains shake, Father?"

"No. All those things happen farther to the north-east. And no, I have not yet captured Apepa. Sharuhen is a mightily defended fort, my son. It will not be defeated soon." He took the boy's chin in his palm. "I have come back to see your mother and your new sister," he explained gently. "Go back to your tutor now. We will talk later."

"She is very sick," Ahmose-onkh whispered. "Mother thinks she is cursed." Herself or the baby? Ahmose wondered. Ahmose-onkh bowed again and turned back to where Pa-she had risen and was standing under the canopy, anxiously watching their interchange. Ahmose called a greeting to him before moving on and was rewarded with a reverence.

The Captain of the Household Guards had emerged from the house and was waiting for him as he approached the side entrance. "Welcome home, Majesty," he said. "If I had known of your coming, I would have cleared the river path and placed more men at the watersteps. I will warn the rest of the household that you are here."

"Thank you, Emkhu," Ahmose answered, concealing his impatience. "I appreciate your conscientiousness. But I want to go to the Queen at once. Where is she?"

"Her Majesty spends most of each day in the nursery once the morning audiences are over," Emkhu told him. He hesitated. "Majesty, I ... we ... I am very glad that you are here."

"I understand," Ahmose said quietly. "Make sure we are not disturbed."

He passed rapidly through the house, startling the servants, who barely had time to recognize and bow to him before he was gone. A growing murmur of surprise and speculation had begun to grow behind him by the time he came to the women's quarters and saw Uni rising from a stool outside Aahmes-nefertari's door, eyes widening fleetingly with shock. "I am most relieved to see you, Majesty," the steward said, his face already falling back into lines of customary politeness. "I had hoped that your mother's letter might bring you home."

"Did she exaggerate?" Ahmose demanded. Uni shook his head.

"Not at all. The Princess becomes weaker every day and the Queen more despairing. She has been able to continue her governmental duties with Khunes's help, but she herself is near to collapse. She has suffered much over her children." There was no hint of condemnation in Uni's tone. Ahmose had expected none. Uni, like Akhtoy, knew the minds and hearts of his charges better than they knew their own.

"Is she within?"

"She has had the door removed between her sleeping room and the nursery," Uni explained. "She will no longer allow any servant or nurse to touch the Princess, which means of course that she wakes every time the Princess cries. And she cries a great deal. I have tried to reason with Her Majesty but to no avail."

"I will go in now," Ahmose said. "Bring wine and something to eat in about an hour. Don't announce me." Uni pulled open the door and he walked inside.

She was not in her little reception room, nor in her bedchamber beyond. Ahmose went through them quietly. He could hear her singing, her voice soft and low but with a note of such anguished tenderness imbuing it that Ahmose paused, unwilling for a second to intrude upon her privacy. He approached the doorway. He could see her through it, bending over a high cot on which a basket had been set. There was no one else in the room and the only furniture was an armless chair.

She must have sensed him standing there, for all at once she stopped singing and glanced up sharply, at first without recognition. Her face was pale, her eyelids swollen. Dark purple patches under the eyes themselves made it seem as though some scribe had smudged her with ink. Her naked collarbones protruded like rails beneath her throat and her arms were thin. Ahmose could see little of her body, for her sheath had billowed out in front of her as she inclined over the basket. Gods, she is dying too, he thought, love and fear suddenly rushing through him in a hot flood. She was staring at him as she slowly straightened, the whites of her eyes becoming visible for a moment as she saw who it was.

"Ahmose?" she choked, then she was rounding the foot of the cot and running towards him, fists clenched. Throwing herself on him, she began beating at him and shrieking his name. He managed to put his arms around her, holding her loosely, not dodging her blows, until suddenly she went limp against him, and laying her head on his breast she huddled there, sobbing harshly. "I hated you, I have been so angry with you, you left me all alone, I cannot bear it, I can take no more," she was half-babbling, half-wailing, her fingernails digging into his skin, her forehead fever-hot where it was pressed to his ribs. His grip tightened around her and he swayed to and fro, dismayed at her fragility, awed by her complete loss of control. For a long time they stood thus, locked together, until the torrent of her pain and rage began to ebb and her sobs became intermittent, then he moved her gently away. "I have composed a new face for the overseers and ministers every morning," she said. "It has been the most difficult challenge I have ever faced. I think I am going insane, Ahmose.

What are you doing here?" There was still an edge of hysteria to her voice. He ran his thumbs across her cheeks, wiping away the tears, and kissed her wet mouth.

"Mother sent me a letter, dearest one," he told her. "It filled me with remorse and anxiety and I knew I had to come. Now show me my daughter." For answer she took him by the hand and led him to the basket. The action was almost shy, and although she was moving ahead of him, he had the impression that he was the one guiding and she a child. He was surprised that her violent outburst had not wakened Sat-Kamose. Any healthy baby would have been screaming at the sound. But he realized at once as he peered into the wicker cot that this Princess was too weak to respond to any shock.

She was lying on her back, arms limp at her sides, black eyes partly closed, breathing rapidly. Ahmose drew down the small sheet covering her and had to repress a start of pity at the sight of the clearly discernable rib cage, the tiny, jutting hipbones. "She looks starved," he murmured.

"She is starved," Aahmes-nefertari answered. "She drinks greedily but then she vomits and curls up her little knees and cries. Oh, Ahmose, my heart is torn apart by her suffering. If there was anything I could do, even to the shedding of my own blood, I would do it! The physicians are impotent. I have consulted four of them. Our own Royal Physician wants to give her poppy, but I said no. It might harm her further. I did not know what to do!"

Ahmose reached down and lifted the body that was lighter than the pectoral he wore around his neck. Sat-Kamose gave a whimper, turning her head towards him, and in the moment that the tuft of her soft hair touched his chest he fell in love with her. Going to the chair he sat and cradled her, rocking slowly. One pale fist like the bud of a flower crept up and found his own wide chest, resting there with such immediate acceptance that he wanted to cry out himself.

But Aahmes-nefertari had sunk to the floor beside him, both arms around his calf, her head pressed to his thigh. She was still shuddering and he dared not add his new-found agony to her own. "Forgive me for my bitterness and my silence," she whispered. "I have been cruel to you and I am sorry."

"No," he said thickly. "It is I who have behaved with the most boorish insensitivity. I love you, my wife, and I love my daughter."

They sat there for some time in a mood of emotional exhaustion, she taking strength and comfort from the warmth of his flesh and he searching for the limits of this strange new passion and finding none. His eyes never left the baby's face. He noted her resemblance to Aahmes-nefertari in the shape of her jaw and the way her mouth quirked as Seqenenra's had done. With a pang he saw that her ears followed the curves and hollows of his own. But most of all he was dismally aware of her pallor, the tinge of grey to her skin, the track the tears of bewilderment had made across the minute indentations of her temples. He wanted to place his lips against hers and force life into her with a gush of his own hot breath, crush her against him so that the beat of life pulsing so steadily beneath his own ribs might flood her with vitality. I am the King, he thought with anguish. I am the Son of the Sun, Amun's Incarnation in Egypt. Every green spear of wheat in the fields, every ox standing drinking in the shallows of the Nile, every peasant, soldier and noble, exists to obey me. Yet I am powerless to command my baby to be healed.

Aahmes-nefertari stirred at last. "Put her back in the basket, Ahmose," she said dully. "She is asleep," and Ahmose saw with a jolt that the baby's sunken eyelids had closed. Carefully he rose and laid her tenderly down. She made a little sucking sound but otherwise did not stir and her flaccid limbs fell loosely onto the mattress. Ahmose covered her with the sheet and turned to his wife.

"I have ordered Uni to bring food," he began, hushing her protest by taking both her hands. "You will eat and drink and then you will go to the bath house and Senehat will bathe you. I will stay here until you return." He saw consternation on her face and he shook her fingers gently. "I must speak to the Royal Physician and Mother, but I will come back afterwards," he assured her. "I intend to have my couch moved in here. We will keep this terrible vigil together, Aahmes-nefertari, and from now on the morning audience will be my responsibility." She began to cry again, but this time with a quiet gratitude.

"I have not asked you about Sharuhen," she started to say. He cut her short.

"Sharuhen is a mirage today," he said. "I only care about you and Sat-Kamose."

There was a knock on the door and Uni entered with Senehat and Hekayib behind him. A fragrant steam rose from the trays they carried. This time it was Ahmose who led Aahmes-nefertari through into her reception room and sat her down beside the table, pouring wine for her as the servants set out the food. "Look, dearest, there is a fresh salad, surely the first of the season," he said. "Lentil soup smelling of coriander, roasted beef with peppercorns, and hot barley bread sprinkled with sesame seeds. We must not waste a single mouthful!" He pushed the platters towards her, dismissing Uni as he did so. The door closed and he drew up another chair beside her. "Eat, Your Majesty, I command you," he said sternly, "or I will have you thrown into Kamose's jail." She rewarded his effort with a wan smile and to his relief, picked up a thin, green onion shoot, twirling it around in her fingers before biting off a piece.

"Thank you, Ahmose," she murmured. "I think perhaps I am a little hungry today. Will you fetch Sat-Kamose if she wakes?" He nodded. Placing his elbow on the table, he rested his chin in his palm and watched her with satisfaction, but long before she had finished the meal there was a thin cry from the nursery. Motioning her to stay where she was, he got up and went to attend to his daughter. He felt as though he were walking to his execution.

When Aahmes-nefertari returned from the bath house, Ahmose left her and made his way to his father's office. Both Akhtoy and Ipi had gathered with Uni outside Aahmes-nefertari's door and Ahmose sent his steward for the Royal Physician and Ipi to Aahotep with a warning that he would come to her apartments presently. Once inside the room that he still thought of as belonging to Seqenenra he felt more calm. Something of his father's serenity lingered here and Ahmose remembered him with a spurt of longing. You never seemed disturbed or agitated, Osiris one, he spoke to him in his mind. You were always meditative in your speech and dignified in your manner, even after Mersu's savage attack left you crippled and paralyzed. Whatever inner turmoil you endured did not reveal itself in your demeanour. Amun give me the same grace and power over myself, and the courage to bear both my wife's despair and my own grief as this tragedy is played out to its inevitable end.

By the time the Royal Physician was admitted and had bowed, Ahmose had recovered his equilibrium. The man looked almost as tired as Aahmes-nefertari. He waited impassively.

"There is no hope for my little daughter, is there, physician?" Ahmose demanded without preamble. The physician wetted his lips.

"None, Majesty," he said frankly. "I am sorry. The Princess keeps down neither her mother's milk nor the wet nurse's nor the goat's milk I was forced to recommend. I am ashamed to say that I do not know why." Ahmose thought for a moment.

"The Queen tells me that you wished to give the baby poppy but that she refused you." The physician raised his shoulders under his yellow tunic, a gesture of futility.

"The Princess is dying a slow and painful death by starvation," he said. "Poppy would not prolong her life but it would ease her pain and give her the gift of unconsciousness." His words were hesitant and Ahmose pounced on them.

"Why do you think the Queen refused such help for a child whose affliction is sapping her own life?" The man looked at the floor.

"I could not say, Majesty." Ahmose stepped closer to him.

"Yes, you could!" he snapped. "You are my Royal Physician. You are wise, and skilled in your profession. Answer me!" The physician raised his head unwillingly.

"I have no definite conclusion," he admitted, "but it seems to me as if Her Majesty is punishing herself for something I do not understand by denying poppy to the Princess. She wishes to drink the dregs of the baby's suffering to the full as an expiation. Perhaps Your Majesty has more knowledge of such a matter than I." Ahmose stared at him, frowning. An expiation, he reflected. Yes, of course. My poor Aahmes-nefertari. You blame yourself for your dead and dying children, don't you? You are terrified that I will reject you because of what you see as your failure and you flog yourself mercilessly with guilt.

"Perhaps I do," he said reflectively. "Prepare the poppy and come to the Queen's apartments later this afternoon. Wait there for me. You are dismissed." I feel as though I have been home for a week at least, he mused as he set out for his mother's rooms, but it has only been a few hours. Yet I do not believe that I will be eager to leave again as I was the last time, nor do I fear the boredom that dogged me then. Sat-Kamose has captured my heart, and because of her my domain shines with the light of fulfilment. I will not have her long. I am resigned to her loss even as I discover the joy of loving her. I embrace the bitter with the sweet, for I suspect that she has begun to show me dimensions of myself to which I was utterly blind. How might Hent-ta-Hent have changed me if I had been with her at her dying?

It occurred to him hazily that his recent, hurtful encounters with Tani might have had something to do with his almost instant recognition of his daughter as something precious, that Tani's unwavering, implausible defection had awakened him to the unpredictability of life in a way that his military escapades never could. He was briefly pondering the matter when his mother's steward saw him coming, saluted him, and he was admitted into her presence.

He was taken aback to see Tetisheri there also, sitting on the chair by Aahotep's couch, her feet resting on a stool and her gnarled hands in her lap. He thought that he had hidden his surprise that was almost alarm very well but as he approached her, bending over to kiss her ring-encrusted fingers, she gave a grunt. "You did not expect to see me, did you, Majesty?" she said. "But it has been a very long time since we met and when I heard that you had arranged to see Aahotep I hurried to be here." Her tone held mild reproof. You should have at least sent me your greetings if you did not intend to visit me, it implied, and Ahmose did his best to quell the familiar irritation mixed with shame that her unspoken criticisms always conjured.

"You are looking well, Grandmother," he murmured, forcing himself to meet the fierce, knowing eyes that still glittered with intelligence although she was nearly seventy years old.

"I have an aching back and I do not sleep well," she retorted. "Other than that I am in good health. I am sorry that circumstances have forced you home, Ahmose. There really is nothing you can do for Sat-Kamose, and as for Aahmes-nefertari ..." She shrugged eloquently, the wrinkled hollows above her collar-bones suddenly deepening with the gesture. "Your wife has fallen apart most regrettably. I love her but she always did lack stamina. She was easily frightened as a girl, and what that baby needs is the care of a strong, calm female. The wet nurse was admirable in that respect, but Aahmes-nefertari sent her away." Ahmose straightened and gazed at her, fighting to keep his temper. Her tongue had sharpened with age, but he made himself remember that she did indeed love Aahmes-nefertari even though her vision of the Queen was made up almost entirely of the memories to which she clung.

"I was not forced to come home," he said steadily. "I came to see my daughter before she died and to support my wife. No better woman has been under so much strain without breaking, Tetisheri, excluding you, of course. Nothing ever breaks you." She had not missed the sarcasm of his words but she did not rise to it. Instead she said unexpectedly, "Kamose's murder broke me. Your father's death in battle almost broke me. My speech is sometimes cruel, Ahmose. Forgive me. It is just so frustrating ..." She trailed off into silence and he turned to his mother with relief. Here at least was an echo of Seqenenra, sane and quietly competent in her actions and intuitive in her decisions and pronouncements. Taking her hand and pressing his cheek to hers, he smiled at her.

"Thank you for the letter," he said simply. She returned his smile.

"I knew you would come," she replied. "It has been dreadful here, Ahmose. She would not relinquish the reins of government to me because you had entrusted the running of the country to her. It was a matter of pride. But if you had tarried any longer, I think she would indeed have broken utterly. I did not have the authority to give her any orders." She indicated the pomegranate wine and shat cakes set out on the table. "Now sit and tell us of Tani," she invited. "Your report conveyed little but shouted much."

Ahmose's heart sank. He had known this moment would arrive but still he shrank from it. Tipping the gleaming red liquid into a cup, he took a swallow of its fragrance before settling unwillingly into a chair. In spite of his desperate searching he could find no way to soften the blow that had already fallen on Aahotep, no little lies to bind up a wound already bleeding. So he recited the events of Tani's refusal to tell him where Apepa had gone, her refusal to take ship back to Weset, her adamant desire to enter Sharuhen and be with her husband, in plain unvarnished language. He did not, however, repeat his sister's all-too-realistic assessment of the reception she might have expected from the women of her family. Aahotep listened motionless, watching his face, raising her cup occasionally to drink but saying nothing. When he had finished, it was Teti-sheri who expressed her disgust.

"The person you describe is unrecognizable as the girl who left here with Apepa so bravely," she snorted. "She allowed the Setiu to corrupt her will. Little coward! Thank the gods her father is not alive to see her betrayal! He would have whipped her and sent her to Weset tied to her cabin wall! We will not refer to her again. Now tell us of Sharuhen and the siege. That news is much more interesting." She had blustered angrily in her old woman's uneven croak, but Ahmose saw her quickly tuck her hands into the folds of her sheath to hide their trembling and he was filled with pity for her. Hastily he began to talk of Apepa's escape, the burning of the palace, Abana's capture of the Setiu and how he had forced them to reveal Apepa's destination, all the drama and excitement on which she throve, and he was rewarded with a series of snorts, laughs and exclamations as she became more and more involved in the tale. Finally she slapped the arm of her chair. "Ha!" she crowed. "Now we have him, that spawn of Sutekh! It is only a matter of time before Sharuhen falls to you and you will be able to cut off his head! Well done, Majesty!" He did not spoil her delight by reminding her of Sharuhen's impregnability. Draining his cup, he rose and bowed to them both.

"Apart from the morning audiences, I shall be spending all my time in Aahmes-nefertari's quarters," he said. "I ask you both to see to Pa-she and Ahmose-onkh. Does he still run off to play in the bricklayers' mud pits?"

"The bricklayers have gone, Ahmose," Tetisheri said. "The old palace needs nothing but whitewash and decoration. Even the gardens have been laid out around it, although they are still new and unlovely. Will you have it blessed soon?" I have dreamed of that moment since Kamose and I sailed north to reclaim Egypt, Ahmose thought sadly. Now it is here and all I can think about is Sat-Kamose. I feel no exultation, no sense of triumph. Fate has stolen it away.

"I do not know," he answered heavily. "Perhaps." He turned to the door but his mother's voice forestalled him.

"Is she well?" Aahotep asked mildly. Ahmose paused.

"Yes, she is well, and more beautiful than ever," he replied without looking at her. He rapped on the wood. Kares opened at once, and sick with desolation Ahmose stepped out into the passage.

The Royal Physician and Uni were waiting for him outside Aahmes-nefertari's door and they went in together. It seemed to Ahmose that she must have been pacing just within her reception room, anxious for his return, the baby in her arms, for she almost ran to him as Uni closed the door behind him, her expression clearing. But when she saw the vial and spoon the physician was carrying, she halted abruptly. "No," she said. Ahmose placed a hand firmly on her shoulder.

"If you must blame anyone for the feebleness of our children, blame the gods, not yourself," he said to her in a low voice. "I do not condemn you. Don't you know that? How can you believe that these losses, horrifying though they are, can possibly erode the love I hold for you? We are one, my dearest sister. We have survived many tests of our unity. We have been angry with each other. But underneath it all there remains a bond that cannot be severed." Gently he eased Sat-Kamose from her grasp. "You are using her suffering to torture yourself and that is selfish of you. We must try to alleviate her pain and ease her passing into the presence of Osiris."

"She will not keep it down," Aahmes-nefertari protested faintly, but she made no further demur. She had gone very pale at his words, but something in her eyes had begun to change as he spoke. It was slender evidence indeed, but he knew that the battle for her sanity was won. Signalling to the physician, he folded the baby's linen wrapping down under her chin. Sat-Kamose was watching him. Her quick breaths were hot on his fingers. Her head with its scant covering of fine black hair seemed to have grown larger, lolling in the crook of his elbow. It is an illusion fostered by the wasting away of her little body, Ahmose thought with a loving compassion that sheared through him like a sword stroke. Amun, you have given much with your omnipotent right hand, but you have taken away with your left.

The physician came close, his small spoon already full of the thin, milky liquid. Carefully he inserted it between the

dry lips. Sat-Kamose wrinkled up her gem-sized nose, swallowed convulsively, coughed weakly, and began to cry.
Ahmose rocked her, crooning a song half-forgotten from
his own nursery days, and all present waited to see her
vomit the drug. But she did not. After a minute her eyelids
drooped. Ahmose felt her tense limbs relax. She fell asleep.
"I will come twice a day and once in the night to repeat the
dose, Majesty," the physician said. "One ro each time and
no more." Bowing, he backed away and left the room.
Ahmose passed the baby to Aahmes-nefertari, who walked
into the nursery. Ahmose turned swiftly to Uni.

"Bring all our meals here," he ordered. "Make them
pretty and appetizing so that the Queen will be tempted.
We will have beer instead of wine. Beer is more sustaining.
Keep everyone away except Akhtoy, Ipi and Khabekhnet,
and admit them only if their need is dire." Uni smiled.

"I understand, Majesty," he said. "I honour your
wisdom." Wisdom? Ahmose reflected ruefully in the
moment when Uni had gone and his wife had not yet reap-
peared. It is not wisdom, my good steward, but blind fear.
What would I do without Aahmes-nefertari? I would be like
a sail with no wind to fill it.

The following weeks assumed a rigid pattern whose shape
was determined by Sat-Kamose's needs and whose sombre
colours were painted by death itself. Every morning Ahmose
rose to the Song of Praise that had been resumed upon his
return. He went to the bath house to be washed, shaved
and massaged, to his own quarters briefly to be painted and
dressed, and then with Ipi and Khunes he proceeded to the
main reception hall, where he dealt with the business
that had always accumulated from the day before.

Back in Aahmes-nefertari's rooms he would greet the Royal Physician who would be waiting and together they would administer the great gift of the gods that had the power to banish pain and bring unconsciousness. Sat-Kamose always cried at its bitter taste and sometimes retched, but as time went by her stomach grew too weak to make the spasm that would expel the poppy. Encouraged, the physician had tried to feed her again with goat's milk, but she could not retain it. She was in Ahmose's or her mother's arms almost continually. Ahmose, bearing his feather-light burden as he walked back and forth between the rooms that had become his whole world, was several times convinced that she had already died, so limp was her body and so faint her breathing.

At first he would return from the audiences to find his wife sitting beside her couch with Uni's food untouched on the table before her and Sat-Kamose on her lap. Once the physician had left, he would be forced to crouch beside her and coax her to take just one mouthful and then perhaps another. She would comply listlessly, her eyelids swollen, her spine hunched over her folded arms, and twice she herself vomited what she had eaten in a fit of violent rejection against that which her child could not do, but gradually her appetite improved until more often than not Ahmose, entering her rooms, was overjoyed to see the platters empty but for a smattering of crumbs. Senehat would escort her to the bath house while Ahmose kept vigil over the basket that held such a precious, such a penetrating hurt for both of them.

At Ahmose's insistence, Aahmes-nefertari submitted to the Royal Physician's examination and his pronouncement was encouraging. "She has gained some flesh, her eyes are less full of the yellow of ukhedu, and her breath no longer stinks," he told Ahmose. "I will not prescribe for her. All she needs is healthful food and rest. She sleeps well?" Ahmose assured him that she did. She had begun the nights in fits of shallow dozes interspersed with periods of wakeful agitation, when he would attempt to calm her with board games and stories by the light of the one lamp always kept burning. But slowly the duration of her sleeping hours became longer, her sleep deeper. One night she did not even wake when the physician entered quietly to give Sat-Kamose her poppy.

Ahmose, himself wakeful, spent many hours sitting by Aahmes-nefertari's bed and watching her, rediscovering his delight in the sheer harmony of her frame, the dark hair foaming back from her wide temples, the delicate bluish tinge to her closed eyelids, the thick black lashes quivering under the influence of her dreams, the aquilinity of their father's nose and the petal fullness of their mother's mouth. The lamp's even glow cast friendly shadows over her throat, heightened the brown cleft between her breasts, and made her shoulders gleam as though her skin had been oiled. It was not lust he felt. The days were too fraught with worries for something so strongly elemental. Tenderness and an awareness of her uniqueness as his wife, his beloved, filled him in these moments, giving him the patience and self-lessness he needed to nurse her and his daughter through the ordeal in which they were all embroiled.

Once, just after midnight when the Royal Physician had gone and Aahmes-nefertari was sunk in unconsciousness, he left the women's quarters, and with a word to Uni on his pallet outside the door should she wake, he set off for the temple alone. The moon was three-quarters to the full and the garden lay peacefully shrouded under its pallid rays. Feeling dazed after his long imprisonment, Ahmose paused to draw the warm air into his lungs before making his way out the watersteps gate, refusing an escort from the gate guards and turning onto the river path, a ribbon of greyness winding beneath his feet into the duskiness of palm trunks ahead.

The moon-drenched sky above was a haphazard pattern of faintly stirring leaves and branches and the Nile itself ran silver-grey and silent beside him. The town of Weset, now almost a city, lay enchanted beyond the shrubs and small fields to his left, its mud houses dark, its streets empty but for a few prowling dogs and an occasional spark of light where some citizen sat up, as sleepless as his King. Yet it murmured and rumbled quietly, its pulse a blend of every life, human and animal, that made up its existence. Far out on the desert a hyena barked sharply once, the sound echoing across the unseen dunes before dying away. I love this place, Ahmose thought as he strode along. Everything that I am has been moulded by its slowly multiplying impact on all my senses. I am the King of Egypt but I am first of all a child of Weset, and so I shall always be.

The temple forecourt was deserted. Ahmose crossed it quickly. The inner court, being roofed by mighty stone slabs, was drowned in darkness. A guard materialized out of the shadows to challenge him but, seeing who he was, retired with a quick apology. Removing his sandals, Ahmose approached the sanctuary. It was closed and sealed, of course, but that did not matter. A faint scent of incense hung in the air and mingled with the smell of dust and wilting flowers.

Ahmose knelt, then prostrated himself, arms outflung, face to the floor. With eyes closed he prayed for Sat-Kamose, for Aahmes-nefertari, for himself, the words coming easily and from a clarity of mind he had not experienced in a long time. After a while he sensed movement behind him but he did not look up. Someone settled beside him and also began to pray, and with gladness he recognized Amunmose's voice. When he had said everything he wished to say to the god, he rose and the High Priest rose with him. "I heard that you had returned, Majesty," he said, his voice falling flat in that small, close place. "Your mother sends Yuf to me with regular reports on the affairs of the house. The Queen asked me to appoint a substitute for her to perform the duties of Second Prophet in her stead until the little Princess recovered or died and I have done so. I gather that she is in poor health herself." What a rigid sense of obligation Aahmes-nefertari has! Ahmose marvelled privately. Egypt could be disappearing under a lake of fire and she would still be concerned that she was unable to undertake her responsibilities.

"I have always valued your tact, Amunmose," Ahmose replied. "She is bowed under a crushing weight but she is recovering. It is good to see you again. At the moment my duties to Amun are performed only in my heart and for that I do not apologize." Amunmose's face was a dim oval looming out of the darkness. Nevertheless Ahmose could read his sombre expression.

"Of course not," the High Priest said. "I have no comfort to offer you, Majesty, unless it is a prediction emanating from the Seer's vase. Sharuhen will fall and Apepa will be yours."

"No comfort in my present distress," Ahmose said heavily, "but I do not doubt the Seer's gift. After all, he foretold today's tragedy."

"He is but an instrument of the god," Amunmose said simply. "Please convey my respects to my Second Prophet."

"I will indeed. And I thank you for your company tonight." The outer court was a rectangle of greyness. Ahmose turned towards it, retrieved his sandals, and began to walk home.

Sat-Kamose died during the night of the thirtieth of Pharmuthi. The Royal Physician had made his accustomed visit just after midnight. Aahmes-nefertari had slept briefly but then had woken and got up, coming to sit on the edge of Ahmose's cot where he was preparing to sleep himself. "A dream disturbed me," she said apologetically. "I don't remember what it was. I cannot rest again, Ahmose. I need to hold my daughter." It would not matter, Ahmose knew. The baby was only semi-conscious most of the time and no longer even whimpered when lifted. He tossed back his sheet and stood.

"I will bring her to you," he said. "Prop yourself up with cushions on my couch. Would you like a drink of water?" She nodded. Before he padded into the nursery, he poured her a cup and passed it to her, waiting to set it back on the table after she had emptied it thirstily.

"You have been wonderful to me," she blurted impulsively. "More than I deserve. I love you so much, Ahmose. Forgive me for everything."

"Everything?" he smiled, noting that the effects of her dream, whatever it was, were still upsetting her. All the same, her face had lost its haggard look and the flush of health was returning to her skin. "I cannot imagine what everything might be. If you are settled, I will fetch Sat-Kamose."

He went through into the dimly lit nursery and bent over the basket, but his intent was stayed. He had seen death many times in the past few years and even on the features of otherwise unmarred soldiers its mark was unmistakeable. Or rather, the absence of its mark, he thought with a wave of terrible forsakenness. No matter how composed the face, how apparently deceptive the image, one glance can confirm that the ka has flown and only a vacant shell is left.

The baby's half-closed eyes glittered but with a borrowed spark of life from the lamp. Her mouth was partly open, the rows of tiny bones across her chest utterly motionless. Ahmose lifted her and crushed her to him. Her body was still faintly warm but it was the heat of any inanimate thing left out in the sun, a cushion, a blanket, not hers, not generated by the meagre spark of life that had smouldered within her. Biting his lip fiercely in an attempt to stem the tears that were already stinging his eyes, he carried her out into the bedchamber.

Aahmes-nefertari gave one soft cry when she saw his face, and held up her arms. Reverently Ahmose placed the pathetic little corpse in them and then sat beside her, taking up one of Sat-Kamose's hands in his and encircling his wife with the other. They did not speak. They stayed huddled together on the couch, both weeping, while the night deepened around them and their child's body gradually became cold to their grieving touch.

Ahmose carried Sat-Kamose to the House of the Dead himself. He wrapped her corpse in clean linen, sent Uni to order his litter brought, and walked quietly through the hushed passages of the house. Standing by the path through the garden, he noted that the moon was waning, that a wind had sprung up and was tossing the tops of the dark palms, that something indistinguishable, insect or frog, was rustling in the grass at his feet. The world has not changed, he thought. No star falls to mark your passing, little one. The trees do not pause in their motion to whisper your name. The river does not cast showers of tears upon us as I wait here with your husk in my arms. We may chart the stars, make use of the trees and the river, we may farm the earth and tame the animals, but those things cannot reward us with a single sympathetic response to human agony.

The litter came, borne by four sleepy servants. Ahmose told them where to take him, got into it, and drew the curtains closed. The House of the Dead was attached to Amun's temple and the distance was not far. In the privacy of the conveyance he uncovered his daughter's face and kissed the slack mouth but it was her soul that he wished to embrace, the essence containing everything she might have become, and in the end he rewrapped her with a sense of frustration.

The litter bearers set him down some way from the heavily guarded entrance to the House. He understood their reluctance to go farther and did not protest. Holding Sat-Kamose tightly, he walked up to the temple guardians and asked for a sem-priest, standing calmly while one of them disappeared into the darkness of the building. The other had extended his spear across the doorway, a ceremonial action, although Ahmose knew that he was perfectly capable of using force to prevent anyone from entering.

Not that anyone sane would choose to pass the gloomy portal. Stale airs blew from it, imbued with unidentifiable odours that nevertheless sent a shiver of apprehension down Ahmose's spine.

There was a flicker of movement in the shadows and a man appeared. He did not cross the stone lintel but he bowed. "What do you want of us, Majesty?" he enquired. Ahmose held out his small bundle.

"I bring you my daughter, the Princess Sat-Kamose, for beautification," he said, his voice trembling.

"We are sorry to hear of her death," the man replied. "Place her on the ground and step away." It was time to let her go, but for an instant Ahmose could not relinquish her. With a groan he lifted her to his neck, resting his chin on her windings, squeezing his eyes shut, feeling his tears run hot down his cheeks. Suddenly he was reminded of the day Hent-ta-Hent was buried, how little he had felt then, how selfishly divorced from any genuine grief for the child or compassion for her mother. All at once it was there like an Inundation long delayed, a rush of love and sadness whose force was different from the pricking of his present agony, more seasoned by the time that had passed, perhaps, diffusing under it, filling empty caverns within himself that he had not known existed. He could hardly breathe for the weight of it. The sem-priest waited impassively. At last Ahmose did as he was commanded, laying Sat-Kamose gently down and moving away. The priest at once emerged, picked her up, and quickly regained his place beyond the doorway. "My robe did not touch you but my breath or the emanations of my body may have rendered you unclean," he went on. "Go to the sacred lake and purify yourself."

With another short bow he vanished and Ahmose was left to retreat to the litter. He felt as abandoned as the dry, eviscerated corpses whose company his child would soon be keeping.

He had himself transported to Amun's lake. On its peaceful verge he removed his kilt and headdress and stepped down into the cool water until he was completely submerged, allowing his mouth, ears and nostrils to fill with the god's cleansing touch. Clambering out, he dressed quickly and gave the order to return to the house. I am free of the corruption of her death, he thought, but my soul will always bear the scars of her short life. May the gods receive you joyfully, my innocent little one!

Word of the death had already been spreading through the house by the time he left the litter and made his way back to Aahmes-nefertari's apartments. In spite of the hour, a few servants hung about the passages. They reverenced him as he swept by them, distress on their faces, but he was too heartsick to acknowledge their sympathy. Aahmes-nefertari herself was sitting on the floor with her forehead on her knees when he closed her door behind him at last. She looked up. "It is done," he said flatly, and going to her he pulled her to her feet. For a while they clung to each other, then she released him.

"Share my couch with me tonight," she pleaded. "I want to feel your warmth, Ahmose. I am so cold." For answer he held open the sheets and she climbed between them. He did not bother to undress. Suddenly very weary he lowered himself beside her and at once her arms went around him. There will be no sound from the nursery tonight, he thought, and with the sadness came a sliver of relief.

Next day he moved back into his own rooms and the seventy days of mourning for Sat-Kamose began. Ahmose continued to attend to matters of government every morning. He consulted with Pa-she regarding Ahmose-onkh's steady progress and set aside several hours each day to spend with the boy. He often joined his mother and Tetisheri in the garden in the late afternoons which were becoming increasingly hot as spring gave way to summer. There was no music and no feasting.

He had expected Aahmes-nefertari to suffer a relapse into depression and sleeplessness and indeed a part of him missed the intense hours they had endured together when he had become her nurse, but she was going about her business calmly and, according to her steward, was eating and resting well. Ahmose saw little of her. She did not avoid him. They often met when their paths crossed outside the reception hall or they were moving in opposite directions through the house, and once he had invited her for a short sail on the river to enjoy the sunset. She was tranquil and smiling but somehow distant, and something told him to leave her alone.

Reports from Sharuhen arrived regularly, each one much the same as the one before. The army was now firmly entrenched around the city. The men were fit. The water was being delivered in scant but sufficient quantity under Abana's supervision. There were no skirmishes with the mountain tribes and Sharuhen itself seemed entirely oblivious to the Egyptian presence. Ahmose sighed with every seal Ipi broke and exclaimed in disgust after every reading. It will take an act of the gods to open those gates, he reflected glumly. Amunmose told me of the Seer's prediction, that Sharuhen would fall and Apepa would be mine, but the Seer neglected to tell me exactly when these things would happen. I might be in my sixtieth year and Apepa dead of old age. Seers irritate me. They speak in riddles and still expect to be paid. But he remembered the man's daunting words regarding Sat-Kamose, unborn and unnamed at the time, and silenced his sacrilegious thoughts.

His attention turned at last to the old palace. He had not wanted to enter it until he was able to revive the many memories and their attendant emotions that its rough walls and echoing rooms had spawned in him. Its past glory had brought melancholy dreams, its ghosts a thrill of fear when he and Kamose crept into it at night as children, its rubble-strewn roof where his father had been attacked an overwhelming weight of anger and loss. But during the weeks of mourning for his daughter he found himself often standing in his garden and staring at it across the now smooth and unbroken run of lawn where the wall between it and the house used to be. It is mine by right of my birth, he told himself. It is a King's mansion, and by moving into it I shall be re-establishing the law of Ma'at in Egypt after so many years of Setiu occupation. But not until one bright, hot morning when he saw Ahmose-onkh come racing around one of its corners and fly, laughing and shrieking, towards the pond with a smiling Pa-she in pursuit did he make up his mind.

He sent for Prince Sebek-nakht, meeting him in the shadow of one of the palace's towering frontal pillars that now rose straight and true to a dazzlingly blue early summer sky. "Some of the interior walls have been white-washed, Majesty," the Prince told him as they walked inside, "but of course no more work is possible until the Princess's funeral. I am satisfied with what I have done. I hope you will approve of it also." Ahmose did not reply. Silently he paced the burnished floors that ran away before him into vast, dim caverns, brushed his fingertips along the smooth walls that echoed to his footsteps, stood pensively in pools of white light splashing down from the clerestory windows high above, mounted wide stairs that led to more lofty chambers, and finally found himself on the roof with Weset spread out beneath him in its forest of palms and the Nile glinting between its sandy banks. A shout from below made him turn. Ahmose-onkh had seen him and was waving, a toy child standing in the middle of a little garden. Already Ahmose's concept of proportions had changed. He waved back. "You will see that I have obeyed your command regarding the narrow stairs leading up to that portion of the roof that sits over the women's quarters," Sebek-nakht was saying. "There are doors at its foot and its top and the steps themselves have not even been cleared of rubbish, let alone repaired. Does Your Majesty wish to inspect the new administrative offices to the rear? They are all now complete." He spoke with a pardonable pride. Ahmose shook his head.

"I am awed by your accomplishment, Prince," he said. "The palace retains its air of ancient authority yet it is somehow lighter, bigger, the new in harmony with the old." He spread his hands helplessly. "I cannot express my meaning other than to say I am delighted." Sebek-nakht smiled.

"It is a dwelling for a god and will be a fit setting for all your divine descendants," he assured Ahmose. "Apepa's palace in Het-Uart was a shack compared to it. The Queen has hired the most accomplished artists in the south to decorate its pillars and walls. She has also commissioned tiles of lapis for the floor of the throne room and sheets of gold for its walls. She tells me that sufficient silver and gold is coming into the Royal Treasury to forge the waterstep gates of electrum as you desire. They will shine with the reflected glory of the sun and blind every helmsman trying to steer his craft past them."

"Aahmes-nefertari has done that?" Ahmose was astonished. Sebek-nakht sobered.

"She gave the orders before the Princess was born," he said. "Much of her heart has gone into this edifice, Majesty. She has insisted on her personal involvement in every decision that was made. She and your mother have even consulted the gardeners regarding the placing of the surrounding lawns and flowerbeds and they have brought sculptors from Swenet to fashion the fountains." Ahmose did not trust himself to comment for fear the swelling of his throat might betray him. I am ashamed, he thought. I cared nothing for the dispatches from Weset while I was besieging Het-Uart and marching on Sharuhen. I gave them no more than an impatient few moments. My wife, my family, were less to me than an evening of wine and conversation with my generals by the army's cooking fires. Amun forgive me. Nodding brusquely he swallowed and started back down to the sun-drenched courtyard below.

On the eleventh day of Epophi, two and a half months after Ahmose had carried Sat-Kamose to the House of the Dead, she was escorted across the river by the whole court and the temple staff and laid in her tiny coffins beside

Hent-ta-Hent. Ahmose could not help comparing this funeral with the last. Outwardly it was the same. The women wore mourning blue, cast soil upon their heads, and keened. The red oxen of custom, dragging the sled on which Sat-Kamose lay, plodded towards the tombs on the western bank in clouds of dust. Amunmose wielded the pesesh-kef and the netjeri-blades to open the girl's mouth and restore life to her five senses. Incense rose shimmering in the heat and the singers and dancers twirled.

But this time every sound and movement, every word of the ritual pains me, Ahmose thought. Hent-ta-Hent's funeral did not penetrate my restless callousness. Now I am bereft of joy, I am wounded by them both, and all because of a little creature whom I could comfortably hold on the two outstretched palms of my hands. While he ate the feast afterwards with Aahmes-nefertari, he watched Ahmose-onkh edge towards Kamose's tomb where Behek still kept his vigil. The dog rose with difficulty to greet the boy who knelt and began to caress the grey head. Behek is growing old and stiff, Ahmose mused. One day the priests who tend the tombs will come to offer sacrifices to Kamose and find him dead. I must warn them that he is to be embalmed and buried with honour, close to Kamose. Such faithfulness deserves a reward.

Aahmes-nefertari had said nothing at all during the days spent performing the required rites. Occasionally she wept and Ahmose would pull her close to him, but for the most part she stood with her hands clasped loosely before her, staring at the ground. He was no longer concerned for her health or safety. He knew that there was no desperation in her grieving, because he was sharing it with her. But he also sensed that she was thinking, deeply and fiercely.

Once back at the house he was immediately aware that its atmosphere had changed. It was always so after a funeral. Mourning would begin and a weight of oppression would settle over everyone, to be magically dispelled when the boats returning from the west bumped against the water-steps. He disembarked and he and Aahmes-nefertari walked arm in arm towards the pillars of the front entrance, the other members of the family drifting behind.

Suddenly she tugged him to a halt, and waiting until Aahotep, Tetisheri and a yawning Ahmose-onkh had passed, she let him go. "I have something to say to you, Majesty," she began in a high, hurried voice. "There has always been a lick of the coward in me. When I was younger I was afraid of almost everything—a threatening omen, the prick of a thorn, a harsh word. I waited constantly for the gods to strike me. Then the war began and I was forced to grapple with real danger, separate it from the phantoms of my mind." She bit her lip. "I was not very successful. It was not until Kamose was murdered and you were wounded that I discovered a spark of genuine bravery and recklessness in my character. It freed me. But with Hent-ta-Hent's death all the old terrors returned." She folded her arms, gripping herself tightly as though she were cold. "I drowned in them. I did not fight. When I became pregnant with Sat-Kamose, the dark waters of self-pity and extreme caution had already closed completely over my head, and by the time she was born I was so ill I could no longer eat, sleep or walk without hatred for myself and for you." Ahmose made as if to hold her but she stepped away.

"No," she said loudly. "Let me finish. None of it was your fault. None. Then you came home and you were gentle and loving and you saw her and cared for her, for both of us, and something in me began to be ashamed." Tears were trickling down her face but she was smiling. "I have found my courage again, Ahmose. We have lost our daughters but we will have more children and I will never again be afraid. I will not deny life itself. Will you come to me tonight and make love to me? It has been too long." Astounded and deeply moved, Ahmose drew her to him, cradling her warm head against his chest.

"Not all the blame is yours, dearest sister," he said hoarsely. "I have been unforgivably selfish. It would delight me to come to you tonight. I would like nothing better." He felt her give out a sigh. Still crushing her against him, he turned her towards the house.

He wondered if her outpouring had simply been an extreme reaction to the strain of Sat-Kamose's funeral, but as the days passed and she remained cheerful and affectionate he came to believe that whatever fires of self-condemnation and revelation had been lit in her had burned themselves out, leaving her permanently changed. She and he were closer than they had ever been, making love happily every night, sitting in audience together, watching Ahmose-onkh learn to swim, and presiding over the increasingly elaborate feasts for the foreign dignitaries, ambassadors and wealthy merchants who had begun to pour into Weset like miners catching a glimpse of a vein of gold in what had been a secluded cave.

Ahmose would have been entirely content if it were not for the problem of Sharuhen. Every time a herald arrived with scrolls from his generals, he would secrete himself in his father's office until the cloud of frustration they brought had been dissipated. Sharuhen was an unfinished task. Apepa was a living growth inside a monstrous cocoon attached to the border of Egypt that must be ripped away and trodden upon, and Ahmose knew that soon he must leave Weset once again and take the Horus Road east.

He waited to discuss the matter with his wife until the beginning of Thoth when the New Year celebrations were over and the Inundation had begun. A rich harvest had been gathered. Overseers and governors everywhere sent word of Egypt's return to fertility and peace together with gifts for their King. The Treasury was filling. The gold routes were stable. It was a good time to go, Ahmose reflected, and Aahmes-nefertari would rule with calm efficiency while he was away. He chose an evening when no guests had been entertained and he and Aahmes-nefertari were free to sit in the garden, sharing a last cup of wine before going to their quarters. The heat that day had been intense. They had swum in the river at sunset and were now wrapped in a companionable silence while dusk slowly filled the trees beyond them and seeped across the grass. Aahmes-nefertari had perched on a stool and Senehat was combing out her wet hair. Ahmose sprawled at her feet, tracing their delicate bones with one pensive finger. He had just summoned up the courage to speak when she forestalled him. "I have good news for you, Ahmose," she said. "I am pregnant again. The baby will be born in the spring, at the end of Pharmuthi. Are you pleased?" He glanced up. She was looking down at him and smiling. He made himself grip her foot, concentrating on the action of his hand so that his dismay would not show on his face.

"Indeed I am pleased," he said heartily. "Are you sure?"

"Perfectly sure. And perfectly happy." She nudged him playfully with her toe. "I have already been to the Seer for a prediction. He says that I may expect a healthy boy who will live a long life." Was he lying? Ahmose thought immediately, and then was ashamed. He scrambled up and kissed her softly on her mouth.

"Oh, Aahmes-nefertari, you deserve this," he said. "We both do. We will go to the temple tomorrow and make an offering to Amun." She signalled to Senehat to leave them, and pulling her hair forward she began to braid it with quick, deft movements.

"I have one favour to ask of you, Ahmose," she said, not meeting his eye. "You may refuse if you wish."

"I do not want to refuse you anything," he protested. "What is it?" She still did not look at him.

"I want you to stay with me until this baby is born," she said. "Do not mistake me, I am not afraid. But I need you here. Will you stay?" Both hands froze on the braid and she became motionless, a curve of loose robe and one pale cheek. Ahmose could feel her tension.

Suddenly he realized that everything important to her hung on his answer. It was not a test. She had not set out coldly to prove his loyalty, with anger or assurance as the goal depending on his words. She was risking all her future well-being in this moment and she had chosen the perfect time to do it. She was well aware that his men did not need him, might never need him, at Sharuhen. Nor was his presence required in Weset, where the wheels of government could go on turning without him, providing someone in authority stood ready to guide it when necessary. Only she truly needed him and he was being asked if her need was as vital to him as it was to her. Kneeling, he lifted her hands and brought them up, imprisoned in his own, under her chin. Her face was already dim in the fading light and her eyes were huge and dark. He smiled slowly.

"Of course I will stay," he said.

16

IN THE MONTH of Pharmuthi the following year Aahmes-nefertari gave birth to a lusty, healthy boy. Her pregnancy had proceeded normally. The phantoms of doubt and fear that had plagued her while carrying Sat-Kamose had returned occasionally during the long nine-month wait for the new baby but she had mastered them well, sharing them with Ahmose so that their sting was rapidly drawn. He himself settled determinedly into the routine of court life, at first willing himself to be content but later reading the scrolls from Sharuhen with a sense of relief that there were no changes in the east. He was happy with his wife, happy with Egypt's growing peace and prosperity, and if he woke in the night full of a fleeting dissatisfaction, it was because the old palace remained empty of both Throne and Royal Regalia.

He and Aahmes-nefertari spent a portion of every morning wandering the gracious halls and lordly passages of the place that would be both their home and a shrine to the Divine Incarnation of a renewed Ma'at. The lapis tiles for the Throne Room were finished and laid. Its walls were at last covered with sheets of gold on which were etched giant representations of the King in the Double Crown smiting his enemies with an axe while a smaller Aahmes-nefertari clung to his heel with one hand and raised the ankh in the other. The artists swarmed the precincts with their pots of bright colours, turning pillars into grapevines, ceilings into birds and stars, and corridors into rivers and pools of blue water in which fish swam and on which delicate lotus and lily blooms floated.

Ahmose was exultant when Chief Treasurer Neferperet announced that there was now sufficient gold and silver in the treasury to begin work on the gates of electrum and the goldsmiths were ready to offer a choice of designs for it to the King. Trade was becoming well established. Gold, ivory, ebony, ostrich feathers and the pelts of exotic animals came north from Wawat, oxen from Tjehenu, gold and silver rhytons, ewers, and bowls, bronze inlaid ceremonial swords and daggers, ceramics of eggshell thickness adorned with octopi, dolphins and urchins, dyes, and of course the precious poppy flowed in from Keftiu, but as yet there was no cedar from northern Rethennu or a fresh influx of horses from the tribes even farther east with which the Setiu had dealt. Ahmose wondered gloomily if there ever would be, but he did not dwell on the lack. The gods had looked on him with favour and he was careful to be grateful.

The astrologers chose the name Amunhotep for Ahmose's son. Aahmes-nefertari, cuddling the chubby baby while the nursery attendants twittered and clucked around her, was overjoyed when Amunmose brought the news himself. "'Amun-is-satisfied'!" she exclaimed, bending to rub her nose playfully against her son's. "What a wonderful name! Surely it means that the god has ceased to test our ability to endure, Ahmose! He is satisfied with all we have done for him!" Ahmose peered at Amunhotep and after a moment the baby gurgled, smiled, and thrashed his fat arms.

"They should have named him Mighty Bull of Weset," he teased her. "He eats and kicks like one."

"The Seer has predicted a glorious future for him, Majesty," Amunmose put in. "Long life and stability."

"I am so glad," Aahmes-nefertari whispered. "So glad, so glad." She met her husband's eye over the bundle in her arms. "Prince Amunhotep. He will be a great warrior and a fine governor like his father."

"And brave and stubborn like his mother," Ahmose retorted, grinning. He kissed her flushed cheek. "When you have finished adoring your accomplishment, come on the river with me. The evening is cool and sweet and I need some attention, too."

He remained at home for another three months to make sure that both Aahmes-nefertari and his son continued in good health. The season of Shemu had begun, with its breathless heat. Pakhons and Payni went by, and then it was the beginning of Epophi, when all over Egypt the peasants took to the fields with their scythes, the threshers stood ready to flail the chaff from the grain, and the vintners waited to trample the dusty, bursting grapes being tumbled into the vats.

Ahmose went to his wife's apartments and, finding her absent, climbed the stairs leading to the roof above them. She was there with Senehat, sprawled indolently on a mat, her head on a cushion, gazing up at the blaze of summer stars flung across a black sky. Hearing him come, she turned to look at him but she did not rise. He lowered himself beside her and took the cup of water Senehat immediately proffered. "The house was unbearably hot today," she murmured. "It is time to start sleeping on the roof. Even the draught blowing through the pillars of the reception hall at the feast tonight seemed too warm. How lovely it is up here, Ahmose!" He swallowed his water and nodded an agreement, slowly scanning the length of her naked body illumined by the soft glow of the single lamp. It had been placed well away from her so that the insects it attracted might not annoy her, and the golden half-light it cast made silken highlights of her knees and hips, the slight mound of her stomach, the well of her breasts, leaving the rest hidden in a tantalizing shadow. She was beautiful and she was his. He felt her hand slide over his where it rested beside her.

"Dear Ahmose," she said. "I know why you are here. You want to go north again, don't you?" Startled at her perception, he leaned closer so that he could see her expression. She was smiling at him wistfully.

"I don't want to, Aahmes-nefertari, and that is the truth," he replied. "But I must. It is time."

"I know." She curled up into a sitting position and wriggled around to face him. "I shall miss you terribly," she admitted. "This year has been a blessed one, has it not? And you will miss Amunhotep's first words, his first steps. That is a pity." There was no rancour in her words, only regret. She laughed shortly. "Ahmose-onkh has begun to call him Ahmose-onkh-ta-sherit. He sits by the basket and tells him to hurry up and grow so that they can shoot the bow and read stories together. He has been lonely, I think." Ahmose touched her calf.

"I think so too. Ahmose-onkh-the-younger. That is charming. But I do not intend to miss a moment of Amunhotep's progress if I can possibly avoid it. I go to

Sharuhen only to dismantle the army and bring Weset's divisions home."

"Ahmose!" She swayed back in surprise. "You will give up the siege? Leave Apepa safe forever in that city? But why?" He pursed his lips.

"Because Sharuhen cannot be taken. I could sit up there for years while the inhabitants ate the fruits of their gardens and drank from their wells. I suppose in time some misfortune would overtake them. The population might become too large for the food supply or a plague might strike them, anything, but those things cannot be predicted. The Keftiu cannot go on shipping water to the troops forever and the men themselves cannot be expected to die of old age, inactivity and frustration." He shrugged. "I will leave a division permanently stationed at the Wall of Princes and across the Horus Road, just within our border. The rest I will distribute to garrisons in the Delta and Iunu and Mennofer, perhaps one at Khemmenu, so that they can be rotated and yet called up as they are needed. Amun and Ra will come back with me and go into the new quarters with their wives and families."

"But what of Apepa?" she pressed. "He was the symbol of every oppression to Kamose and to you also. Leave him alive and the work is unfinished. And what of his sons? They will claim the kingship of Egypt if you allow them to survive."

"I know," he said quietly. "I have spent the last few weeks thinking about little else. But there is no alternative, Aahmes-nefertari, no way to reach in and pluck Apepa and his sons from within those stone walls. I will keep scouts in the vicinity and I can use the divisions that will be at Iunu and Mennofer to march on Sharuhen quickly if the opportunity arises, but I will not waste my life sitting in a tent and waiting for something to happen. I want to be here with you and the children, with my ministers and overseers, watching Egypt blossom under my hand." He lay down and pulled her after him, dismissing Senehat as he did so. "I will commission a new throne, new regalia, and try to forget that at the very end I failed. I have decided that it is a price worth paying in exchange for everything I hold dear." She lay silently in his arms for a long time and he wondered if she had fallen asleep, but presently she stirred against him.

"Nevertheless," she breathed, "it is the will of the god that determines our fate. Go into the temple before you leave, and sacrifice a bull to Amun, and pray that our vengeance may indeed be complete. He will not desert you now, at the end, Ahmose. I am his Second Prophet, remember. I have a feeling that the war is not yet over."

"I respect your intuitions," Ahmose said without much conviction. "I will do as you say, but without your confidence, Aahmes-nefertari. Now you must do as I say. Kiss me. This may be the last time we make love on the roof of the old house. Move into the new house while I am gone and see the electrum gates hung so that their fire may greet me when I come sailing home again." At once she raised herself on one elbow and placed her mouth on his and his arms encircled her. I am right to admit this small defeat, he thought before his senses slipped away from his control. It is a matter of priority. But he knew that he would carry a tiny seed of bitterness in his soul for the rest of his life.

He set out on the twelfth of Epophi with Akhtoy, Hekayib, Ipi, Khabekhnet, Ankhmahor and the Followers, one day after the anniversary of Sat-Kamose's funeral. He and Aahmes-nefertari had taken offerings of flowers, oil, fruit and bread to lay outside the tomb. They had stood in the baking sun with Amunmose in front of the sealed entrance, saying the prayers of remembrance and petition for the girl's ka, and there was no sadness in Ahmose as he held his wife's hand, only love for the baby who had melted his heart and a belated understanding that her brief life had been responsible for healing the breach between himself and Aahmes-nefertari.

Afterwards he had said goodbye to Aahotep and his grandmother, taken Ahmose-onkh out on the desert in a chariot and given him his first driving lesson, and then made his way to the temple to perform his sacrifice as he had promised his wife. Watching the bull's blood pour into the waiting bowl, he did his best to pray with fervour for a final vindication but his thoughts would not stay centred on the words he was saying and in the end he fell silent. Do what you will, King of All Gods, he told his totem resignedly. You have led us from occupation to freedom at the cost of many lives and much suffering. If at the last you choose to spare our enemy, then it is your sublime prerogative to do so.

He spent the evening with Aahmes-nefertari discussing the matters of government to be dealt with while he was away, then he went through into the nursery, kissed his sleeping son, and retired to his own rooms. Lying on his couch in the darkness, he felt homesickness already creeping towards him and he welcomed it as a sign that he was indeed fully reconciled to his decision to leave Sharuhen to its isolated peace.

He slept deeply and dreamlessly until Akhtoy roused him two hours before dawn. "The ships are loaded and ready, Majesty," the steward told him, "and there is hot water in the bath house. Uni will not wake the Queen, as you requested. Will you eat now?" Ahmose swung his legs to the floor. The air was thick and hot in his bedchamber and his head was aching gently.

"I will eat on the boat when the sun rises," he said. "But I will wash. Has Khabekhnet sent out a herald to warn the generals?"

"He has. The High Priest is waiting above the watersteps to purify your way with blood and milk." Ahmose rubbed his face and came fully awake.

"Is he? But why? I am not embarking on a fresh venture or undertaking a formal progress."

"Queen Tetisheri commanded it," Akhtoy replied. "She was carried to the temple in her litter just after the afternoon sleep yesterday. She also awaits you." Ahmose exchanged a rueful glance with his servant.

"Very well," he said. "Give me that kilt, Akhtoy, and I will go to the bath house. So much for making a quiet departure."

They were both standing patiently by the open watersteps gate. Tetisheri's servant Isis held a lamp. The night was still fully dark, with no hint of the dawn. Tetisheri was swathed in a cloak as though it were winter. Ahmose approached them diffidently, not knowing what to expect from his grandmother. He had not told her of his intention to withdraw from Sharuhen for fear the news might bring down an avalanche of harsh words on his head, but perhaps she had found out by some mysterious means and was about to heap imprecations on him now.

But when he came close, her arm shot out and imprisoned him in a strong, bony grip. "During my rest yesterday afternoon I dreamed that you were killing a goose," she said without preamble. "You had the creature firmly held under your arm with its head in your hand. First you plunged the knife into its breast and then you severed its neck with one swift blow. Blood spurted over your chest and ran down your legs. So wet and red and rich, Ahmose, and the feathers gleaming white and the knife glinting as you slashed." Her unpainted face was turned up to him solemnly. "I did not know when I dreamed that you were going north to disband the army, I swear it. Ahmose-onkh told me later that you had promised to see him very soon. Then I knew." Her hooded eyes were alight with triumph. "Such a dream is very rare and its interpretation clear. You will kill your enemy. There is no doubt."

"Tetisheri," he said as kindly as he could, "I am impressed by your dream. Akhtoy had a similar one some time ago, just before the gates of Het-Uart opened. But if you tell me in order to persuade me to stay at Sharuhen, you are mistaken. I go to end the siege. My mind is made up." He tensed against the flood of protest he believed would come but she merely nodded once and dropped her hand.

"You are the King," she said utterly unexpectedly. "Your decisions are in the way of Ma'at. Yet you sacrificed a bull in the hope that Amun would grant you this one last victory, did you not?"

"I did, but ..."

"Amunmose has brought milk mixed with the blood of your offering," she interrupted him imperiously. "It will sanctify your going and consecrate your feet to speed you to Apepa's death. I know it. All I ask is that you tarry one week in your tent outside Sharuhen. One week. Will you do that for me?"

"It will take more than a week for the army to pack up and prepare to march," he answered. "But yes, Grandmother, I can promise that."

"Thank you." She spoke with such uncharacteristic humility that he was disarmed. Scooping her up bodily, he planted a kiss on her leathery cheek before setting her back on her feet. She bore it with dignity, signalling to the High Priest to begin the rite. At once he began to sing, walking ahead of Ahmose, the pink milk and blood splashing the stone and cascading down the steps to be diluted in the dark water below the ramp. "Go, Ahmose, leave now!" Tetisheri urged. "The ramps of the servants' ships are already drawn up, as Apepa draws near to his doom. I will pray for you every day. Do not wash the mixture from your sandals. Carry the god's blessing with you all the way to Rethennu."

"Watch over my sons," Ahmose managed, and she smiled.

"Always," she said.

The blood and milk were not sticky under his sandals, for the stone paving was cool. Nevertheless he felt the liquid moisten the sides of his feet and seep under his soles as he descended the steps. He ran up the ramp, and turning saluted Amunmose and his grandmother. She did not wave back. She had gathered the cloak tightly around her again, her grey hair straggling stiff and untidy on her shoulders, her aging but imperious features soft in the light of the lamp Isis held high, and for once Ahmose loved her unreservedly.

The mooring ropes were cast adrift. Qar called to the helmsman and the rowers lowered the oars. Ponderously the *North* swung out into the sluggish current. The last he saw of Tetisheri was her proud carriage as she walked back towards the shrouded bulk of the sleeping house.

The journey to the Delta was uneventful. Ahmose did not hurry but neither did he put in at Khemmenu to see Ramose as he had wanted to do on the way south. He arrived at Het-Uart at the end of the first week of Mesore, having spent long, pleasurable hours hanging over the railing of the *North* to watch the fields being harvested as she beat her way down the Nile. Villagers were busy in the Delta also, picking fruit from the laden trees and stripping the grapevines. Ahmose felt to his bones the new harmony his beloved country was making. Everywhere the atmosphere was one of hope and abundance, a new trust in the security he was creating. Whether Sharuhen fell or not, he reflected, the past hentis of foreign rule were fast disappearing from the minds and memories of his subjects. But not from mine and not from my descendants, he vowed as he moved from his cabin to the railing and to the shore in the quiet evenings. I will make sure that no future King ever forgets these times so that never again will Egypt become the prey of rapacious men who live-without-Ra.

At Het-Uart word of his coming had preceded him and Mesehti was waiting with his chariot. After a few hours consulting with Khety and Sebek-khu regarding the continued demolition of the city walls and its reclamation, he set out along the Horus Road, his baggage and his entourage strung out cheerfully behind him. Abana had not been in the Delta. He was on his way to Rethennu on one of the water ships and Ahmose looked forward to greeting him later. This late in the summer the flood plains were dry and hard and even the Sea of Reeds had shrunk. Ahmose made good time. At the Wall of Princes he spent a pleasant night with Generals Iymery and Neferseshemptah in one of the forts, hearing over beer and coarse bread how the restoration and re-manning of the Wall was proceeding steadily. It was good to be back among soldiers, he thought to himself contentedly, but not as good as sitting with Aahmes-nefertari and their son in the garden at home, sharing gossip after a long, hot day. He missed them already.

Eight days later he was met by Standard Bearer Idu and an escort from his Division of Amun, and surrounded by the Followers he entered the perimeter of the camp. He might have left it only yesterday. There were the same neat rows of tents, the same aroma of roasting meat, the same toing and froing of soldiers sauntering in noisy groups or hurrying on errands, the same flash of chariot wheels as officers came and went. A cloud of dust far to his right where the bivouacs ended and the gravelled desert began told him that a contingent of troops was drilling, although the distance was too great for him to hear the shouted commands of the captain.

While Akhtoy oversaw the erection of his tent and Khabekhnet went to summon the generals, Ahmose had himself driven closer to Sharuhen. The camp has remained true in my memory, he thought, but for some reason I imagined Sharuhen itself to be smaller as the months passed. Perhaps because I so desperately desired to conquer it. But it is larger than I remembered. Its walls are higher and sturdier, its impression of inviolability stronger. I am doing the right thing in accepting a limit to the extent of my retribution. I wonder if my commanders will agree?

They gathered outside his tent in the long shadow it cast. The late afternoon was hot and they gladly accepted the water and beer Akhtoy poured for them. Ahmose, scanning them carefully as one by one they arrived, reverenced him, and took their places around the table, thought that they seemed subdued. Although happy to see him return, there was no laughter or idle talk among them. He brought them to order with a greeting and asked for their reports. Kagemni was the first to speak. Under his crumpled red linen helmet his brow was furrowed and shining with sweat, and dust had settled in the creases around his long nose. "There has been no word from the city, Majesty," he said. "We are watched occasionally, almost casually, from the top of the walls but otherwise we are ignored. We need more water. The summer heat here is intense and the wind has veered from the west, off the ocean, and now blows from the north, stirring up the desert and making the soldiers irritable. They cannot bathe to relieve their distress."

"We have begun to send them to the ocean in shifts," Akhethotep added. "There they can disport themselves in the Great Green and wash, but many of them fear the size and force of the sea. Food is not a problem, however. General Hor-Aha has turned the Medjay into hunters. They range the mountains and regularly bring in much game."

"There has been an increase of eye sickness, Majesty," Baqet interposed. "The physicians sent to the Delta for more unguents. The constant glare of light off the sand is responsible, of course, and the dust. There is no shelter here, nothing green."

"The Medjay do not care for such shelter," Hor-Aha said. "They are content. But the rest of your troops complain to their officers every day. Also it must be the season of locusts. My tribesmen have encountered large swarms of them in the thin strip of fertile land at the foot of the mountains. They do not fear them, but their black clouds can be seen from the camp and the sight of them stirs a superstitious dread in the other soldiers. They are seen as an omen of disaster."

Ahmose studied his friend. He alone of all the generals appeared to have benefited from his stay in this dry, forsaken place. His black skin had a sheen of health to it and his dark eyes were clear. His hair had grown again to its former length and lay gleaming on his broad shoulders. Unlike the others, he was not sweating. Ahmose rapped the table. "I had already decided to give up the siege," he said, "and everything I hear from you reinforces that decision. It is time to admit a bloodless defeat, my Generals, and retire behind the Wall of Princes. I will lose face but my soldiers will doubtless bless me. No Egyptian likes being away from his land for too long." No one objected and in their silence he read relief. "I see that you agree," he continued dryly. "Then you may inform your officers that we will march one week from today. I will give you the redistribution of the divisions later. Now I invite you to eat with me and we will talk of other matters. I am pleased to be in your presence again."

After they had gone, he was reluctant to enter his tent. The light was fading and with it the heat, although the wind still gusted, flattening his kilt against his thighs and tugging at the lappets of his helmet. Taking Ankhmahor, he strolled in the direction of the fort. He was drawn to the rugged adamant of its stone, its aura of complete indifference. He tried to imagine its gates open, its citizens coming and going along the road to the ocean, the ox carts of traders rattling as they drew near, the cries of its children and the chatter of its women, but he could not. Sharuhen was too solid, too real to be a mirage, yet there was a dreamlike quality about it that troubled him. I shall never see what is inside it, he thought. Somewhere within its mute defences Apepa and Tani eat and sleep, walk and talk, but my mind sees them standing stiffly motionless while the sun rises and sets, a pair of statues who neither breathe nor blink. I suppose the rock walls muffle all sound, particularly with the gates closed, but I cannot rid myself of the fancy that Sharuhen is crowded with lifeless figures.

For three days he rose early, had himself driven as close to the city as was safe, and spent the morning hours sitting under a canopy with his gaze on the southern gate. He had no duties to perform. A wave of excitement had rippled through the camp with the news that the siege was to be lifted, but Ahmose remembered the sneering arrogance of the man who had spoken from the wall and would not give his name and a part of him regretted this retreat. I would have liked to see him humbled, he thought. For what is he but the petty ruler of a single city? Yet I, King of Egypt, must slink away from his haughty disregard like a whipped dog.

But on the fourth day, as he was slumped in his chair with the thin protection of the canopy flapping above him, he saw a man suddenly appear on the top of the wall. Ankhmahor uttered an exclamation that was echoed by the Followers clustered around. Ahmose came to his feet,

his mind all at once filling with his grandmother's dream
and his promise to tarry outside Sharuhen for seven days.
Excitement flooded him. The man lifted a horn to his
mouth and blew. "Egyptians!" he shouted. "The Queen
Tautha desires audience with her brother! Let her approach
him unharmed!"

A hundred ideas flashed through Ahmose's head, but
one was uppermost. They will open the gate to let her out,
we could rush them then, but no, it would take too much
time to muster an assault, can I and the Followers make the
attempt? The man had not waited for a reply. He had disappeared as quickly as he had come. Already the gate was
inching open and a small figure was emerging. It was Tani,
unescorted, a lone woman crossing the hot waste towards
him, the tassels of her robe flicked by the wind, stray
strands escaping from her bound hair and being flung
against her neck.

"Mesehti, the chariot!" Ahmose called. The Followers
were also watching Tani come nearer, their hands on the
hilts of their swords. Do they expect her to lunge at me with
a dagger? Ahmose thought idiotically. Then she was before
him, eyes narrowed against the sunlight, holding her hands
wide.

"I bring no weapon," she said to Ankhmahor, a hint of
sarcasm in her voice. "Greetings, Ahmose. I must speak to
you immediately and privately. Am I permitted?" For
answer he indicated the chariot. She stepped up onto its
floor and he followed. Mesehti clucked at the horses and
they set off towards Ahmose's tent. He had not said a word.

Once inside he dismissed Akhtoy and turned to face
her. "Have you brought me the surrender of Sharuhen?"

he demanded, without much hope. She laughed once in shock.

"No, of course not!" she said sharply, then she softened. "It is wonderful to see you again, Ahmose." He would not respond to the tenderness of her tone.

"What do you want?" he asked roughly. "Have you had enough of the Setiu? Have you come to beg me to send you home? I will do it gladly, Tani." She bit her lip and looked away.

"I need your help," she said in a low voice. "My husband is very ill. He needs poppy to ease his pain but there is none in the city. Sharuhen's supply has always come from Keftiu, but the siege has put a stop to it. May I sit down?" He nodded and she collapsed into a chair. "I know how you hate him," she went on urgently, "but I pray that you will take pity on a fellow man in great distress."

"He is ill?" Ahmose repeated in astonishment. "Apepa? What is the matter with him?"

"There is a steep stone stairway leading from the house where we live, down to the street entrance," she said. "He was descending it when he tripped on something, a pebble perhaps, I don't know. He fell. The guards caught him at the bottom but it was too late. He had broken his leg."

"A broken leg? But surely …"

"He broke it in three places," she blurted. "Not cleanly. Shards of bone were sticking out of his skin. He was screaming. Oh, Ahmose, it was terrible. He went on screaming while he was carried back into the house and laid on his bed. His physician tried to push the bones back into place and he fainted. It was useless. That was three days ago. Then the ukhedu started to spread. Washing his leg and putting salve on it did no good. It swelled and oozed. He can hardly be touched without his shrieking with the pain. This morning I left him drowned in sweat and shaking as though it was winter." Her face worked and she burst into tears. "His physician is a fool!" she cried out. "He is dying, and in such agony you cannot imagine! Please, Ahmose, give me poppy!" Grabbing up a piece of linen from the table, she held it to her eyes. Her shoulders were heaving with her sobs.

Ahmose stood watching her. He was not untouched by her distress, but a tide of sheer malicious joy was filling him, making him smile. A part of him saw it grow with righteous horror but he could not control it. Apepa was dying. Not the quick and easy death of an arrow through the chest or a sword thrust through the neck but slowly, in exquisite torment. It was a vengeance better than any he could have conjured up himself. Amun had seen the impregnability of Sharuhen. He had reached inside the city and struck Apepa down. He had honoured the trust and perseverance of his servants. He had answered their petitions and had sent Tetisheri the dream to tell them so. By this act of divine retribution the god had set his mighty seal on Egypt forever and Ma'at was finally made whole. Let him suffer, Ahmose thought savagely. Let Amun's hand squeeze ever tighter about him until he has drunk the bitter wine of anguish to the lees and life has fled.

But then another notion insinuated itself beneath the turmoil of hostility and dark pleasure and he took one step towards his sister. "No," he said firmly. "I will not give you poppy to take into Sharuhen. I do not care whether Apepa dies in torment or happily unconscious under the spell of the drug as long as he makes an end. However, if you will bring him here to me together with the Horus Throne and the Royal Regalia, he can have all the poppy he needs." Her head jerked up. He saw the colour drain out of her cheeks until she was ashen under the delicate brown of her skin. The fingers clutching the linen convulsed.

"Ahmose!" she choked. "Have you no pity?"

"None." He dragged the stool over and sat so that their knees were almost together. "This is the man in whose name our father was crippled, for whom Kamose was murdered," he said harshly. "This is the man who would have had Aahmes-nefertari married to a commoner, Grandmother sent to a harem for old women, and Kamose posted forever to the border fort at Sile. He condemned me to live out my days in Kush under Teti-En, fighting the tribes who would not submit to him. If Kamose had not taken hold of his courage and begun his revolt, the family would have been not only divided but utterly humiliated." He sat back and folded his arms. "And this is the man for whom you plead. No. My compassion does not extend that far. I have given you a choice. Go back empty-handed or bring him out with the sacred things he stole. How much compassion have you?" She flung the sopping linen away and came to her feet. Sobs spasmodically racked her but she had regained control of herself.

"I did not come to bargain!" she flared. "I came believing in the mercy of a brother. But he has eaten his heart and there is nothing left but a demon!"

"Believe what you will," Ahmose retorted coldly. "I care nothing for Apepa and very little for you."

"You will kill him as soon as he appears!"

"Don't be ridiculous. Unless you lie, he is dying already. You have my word that my physician will assume his care if my throne and my crown come with him. Now what will you do?" She stumbled to the tent flap and he swivelled on the stool to watch her.

"You have become more cruel than I could ever have imagined, Mighty Bull of Ma'at," she said in a strangled whisper. "You have gored me to the marrow. Of course, I will bring him out. Only the most hardened criminal could bear to sit beside him and watch his suffering and I love him. His family will curse you, and I curse you too." She fumbled with the flap.

"Bring him at once," Ahmose called as she pushed her way out. Jumping up, he ran after her. She was fleeing towards the city, her hair coming loose, her robe dragging on the ground. "Send Mesehti to pick her up with the chariot and drive her the rest of the way," he ordered Ankhmahor. "Then find Turi. He is to assemble fifty men and wait outside the southern gate. She will reappear with Apepa. Turi will escort them back here." Ankhmahor's eyes lit up.

"Majesty, how did you make this happen?" he asked. Ahmose blew out his lips.

"You will see how very soon," he said. He felt ill himself. A sudden pang of guilt shot through him, but he straightened his shoulders and it faded. I am sorry, Tani, he said to her silently. It is not true that I no longer care for you, but I could not see this opportunity go by. You are less important than the symbols of Egypt's stability. Akhtoy was hovering nearby and Ahmose crooked a finger at him. "Have another tent erected next to mine and summon my physician," he ordered. "And tell Hekayib to bring a jug of wine. This day promises to be very long."

He lay on his couch with the wine cup balanced on his naked chest, listening to the servants raising the other tent and carrying cot, table and chairs inside. He had opened his shrine, lit incense, and prostrated himself in thanksgiving to his god. He had also prayed that Tani would not be prevented from bringing him his prize. What if Apepa's sons objected or his Chief Wife Uazet threw herself on her husband and refused to let him go? But surely if the man was in such agony they would all be glad of a chance to see his pain relieved. What this might mean regarding the fate of Sharuhen itself he did not know. Nor did he care. Heart pounding erratically, he felt the culmination of his destiny come swiftly to a climax. The god had moved. The chain of events resulting from his action were up to the King.

It was evening before he heard the sounds for which he had been waiting. A swell of excited voices, the rattle of chariot wheels and the tramp of many feet brought him hurrying outside. Two curtained litters were being set down and Turi was dismissing his curious men. Tani was dismounting, and with a shake of the reins Mesehti turned the horses back towards their stalls. Tani did not look at Ahmose. Beckoning to several of the Followers, she drew back the first litter's drapery. At once the air was filled with the stench of rotting flesh. Several of the Followers flinched as they bent and lifted the pallet and its groaning burden within but Tani did not. Neither did Ahmose.

The physician and his assistant were waiting by the cot. Gently the Followers laid Apepa down and withdrew. Tani collapsed into one of the chairs. The physician drew back the stained sheet, and in spite of himself Ahmose gave a cry. Apepa was naked but for a loincloth already soiled with his excrement. One leg was shaking and trembling uncontrollably. The other was an almost unrecognizable mess of weeping pus. Maggots were wriggling and crawling over the pieces of streaked bone protruding from the suppurating perforations and the odour in that enclosed space was now overpowering. Only the physician seemed unmoved. "Bring a bowl," he snapped at his assistant. "First we must pick off all these parasites. While I am doing that, you can get hot water to wash him." He already had the poppy ready. "You realize, Majesty, that he will die in a matter of hours," he said to Tani. "Nothing can be done for a fracture of this kind. Not even Egyptian physicians would have been able to save him. All I can offer him is the blessing of unconsciousness." She swallowed and nodded, her features twisted with grief.

Ahmose stepped closer, trying to find a point of affinity between his memory of Apepa's face and the contorted image on the pillow. The man whose likeness had been seared into his mind had been taller than most, with long, shapely legs and broad shoulders. His neck had been long also, almost too precarious to support a most un-Egyptian head of high cheekbones, a pointed chin, brown eyes set too close together and a mouth whose corners turned down to give him a sullen look. Laugh lines had fanned out across the temples. Ahmose remembered them vividly. But the face shiny with fever sweat, the mouth drawn back in a rictus of pain, the sunken eyes, bore no resemblance to the King draped in gold-shot linen and hung with jewels who had mounted the Throne he had brought with him to

Weset from Het-Uart and had sat in judgement over the family. This was a human being reduced to the condition of a wounded animal.

All at once Apepa's eyes opened. He was panting rapidly, each outward breath a whimper, but he was struggling to speak. Slowly he focused on Ahmose. In spite of Ahmose's revulsion he bent lower, seeing Tani grasp her husband's hand on the edge of his vision. "Ahmose Tao," Apepa whispered. "Little did I know on that day when you stood before me in Weset what forces of bitterness and desperate obstinacy I was releasing with the pronouncement of my sentence against you and your family. I have paid dearly for my blindness."

"So did my father and my brother, Awoserra Apepa," Ahmose replied. "So did a great many Egyptians. It has been a bloody and vicious few years."

"And now you are King. I underestimated both your pride and your perseverance. My gods have deserted me. They have left me to die in your tent like an unwanted beast. I fled to Sharuhen but I am back in Egypt. I am back in Egypt!" His voice trailed away into a series of cries and mumbles and his eyes rolled back in his head. Ahmose straightened.

"Give him the poppy if he can swallow it," he ordered. The assistant was behind him with the bowl. Ahmose stepped away. He did not think that his stomach would allow him to watch the maggots being caught without rebelling in disgust. Holding his breath, he left the tent.

Turi and his soldiers were still clustered protectively around the second litter. Ahmose strode to it, taking in deep breaths of the warm, unscented air as he went. He nodded once and the curtains were pulled open. The red light of the westering sun struck the Horus Throne, turning its gold to fire. A ripple of amazement ran through the men. Some of them knelt. "Lift it out," Ahmose ordered. Several soldiers raised it gingerly, set it on the ground, and hastily stepped away. Two boxes lay on its seat. Ahmose hesitated before exposing their contents, then gathering his courage he opened the first. The Double Crown lay beneath his gaze, the smooth, conical white hedjet of Upper Egypt glowing a delicate pink with the red deshret beside it. He touched them reverently.

"It is the pshent," Turi exclaimed in awe. Ahmose could not answer. His heart was too full. Lovingly he opened the second. Banded in gold and lapis the heka and the nekhakha nestled in their beds, bathed in Ra's scarlet glory. Scarcely able to believe that they were there before him, Ahmose traced their shapes with one adoring finger.

"The Crook of Mercy and the Flail of Justice," he breathed. "Amun, I thank you for these gifts though they come in the midst of pain and death. I pray that I may always be worthy to wield them, remembering that though I am your Incarnation I myself am but a servant of Ma'at."

He did not sit on the Throne. The temptation never crossed his mind. It was neither the time nor the place and the beautiful chair itself seemed to forbid him to do so. But hungrily he scrutinized every intricate detail: the turquoise and lapis wings of Isis and Neith on the gold of its sides where the goddesses raised their arms to protect and enfold the King, the backrest of finely tooled gold inlaid with jasper and carnelian made into the likeness of the stool of wealth and the staff of eternity from which many ankhs hung, the mighty Eye of Horus at the rear and the snarling lions' muzzles on which his hands would lie. "Turi," he called, his voice thick with emotion. "Have these things packed securely and escorted to Weset with a suitable number of troops to guard them. See me when you are ready to go. I will dictate a scroll to the Queen to go with them." He thought of the room in the new palace where the Throne would sit on its lordly dais, its aura of power and splendour filling the awesome space, the light of dozens of lamps sparkling in the traceries of pyrite on the lapis floor and being magnified by the golden walls. He could not quite believe that all the symbols of his kingship were here, sitting on the uneven gravel of a foreign desert, exuding a dignity that rendered their poor setting completely insignificant. For some minutes he simply stared at them, unwilling to move out of the circle of their mute influence, and he stumbled when finally he turned away and took the few steps into his tent.

Suddenly hungry, he asked Akhtoy to bring him food, and he had just finished his meal when the physician was announced, a faint odour of decay wafting with him. The man bowed. "The patient has fallen into a coma," he told Ahmose. "He will not wake again, I think. I could not help him, Majesty. I am sorry."

"Stay with him though and have more poppy ready in case he does become conscious," Ahmose said. "I promised Queen Tautha that he would be cared for until he dies." The physician heard the hint of a query in his words.

"I will be very surprised if he survives until dawn," he offered. "He is rotting even before his ka leaves his body. He does not look strong but he has a great determination to live."

"That is strange considering he has lost everything." Ahmose paused. "Thank you. You are dismissed. Send the Queen to me."

It was some time before Tani was admitted. Dusk was falling and Hekayib had trimmed and lit the lamp, removed Ahmose's sandals and kilt, and helped him into a sleeveless tunic before taking up his post outside. Ahmose saw her approach him with a concern which he hid. She looked exhausted, her eyes hollowed, her lips pale. "Come and sit," he said. "You need sleep, Tani. Are you hungry? Let me pour you some wine." She found a chair, took the cup from him listlessly and sat staring into the depths of the liquid as though she was not sure what it was.

"The physician told me that he will be dead by morning," she said tonelessly. "I am bereft, Ahmose. Without him I am utterly adrift. To the Setiu I am an Egyptian foreigner and to Egyptians I am a woman who has relinquished her birthright. He loved and protected me. What can I do now?" He eyed her cautiously. She was not usually given to self-pity.

"What do you want to do?" he asked noncommittally. "I presumed that you would take his body back inside Sharuhen and rejoin his family there." Her head shot up.

"Take him back inside Sharuhen?" she repeated as though he had said something insane. "But, Ahmose, he must have a fully royal Egyptian burial!"

"What?" He set his cup down on the table with such force that the wine slopped over his hand. Roughly he shook off the drops. "Will you add blasphemy to your foolishness, Tani? The man not only came from a long line of usurpers but he was Setiu. A foreigner. Let his own people burn him or dig a hole for him or whatever the inhabitants of Rethennu do with their corpses. What is the matter with you? Have you lost your wits?" He had spoken as though Apepa were dead already, and Tani's mouth set in a thin line.

"You have no choice," she said calmly. "If you refuse him a royal interment, you will be casting doubt upon your own divinity."

"How so?" He wiped his fingers on his tunic with quick, fierce movements. If grief is poisoning her mind, she will come under the special protection of the gods, he was thinking. As a madwoman her person will be sacrosanct and I can take her home and end this absurdity. Everyone at Weset will pity her for living among the Setiu so long that she has become unhinged. Oh, Tani, to see you sitting laughing on the verge of the pool with your bare feet dangling among the waterlilies and Ahmose-onkh beside you! She had taken a judicious sip of her own wine and he noticed critically that her hand was trembling.

"It is like this," she went on. "You are a King by right of lineage, are you not?" He nodded. "And I am a fully royal Princess. The right of legitimization passes through the female blood, not the male, Ahmose. You married Aahmes-nefertari, also a fully royal Princess. You had to in order to become eligible for divinity. Apepa married me. That made him a fully royal Egyptian King." Rage boiled up in him and he clenched his fists.

"How dare you suggest that Apepa had any claim upon the throne of Egypt at all!" he shouted. "I wait for Amun to strike you dumb! Does all that the family has been through mean nothing to you? When did your Egyptian soul desert you in shame and leave a Setiu ka to slither into its place?"

"He was not so until he married me," she said loudly, emphatically, cutting across the explosion of his anger. "But as soon as I signed that contract, Apepa became a rightful King of Egypt. If you refuse him the full honours due to such a King, you will be calling your own legitimacy into doubt." Ahmose sat back. All at once he had gone cold.

"You whore," he whispered. "I see the logic in your argument but it is evil, perverse." Her face puckered but she did not cry. "I will do anything to ensure that his ka is not annihilated," she said passionately. "He is a good man, Ahmose. A kind man. If the Setiu bury him, our gods will not recognize or acknowledge him, and that I could not bear! I want him to reach the fields of Osiris and sit under the sycamore tree in peace for all eternity! I am ruthless in this desire!"

A soft tongue of admiration licked him briefly. She may be Setiu but the blood of her stubborn grandmother surges through her veins, he thought. And she is right. To fling Apepa onto a dung heap somewhere is to deny her royalty and my divinity. Damn you, Tani!

"He cannot be beautified," he reminded her crisply. "There is no House of the Dead here, no sem-priests, no natron enough for embalming. He rots even as he dies, and when he dies the process of putrefaction will be swift."

She answered him eagerly, obviously sensing victory. "He can be packed in sand and transported quickly to Het-Uart," she urged. "There is a House of the Dead in the city, built for the Egyptians who lived within its walls. Surely the sem-priests are still there! They could do something, and then I could lay him in the tomb outside Het-Uart with his ancestors."

The irony was not lost on Ahmose. Moodily he tipped more wine into his cup.

"Supposing that I agree to this ... this travesty," he said. "I will allow you to travel with him, but not the rest of his family. I want no Setiu Princes loose again in Egypt."

She drank, twirled her cup between her fingers, and raising it to her breast she held it there like a shield. "I do not care if you leave them here," she said woodenly. "I only care about Apepa. His family never truly accepted me. His Chief Wife was jealous and his sons treated me with barely concealed disdain. Now they have repudiated me altogether for lowering myself so far as to beg for your help. They wanted him to die like a warrior."

"Warriors do not die by falling down a set of stairs," he retorted caustically. "Congratulations, Tani. It seems that you have managed to earn the contempt of Egyptian and Setiu alike. That is quite a feat."

She flushed. "You are cruel, Ahmose," she half-whispered. "Do you also hold me in derision?"

The soft tongue of pity licked him briefly. "No," he said more gently. "You have sold the pride in your blood and heritage you once had and for that I can no longer respect you, but you are still my sister. There is still the affection of one family member for another."

"Cold comfort," she murmured. "But I suppose it must be enough."

"Enough? It is a great deal considering the depths of self-ishness and stupidity to which you have fallen!" he snapped, his moment of compassion gone. "Now tell me of Apepa's sons. I need to know what they are like." He saw the question in her eyes and the caution which forbade her to give it voice.

"He has several by his concubines," she said, "but only two by his legitimate wife Uazet. Apepa the Younger and Kypenpen. Kypenpen is very like his father in temperament, mild and intelligent, but Apepa the Younger is arrogant, brash and impulsive. Before my husband had the fall that has destroyed him, his elder son pestered him constantly to confront your army, issue challenges, open the gates and fight. It was a ludicrous idea and Apepa knew it, but he could not silence his son's loud importuning. I do not like Apepa the Younger, and he has hated me for being your sister."

"Why was the idea ludicrous?" Ahmose pressed. Something in his tone alerted her and she closed her mouth, fixing her gaze on the tip of her sandals under the folds of her patterned robe. "Let me guess," he went on slowly. "Could it have been because Sharuhen is mostly full of common citizens and its garrison is very small? Rethennu as a whole is decidedly denuded of soldiers. My army killed most of them when they ventured into the Delta. Am I right?" She continued to stare at her feet without answering. Ahmose regained his chair and crossed his legs. "Look at me!" he demanded sharply. Reluctantly she met his eyes. "I am willing to command a royal burial for your husband," he said. "A box full of sand will be waiting outside his tent within the hour. As soon as he expires, you will set out with him to Het-Uart and I will give you a scroll to General Sebek-khu giving you permission to go to the House of the Dead, mourn formally for seventy days, and engage whatever High Priest you can find to perform all the necessary rites before the tomb of Apepa's ancestors. Then you are banished. You are never to return to Egypt. If you do, you will be killed. I will instruct Abana to arrange passage for you to Keftiu with sufficient gold to enable you to live comfortably. Marry again if you choose. In return you will tell me how many troops are stationed inside Sharuhen."

She had gone very still while he was speaking. Even her breathing became almost imperceptible. But her eyes were fixed on his face with a persistent intensity.

"And if I refuse?" she whispered.

He shrugged. "Then I will have your husband's body burned as soon as he is dead and I will imprison you at Weset for the crime of treason."

"Ahmose!" she burst out. "You would not!"

"Yes, I would," he replied with cold force. "Make up your mind now, Tani. The night passes."

"What a magnificent choice," she said bitterly. "What glorious alternatives. Damn my husband's ka to annihilation or betray my benefactor the Chieftain of Sharuhen and go into exile. How merciful you are, Son of the Sun, upholder of Ma'at! How benign! Once more you have rubbed salt into a wound already throbbing with unbearable pain. Very well." She rose, drawing her robe around her with graceful, regal gestures. "The garrison within Sharuhen holds no more than five thousand soldiers. They are well armed but not well disciplined. They are certainly no match for your army, as Apepa knew when he refused to listen to his son's rash pleading. But they will not come out, Ahmose. The Chieftain will not release them."

"Who rules in Sharuhen?" Ahmose urged. "Does the Chieftain or his brother to whom he gave sanctuary?"

"The Chieftain will bow to Apepa the Younger's authority," she admitted. "Now let me return to my husband's bedside. I hope we will not meet again." She did not wait for a dismissal. Gliding to the tent flap with head down, she left him.

I refuse to feel ashamed, he told himself sternly. I did what I had to do. I did more for her than many in my position would have done. Perhaps one day she will realize that my own choices were as limited and terrible as hers, and she will forgive me. Going to the tent opening, he shouted for Khabekhnet, and when the herald appeared and bowed, he issued his instructions. "I want a coffin full of sand for Apepa delivered at once," he said. "See the Scribe of Distribution about it. Tell General Turi that as well as the Throne he will be escorting Queen Tautha and her husband's corpse as far as the Delta. Send Ipi here at once and then find Prince Abana if he has returned."

It did not take long for Ipi to appear, settle his palette across his knees, and prepare to take the dictation. Ahmose composed a letter to Aahmes-nefertari regarding the recovery of the Throne. He could not avoid describing Tani's part in it but he did so as tactfully as possible, his mind filling with a vision of his wife and his beautiful little boy. The sanity of their images served to calm him, and he finished the letter to Sebek-khu at Het-Uart in a more collected mood.

Abana was already waiting by the time Ahmose had finished, and bidding Ipi stay and record the conversation, he invited his Admiral to enter. Abana bowed and took the chair Ahmose offered. His weeks at sea had etched a few lines more deeply into his face and turned his brown skin even darker, but he filled the tent with an aura of well-being and masculine vitality that Ahmose drank in with gratitude. "The shipments of water are to cease in three days," Ahmose told him. "Before they do, I want you to fill every barrel we have. I am withdrawing the army."

"So I hear." Abana stretched out his legs, crossed them at the ankles, and regarded his King speculatively. "But the army will not need so much water to simply march to the Delta where there is plenty. Your Majesty has a plan." Ahmose smiled at him.

"I have indeed. I have learned that the garrison inside Sharuhen is small and the city itself is commanded by a very arrogant, very rash young man. I intend to take three of my five divisions back to Egypt, leaving one in full view of Sharuhen and one hidden a few miles away behind the dunes to the west. I want you to become an infantry soldier for a while, Prince." Abana nodded equably.

"I am yours to command," he said. "This sounds intriguing. You will attempt to lure this stupid young man into pitched battle and, having persuaded him to come out, reinforce your troops and defeat him. Is Sharuhen to be sacked, even though Apepa is as good as dead?"

"You are the one who will entice him out of his stronghold," Ahmose said. "You have a way with impudence, Prince. Every day you will parade beneath the walls shouting insults. It is only a matter of time before the gates open." Abana looked thoughtful.

"How many troops does the fort have?" he wanted to know. "And who am I mocking?"

"Five thousand, which is why I will leave a full division, five thousand men, in plain sight and another five thousand secreted in the dunes. The man who will not be able to resist your challenge is Apepa's eldest son, Apepa the Younger." Abana's eyes narrowed.

"You cannot afford to let them live, can you, Majesty?" he said softly. "Apepa dies but his sons live on, a threat to everything you have accomplished. When the battle is over and I am victorious, I am to execute them?"

"In this I have no choice," Ahmose replied. "The soldiers may loot Sharuhen. They deserve it. But no citizen is to be murdered. I care only that Apepa the Younger and his brother Kypenpen are correctly identified and killed. Leave the children of Apepa's concubines alone. They have no claim to Egypt. Am I understood?"

"Perfectly," Abana assured him.

"There is one more thing," Ahmose went on. "My sister is to take ship to Keftiu after Apepa is buried. I have given her permission to conduct his funeral rites in Het-Uart but then she must leave Egypt. You have become acquainted with many Keftiu traders. Arrange a safe passage for her. I will give her a letter to the Keftian ruler." He could see one conjecture follow another behind Abana's alert, dark eyes. I do not have to explain any of this, he thought with relief. Abana is astute enough to reach his own conclusions regarding the source of my information and how I bartered for it. "She will mourn for the full seventy days," he finished. "Surely in that time you will have humbled Sharuhen and returned to the Delta. Take any of Apepa's officials with you. They will provide Tani with company on her journey and form the core of her new household when she arrives."

"The Keftians and the Setiu have always respected one another," Abana said, rising. "You may trust me to do all as you would wish, Majesty."

"Good. Then you are dismissed."

He went to his couch early but he could not sleep. No sounds came to him from the tent next door, but he was preternaturally aware of what it contained and his mind insisted on supplying exaggerated pictures of the physician bending over Apepa's decaying form on one side and Tani on the other, both of them casting grotesque shadows on the tent walls. When his imagination supplied a third shadow, tall and sinister, he got up, wrapped himself in a cloak, and leaving his own tent he let himself quietly into the other.

The physician was dozing in a chair and Tani was asleep on her stool beside the couch, one arm stretched across her husband's shallow chest, her head resting on the pillow next to his. Unconsciousness had erased the evidences of weariness and sadness from her face and in the dim lamp-light Ahmose saw again the young, unsullied girl she had been. He wanted to go up to her and stroke the dishevelled hair back from her brow, murmur words of reassurance and comfort, but instead he sank to the floor just inside the entrance and watched her.

The physician had been roused by Ahmose's small noises. Yawning, he stood and bowed. "His breathing has become very faint and erratic, Majesty," he said in a low voice. "It is a matter now of moments, not hours." Ahmose nodded and put a finger to his lips. The physician moved back to his chair.

Ahmose was woken by Tani's cry. She had overturned the stool and was half-sitting, half-lying on the couch, Apepa cradled in her arms, rocking him and wailing. Finding himself curled up on the floor of the tent, Ahmose struggled blearily to his feet. The physician was tidying away his phials and spoons. "Give me leave to go to my quarters, Majesty," he said. "It has been a long night. I will see that the bed linen is burned in the morning." Ahmose waved his permission and turned to Tani, intending to say some word, make some gesture of commiseration, but he hesitated. She was oblivious to all but her grief, her eyes closed, her whole body mutely shouting her pain as the tent filled with her keening. Nothing I could say or do would be sincere, Ahmose thought. I am glad he is dead, and any expression to the contrary would be a lie. He slipped away as noiselessly as he had come.

He sent a warning to Turi to be ready to set out at once, but he gave Tani another hour to exhaust the first hysterical outpouring of her grief before allowing Apepa's body to be carried out and put in the sand-filled coffin. By the time she emerged, swollen-eyed but silent, the box had been fastened shut and loaded onto an ox cart, the Throne and Regalia occupied another, and Makhu had a chariot waiting for her. Turi and the escort stood waiting also, their faces solemn in the leaping orange light of the torches. Ahmose went to her, but she strode past him without a glance, stepped up into the chariot, and arranged herself on its floor. At Ahmose's signal Turi called a command, the soldiers formed ranks, and the cavalcade began to move. Ahmose strained after it until the flare of the torches was no more than a vanishing flicker, then he began to walk away. "Go to bed, Akhtoy," he said over his shoulder. "I shall not need you until sunrise."

He kept walking, tripping occasionally on the uneven ground, through the neat rows of the army's tents, past the horses' stalls, past the stores of grain, until he came to the outer perimeter of the camp. He was challenged and he answered. He could feel the sentry's curious gaze on his back but he went on. At last he realized that he was beyond sight or sound of his host and he came to a halt. The moon was setting, a pale, misshapen disc about to sink into the ocean far to the west. It gave no light but the stars were a crowded white glory flung wide above his head and all around him the desert lay peacefully still. Not even the air was stirring.

There was the vague hump of a rock close by. Ahmose sat down and rested his forehead on his knees. It is over, he thought. It is really over. He felt something give way inside him at the words, like a tight band tearing loose, and suddenly he was weeping, hot tears sprinkling his feet, sobs rising from some place long frozen deep within his soul, and he did not stop until the last vestige had shattered, melted, and been washed away.

17

DAWN WAS BREAKING when Ahmose returned to his tent. Before he washed or ate, he summoned Khabekhnet. "Appoint four heralds to stand beneath the city's four walls and call Apepa's death at noon, at mid-afternoon, and at sunset," he ordered. "Have them say, 'This night Awoserra Apepa was gathered to his gods.' There is no need for offence. We must consider the grief of his family." He saw Khabekhnet quickly scanning his face before dropping his gaze and retreating and he realized that the marks of his weeping must still be evident. So be it, he thought, as Hekayib shouldered his way into the tent with a bowl of steaming, scented water and a vial of oil. Let my people see that a King may be human enough to shed tears while still holding over them the ultimate authority of a god. Hekayib removed the rumpled tunic and began to bathe away the rigours of the night. The water felt good on Ahmose's skin, refreshing and cleansing, and it came to him that the water of his tears had also cleansed him, scouring his heart and mind free of every invisible accretion laid slowly on them by the years of tension and pain.

He spent the morning being driven through the camp. The soldiers had already received word that they would be leaving and he was cheered as he passed. In the afternoon he met with the generals, outlining his plan to them carefully and emphasizing Abana's role. "The Division of Amun and Division of Ra will accompany me home to Weset," he told them. "Ptah will be disbanded temporarily, but do not tell your men yet, Akhethotep. They must still march back to Egypt sober and in good order." His men laughed. "You, Baqet, will keep the Division of Thoth here in full sight of Sharuhen, and you, Meryrenefer, will appear to leave but you will deploy your men on battle alert behind the dunes. Keep them well hidden but ready to respond when Baqet sends word that Apepa the Younger has opened the gates. I have decided to station you permanently at Khemmenu when this is over, Baqet. I will send word to Ramose to begin building barracks there for the soldiers and their families. One division still in the Delta will also be disbanded, subject to immediate recall if necessary, and the other will continue to guard the Horus Road and man the forts of the Wall of Princes. Sebek-khu will eventually take permanent control of Het-Uart and Khety will take his division to their new home at Mennofer. Thus the whole of Egypt will have a military protection. Are there any questions or objections?"

"What of the Medjay, Majesty?" Hor-Aha asked testily. "They have been your faithful allies since your father's day. Will you send them back to the nothingness of Wawat?" Ahmose glanced at him quizzically.

"You fear the nothingness of Wawat, General?" he asked evenly. "But do not worry. The Medjay have their village on the west bank at Weset. They are not forgotten and their long service will be rewarded. All of you," he said raising his voice. "All of you will be rewarded. Without you the sun would be rising each day on a very different Egypt. Without your presence my crowning will be a poor event indeed. I shall send you word as soon as the astrologers have chosen a propitious time." They looked at him blankly. Then Kagemni snorted.

"How stupid we are, my friends!" he exclaimed. "Apepa is dead, the Horus Throne is on its way to Weset, the fighting is all done. It is all done! Wake up! Egypt will rejoice in a true Incarnation. We have endured and we have the victory!" Roars of laughter and an explosion of chatter followed his speech, and Hor-Aha leaned close to Ahmose.

"They knew but did not know," he commented. "Full understanding did not strike them until you mentioned your crowning. Will they settle well to peace, do you think?" Ahmose met the man's black eyes.

"Peace is only maintained through a watchful strength," he replied. "Egypt has learned this tragic lesson well. She will not forget, and neither will they." He scanned the noisy, delighted men around the table. "Your bow may hang on a wall and your dagger only leave its sheath to dispatch a hyena, Hor-Aha, but you and they will still be Egypt's defence. Be assured that the knowledge will never be far from my mind."

On the morning of the fourth day the divisions rose, shouldered packs, tightened belts and sandals, and marched away from Sharuhen, leaving Baqet and his five thousand men ranked rather forlornly in the littered waste they had left. The city bulked like some vast monster behind them and on every side the stony desert ran away, shimmering malevolently in the heat. There had been no acknowledgement of the heralds' cries but men had appeared briefly above the walls before vanishing again with ghostly speed. Ahmose, sparing one swift glance behind him at the standard of Thoth framed bravely against those uncompromising bastions, prayed that even its memory might eventually be erased from his mind.

In eight days his forces were making camp again, this time around Het-Uart. The Division of Osiris had obediently left the main body of the army once Sharuhen was out of sight and had dug itself into the base of the dunes a little more than five miles from the city. The three remaining divisions had moved on rapidly, optimism lending speed to their feet, and the journey had been uneventful.

Outside Het-Uart, Ahmose sent Kagemni and the Division of Ra on to Weset together with the Medjay. He dismissed Akhethotep and the Division of Ptah amid the soldiers' wild rejoicing and saw the Division of Horus under General Khety march south to Mennofer. All he had left was the Division of Amun, less the contingent that had escorted Tani and then gone on to Weset, and Sebek-khu whose men were still busily engaged in tearing down Het-Uart's walls. Although he reminded himself many times that the years of war were over, that no more blood would be shed in Egypt, that the need for vigilance was past, he felt naked and defenceless. He also felt oddly purposeless. The end had come so quickly, a sudden halt that saw the constant apprehension that had always tautened his body and his heart alleviated, that his mind still ran ahead to the next battle, the next military decision to be made.

He had his tent set up outside Het-Uart. He had no desire to enter the city, although from where he sat in the stifling evenings he could now see far beyond the truncated remains of its defences to its narrow streets and cramped houses. They seemed alive again with soldiers, new citizens and old, dogs, donkey carts and grubby children who squatted in the dirt. He could even catch a glimpse of the Temple of Sutekh and regretted his decision to allow it to stand. He had met with Sebek-khu who had told him that Tani was living in an anteroom of the temple. Apepa had been taken to a House of the Dead, and Sebek-khu himself had coerced a priest of Ra from Iunu to perform the funeral ceremony when the period of mourning was over. "I trust I did the right thing, Majesty," the General had said apologetically. "The priest was most reluctant to help your sister. He was afraid that in granting the usurper the blessing of an Egyptian burial he would be incurring your wrath."

"You did well," Ahmose told him. "And is the Queen in good health?"

"She seems so," Sebek-khu had admitted. "She seldom leaves the temple. I have appointed a guard and a servant for her. Would you like an officer to bring her to you?" Ahmose had considered but declined.

"No. Send me word when Apepa goes to his tomb. I will see her then."

He was content to wander along the tributary, now filling gradually with the power of the Inundation, enjoying the song of birds and the welcome shade of the river growth with Ankhmahor and the Followers. He sat with them in the evenings drinking wine and reminiscing, a luxury they could all afford now that no danger threatened them. He lay on his couch through the dark hours, listening peacefully to the quiet rumble of Het-Uart, a sound composed of so many familiar elements that reminded him of his home.

He had requested sentries to be posted at strategic points along the nearer end of the Horus Road, more from habit than from necessity, and he had not withdrawn the scouts in Rethennu in case Abana or Meryrenefer needed to communicate urgently with him, but he found his mind at last slowing, rejoining the growing relaxation of his body and heart, and he knew there would never again be any sudden alarm to rouse him to some dire necessity in the middle of the night.

The beginning of the new year had been celebrated a day after Ahmose arrived in the Delta, and with it the month of Thoth. The heat continued on into Paophi, not as intense as it was in the south but more uncomfortable because of the Delta's humidity. On the fourth day of Paophi, Abana, General Baqet and General Meryrenefer came striding towards Ahmose where he was sitting by the water lazily contemplating the rush and gurgle of the current. He rose and greeted them warily, unable to read any news from their faces. They accepted his offer of stools with alacrity. "The Sea of Reeds is already becoming difficult to negotiate, Majesty," Baqet said, almost snatching the cup of beer Akhtoy was holding out, and drinking thirstily. "We made less time than we had hoped and the men are covered in mosquito bites and mud. We did not stop to allow them to bathe once we struck the lakes of the Delta but they are splashing about in the canals now. How good it is to be back in Egypt!"

"I am pleased to see you," Ahmose answered. "What happened at Sharuhen?" It was Abana who told him. The other two had fallen silent.

"I performed outside the walls as rudely as you could have wished, Majesty," he began. "I thought I would enjoy taunting Apepa's son but I did not. As the days went by, I found myself shrinking from so ignoble a task. I dreamed of him weeping for the loss of his father. I developed a sore throat, not from shouting I believe but from guilt." He shot Ahmose a sombre glance. "It had to be done but it shamed me. When I get home to Nekheb, I shall purify myself in the goddess's sacred lake and offer her a sacrifice of atonement."

"I know," Ahmose said softly. "It was not a duty for an honest man, Prince, and I am truly sorry for the necessity."

"It worked though," Baqet cut in. "One morning the gates opened and the Setiu soldiers came tumbling out. Apepa the Younger was commanding them. They were disciplined enough for garrison troops but they were no match for us, and Apepa's son was no Pezedkhu. The Division of Thoth cut them down with ease. I had sent a runner to Meryrenefer as soon as I saw the gates move. When the Division of Osiris arrived and realized that I needed no assistance, it marched on into Sharuhen. By the time the skirmish was over, the city was in Egyptian hands."

"Speaking of which, I took a hand in the fight and two women from the fort," Abana said. "The hand was recorded by the Scribe of the Army. I hope you will let me keep the women. My wife will be sorry that the war is over, seeing that I am managing to provide her with a complete household through my captures." His tone was light, an attempt at humour, but Ahmose sensed the discomfiture behind it.

"Tell me the rest," he ordered. None of them spoke. Finally Meryrenefer cleared his throat.

"Prince Abana dragged Apepa in from the battlefield. He was screaming imprecations like an enraged woman. He resembled his father to a great degree, Majesty. Perhaps that made his execution a little easier." He looked hesitantly in Abana's direction but Abana was staring at the ground between his knees. "The Chieftain of Sharuhen was dead already, slain in the fight. In the centre of the city was a palace of sorts built of stone. All Apepa's family was there as well as many of his ministers. More escaped from Het-Uart than we had thought. You had commanded us to harm no one except Apepa and Kypenpen, but there were many children and young men gathered with the women and we did not know which was the younger prince. We were forced to … to … to injure one of the children before Kypenpen gave himself up."

"We tied a rope around its head and twisted it," Abana said hoarsely. "Egyptians do not torture babies. The poor little creature howled and cried. One of the young men came forward out of the sobbing crowd and identified himself as Kypenpen. We know it was he because his mother rushed after him screaming, 'No, Kypenpen, not you! Let the child die but not you!' We took him out into the garden with his brother and we cut off their heads. An officer took their hands and it was recorded. There are many beautiful gardens inside Sharuhen. One would not have thought it, given the desert outside."

"Then there was a day of looting," Meryrenefer said. "The soldiers have many lovely things and a few slaves to take home to their wives."

"Very well," he said firmly. "Meryrenefer, tomorrow you will disband the Osiris Division and you, Baqet, will take the Thoth to Khemmenu. I have already notified Prince Ramose of your coming. You are both dismissed." Hastily they emptied their cups, rose, and retreated. Ahmose turned to Abana. "I intend to muster the divisions once a year for refreshment training," he said. "Do you think this is a good idea?"

"Yes, Majesty," Abana responded woodenly, still gazing moodily out at the churning tributary. Pezedkhu's ring on its gold chain winked at Ahmose in the strong sunlight.

"I think I will leave half the navy in the Delta to earnits keep as transport for trade goods, take a quarter of the ships to Weset, and send a quarter down to Nekheb with you," Ahmose continued. "As my Admiral, does this meet with your approval?"

"Yes."

Ahmose reached across and prodded him gently. "You have too much pride, Abana," he chided him. "You regard yourself more highly than your King." For a moment his accusation had no effect but then Abana swung round, startled.

"You wound me, Majesty," he protested. "I am your most faithful servant. I have risked my life for you. I would die for you."

"Then how is it that you brood over the performance of your duty as though the command and its fulfilment were somehow your responsibility alone? Are you then the King?" The Prince's face fell. He began to smile faintly.

"You are possessed of much wisdom, Mighty Bull," he answered ruefully. "You are of course correct. Forgive my excessive arrogance."

"I have forgotten it already. Now tell me what Setiu you have brought with you." Abana straightened.

"Quite a few fish became entangled in our net," he commented. "My cousin Zaa is guarding them. They are sequestered in a very small tent." His smile widened. "You speak of arrogance, Majesty. These men are supremely arrogant and full of complaints. They grumbled all the way to Het-Uart. If it had not been for Your Majesty's explicit instructions, I would have been happy to abandon every one of them when we passed through the dunes and let the lions and hyenas have them. Zaa is more tolerant than I, which is why he is attempting to care for them. There is Itju, Apepa's Chief Scribe; Nehmen, his Chief Steward; Khian and Sakheta, both heralds; and Peremuah, the erstwhile Keeper of the Royal Seal. With their wives and children, I must add. I left Apepa's Chief Wife behind to bury her sons, and the concubines and their children also."

"Good," Ahmose said. "Tell Zaa to have his prisoners conducted to Queen Tautha's room in the temple. They are to be banished with her and they will provide a mourning party for Apepa. Your task now is to find a ship with a reliable captain to take them all to Keftiu once Apepa is entombed. Ipi will give you the necessary scrolls and gold. Then you will go home to Nekheb." Abana rose.

"But, Majesty, I had thought …"

"Do not think," Ahmose interrupted him mildly. "You need rest, my Prince. Take a quarter of the navy. Take your prisoners. Visit Nekhbet's temple. Prepare for the invitation you will receive to my coronation." All at once Abana knelt, and prostrating himself he pressed his lips to Ahmose's foot.

"You are a great god," he said huskily. "I love you, Ahmose." Then he scrambled up and bowed, and walked briskly away.

In the middle of Paophi the long celebration of the Amun-feast of Hapi began, when the god of the Nile was worshipped and thanked for his bounty. Ahmose, together with hundreds of his subjects, took to the rapidly rising water in his skiff and flung armfuls of flowers onto its surface, poured oil and wine into its frothing depths, and joined in the songs of adoration that rose from the throats of the vast throng and went echoing from bank to bank of the swelling tributary. Every day there was a different rite to be observed, new offerings to be made. It was one of the most beloved of all Egypt's religious observances and it continued to the twelfth day of the following month, Athyr. But on the ninth of Athyr, Ahmose received word that Apepa would go to his tomb the next morning and regretfully he prepared to withdraw from the ceremonies. It would be his last opportunity to see his sister, and whether she liked it or not, he wanted to be present.

He had not set foot in Het-Uart since his return but, surrounded by his Followers, he made his way through the maze of streets. The bodyguard cleared his way and Khabekhnet went ahead calling a warning but everyone wanted to see him and his progress was slow. People knelt as he passed, shouting his name. Children ran up to him despite the Followers' vigilance, thrusting wilting flowers or shiny pebbles at him, even attempting to hold his hands. He was amazed and humbled at the tide of love and admiration that surged around him. This belongs to you also, Kamose, he thought, deafened by the lively uproar. It is a homage to the House of Tao, all of us, for freeing them from the bondage of hentis. How Tetisheri would have enjoyed it!

Once he entered the district of the nobles, however, the crowd thinned. Here many officers had taken up residence and he was saluted as he went, until even they disappeared and the temple of Sutekh reared before him. Its forecourt had been cleared of the chaos he remembered. Looking to his left, he saw a vast stretch of reddish open ground where Apepa's palace and its protecting wall used to be. Only a few trees remained, swaying gracefully, their shade empty. He averted his eyes.

As before, he refused to enter Sutekh's domain. He waited quietly until he saw the procession emerge, first the priest of Ra with his acolytes holding smoking incense burners, then the red oxen of sacred custom drawing the sled on which Apepa's coffin lay, then Tani and the Setiu officials followed by the professional mourners. The coffin itself was of wood but it was lavishly decorated with gold and the eyes painted on its side had been delicately executed. Sebek-khu had obviously taken great pains to provide something suitable from a funerary storehouse in the city. Tani, dressed in mourning blue, was crying and the professional women, some fifty of them, were keening with high voices and casting on their heads the earth they had brought with them. No earth existed in Het-Uart, only beaten dirt as hard as the stones of Sharuhen. Ahmose made a mental note to make sure that Sebek-khu was reimbursed for the amount he must have had to pay to the women. The number of hired mourners reflected directly on the importance of the deceased.

The cavalcade skirted the temple and Ahmose joined it at the rear. It was not far to the tombs of Apepa's forebears. Behind the temple was a mausoleum entered through a gate which now stood open. Beyond it was a city in miniature, paved streets fronted by small houses that at first seemed ready to welcome their occupants to cooking fires and cushioned bedchambers, but as Ahmose passed the first set of tiny entrance pillars and glanced inside he saw that they were empty but for an offering altar. The noble Setiu dead rested under the floors. He did not like the way his footsteps came echoing back to him and the discordant wails of the women woke other wails that returned, thready and faint, like the answering voices of distant spirits being lured to the business of the living who had invaded their realm.

The priest halted at a house close to the end of the central row. Apepa's coffin was removed from the sled and stood upright. Ahmose, peering beyond it into the gloom, saw the deep hole into which the sarcophagus would be lowered, and shuddered. Armed with the pesesh-kef and the netjeri, the priest began the rites and Ahmose closed his eyes. Even the incense did not smell right in this strange place. It seemed to mingle with the odour of damp stone and earth that was never sweetened by the sun. He remembered the stench of Apepa's dying, and clenching his jaw he resigned himself to wait.

The convoluted, intricate rituals took a long time, but at last the coffin was carried inside the mortuary and the attendants gathered around to see it descend. Tani laid a bouquet on its lid, stood a moment in thought, then turned to Ahmose. He had not realized that she was aware of his presence. They eyed one another in the gloom. "I will not stay for the funeral feast," Ahmose said awkwardly. "I have discharged my bargain, Tani." He fumbled at his waist and drew a scroll from the pouch hanging there. "It is sealed with my name and titles," he told her as he handed it to her. "Give it to Keftiu's ruler. Prince Abana has seen to all the details of your journey. You will be perfectly safe and comfortable." She nodded. "I know you expressed the hope that we would never meet again," he stumbled on, "but I wanted to offer you such meagre support as I could on this day. And I had to say goodbye." Suddenly she stepped to him and, astounded, he felt her arms go around him.

"Dear Ahmose," she said brokenly. "We have each done what we had to do. You will be one of Egypt's mightiest Kings, I know it, and I also know that in spite of everything we still love one another. Please, let us also forgive one another and the gods who have decreed that we should live in this terrible age." She withdrew and kissed him softly on the mouth, giving him a taste of her salt tears. "Can we do that?"

"Yes," he replied, seeing her through a blur of his own. "Yes, dearest Tani, Queen Tautha. Dictate a letter to me sometimes. Tell me how you fare. If there is anything you lack and I am able to provide it, I will. Farewell."

He turned on his heel and left her, walking back along that haunted avenue lined with the bodies of those who had crafted the history of Egypt's occupation. They had begot one another in pride and indifference to the country they had enslaved until the last ruler of their House had dictated a letter to an insignificant princeling far away in the desert of the south and in so doing had created the catalyst for his own downfall.

It is finished, Ahmose thought. I have kept faith with you, Seqenenra my father. I have brought your struggle to fruition, Kamose, my beloved brother. I am justified before the gods. It is time to go home.

EPILOGUE

ALTHOUGH IT WAS EARLY and the sun had only just risen, crowds were already gathering to either side of the river road between the palace and the temple and the Nile was choked with small craft of every description. For some weeks the population of Weset had been growing as the day of the King's coronation drew near. Minor nobles and villagers alike from all over Egypt had left their homes and converged on the town, turning it into a noisy congestion. The mayor of Weset, Tetaky, had been forced to request troops from the Division of Amun to police the streets as fights broke out over food or living space, whether litters or donkeys had priority in the narrow alleys, and why only local stallkeepers should be allowed to choose the most favourable sites from which to ply their wares along the route the royal cavalcade would pass.

Ahmose had woken before dawn, and for the first time since the old palace was restored he mounted to the roof by way of the staircase he had ordered closed off and sealed. The wax adhering to the rope on the lower door broke easily under his touch, and as he pulled the door itself towards him and put his foot on the bottom step, he was aware of the musty, stale odour of disuse. The lamp he was carrying illumined the layers of dust, the cracks and rough pieces of broken brick, and he negotiated them carefully, one hand on the wall. He knew that in this place, above all others, his father and his brother were with him and he called to them softly as he went, begging them for their presence in the temple, their prayers and blessings on this momentous day. The upper door had been sealed from the inside. Again he crumbled the wax into which the imprint of his name had been pressed, and emerging at last, found himself above the quarters where his women lay, still deep in their slumbers.

The windcatcher against which his father had placed his back had been cleared of the rubble that had filled it and was once again funnelling the prevailing summer wind down into the palace, so Ahmose was forced to lower himself against its side, facing east. The sky held a faint rosy blush. Ra was about to be born out of the body of Nut. Hunching up his knees, Ahmose waited. He had intended to spend these precious few minutes in remembering his dear dead ones, contemplating the journey they had begun together and only he had been privileged to complete, meditating upon the ceremony that would empower him to become in truth the incarnation of his god, but with the settling of his body a profound joy began to steal over him so that he was unable to maintain a state of inner quietude.

The streak of pink along the horizon widened, deepened, and beneath it a yellow glow threw the edge of the desert into black relief. A wind sprang up. Down below in the gardens that now encircled the palace one bird sent out a piping cry. It was followed by others, and soon a musical harmony of song mingled with the steady, muted murmur of water spouting from the fountains into their stone basins. In the east a rim of fire shimmered, pulsed, and rays of light came racing towards Ahmose, bringing a storm of colours with it. He closed his eyes. Son of Ra, Son of the Morning, he thought. I am that also. Touch me with your golden fingers, Mighty One. I am held in the centre of Ma'at where I belong. This is my destiny, to be the axle around which the wheel of Egypt's equilibrium turns.

He had just blown out the now feeble flame of the lamp when a voice came muffled from the base of the stair. "Majesty, are you up there? It is time for you to go to the temple." Ahmose heaved himself up.

"Akhtoy, I have made you my Fanbearer on the Left Hand," he called back down. "You no longer need to concern yourself with these errands. Leave them to Royal Steward Hekayib and his assistants. Unless, of course, you think you did not train him well enough."

"I am sorry, Majesty," Akhtoy replied as Ahmose reached the bottom and pushed the door closed. "It is an old and precious habit, hard to break."

Just beyond the entrance pillars the litter bearers were waiting, Harkhuf and the Followers with them. Ahmose had greeted them and sat down when Hekayib came running after him. "The Queen and the Hawk-in-the-Nest are being dressed, Majesty," he panted, "and the Princes have already left their quarters." Ahmose nodded.

"Thank you, Hekayib, but you do not need to worry. Everyone will wait until I have gone. Go and eat something. You look strained." The bearers drew the curtains closed and lifted him. He heard Harkhuf bark a command to the guards on the gate and he was carried through. He spared a quick glance back through the drapes as the huge electrum doors were swung ponderously shut. They had been hung the day before he had returned from Het-Uart. He had seen them glinting like fire as his ship approached Weset and with a thrill of pride he had known that he would disembark at the watersteps, walk between them, and enter his new domain for the first time as its inhabitant.

The route to the temple was thickly lined with soldiers to keep the populace back. Ahmose could see nothing, but he could hear the excited speculations as his litter passed. He would return to the palace seated on the Horus Throne, Aahmes-nefertari beside him and Ahmose-onkh at his feet, fully crowned and robed and carried high so that his subjects could see him, but now, naked save for a loincloth, he must remain hidden.

The canal leading to the temple was also heavily guarded. No one but those invited would be allowed inside Amun's precinct, and Ahmose welcomed the stately silence that descended on him as he left the litter, directed the Followers to proceed inside and take up their stations, and walked alone to the sacred lake. Two priests were waiting for him. Stripping him of the loincloth, they led him down into the water, submerged him, and scrubbed him thoroughly with natron. They did not speak and neither did he. The solemnity of the occasion was beginning to creep over him and he submitted to their ministrations gravely.

With plain reed sandals on his feet he was escorted into an anteroom and shaved from his skull to his ankles, still in that same efficient but reverential silence. Only then did Amunmose appear. He was arrayed in the full panoply of his office: a white linen gown of the twelfth grade trimmed in gold, so gossamer fine that its folds trembled with his breath, a white ribbon encircling his head, the leopard skin draped across one shoulder and his gold-tipped staff of authority in his hand. An acolyte was with him. Passing the boy the staff, Amunmose wrapped a new loincloth around Ahmose, then taking him by the hand he guided him through into the inner court.

It was full of the multitude of his nobles, generals, courtiers and the foreign ambassadors, a sea of winking jewels, perfumed linens and kohl-rimmed, expectant eyes glimpsed through the sweet haze of dozens of smoking incense burners. He looked for his family first. Tetisheri and Aahotep were sitting against the opposite wall. His grandmother seemed like a statue, clothed entirely in a silver-leaved sheath covered by an embroidered silver cloak, her hair hidden under a cap of silver whose wings brushed her thin collarbones. Aahotep had chosen to wear scarlet linen hung all over with droplets of gold. Above her painted face the golden stool, symbol of the goddess Neith, rose like a solid crown. Heavy rings glimmered on her folded hands and ankhs adorned her wrists and neck. Tetisheri was staring straight ahead, obviously caught up in the extreme dignity of the moment, but his mother smiled at him briefly, her dark eyes lighting.

Ahmose turned towards the sanctuary. Its doors were folded back and within it Amun sat garlanded in flowers. Lamplight slid over the frills of his two plumes and the golden curves of his body like smooth oil. Other gods stood with him: the falcon-headed Ra with his sharp beak and black, beaded eyes; the vulture goddess Nekhbet of the south; and Wadjet, the cobra goddess of the north whose hood was spread and whose fangs were exposed, ready to spit poison at any threat that might come near the King.

Just outside the sanctuary the Horus Throne rested and

Aahmes-nefertari was herself enthroned beside it, her sheath sparking gold, her pectoral of gold and lapis scarabs netted in gold chains covering her breast, the wings and out-thrust head of Mut, wife of Amun and guardian of Queens, on her head. Mut's claws to either side of Aahmes-nefertari's painted cheeks grasped the shen sign signifying infinity, eternity and protection. Ahmose-onkh sat at her feet on a low stool. His youth lock was wound in gold ribbon sewn with tiny golden lotuses and papyri and a single Eye of Horus rested against his delicate ribs. Ahmose had given him matching gold bracelets, miniature copies of the silver armbands his generals wore, with his name and rank as Hawk-in-the-Nest etched on them, and he was engrossed in turning them proudly round and around his wrists.

The singers had burst into a chant. Following Amunmose, Ahmose approached the god and prostrated himself, lying prone on the floor and then crawling to kiss the golden feet. Rising, he faced the tightly packed throng. An acolyte was holding out two dishes, one of natron and one of water from the sacred lake. Amunmose wet his finger and dipping it into the natron, proceeded to anoint Ahmose on the forehead, eyelids, tongue, chest, hands and feet, murmuring the prayers of purification as he did so.

The figure of Ra stepped out from the sanctuary. In his hands he held a large ewer. His cruel, curved beak brushed Ahmose's ear as he raised the vessel high, and a cascade of cool water poured over Ahmose's head, ran down his belly, and pooled between his legs. "This is the cleansing power of Ra," the god called. "Your purification is complete." A priest came forward hurriedly with a cloth to dry Ahmose. The chant of the singers changed, swelled, and Amunmose lifted a cloth of gold kilt and a jewelled belt from the arm of one of his waiting priests. Wrapping the kilt around Ahmose's waist and fixing the belt in place, he said loudly, "Receive the garment of lucidity and the belt of courage."

"Lucidity and courage belong to the god," Ahmose responded. "I receive them as his son." Next a jewelled cape was laid around his shoulders. It was very heavy and Ahmose instinctively straightened his spine in order to bear its weight.

"Receive the mantle of authority," Amunmose intoned and Ahmose answered obediently,

"Authority belongs to the god. I receive it as his son." Amunmose indicated the Throne and at last Ahmose sank onto it and laid his hands along the lions. He felt his fingers briefly enclosed. Aahmes-nefertari was looking across at him and smiling tremulously. "Egypt will honour you as her salvation through every age," she whispered. "I want to cry but my kohl will run if I do. I love you, my King." Amunmose was kneeling, the sandals in his grasp. Made of gold leaf, set with lapis and jasper, they had once been painted with a likeness of Apepa on each sole so that Ahmose might crush his enemy as he walked, but Ahmose had requested that it be expunged. He had no desire to trumpet his vengeance on this day.

"Receive the sandals of wisdom," Amunmose pronounced.

"Wisdom belongs to the god," Ahmose replied. "I receive it as his son."

He was adorned with a pectoral his mother had commissioned, a great square of gold representing a sacred kiosk inlaid with carnelian, lapis and turquoise depicting the

Lake of Heaven on which a solar barque sailed. Falcons flew over it to left and right and in its centre Ahmose stood while Ra and Amun poured streams of libation over him. A gold and turquoise bracelet, also a gift from Aahotep, was fastened around his forearm. It was hinged in two parts. On the right Ahmose was shown being crowned by Geb, God of the Earth, and on the left Seqenenra and Kamose knelt in the jackal masks of the dead, their arms raised in ecstasy. Deeply moved, Ahmose kissed it.

Now Ipi came forward, crouched low. Ahmose had appointed him Overseer of Protocol and Guardian of the Royal Regalia. He was sorry to lose the man's skill as a scribe, but he felt that Ipi deserved recognition for his trustworthiness. Laying his two charges before the Throne, Ipi opened them, bowed to them and to Ahmose, and retired. The two goddesses who had remained in the sanctuary now came gliding forward and the singers fell silent. A hush fell over the assembly. Out of one chest the goddess Wadjet removed the Red Crown. Setting it solemnly on Ahmose's head she called, "Receive the deshret and rule the Red Land unto millions of years." Leaning forward she kissed first the crown and then Ahmose's forehead. Nekhbet already had the White Crown in her hands. Placing it gently inside the Red Crown she said, "Receive the hedjet and rule the Black Land unto millions of years." After making her obeisance, both she and Wadjet removed the Uraeus, the cobra and the vulture, from its bed and sank it into its niche in the centre of the Red Crown. "Receive the Lady of Dread and the Lady of Flame," they chorused together. "Death to your enemies and a shield to Your Majesty."

The final act was again performed by Amunmose.

Placing the Crook and the Flail in Ahmose's hands, he flung
up his arms in triumph. "Behold Uatch-Kheperu Ahmose,
Son of the Sun, Horus, the Horus of Gold, He of the Sedge
and Bee, He of the Two Ladies, the Mighty Bull of Ma'at,
God in Egypt!" he shouted. "Life, Health and Prosperity to
him forever!" Ahmose rose, and the Queen with him. At
once the temple exploded into a roaring tumult. The singers
sang. The dancers swayed. Shouts of acclamation resounded
to the roof. Ahmose waited but the noise did not abate. It
continued to rise, thrilling and deafening, until he raised the
Crook and Flail and held it over the host. Then every knee
bent, every forehead touched the ground, and Ahmose and
his family walked slowly through the ocean of adoration and
out into the blinding sunlight of a summer day.

Ahmose was carried back to the palace on an hysterical
tide of enthusiasm, high above the seething, yelling people.
Ankhmahor stood beside him as his Fanbearer on the Right
Hand and Akhtoy held the ostrich fan on his left. Ahmose-
onkh leaned against his calf and waved happily at the
crowd. Aahmes-nefertari was following on her own throne
behind them, with Tetisheri and Aahotep behind her in
uncurtained litters. Harkhuf and the Followers together
with Khabekhnet strode imperiously ahead. It would take a
long time for the rear of the straggling procession to reach
the reception hall where the guests would feast for the rest
of the day and far into the night. As the palace hove into
view and the gates were swung open, Ahmose glanced up.

Two figures were watching him from the roof of the
palace. One was sitting with his back against the opening
of the new windcatcher which was, Ahmose thought bewil-
deredly, impossible. The other was standing with his arms

folded, gazing pensively out over the glittering expanse of the Nile to the line of rugged cliffs on the west bank. Ahmose blinked, then looked again. The roof was empty, of course it was, baking in the noon heat.

The bearers set him down, and at once Ipi was issuing orders to his assistants to remove the Horus Throne to its accustomed place inside on the dais and holding out one of the chests so that Ahmose could lay in it the Crook and the Flail. Aahmes-nefertari came close, slipping her arm through his. "Chief Treasurer Neferperet tells me that there are literally mountains of gifts about to be formally presented to you from foreign ambassadors and your grateful nobles," she said. "I know that this is a very sacred and important day, Majesty, but it is also fun, is it not?" He smiled and kissed her hennaed mouth.

"Indeed it is," he answered lightly. "Shall we go to the nursery and worship our son before parading into the reception hall for our own share of veneration?" Ahmose-onkh was tugging at his kilt.

"Majesty Father, the frogs have not yet found their way into the new pool," he complained. "Some of them have, but the big ones, my favourites, are very slow." Ahmose ran a loving hand over the boy's brown skull and down the thick youth lock.

"The kerer are symbols of rebirth," he said. "Be patient with them. They will come when they are ready. There is a perfect time for everything within the omniscience of Ma'at. Now let us go in." The shade beneath the pillars was inviting. Hand in hand, the three of them left the brilliance of the courtyard and made their way into the coolness of the palace beyond.

SELECT BIBLIOGRAPHY

BOOKS

Aldred, Cyril. *Jewels of the Pharaohs: Egyptian Jewelry of the Dynastic Period*. rev. ed. London: Thames and Hudson Ltd. 1978.

Aldred, Cyril. *The Egyptians*. rev. ed. London: Thames and Hudson, 1987.

Baikie, James. *A History of Egypt: From the Earliest Times to the End of the xviii Dynasty*. Vol 1 and 2. Freeport, New York: Books for Libraries Press, 1971.

Baines, John, and Jaromir Malek. *Atlas of Ancient Egypt*. New York: Facts on File, 1987.

Bietak, Manfred. *Avaris, the Capital of the Hyksos: Recent Excavations at Tell el-Daba*. London: British Museum Press, 1996.

Breasted, James H. *A History of Egypt: From the Earliest Times to the Persian Conquest*. New York: Charles Scribner's Sons, 1905.

Breasted, James H. *Ancient Records of Egypt*. Vol. 2 and 4. London: Histories & Mysteries of Man Ltd., 1988.

Bryan, Cyril P. *Ancient Egyptian Medicine: The Papyrus Ebers*. Chicago: Ares Publishers Inc., 1930.

Budge, Wallace E.A. *A History of Egypt: from the End of the Neolithic Period to the Death of Cleopatra VII. B.C. 30*. Vol. 3, *Egypt under the Amenemhats and Hyksos*. Oosterhout: Anthropological Publications, 1968.

Budge, Wallace E.A. *An Egyptian Hieroglyphic Dictionary*. Vol 1 and 2. rev. ed. New York: Dover Publications, Inc., 1978.

Budge, Wallace E.A. *Egyptian Magic*. London: Routledge & Kegan Paul, 1986.

Budge, Wallace E.A. *Legends of the Egyptian Gods: Hieroglyphic Texts and Translations*. New York: Dover Publications, Inc., 1994.

Budge, Wallace E.A. *The Mummy: A Handbook of Egyptian Funerary Archaeology*. New York: Dover Publications, Inc., 1989.

Cottrell, Leonard. *The Warrior Pharaohs*. New York: G.P. Putnam's Sons, 1969.

David, Rosalie. *Mysteries of the Mummies: The Story of the Manchester University Investigation*. London: Book Club Associates, 1979.

Davidovits, Joseph, and Margie Morris. *The Pyramids: an Enigma Solved*. New York: Dorset Press, 1988.

Gardiner, Sir Alan. *Egypt of the Pharaohs*. Oxford: Oxford University Press, 1964.

James, T.G.H. *Excavating in Egypt: The Egypt Exploration Society 1882–1982*. London: British Museum Publications Limited, 1982.

Mertz, Barbara. *Temples, Tombs & Hieroglyphs: A Popular History of Ancient Egypt*. rev. ed. New York: Peter Bedrick Books, 1990.

Murnane, William J. *Guide to Ancient Egypt*. New York: Penguin Books, 1983.

Murray, Margaret A. *Egyptian Religious Poetry*. Westport: Greenwood Press Publishers, 1980.

Murray, Margaret A. *The Splendour that was Egypt*. rev. ed. London: Sidgwick & Jackson, 1972.

Nagel's Encyclopedia-Guide. *Egypt*. Geneva: Nagel Publishers, 1985.

Newberry, Percy Edward. *Ancient Egyptian Scarabs: An Introduction to Egyptian Seals and Signet Rings*. Chicago: Ares, 1979.

Newby, Percy Howard. *Warrior Pharaohs: The Rise and Fall of the*

Egyptian Empire. London, Boston: Faber and Faber, 1980.

Porter, Bertha, and Rosalind L.B. Moss. *Topographical Bibliography of Ancient Egyptian Hieroglyphic Texts, Reliefs, and Paintings*. Vol. VII, *Nubia, The Deserts and Outside Egypt*. Oxford: Griffith Institute Ashmolean Museum, 1995.

Richardson, Dan. *Egypt: The Rough Guide*. London: Penguin Books, 1996.

Shaw, Ian, and Paul Nicholson. *The Dictionary of Ancient Egypt*. London: Harry N. Abrams, Inc., 1995.

Spalinger, Anthony J. *Aspects of the Military Documents of the Ancient Egyptians*. London: Yale University Press, 1982.

Watson, Philip J. *Costumes of Ancient Egypt*. New York: Chelsea House Publishers, 1987.

Wilson, Ian. *The Exodus Enigma*. London: Guild Publishing, 1986.

University Museum Handbooks. *The Egyptian Mummy Secrets and Science*. Pennsylvania: University of Pennsylvania, 1980.

ATLASES

Oxford Bible Atlas. 2nd ed. London; New York: Oxford University Press, 1974.

The Harper Atlas of the Bible. Edited by James A. Pritchard. Toronto: Fitzhenry and Whiteside, 1987.

The Cambridge Atlas of the Middle East and North Africa. Cambridge, U.K.: Cambridge University Press, 1987.

JOURNALS

K.M.T. a Modern Journal of Ancient Egypt. San Francisco.

Volume 5, number 1, *Hyksos Symposium at the Metropolitan Museum*.

Volume 5, number 2, *Amunhotep I, Last King of the 17th Dynasty?*

Volume 5, number 3, *Decline of the Royal Pyramid*.

Volume 6, number 2, *Buhen: Blueprint of an Egyptian Fortress*.

ACKNOWLEDGEMENTS

 HEARTFELT THANKS to my researcher, Bernard Ramanauskas, without whose organizational skill and meticulous attention to detail these books could not have been written.

Thanks also to Dr. K.F.M. Jackman, M.D., B.F.C., for his timely advice.

Read More
PAULINE GEDGE
Stunning New Editions

THE HIPPOPOTAMUS MARSH
ISBN-13: 978-0-14-316745-7
Volume One of the Lords of the
Two Lands Triology

THE OASIS
ISBN-13: 978-0-14-316746-4
Volume Two of the Lords of the
Two Lands Triology

THE HORUS ROAD
ISBN-13: 978-0-14-316747-1
Volume Three of the Lords of the
Two Lands Triology

HOUSE OF DREAMS
ISBN-13: 978-0-14-316742-6

HOUSE OF ILLUSIONS
ISBN-13: 978-0-14-316743-3

SCROLL of SAQQARA
ISBN-13: 978-0-14-316744-0

More than 6 million copies sold

penguin.ca